Before he could it, Lucas reached out and pulled her into his arms.

"I'm just so scared," she admitted. "Not for me but for Camden and you. For your family."

"No one is going to hurt Camden or my family," he assured her. Not that he was in a position to give that kind of assurance. Not with hired guns after them. Still, those hired guns would have to get past him, and since he was protecting his son, Lucas had no intentions of making that easy for them.

Hailey looked up at him at the exact moment he looked down at her. He was so not ready for this. Well, his mind and heart weren't anyway, but the rest of him seemed to think it was a good idea to kiss her or something.

Especially something.

The heat came. Memories, too. Vivid memories of Hailey naked and beneath him in his bed.

The very bed that was just up the hall.

LUCAS

BY
DELORES FOSSEN

HarperCollins
PUBLISHERS
Since 1817

First Published in Great Britain 2017
By Mills & Boon, an imprint of HarperCollins*Publishers*
1 London Bridge Street, London, SE1 9GF

© 2017 Delores Fossen

ISBN: 978-0-263-92882-2

46-0517

Our policy is to use papers that are natural, renewable and recyclable products and made from wood grown in sustainable forests. The logging and manufacturing processes conform to the legal environmental regulations of the country of origin.

Printed and bound in Spain
by CPI, Barcelona

Delores Fossen, a *USA TODAY* bestselling author, has sold over fifty novels with millions of copies of her books in print worldwide. She's received a Booksellers' Best Award and an RT Reviewers' Choice Best Book Award. She was also a finalist for a prestigious RITA® Award. You can contact the author through her website at www.deloresfossen.com.

Chapter One

Texas Ranger Lucas Ryland stared at the bed in the room at the Silver Creek Hospital.

It was empty.

He touched his fingers to the sterile white covers, already knowing they wouldn't be warm. According to the doctor, no one had been in that bed for at least the last fifteen minutes.

Maybe longer.

Mumbling something that Lucas didn't catch, Dr. Alfred Parton paced across the room. The doctor had already told Lucas that he wasn't sure how long the *patient* had been missing. That was one of the first things he had told Lucas when he called him. Of course, first Dr. Parton had dropped the bombshell.

Hailey Darrow is gone.

Lucas had rushed to the hospital to see for himself. And now that he had seen the empty bed with his own eyes, it didn't help with the jolt of adrenaline he'd gotten.

"How the hell did this happen?" Lucas demanded.

"No idea." Dr. Alfred Parton scrubbed his hand over his balding head, something he'd been doing a lot since Lucas had arrived. "I've asked everyone on the staff, and no one knows. But Hailey must have had some help. She wouldn't have been able to get up and just walk out of here."

No. Not after being in a coma for three months. She wouldn't have been able to stand on her own, much less get out of the bed and leave the building.

Of course, that only brought on a boatload of questions for Lucas—had she awakened and managed to talk someone into helping her leave? It was a valid concern, because the last time Lucas had seen Hailey conscious, she'd been nine months pregnant with their child and running. Not just from some guy who'd been chasing her.

But also running from him.

He'd found her, finally, unconscious from a car accident. She'd plowed into a tree, and a limb that'd come through the windshield had given her a nasty head injury. She'd also had a fake ID and enough cash for Lucas to know that she had planned on disappearing.

Even now, three months later, that felt like a punch to the gut, but a "punched gut" feeling pretty much described his entire relationship with Hailey for the year he'd known her.

"We have some security cameras," the doctor explained, "but none back here in this part of the hospital. They're at the front entrance, the ER and the pharmacy. We're still looking, but she's not on any of that footage."

Which meant she might still be inside the place. It wasn't a huge hospital, but there were clinics, storage closets and probably some unoccupied rooms.

"You think she'll try to go to the Silver Creek Ranch?" the doc asked.

Lucas cursed and yanked out his phone. He'd been

so shocked by the news that Hailey was missing that he hadn't even considered the next step of how this might play out.

But, yeah, if she was capable of moving, she would almost certainly try to get to his cousins' ranch, where Lucas now lived. Hailey would try to get to the baby.

Camden.

His three-month-old son.

But he was Hailey's child, too.

And Hailey would go after him. Or rather, she would try. As far as Lucas was concerned, Hailey had given up her rights to their precious little boy when she'd gone on the run before Camden was born. Hailey had endangered herself and the baby in that car wreck.

"Search every inch of the hospital," Lucas ordered the doctor, though that was just the frustration talking because the staff was already looking for Hailey. "And let me know the second you find her."

Lucas headed out the door, hurrying, but he didn't call Camden's nanny because he didn't want to alarm her, yet. Instead, he called his cousin, Mason Ryland. Mason was a part-time deputy in Silver Creek, but since it was nearly 8:00 p.m., he'd already be home, and his house was just up the road from Lucas's new place.

"I'm not coming into the office," Mason said instead of a greeting. His cousin wasn't the friendliest of the Ryland clan, but he would protect Camden with his life.

Lucas prayed it didn't come down to that, though.

"Hailey's missing from the hospital," Lucas tossed out there. "I'm on my way home now, but make sure she doesn't get anywhere near Camden."

Mason cursed, too, and it was ripe enough that Lucas

heard Mason's wife, Abbie, give him a scolding about saying such things in front of their two young sons.

"You can explain when you get here," Mason said. "I'll head over to your place now."

Lucas thanked him and hoped he did indeed have something to explain—like Hailey's whereabouts and how she'd managed to escape. Right now, he didn't know nearly enough.

He ran out of the building and across the parking lot to his SUV. The November wind swiped at him, but he didn't duck his head against it. Lucas kept watch around him. A habit that had saved him a time or two while he'd been a Texas Ranger. But nothing seemed out of the ordinary.

The moment he was behind the wheel, Lucas started the engine. However, before he could throw the SUV into gear, he caught the movement from the backseat. Lucas whirled around, already reaching for his gun.

But it was too late.

Hailey was there.

She was sitting right next to the baby's empty car seat, and thanks to the security lights, he could see that she had a gun pointed right at him. *His* gun. The one he kept as a backup in the glove compartment. Since he hadn't seen her when he first approached the vehicle, it likely meant she'd ducked down out of sight. Hiding from him so she could—well—do whatever the heck she was doing.

"Leave your weapon in your holster," she ordered, and it was indeed an order.

That was a hard look Hailey gave him. But the hardness didn't mesh well with the beads of sweat on her forehead. It was chilly, definitely not warm enough weather for sweating, so this must have been from exertion. There was no color in her cheeks. She looked weak, and no doubt was, but she didn't need much strength considering the gun she had in his face.

Lucas had no idea if she'd actually shoot him, because she clearly wasn't thinking straight. Couldn't be. Or else she wouldn't have him at gunpoint. Then again, she had run from him three months ago, so it was obvious she hadn't trusted him.

Still didn't, apparently.

The head injury that had put her in the coma had healed with the exception of a thin scar near her scalp. Her blond hair was pushed back from her face now so the scar was easier to see, but in another month or two, it'd be practically gone. No signs of the trauma that had nearly killed her and the baby.

No visible signs, anyway.

Lucas would always remember. *Always.*

"Start driving," Hailey insisted. "We can't stay here."

Because the hospital staff would look in the parking lot. But that didn't explain why she was hiding and clearly trying to escape.

Hell, it didn't explain a lot of things.

Lucas did drive. Not far, though, and only after he hit the child safety button to lock all the doors so that Hailey wouldn't be able to get out. He drove out of the parking lot and went two blocks up before pulling over.

He purposely didn't choose a spot in front of any businesses in case something went wrong when he wrestled that gun away from her. Instead, he stopped in front of the town park. Since it was already dark, the park was empty.

"All right. Now talk." Lucas had a string of questions but went with the easiest one first. "How'd you get from your room to my SUV?"

"I walked."

"Impossible," Lucas fired back. He glanced around to make sure someone wasn't out there ready to help her with more than just getting out of that hospital bed. "People who've been in a coma for three months just don't get up and walk."

She nodded. Dragged in a thin breath. That's when he noticed she was shaking. "I've been out of the coma for nearly a week now, and I've been exercising my legs when no one was watching."

Nearly a week.

Damn.

"And none of the medical staff noticed?" he snapped.

"I was never in a vegetative state, just a deep coma, so the monitor already showed plenty of brain activity for me. The activity increased when I woke up, but I tampered with the machine so that it looked as if it malfunctioned. I kept doing that, and the staff thought they had faulty readings."

A nurse had indeed told him about the readings, and the hospital had called in someone to repair the machine. The Silver Creek Hospital wasn't big or modern by anyone's standards so they hadn't had another monitor to use on Hailey. That's why the nurses had been keeping a closer watch on her. Obviously, they hadn't watched nearly close enough.

"How'd you know how to tamper with the monitor?" he pressed.

She glanced away. "I'm good with computers and such."

This was the first Lucas was hearing about that, but

it didn't matter. Not when there were so many other things they needed to talk about.

"When I was trying to regain my strength, I made sure no one else saw me," she added.

Obviously. Just as she'd made sure he hadn't noticed her before he'd gotten in his vehicle.

Her gaze dropped to her stomach for just a second. "I listened to try to find out if I'd had a boy or a girl, but no one mentioned it. Not even you when you visited me on Monday."

Clearly she'd known he was there. Lucas had indeed visited her, something he did a couple of times a week. Why, he didn't know, because he couldn't get answers from a woman in a coma. It riled him to the core, though, that she'd been awake during that visit and hadn't said anything.

But what had he said?

Lucas wasn't even sure—maybe nothing—but he'd almost certainly glared at her. He still was glaring now.

"So, you faked being in a coma for the last week, built up your strength, and just walked out of the hospital?" he asked, going through the probability of that as he said it.

He was skeptical.

Hailey nodded. "I ducked into a supply room, and when I heard the doctor call you, I knew you'd be arriving soon. I made my way to the parking lot and hid behind some shrubs."

"And then you broke into my SUV," Lucas snarled.

"The back door was unlocked," she answered as if that was something she did all the time. To the best of his knowledge, she didn't, but then, he really didn't know much about this woman.

The mother of his child.

"Why didn't you let me know you'd come out of the coma?" Lucas demanded.

Hailey stared at him a long time. "I'll tell you that if you'll tell me what I had—a boy or a girl?"

He debated bargaining with her. Even with that gun aimed at him. But it was probably best to give her the information so they could move on to something else. Something that involved his ripping that gun out of her hand.

"You had a boy," he finally said. "He was born three months ago."

"Three months?" she repeated. It sounded as if she had to choke back a sob. "That long."

Yeah, that long. "The doctors had to deliver him by C-section because you weren't conscious when you went into labor."

She shook her head, her breath shuddering. "I don't remember."

"Comas are like that," he said, and he didn't bother to sound even marginally sympathetic. "I named him Camden David. But I have sole custody of him," Lucas added.

Not a lie, exactly. He did have custody of him and had tried to make it permanent, but the judge had refused on the grounds that Hailey might come out of the coma and her parental rights could be reinstated.

Could be.

Lucas would make sure that didn't happen.

Something went through her pale green eyes, and Hailey made a sound, part groan, part gasp. At first he thought maybe the reaction was due to his custody comment, but the tears proved otherwise. It was the reaction of a woman who'd just learned she had a son.

But she was a mother in name only.

"And he… Camden's all right?" Hailey asked, still blinking back those tears. "There were no problems with the delivery?"

"Yeah. No thanks to you."

"Is he safe?" she asked before Lucas could finish what he was about to say.

"Of course he is." Lucas couldn't stop himself from cursing. "What the hell were you thinking when you went on the run like that? And what happened to you? Were you driving too fast? Is that what caused the accident—and that?"

He pointed to her scar, but Lucas didn't pull back his hand. He knocked the gun away from her, and it fell on the front passenger's seat. Hailey immediately scrambled to retrieve it, but Lucas was a whole lot faster. He dropped it on the floor, well out of her reach.

"Don't make me draw my gun," he warned her and took hold of her wrist in case she was about to try to get out the door.

But she didn't try to escape.

A hoarse sob tore from her mouth, and Hailey eased away from him. Just in case she had another weapon back there, Lucas leaned over the seat and did a quick check around her. He frisked her, too. Since she was wearing a pair of loose green scrubs, a thin sweater and flip-flops, there weren't many places she could conceal a weapon.

Still, after what'd happened three months ago, Lucas looked.

His hand brushed against the side of her breast, and

she made a soft sound. Not the groan she'd made earlier. This one caused him to feel that tug deep within
his body. But Lucas told that tug to take a hike.

Their gazes connected. Not for long. Lucas finished
the search and found nothing.

"Now, keep talking," he insisted. "Tell me what happened to you. Why did you go on the run, and why
didn't you tell anyone before now that you were out of
the coma?"

She opened her mouth and got that deer-in-the-head-
lights look. What she didn't do was answer him.

"Enough of this," he mumbled.

He took out his phone to call Mason and then the
sheriff, but as he'd done with her earlier, Hailey took
hold of his hand. "Please don't tell your cousins. Not
yet."

Since most of his Ryland cousins were cops, that
wasn't what he wanted to hear. "Did you break the law?
Is that why you were on the run?"

"No." She closed her eyes and shook her head. Her
head wasn't the only thing shaking, though. She started
to shiver, the cold and maybe the fear finally getting
to her. "But I'm in trouble. God, Lucas, I'm in so much
trouble."

He was about to curse at her for stating the obvious,
but something else went through her eyes.

Fear.

"It won't take long for word to get out that I'm
awake," Hailey said, speaking barely louder than a
whisper. "And he'll find out."

"He?" Lucas snapped.

Hailey's voice cracked. "There's a killer after me."

Chapter Two

Hailey closed her eyes a moment, hoping it would help with the dizziness.

It didn't.

It was hard to think with her head spinning, the bone-deep exhaustion and the muscle spasms that kept rippling through her body.

Hard to think, too, with Lucas glaring at her as if she were the enemy. Of course, in his eyes, that's exactly what she was.

He obviously didn't believe her. Didn't trust her, either, but somehow Hailey had to make him understand. First, though, he had to take care of what was most important—the baby.

"Are you sure Camden is safe?" she asked.

That caused a new slash of anger to go through his eyes. Probably because he believed she was dodging the news she'd just dropped on him.

There's a killer after me.

"He's safe," Lucas finally said, but he spoke through clenched teeth. "Now, tell me why you need to make sure of that. Does it have something to do with the so-called killer?" He didn't give her a chance to say a word, though. "Or are you trying to lie your way out of why you ran from me three months ago?"

"It's not a lie." She wished it was. "But I didn't tell the truth about some other things."

That tightened the muscles in his jaw even more. "Start from the beginning, and so help me, there'd better not be any lies this time."

Hailey nodded but glanced around them. Since it was Tuesday and a school night, Silver Creek wasn't exactly teeming with activity, but she did spot someone jogging in the park. She kept her attention on him until he disappeared around the curve of the tree-lined trail. Maybe it was nothing. Maybe the guy was just that— a jogger—but he could have been someone after her.

"We need to find a better place to talk," Hailey told him.

Lucas gave her a flat look. Cursed. "I'm not taking you to the Silver Creek Ranch."

That was no doubt where the baby was.

Camden.

Hailey mentally repeated that, something she'd been doing since Lucas had first mentioned her precious son's name. Learning something—anything—about her baby caused her heart to ache. It felt as if someone was squeezing it hard.

Mercy, she'd lost so much already. Three months. And there was a lot more she could lose. Thank God the baby was okay, but it was up to her to make sure he stayed that way.

"I can't see Camden," Hailey answered. Saying it aloud added an even deeper pain. "Not until I'm sure it's safe."

"You won't see him at all," Lucas snapped. He

spewed out more of that profanity. "You don't have a right to see him."

No, in his eyes, she didn't. But if and when this was over, she would see her son. Even if she had to push her way through an army of Ryland lawmen. No one would keep him from her.

Since it was obvious Lucas wasn't going to budge, Hailey tried to figure out the fastest way to convince him that it wasn't safe for her to be out in the open like this.

That meant starting from the beginning.

"I'm not who you think I am," she said.

A burst of air left his mouth, but it wasn't a laugh. "Obviously. You slept with me and then sneaked out, leaving me a note saying you couldn't see me again."

Hailey didn't need a reminder of that. She could have recited the note word for word.

Lucas, I'm sorry, but this was a mistake. I can't get involved with you.

"That was the truth," she continued. "I shouldn't have let things get so…intimate between us."

"But you did, and you got pregnant."

Yes, she had. Since they'd used a condom, the pregnancy definitely hadn't been something Hailey had been expecting. But that hadn't stopped her from wanting the child right from the start.

"Mistakes aside," Lucas continued, "you had no right to run away from me while you were carrying my baby." He cursed again. "If you hadn't had that car accident, I might have never found you. Of course, that was probably the plan, wasn't it? To run away so that I'd never be able to see my child?"

Hailey didn't even have to think about that answer. "No. That wasn't the plan."

He didn't believe her, but it was the truth.

"I was trying to stay alive, trying to keep the baby from being hurt," Hailey explained.

He tapped his badge. "I'm a Texas Ranger." That was probably his way of saying that if something was wrong, she should have gone straight to him.

But Lucas had been in danger, too.

Something he didn't know.

Yet.

Figuring she would need it, Hailey took another deep breath. "Two years ago, I was employed as a computer systems analyst in Phoenix for a man named Preston DeSalvo. I found out he was working with someone in the FBI. A dirty agent. And they were selling confiscated weapons. I went to the cops, DeSalvo was eventually arrested, and after I testified against him, I was placed in witness protection and given a new identity. The marshals relocated me here to Silver Creek."

She paused, giving him a few moments to let all of that sink in, but Lucas didn't take the time. He whipped out his phone again, and before she could stop him, she saw him press the contact for one of his cousins.

Sheriff Grayson Ryland.

"Don't tell him I'm with you," Hailey insisted. "The sheriff's office could be bugged."

She saw the debate Lucas was having with himself, but he didn't stop the call. He did put it on speaker, though, and it didn't take long before Grayson answered.

"I heard about Hailey," Grayson said right off the bat. "I've sent two of the deputies to the hospital to help look for her."

"Thanks," Lucas said. And he paused. A long time. "Can you look up info on a guy named Preston De-Salvo?"

Grayson paused, too. Hailey knew the sheriff well because she'd worked for him as an emergency dispatcher shortly after her arrival in Silver Creek. Grayson had a lot of experience as a lawman and was probably suspicious.

"Is DeSalvo connected to Hailey?" Grayson asked, though she could hear the clicks of his computer keys.

"Maybe."

More keyboard clicking sounds. "Well, Preston De-Salvo was sent to prison about eighteen months ago. He's dead. Killed in a fight at a maximum security prison in Arizona a little over three months ago."

"Why was he in prison?" Lucas pressed.

"A laundry list of charges, including murder, extortion and gun running. An employee, Laura Arnett, testified against him, and she's in WITSEC." He huffed. "Now, what does this have to do with Hailey?"

"Maybe everything. I'll call you back when I know more. In the meantime, can you make sure the ranch is on lockdown?"

"Already have. Mason called and said you'd asked him to go to your house. You think Hailey could be headed there?"

"I'll call you back," Lucas repeated, probably so that he wouldn't have to lie to his cousin.

But the stalling wouldn't last long. Soon, very soon, his cousins would be demanding answers. Especially

Lucas

Grayson, since he wasn't just the sheriff but also the head of the Ryland clan. However, Lucas would be demanding them first.

"Laura Arnett?" Lucas repeated. "That's your real name?"

She nodded. "I haven't thought of myself as that since all of this happened. I'm Hailey Darrow. For now, anyway. But I'll have to come up with another identity. DeSalvo's dead, but no one knows who his partner was," she added.

"The dirty FBI agent," he spat out like the profanity he tacked onto that. "And you believe he's after you?"

"I know he is. Well, one of his henchmen, anyway."

She glanced around again, praying that one of those thugs wasn't nearby, looking for her.

"I don't know how he found me," Hailey continued. "Maybe he hacked into the WITSEC files, or he could have bribed someone to give him the info. But three months ago, I found an eavesdropping device in my house here in Silver Creek, and I knew my identity had been blown."

"You should have come to me." His jaw muscles were at war with each other again. "Or since you were in WITSEC, you could have called your handler."

"I didn't get a chance. Before I could do anything, a hired gun showed up at my house. I hid, but he yelled out that if I didn't give myself up, he'd go after you and use you to get me to cooperate."

The skepticism was still written all over his face. "Cooperate with what?"

Oh, he was not going to like this. "I have some computer files that I didn't turn over to the cops. Files that incriminate Preston's son, Eric. Nothing as serious as murder, but it would have put him away for a few years."

"I'll want to see those files." And it wasn't a suggestion.

She nodded. "It'll take a while to access them. I put them in online storage with some security measures. I set it up so the files won't open until twelve hours after I put in the password."

"Clever," he mumbled, but Hailey didn't think that was a compliment. No. Lucas was silently cursing her for not bringing this to him sooner.

"I let Preston know I'd leak the files if anything happened to me," Hailey explained, "and that his son would head to prison right along with him. It was my insurance, a way of making sure he didn't send his hired thugs after me."

Lucas lifted his shoulder. "But he sent them anyway?"

"No. Preston was dead by then. I think the person who sent the thugs is the dirty agent. First, though, he wants those files."

"Or it could be his son who's after you," Lucas quickly pointed out.

"Maybe. But I didn't personally mention anything to Eric about having incriminating info on him."

Of course, that didn't mean Eric hadn't found out. Eric hadn't visited his father in prison. Not once. But Preston could have said something to one of his lackeys, who in turn passed the info on to Eric. Which wouldn't have necessarily been a bad thing. Because it could have kept Eric off her back, too, had he ever decided to come after her.

"How did you get away from that hired gun?" Lucas asked a moment later.

"I sneaked out the back of the house. I had a car, some cash and new identity papers in a storage unit." Hailey huffed. "I'll answer all your questions. I promise. But we can't stay here. In fact, you can't be with me."

He looked at her as if she'd just sprouted wings. "You think I'm going to dump you out here on the street?"

"No, but I was hoping you'd arrange to get me a car. Or let me use this SUV for a couple of hours."

"That's not going to happen. But I am taking you somewhere—to the sheriff's office."

"No." She couldn't say it fast enough, and Hailey went to the edge of her seat so she could take hold of his arm again. "Didn't you hear me? The office could be bugged. My hospital room was. That's why I didn't say anything to any of the medical staff. I wasn't sure who'd put it there or if I could trust any of them."

Lucas had already put the SUV in gear to drive away, no doubt to head toward the sheriff's office, but that piece of information stopped him. He turned, studying her, probably to decide how much of this was the truth.

Before he could make up his mind, his phone rang, and again she saw Grayson's name on the screen. She doubted Lucas would keep her secret much longer. He would spill everything to the sheriff.

And that meant she had to get out of there—fast.

But how? Lucas had all the doors locked, and she wasn't nearly strong enough to break the windows.

"We might have a problem," Grayson said when Lucas answered, and he put the call on speaker. "Dr. Parton called, and he said right after you left, a man showed up looking for Hailey. He claimed he was her brother."

Oh, God. "I don't have a brother," she mouthed.

"Doc Parton got suspicious," Grayson went on. "And he just sent me the surveillance footage of the guy coming in through the ER entrance. I put his photo into the facial recognition program and got an immediate hit."

Lucas groaned, no doubt because he knew what that meant. If the guy was in the system, he had a record. "Who is he?" he asked the sheriff.

"Darrin Sandmire. A low-life thug." He paused. "Sandmire often works as a hit man."

Her heart slammed against her chest. It was happening. Her worst fears. The killer wasn't just after her. He was here in Silver Creek.

"Sandmire left the hospital before the security guard could stop him, so he could be anywhere in town. Now, you want to tell me what this is all about?" Grayson demanded.

"Yeah. I'll be at the sheriff's office in a few minutes." Lucas paused. "Hailey's with me."

The panic shot through her, and she tried the door handle even though Hailey knew she was trapped. If Lucas took her to the sheriff's office, she might be putting not only herself in danger but also all of them. Lucas put the SUV in gear again, but something must have caught his eye, because his attention zoomed to the driver's side window.

To the park.

Hailey saw it then, as well. The jogger she'd spotted earlier. But this time, he wasn't on the trail. He was coming straight toward the SUV.

And he had a gun in his hand.

Chapter Three

"Get down!" Lucas shouted to Hailey.

His first instinct was to draw his gun and take aim at the man running toward them. But Lucas didn't want to get into a gunfight on Main Street where innocent bystanders—or Hailey—could be hurt.

Lucas wasn't sure he believed everything she'd just told him, but it was obvious she had someone after her. Later he'd find out who that was, but for now he wanted to put some distance between this armed man and them. He hit the accelerator.

Just as the guy took aim.

And fired.

The bullet slammed into the side of the SUV, missing the window and Lucas by only a couple of inches.

"I need a gun," Hailey said, climbing over the seat to get to the passenger side. She started to fumble around for the weapon that he'd knocked away from her.

"Stay down," Lucas warned her, but her search took care of that. Hailey crawled onto the floor.

At least, it took care of it for a couple of seconds. Once she had the gun, she got back in the seat and took aim out the back side window.

She fired.

The sound blasted through the SUV, causing Lucas to curse. He hadn't actually expected her to shoot. Too bad she missed, because the gunman sent another bullet their way.

Lucas sped off. The thug got off one more shot before Lucas took the first turn he reached. He wasn't driving in the direction of the sheriff's office, but he could double back.

Lucas tossed Hailey his phone. "Call Grayson and tell him there's an armed man near the park at the intersection of Main and Everett Road."

Hailey made the call, but she kept watch behind them, making sure that goon wasn't in pursuit. The moment Grayson answered, she rattled off the information. Then she hit the end call button. No doubt because she didn't want to answer Grayson's questions. That was okay. For now.

But as soon as they reached the sheriff's office, Hailey had better come clean about everything.

Lucas took another turn. Then another, meandering his way back to Main Street. That particular part of the park was only about seven blocks away from the sheriff's office, so it wouldn't take Grayson long to get a pair of deputies there to catch the guy.

"Do you know if that was Darrin Sandmire?" Lucas asked her.

"I have no idea. But I'm pretty sure that was the same man who came after me three months ago."

Hell.

Lucas had to rein in the anger that sliced through him. That was the SOB who'd put Hailey—and therefore, Camden—in danger. Too bad Lucas hadn't managed to shoot him. But then he rethought that. He didn't want the guy dead, not until he had answers from him.

Like who hired him.

Thugs like Darrin Sandmire always worked for bigger thugs. Maybe DeSalvo's son, Eric. Maybe that unidentified rogue agent. Soon, Lucas intended to find out who'd paid this killer to come after Hailey.

Lucas took another turn, the tires squealing against the asphalt. The moment he was on the side street, he saw something he didn't like.

A truck.

It wasn't right in the middle of the road, but the front end was jutting out from the parking space in front of a motorcycle repair shop.

Lucas hit his brakes.

"You think someone's inside the truck?" Hailey asked. Her voice was shaking like the rest of her.

Lucas didn't know, and it was next to impossible to see inside the truck's cab. There was a streetlight and a lit sign for the motorcycle shop, but the tint was so dark on the windshield that he couldn't tell. He pulled up a little farther though so he could get a better look at the front license plates.

"Out-of-state plates," he mumbled under his breath.

Maybe that in itself meant nothing, but Lucas got that feeling in his gut. The feeling that told him to get the heck out of there.

He threw the SUV into Reverse.

But the second he did that, the truck door opened, and a man bolted out.

The guy had a rifle.

"Get down," Lucas repeated to Hailey. "And this time, stay there."

Whether she would or not was anyone's guess, but he didn't want to have to worry about her being shot. He hit the gas, the SUV speeding backward. But he didn't get out of the path of that rifleman fast enough.

The bullet slammed into the windshield.

Since this wasn't the vehicle he used for work, the glass wasn't reinforced. The shot tore through the safety glass, the bullet exiting out the back.

Great. Just great.

Now he had two thugs after them, and Lucas had no choice but to go back in the direction he'd seen that other shooter in the park. Maybe the guy was long gone by now. Or better yet, maybe one of the deputies had managed to capture him.

When Lucas reached the side street, he spun the SUV around so he could drive forward. He definitely didn't want to head right into the middle of an ambush, so he headed for a better lit area.

"The truck's coming after us," Hailey said.

And that's when he realized she'd lifted her head and was looking out the side window.

Lucas pushed her right back down. "Don't make it easier for them to kill you," he snapped. Yeah, it was harsh, but Hailey was clearly the target of some very determined attackers.

Whoever was in the truck fired another shot at them, this one slamming into the rear end of the SUV. A second shot quickly followed.

Then a third.

"There must be two of them," Hailey muttered. She hadn't figured that out by looking at them, though. She was still on the floor.

But Lucas knew there had to be two, as well. Those

shots were too well aimed for someone who was trying to negotiate the turns and dodging the cars parked
along the street.

"Hang on," Lucas told her a split second before he
turned onto another side street. He was thankful he'd
grown up here and knew these streets like the back of
his hand.

His phone buzzed, and since Hailey still had hold of
it, she answered it and put it on speaker.

"Where are you?" he heard Grayson immediately
ask. "Someone just called about shots being fired near
Henderson's Motorcycle Shop."

"Someone in a blue pickup is shooting at us. We're
on Bluebonnet Street, coming up near the Corral Bar."
It was a risk since there'd be customers still inside, but
Lucas didn't plan on stopping or even slowing down.
"I'll turn back on Main Street and head in your direc-
tion. Please tell me you found the first shooter."

"Not yet. But I'll send Dade and Josh your way to
help," Grayson said, and he ended the call.

Good. Dade and Josh were both cousins, both deputy
sheriffs, and maybe having backup would cause these
thugs to quit firing.

The parking lot of the Corral Bar was lit up better
than the rest of the street, and Lucas glanced in his side
mirror at the truck. Definitely two men. And the one on
the passenger side was doing the shooting.

"I can return fire," Hailey insisted, already climbing
into the seat and lowering the window. "Please don't
stop me. This is all my fault, and I have to do something to stop them."

"No way." And he meant it. It might indeed be partially her fault for not coming to him sooner, but she wasn't sticking her neck out to fire any shots.

Hailey didn't get a chance to argue with him. That's because the sound of sirens stopped anything she was about to say. In the distance, behind the truck, Lucas saw the flashing blue lights of a police cruiser.

Dade and Josh, no doubt.

The driver stopped following Lucas and took a very quick turn off a side street. A street that would lead them straight to the highway.

No, hell, no.

Lucas didn't want these clowns getting away, but it wasn't smart to go in pursuit with Hailey in the vehicle. Besides, Dade and Josh went after them, and Lucas could only hope they'd catch them.

"Keep watch for the other shooter," Lucas told Hailey.

He hated to rely on her for help, but with the glass in the front, back and side windows cracked and webbed, they had reduced visibility. That would make it hard for them to see the guy hiding between one of the buildings where he could shoot at them as they drove by.

Lucas held his breath, going as fast as he could, and he didn't release that breath until he made it back onto Main Street. Definitely no sign of the shooter, so he headed for the sheriff's office.

"Can you run?" he asked her.

"I'll try," she assured him. Which meant she couldn't. "I had to use a cane to walk to your SUV."

Definitely couldn't.

The SUV squealed to a stop directly in front of the door to the sheriff's office, but he didn't get out. Lucas waited until Grayson hurried to the door and threw it open.

"I'm carrying you in," Lucas insisted, and he didn't leave any room for argument.

He scooped her up in his arms and rushed her inside the building, with Grayson locking the door behind them. But Lucas didn't stop there. He hurried her past the squad room to the hall that led to Grayson's office and the break room. That way, if someone did come in with guns blazing, she'd have some protection.

"Dade and Josh are in pursuit," Lucas told Grayson. "Arizona plates, but there was something covering the numbers. Mud, I think." Probably not an accident.

"Arizona?" Hailey repeated.

Lucas knew the reason for her concern. DeSalvo had been from Arizona, which meant his son, Eric, likely was, too. So, had Eric sent those goons after Hailey?

Now that they weren't in the SUV, Lucas got a better look at her. Especially a better look at the fear in her eyes. And the fact that she was having to grip the door to steady herself.

"As soon as it's safe, I'll have the doctor come over to see you," Lucas told her.

But she was shaking her head before he even finished. "I can't trust Dr. Parton. Or anyone in the hospital. Someone planted that bug on the table next to my bed."

Lucas certainly hadn't forgotten about that. The device needed to be checked, but that would have to wait, because Grayson no doubt had every available deputy on this manhunt for the shooters.

"When there's time, Hailey will need to give you a statement," Lucas told Grayson.

Grayson nodded. He still had his gun drawn, was

still keeping watch on the area just outside the building. "Is she in WITSEC?"

"Yes," Hailey answered. "But I don't want the marshals to know I'm here."

Grayson mumbled something Lucas didn't catch, but he didn't need to hear the words to know that Grayson wasn't pleased about all this going on right under his nose.

"Hell, you worked for me," Grayson added.

She nodded. "I figured it was a way to keep an eye on what was happening in town, just in case something went wrong." Hailey paused. "And something did go wrong."

Yeah. And Lucas wondered if sleeping with him was in that something-gone-wrong category.

"I'll call Mason and give him an update," Grayson said after he shot Hailey a glare.

Hailey dropped back a step, holding onto Grayson's desk. Lucas was volleying his attention between her and the outside. However, she got his complete attention when she made a soft gasp.

Lucas hurried to her, following her gaze to the computer on the desk. It was obviously the security feed that the doctor had sent Grayson. In the shot, the tall, lanky man was coming through the glass doors of the ER. Grayson had paused it and zoomed in on the man's face.

Darrin Sandmire, no doubt.

Lucas had no trouble seeing the renewed fear in Hailey's eyes. "That's definitely the man who came to my house three months ago. And the man who ran me off the road that night."

Lucas hadn't needed to hear anything else about the

guy to know that he wanted him caught, questioned and punished.

Hailey touched the screen to get the security feed moving again. Darrin disappeared from view when he walked past the camera and to the hall. Since it would have taken him several minutes to get to her room, Lucas sped up the footage, watching for Darrin to re-emerge.

He did.

But the man wasn't alone.

There was a woman with him, walking right by his side, and it was obvious they were talking. The woman was a blonde, and she kept her head down. Right until she was close to the camera.

Now Hailey's gasp wasn't so soft.

"I know her. That's Colleen Jeffrey."

The name meant nothing to Lucas, and he didn't recognize her, either. "Who is she?"

There were tears shimmering in Hailey's eyes when she looked up at him. "My half sister."

Damn.

Lucas was about to assure her that maybe this was a coincidence. But it didn't look like that to him. He needed to get this woman in for questioning right away.

He heard the footsteps. Hurried ones, and they put Lucas right back on alert again. Though he hadn't exactly been relaxing.

"We've got a problem," Grayson said, stepping into the doorway. "Someone tripped the security sensor near the back fence at the ranch. One of the ranch hands spotted a gunman."

Chapter Four

Hailey's breath froze. She wanted to scream, to shout out for Lucas to hurry to the ranch so they could protect their son, but the words and sounds were wedged there in her throat.

No. This couldn't be happening. This monster couldn't get to her baby.

Even without her warning, Lucas thankfully understood just how dangerous a situation this could be, because he took off running toward the front of the building. Hailey followed him. Or rather, she tried.

Lucas must have remembered she was still hobbling, because he spun around, scooped her up in his arms and hurried toward his shot-up SUV still parked just outside the door.

"We need to use a cruiser," Grayson called out to them. "Because this could be a trap to lure you into the open."

Lucas stopped, and while everything inside Hailey wanted to move, to hurry to the ranch, she knew Grayson was right.

"Wait right here for me," Grayson insisted. "I'll bring the cruiser around to the front."

Hailey didn't want to waste precious minutes while

he did that, but they didn't have many options here. Lucas and she waited, the time crawling by slower than a snail's pace, and it seemed to take an eternity for Grayson to drive up. Even before the cruiser came to a stop, Lucas and she jumped into the backseat, and Grayson took off again.

"I'll call the ranch and get an update," Lucas said.

As much as she wanted to know what was going on, Hailey didn't want anyone there distracted right now. She wanted all the focus on protecting the baby.

Camden.

The name seemed foreign to her. Probably because she'd yet to see her son, but maybe that would change soon. Maybe they'd get to the ranch and put an end to the danger.

"Tillie," Lucas said to whoever answered his call.

"One of the nannies," Grayson provided to Hailey, but he didn't even glance back at her when he spoke. He looked all around, no doubt in case someone was trying to follow them.

Or attack them again.

Hailey couldn't hear what the nanny was saying, but since Lucas's arm was pressed against her, she felt his muscles relax just a little. "We'll be there as fast as we can." He paused. "Hailey's with me."

The nanny perhaps hadn't even heard she was out of the coma, so this could be a real shock. An unwanted one. Hailey didn't know Tillie, but she doubted she was going to get a warm reception from anyone at the Silver Creek Ranch. It wouldn't matter that she thought she'd done the right thing.

Still did think that.

But a family of lawmen wouldn't see it that way.

They would believe she should have trusted them. However, maybe they could see now that all the trust in the world wouldn't have put an end to the danger.

Oh, mercy.

That reminder came at her hard, like a heavyweight's fist. The reason she'd tried to escape was to avoid this. To keep her child safe. And now he wasn't safe because of her.

"Whoever's behind the attacks will use Camden to get to me," Hailey said under her breath.

She hadn't intended to say that aloud, and it stung even more when Lucas made a sound of agreement. He'd finished his call with the nanny and now was keeping watch. Along with glancing at her.

"That doesn't mean you're going to try to take him and disappear," Lucas snapped. There wasn't a shred of gentleness in his tone. In fact, it was the same tone he likely used with criminal suspects.

"It's too late to take him and hide," Hailey agreed. "Too late for me to disappear, as well. Because now that they know I'm awake, they won't stop, and they'll try to use the baby to come after me."

That meant she needed to find out who *they* were. And fast. For that to happen, she needed to rely on Lucas.

Something that wouldn't please him.

It didn't please her, either, but no one would work harder than Lucas to keep Camden safe. Of course, once that happened, and this snake was captured and behind bars, Lucas and she would have another battle to fight.

For custody.

But that was a fight that would have to wait for another day. Right now, Hailey had enough to deal with.

"The fences are all rigged with security alarms?" she asked.

"Yeah," Grayson and Lucas answered at the same time. It was Lucas who continued. "There are also sensors on the grounds. Cameras, too. Since this clown tripped a sensor, the ranch hands and my cousins will be able to pinpoint his exact location before he can get near one of the houses."

Good. But pinpointing him wasn't the same as stopping the threat.

"Hurry," Hailey said to Grayson. She was speaking purely out of frustration, because he was going as fast as he safely could.

The rural roads that led to the ranch weren't exactly straight. Plenty of sharp curves and turns, and it certainly wouldn't help them if Grayson wrecked.

Something she knew all too well.

Hailey couldn't quite choke back a gasp when the cruiser tires squealed around one of those turns and it felt as if Grayson was losing control of the vehicle. All the memories of that other night came flooding back.

The frantic rush to get away from the person trying to kill her. The adrenaline and the fear. Even the feeling of the impact.

The pain.

But more intense than the pain and the fear had been the sickening dread that she'd failed.

"Flashbacks?" Lucas asked.

She nodded. "I remember that you're the one who found me that night. If it hadn't been you…"

Hailey didn't finish that thought. No need. Lucas had found her, and while it hadn't made things perfect, it had allowed her to deliver the baby safely.

Grayson took the final turn, and Hailey saw the ranch come into view. To say it was sprawling was an understatement. It'd been huge, but now that the Ryland cousins were buying up the adjacent land and building their own homes, the place stretched out for miles and miles.

They'd also added more security since the last time she'd visited. There was now a large security gate, and she saw several men near it. Ranch hands, probably, since she didn't recognize any of them.

"Get down," Lucas told her as they approached the gate. He lowered the window. "Anything?" he asked the men.

"Yep. Just a few seconds ago Sawyer called to say he shot at a guy who'd crossed over the fence. He and two of the other hands are chasing him."

Hailey sucked in her breath. Sawyer was his cousin as well as an FBI agent. "Did Sawyer have to fire shots anywhere near the houses?"

The guy volleyed glances among Lucas, Grayson and her. Maybe he was trying to figure out if it was okay if he answered since he probably didn't even know who she was.

"No, the shooting happened in the back pasture," the guy said after Lucas gave him a go-ahead nod. "Mason said, though, that y'all should wait down here until they've made sure there's only one."

Oh, mercy.

As hard as that was to hear—and it was even harder for her to stay put—Hailey knew he was right. The attacker might not be alone. Heck, he could have brought an entire army with him, and it was best to aim that army at her rather than launch an attack near the houses.

Still, waiting was hard.

Even if she lifted her head, something Lucas wouldn't like her to do, Hailey couldn't see Lucas's house from this part of the road, but she knew it was less than a half mile away. She knew because he'd taken her there for the one night they'd been together. The night she'd had a serious lapse in judgment and gotten way too personal with a man she should have avoided. Or so it'd seemed at the time. But without that night, she wouldn't have her son, and despite everything that'd gone on, the one thing she was certain of was that she loved her baby.

Lucas didn't seem to be having an easier time waiting than she was. He put the window back up, mumbled some profanity and took out his phone. This time she saw that he was calling the nanny again.

"Just checking to make sure everything is okay," Lucas said when Tillie answered.

Hailey automatically scooted closer so she could hear what the nanny had to say, but that only earned her a scowl from Lucas. He put the call on speaker, her cue to inch away from him. She did.

"The baby's fine," Tillie assured Lucas. "He went straight to sleep after his bottle. And Mason's still here just in case."

Just in case everything went from bad to worse. Hailey hated that it was a possibility, but Mason was another lawman, so it was good to have him there. She prayed, though, that he wouldn't be needed and that the danger would end soon. With this idiot intruder not just in custody but also willing to tell them the name of the person who'd hired him.

"You said earlier that Hailey was with you," Tillie

went on. She paused. "Is, uh, everything okay? Did that man try to get onto the ranch because of her?"

"Yeah," Lucas admitted. Now he was the one who paused. "I'll need to take the baby someplace safe. Will you be able to come with us?"

"Of course," Tillie quickly agreed.

Hailey was shaking her head before the nanny even answered.

The head shaking caused Lucas to scowl again. "I'm going to protect my son," he snarled as if she didn't want the same thing.

She did. More than anything, she wanted him safe. Lucas and his family, too. "But I want to see him."

That got Lucas's muscles tightening again. "And then what?"

It was a good question. Hailey didn't have anything resembling a good answer. "I don't know," she admitted. "I need some answers, and I think the place to start is with my sister."

"I agree," Lucas said without hesitation. "I'll want her contact info and anything recent you have on her. I'll especially want to know why she could want you dead."

"I don't know any of those things," Hailey had to admit. "I haven't seen or heard from Colleen since I've been in WITSEC."

Lucas huffed, clearly not pleased that she hadn't given him something to go on. "You two were close?"

"Once." But that was another round of bad memories. "We were both working as computer systems analysts for Preston DeSalvo's company. I testified against him, but Colleen didn't. She claimed she didn't see the incriminating evidence that I found."

Lucas jumped right on that. "She lied?"

"Maybe. But I can't believe she'd be the one behind this. I'm still her sister."

He gave her a flat look. "Cain and Abel were brothers, and you know how that ended."

Yes, with one murdering the other, but Hailey had to hang on to something, and that something was that her only sister hadn't betrayed her like this. Still, she wanted to talk to Colleen and get this all sorted out.

She nearly reached for his phone to make a call, but there was no one who came to mind that she could trust. Well, no one other than Lucas.

"I'll bring Colleen in for questioning," Lucas said as if reading her mind. He didn't get a chance to add anything else because the sound got their attention.

A shot.

Even though it was in the distance, it still caused Hailey's heart to slam against her chest. She held her breath, waiting, and even though she tried to steel herself for whatever would happen next, she still gasped when Lucas's phone buzzed.

"Mason," he said looking at the screen before he answered it and put the call on speaker.

She hadn't thought her heart could beat any faster, but she'd obviously been wrong. Mason was with the baby, and if he was calling then maybe that meant the shot had been fired close to the house.

Or in it.

Hailey pressed her fingers to her mouth and listened, praying.

"Sawyer fired the shot," Mason said. "The guy's alive for now."

"Is he talking?" Lucas asked.

"No, but I just called an ambulance, so maybe he'll

say something on the way to the hospital. Sawyer has a way of getting dirt to talk."

Good. But that didn't mean this was over. "Are there any other attackers out there?" Hailey pressed.

Just as the ranch hand had done, Mason hesitated. "No. Nothing else is showing up on any of the security feeds, either. It looks as if this clown came alone. And I don't think he came here to kill anybody. He had surveillance equipment on him."

So there could be others on the way. It was too much to hope that this guy's injury and arrest would get the person behind this to back off.

"It's safe for you to come to the house," Mason continued. "If you want to come, that is."

She knew what he meant by that. Mason was giving his cousin an out in case Lucas didn't want her to see the baby. Hailey was about to insist that happen when Lucas gave Grayson the go-ahead to get moving.

Toward the house.

Hailey sat back up, keeping watch around them, but she was also looking for the house. It finally came into view since it was the first building on the ranch road. All of the interior lights were off, probably as a safety precaution, but there were security lights on all four corners of the property. Enough for her to see the barn and corral that hadn't been there a year ago.

Lucas was making this place a home.

Part of her was thankful for that. Their son deserved it. But she was betting there was no place in this home for her.

Grayson pulled to a stop directly in front of the porch, and the door opened. Mason. Yet another unfriendly face, but then, Mason usually looked unfriendly. As he'd done at the sheriff's office, Lucas got her in—fast. This time, though, he didn't carry her. He looped his arm around her waist to steady her, and the moment they were inside, he moved away from her.

Hailey immediately looked around for the baby. But there was no sign of him or the nanny. She was about to demand to see him, but Mason stepped in front of her.

"Just got a text from Sawyer," Mason said, his voice low and dangerous. "The guy he shot is drifting in and out of consciousness, but this is what the guy said."

He held his phone screen up for her to see, and the words there caused her to drop back a step.

Hailey Darrow paid me to take the kid.

Chapter Five

Lucas didn't know who looked more shocked by the accusation that the wounded gunman had just made. He or Hailey.

"I didn't," she said, her gaze firing between Mason and him. "I only left the hospital a couple of hours ago."

Mason didn't seem convinced. "You were conscious for a week. You could have called someone and set this whole thing up."

The anger flared through Hailey's eyes, and she opened her mouth as if ready to return verbal fire, but she was obviously spent. Heck, so was Lucas, and while part of him hated to defend the woman who'd tried to run from him, he couldn't see how this would have played out.

"There was no phone in her hospital room," Lucas explained. "And yes, she could have borrowed one from someone on the staff, but that kind of thing doesn't stay a secret very long."

Lucas could have gone on and mentioned the part about Hailey not having touched her bank accounts since she'd been in the coma, and it wasn't as if she'd had wads of cash lying around the hospital to pay someone to carry through on something like this.

Even Lucas's own explanation didn't seem to convince Mason. "You trust her, then?" Mason asked.

"No," Lucas readily admitted. "But if Hailey intended to take the baby, she wouldn't have done it this way."

At least, he hoped like the devil that she wouldn't. The baby and other members of his family could have been hurt by the thug who'd trespassed onto the ranch.

"Thank you," Hailey said to him.

For some reason, that riled Lucas. Maybe because he didn't want to do anything for her that would cause her to say something like that.

"So, who did hire the *lying* sack of dirt?" Mason asked.

Hailey shook her head, but it was clear from the way she was looking around that her attention was elsewhere. She obviously wanted to see the baby, and Lucas tried to remind himself that if their positions were reversed, he would have wanted the same thing.

Of course, their positions would never be reversed because he would have never gone on the run from the law.

"I'll question Hailey's sister, Colleen, and Eric DeSalvo in the morning." Lucas tipped his head to the hall that led to the bedrooms. "Is Tillie in the nursery?"

Mason lowered his phone and nodded. Even though he didn't voice his disapproval as to what was about to happen, it was on his face. "I'll wait here until I get the all-clear from Sawyer."

Lucas thanked him and made a mental note to thank all the others who'd pulled together to keep Camden safe. For now, though, he had to focus on getting through this. And *this* was having Hailey see the baby.

From the moment Camden had been born, Lucas had

known it might come down to this. But as every day had passed with Hailey in a coma, he'd also considered that she might never wake up. That she might never have a claim on their child. Now, here she was, and Lucas was having to face one of his worst fears.

That he might lose his son.

Not to a kidnapper, either. But to Hailey. She wouldn't be able to get full custody of Camden. No way would Lucas allow that, but she would be entitled to visitation rights. Considering she was in WITSEC, that was going to be tricky. And not very safe for any of them.

Moving ahead of her, Lucas led her down the hall. She caught onto the side of the wall to steady herself, and she was probably moving as fast as she could go.

When they reached the nursery, Lucas stepped in, his gaze immediately connecting with the nanny's. There was just as much concern in Tillie's expression as there had been in Mason's. But she stepped aside so that Lucas—and Hailey—had the crib in their direct line of sight.

Where Camden was sleeping.

"I'll be in the living room if you need me," Tillie said, but her offer seemed to be a question, as if maybe he wanted her to stay.

Lucas nodded, giving her the go-ahead to leave, but Hailey didn't wait for Tillie to be out the door before she hobbled her way to the crib. The sound that left her mouth crushed at his heart. Part moan, part sigh.

All love.

It was a sound and a look that Lucas felt all too well because he got that same punch of emotion every time he was near his son. And even when he wasn't.

"He's so beautiful," Hailey whispered, touching her fingers to the wispy strands of dark brown hair.

Lucas had to agree with her, but he was certain that was the reaction of most parents. Certain, too, that Hailey would want to do more than just touch his hair. She looked back at him, as if waiting for permission. She didn't wait long, though, before she scooped Camden up in her arms.

She made that sound again and kissed his cheek. Even though Camden stirred a little, he went right back to sleep. Good. Even though his son was too young to know what was going on, Lucas didn't want to risk Camden being upset by having his sleep interrupted. He also didn't want to risk Hailey falling with the child, and since her legs were obviously still wobbly, he helped her to the nearby chair.

"Is he healthy?" she asked.

"Yeah." It was hard for him to talk about something so—well—normal. "He's right on target for his height, weight and milestones."

She nodded and looked up at him, and that's when he saw the tears in her eyes. "I was so scared that he'd been hurt in the accident."

"He could have been," Lucas quickly pointed out, but then instantly regretted the jab. It was the truth, but stating the obvious didn't make him feel any better.

"I know. I'm so sorry. When I ran, my only thought was to keep him safe."

Lucas nearly went for another jab by reminding her that the safe thing to do would have been to come to him, but that ship had already sailed. They were here now and had to deal with this. Not just the danger, either. But all those old feelings.

He'd been attracted to her once and vice versa. That's what had landed them in bed in the first place. And while there were still some lingering traces of the attraction, it wouldn't play into this. He hoped the bitterness he felt over what'd happened wouldn't, either. Right now, bitterness wouldn't help.

He was about to question her more about the night of the accident, to see if she remembered any details that would help them find out who was responsible for the attacks, but Hailey spoke before he did.

"Tell me about the delivery," she said.

Lucas paused, not because he intended to hold anything back, but because remembering that night still felt like a punch to the gut.

"I was scared," he admitted. "We didn't know if there'd been trauma to the baby, and since you were so close to your due date, the docs did a C-section on you. But everything turned out okay. Everything except that you were in a coma," Lucas added.

She, too, paused. Then nodded. "I've heard that some people remember and hear things while they're in comas. I didn't." She brushed another kiss on Camden's cheek. "I wish I could remember seeing him as a newborn. He's already so big."

Camden was, but while Hailey had indeed missed a lot, the baby wasn't old enough to have noticed that his mom hadn't been around.

Hailey looked up at Lucas again, those tears still shimmering in her eyes. "I know this is hard for you. You haven't had to share him with anyone for the past three months."

Lucas wasn't sure how to respond to that and didn't get a chance to say anything anyway, because Mason appeared in the doorway. One look at his cousin's face and Lucas knew something else had gone wrong. Apparently so did Hailey, because she slowly got to her feet, her attention nailed to Mason.

"The gunman died on the way to the hospital," Mason said.

Hell. Lucas had wanted him alive so they could get answers. But maybe they could still do that. "Did he have a phone on him? Maybe his boss's number is in his contacts?"

Mason nodded. "Grayson will check for that, but there's more." He paused. "The ranch hands did a thorough search of the fence line in that back part of the ranch, and it appears the dead thug didn't come alone. There were enough tracks back there for three people."

Lucas bit back the profanity that he nearly blurted out, something he'd been training himself to do now that he was a father. Still, it was hard not to curse about that. "Any other signs of the men?"

"No. They're apparently gone. For now, anyway."

That didn't mean they wouldn't be back. Maybe even tonight, since the darkness would give them an advantage for an attack.

"I've got men patrolling the entire ranch," Mason went on. "I also called everyone and told them to lock down and stay inside."

By "everyone" he meant his brothers and their cousins. No one would be leaving and coming onto the ranch unless Mason gave the okay. Which he wouldn't do until he was certain it was safe. And Lucas knew what that meant.

This time he wasn't able to stop himself from cursing.

Because it meant Hailey would have to stay there.

Of course, he probably wouldn't have been able to talk her into budging since she'd want to be near the baby, but Lucas had planned on having her sleep far away from the Silver Creek Ranch. Far away from Camden, too.

"I'm so sorry," Hailey whispered. Maybe she was apologizing again for the danger. But one look in her eyes and Lucas knew the reason for this "I'm sorry." She had also figured out what the sleeping arrangements would be.

"You can stay in the guest room," Lucas growled. It was at the end of the hall, as far away as he could get her while still having her under the same roof.

Hailey mumbled a thanks, and while Lucas thought part of her looked relieved, that was still fear he saw in her eyes. Worry, too. Especially worry when she looked at Mason again. His cousin wasn't budging. Mason continued to stand there, his hands bracketed on the doorjamb.

"What else happened?" Hailey asked Mason. Her voice was shaky again, probably because she knew they were about to get another dose of bad news.

"Grayson tried to get in touch with Colleen, so he could bring her in for questioning." Mason paused again. "But there's a problem. Colleen is missing."

HAILEY HOPED THIS medical exam wasn't a mistake.

She wasn't certain about the ER physician, Dr. Parton, but Lucas had assured her that Parton wasn't the one who'd planted that bug in her hospital room, that the doctor was trustworthy. So, that's what Hailey was going to do—trust him. Besides, she needed to make sure she was okay. Not just for her sake but to soothe some of the concern on Lucas's face.

Of course, she had plenty of her own concerns, too.

There were so many things for her to worry about, and that's what she'd done through the night and now the morning. The constant threat of an attack. Her missing sister. The obvious tension between Lucas and her. Between her and his family, too.

But it was hard for Hailey to focus solely on all of that when she was looking at her son's face while Lucas was holding him.

For the entire time she'd carried him, she had considered how he might look. Considered as well the love she would feel for him, but she'd way underestimated that love. She couldn't believe how deep it was for this child, and even though it crushed her heart, she knew that same feeling of love was the very reason that Lucas would do everything to hang on to his child.

Everything, including attempts to exclude her.

Those attempts wouldn't work, of course. Or maybe they wouldn't. If they couldn't stop the threat of another attack, then she might have no choice but to disappear. She'd do that if it meant keeping Camden safe.

She'd started that process by using Lucas's laptop and putting in her password for the storage cloud for the files she'd gathered on Eric DeSalvo. It'd be a few more hours before she could open them, but once Lucas had a chance to go over them, maybe he could find something he could use to arrest Eric. It might not put an end to the attacks, but at least it would get him off the streets for a while.

"Follow the light with your eyes," Dr. Parton instructed her.

Hailey did, though it meant taking her attention off her son. And Lucas. Lucas was feeding the baby his bottle while he had his phone sandwiched between his shoulder and his ear. She wasn't sure who was on the other end of the phone line this time, but Lucas had obviously adapted to juggling his work with fatherhood.

"From what I can tell, you're fine," the doctor said, stepping back from her. "You'll need a thorough exam, though, and some tests that I can do only at the hospital. Any idea when it'll be okay for that?"

It was the million-dollar question, and Hailey didn't have a clue what the answer was. She shook her head. "We're waiting on some information." Information that would ideally lead to an arrest.

The doctor didn't seem especially pleased with an indefinite delay to those tests, and Hailey knew why. There could be brain damage. And damage to her legs. The muscles felt a little stronger, but she was nowhere near a hundred percent and might need physical therapy to regain all her strength. No way could she risk going to PT or taking those tests now, though, and she didn't want to speculate how long it would be before that happened.

The doctor gathered his things and headed to the door, where Mason was waiting to escort him back to town. They left, leaving Hailey to sit there and watch as Camden finished his bottle. As if it were the most natural thing in the world, Lucas put the bottle aside and moved the baby to his shoulder to burp him.

A year ago, if someone had told her that the tough cowboy cop would be the doting father, she wouldn't have believed it. Lucas likely wouldn't have, either.

Tillie came out of the kitchen and made eye contact with Lucas. "You want me to take him?" Tillie mouthed.

"No, thanks. I'm finished with my call." He put away his phone and looked at Hailey. "That was Grayson. Still no word on your sister, but Eric DeSalvo should be arriving at the sheriff's office any minute now."

Good. Hailey figured the best place to start with getting those answers would be with Eric. And Colleen. It sickened her to think that her sister might be involved in this.

"What about the other gunmen who were around the ranch last night?" she asked. "Any signs of them?"

"No. And the dead guy, Darrin, was using a burner cell phone and didn't have any contacts stored there. In fact, the phone hadn't been used, so there's nothing to trace."

Another dead end. Literally. Since Darrin had lived only long enough to accuse her of hiring him.

"Grayson had the medics take Darrin's picture," Lucas went on. When he reached to take his phone from his jeans pocket, it caused the baby to move, and Camden stirred, lifting his head just a little.

Hailey figured Camden was too young to see her from across the room, so she went closer. Lucas didn't scowl, exactly, but it was close. He took out his phone and handed it to her.

"Take a look at the picture Grayson sent, and see if you recognize Darrin. Is he the same man who went after you the night you were trying to get away?"

She took the phone, her fingers brushing against his. Lucas noticed. Noticed, too, that she was volleying glances between the baby and him. He pulled in a long, weary breath.

"Sit down," he growled. "You can hold Camden while you tell me about the picture."

Hailey moved as fast as she could, making her way back to the chair. Lucas went to her, easing the baby into her arms.

There it was again. That punch of emotion.

Though it was hard to focus with Camden staring up at her, Hailey studied the photo. It wasn't the best shot since the man's face was twisted with pain, but Hailey picked through the features.

And remembered.

She sucked in her breath so fast that she nearly got choked. "He definitely looks like the man who ran me off the road."

Other memories came flooding back. The car following her. Her frantic attempt to get away. Then the crash.

"He rammed into the back of my car, forcing me into a ditch," she explained. "That's when I hit my head."

Thank goodness she'd been wearing a seat belt. That had prevented her from being thrown from the car, but it hadn't stopped the tree limb from coming through the windshield and hitting her.

Lucas stared at her, clearly waiting for more details. Hailey had more, but she had to fight the panicky feeling rising in her again. It wasn't that night, but it suddenly felt as if it was.

"After I crashed, Darrin came to the side of the car," Hailey continued. "He looked at me." But then she stopped, her attention going back to Lucas. "Why didn't he just kill me then? I was helpless, barely conscious."

"Maybe he didn't want you dead," Lucas said. "He probably wanted those computer files and would have been willing to torture you to get them."

Yes. That had to be it. "But he didn't get a chance to kidnap me, because that's about the time you drove up. Did you see Darrin leave?"

"I saw his SUV speeding away. I couldn't go in pursuit."

That's because she had needed medical attention ASAP. Lucas had saved her life. Camden's, too, by staying with them. Lucas didn't seem any more comfortable thinking about that night than she did, and he looked relieved when Tillie came back into the living room.

"Is Camden ready for his bath?" the nanny asked, her voice tentative, probably because she knew that Hailey wanted to continue holding him.

Lucas nodded. "Best if he sticks to his routine," he told Hailey. "Plus, we need to do reports for the attack."

Yes, paperwork. Necessary, but she still hated having to hand her son over to the nanny. She'd gotten so few minutes holding him. Of course, a lifetime would be too few.

"You can watch," Tillie added, glancing at Hailey. "That way, you'll know how to do it." She also glanced at Lucas, and Tillie seemed to ignore the slight scowl that was on his face.

Maybe a scowl because it would mean a delay in doing those reports, but also because Tillie was including her.

Hailey didn't give Lucas a chance to veto Tillie's offer. She stood, following the woman as best she could to the bathroom just across the hall from the nursery. Lucas followed, too. Good thing, because just before Hailey reached the door, she stumbled and would have fallen flat on her face if Lucas hadn't caught her.

And just like that, she was in his arms.

The memories came. No way to stop them. Not with Lucas and her being body to body. Hailey got some flashes of even more body contact. Of when they were naked in bed.

Mercy, that caused the heat to flood through her again. Worse, Lucas noticed, and he looked as if he wanted to curse again. He didn't. He moved her away from him. Well, he moved so that her breasts were no longer pressed against his chest, but he looped his arm around her waist to steady her.

"You should be resting," he grumbled.

"Would you rest if you were in my shoes?" she countered.

That only deepened his scowl. Both knew the answer to that—no, he wouldn't.

Lucas kept his arm around her when they went to the doorway, but it was obvious that he was trying to touch as little of her as possible. Hailey soon didn't notice it because her attention was on the baby. Or at least, it was until Lucas's phone buzzed. She was close enough to see Grayson's name on the screen.

She felt the muscles in Lucas's arm tense. Probably because this could be bad news. He stepped back into the hall, answered the call and put it on speaker.

"Is Hailey there?" Grayson said without even issuing a greeting. Yes, this was bad news. Hailey could tell from his tone.

"I'm here," she answered.

"San Antonio PD found your sister," Grayson continued.

"Where is she?" Hailey immediately asked.

"The hospital. She's hurt, and she's asking to see you. Colleen says she knows who's trying to kill you."

Chapter Six

A car accident.

That's what had put Colleen in the hospital. And not just any ordinary accident, but one that'd happened on the same stretch of road where Hailey had nearly been killed. Lucas figured that was either an eerie coincidence or someone was trying to send them a message.

If it was a message, Lucas hadn't needed it. He knew just how much danger they were in. That's why it was almost certainly a mistake to take Hailey off the ranch and to the hospital, with the threat of an attack still hanging over their heads. But he also knew this meeting with Colleen could give them critical information to put an end to the danger.

Maybe an immediate end.

If Colleen confessed to helping Darrin when he tried to run Hailey off the road.

Lucas doubted that would actually happen, but he wouldn't rule it out. Heck, he wasn't ruling out anything right now. After all, he'd sworn that Hailey would never be under his roof again, and she'd not only spent the night there but also was back in his arms. Sort of. As he'd done earlier, he had to help her out of the cruiser, and that involved touching her.

He didn't have to remind her to hurry, and she did. As much as a hobbling woman could hurry. Lucas only hoped all this moving around wasn't doing anything to harm her leg muscles. The sooner he put some physical distance between them, the better, and that started with her getting back to a hundred percent.

Lucas believed her story about someone trying to kill her. And he felt a little sorry for her. But he wasn't ready to welcome her back into his and Camden's lives.

There was a deputy at the door to the hospital. Another inside. Since his cousins Dade and Gage had escorted Lucas and Hailey to the hospital, that meant Grayson had three other lawmen plus himself tied up with this.

"Thank you for not saying it was a stupid idea for me to come here," Hailey whispered as they made their way down the hall.

Lucas glanced at her from the corner of his eye. "Just because I didn't say it doesn't mean I agree with this. You could have demanded that Colleen tell you everything over the phone."

She glanced at him, too. "I did demand," she reminded him.

Yeah, but Hailey hadn't stood her ground when Colleen had insisted that she speak to her sister in person. This felt like a trap, and while the baby wasn't in danger at the moment, Hailey clearly was.

When they reached the patient ward of the hospital, Lucas spotted yet another lawman cousin. Josh. But he wasn't alone. There was a lanky, dark-haired guy in a black suit standing next to him. Judging from their scowls, neither Josh nor the suit were happy.

Hailey had an equally unhappy reaction to the man.

She sucked in her breath. "That's Brian Minton. He was one of the FBI agents who worked on the DeSalvo investigation."

Even though they were only a few yards from Minton, Lucas stopped. "You don't trust him?"

The question was valid, considering Lucas could feel Hailey's suddenly tight muscles. She hadn't exactly been relaxed on the trip over, but the tension was even worse now.

"I don't trust anyone involved in that," Hailey answered without taking her attention off Minton. "Remember, Preston DeSalvo had a dirty agent on his payroll. I'm positive of that."

No way could Lucas forget it, especially now that he'd read the file about it. The problem was, there'd been at least a dozen agents involved in that case and countless others who might have distanced themselves from it just so there'd be no obvious connection to the DeSalvo family.

"Any proof that Minton's dirty?" Lucas pressed.

"No," Hailey readily admitted, and she got moving again. "What are you doing here?" she asked the agent.

"I've asked him the same thing," Josh provided. "I've also told him he's not getting into Colleen's room until I get the okay from the sheriff. I haven't gotten that okay," he added, directing his glare at Minton.

Minton tapped his badge. "I'm here to interview two witnesses—Colleen and Laura—or, rather, Hailey, as she's going by these days. This investigation belongs to the FBI."

"How do you figure that?" Lucas said, but he didn't wait for an explanation. "Hailey is in WITSEC, and the marshals are in charge of that. As for Colleen, she was in a car accident in the jurisdiction of the Silver Creek Sheriff's Office."

Minton gave him a blank stare and huffed. "You and I both know this is connected to the DeSalvo family."

Lucas almost hoped this guy was dirty just so he could arrest him. "I know no such thing. I'm just bringing Hailey here to visit her sister."

"A sister who could have information I need," Minton countered.

Welcome to the club, but Lucas was first in line to question Colleen.

"Who ran Colleen off the road?" Minton asked, volleying his gaze between Hailey and Lucas.

Lucas shrugged. "Don't have a clue. Yet. How about you? Do you know who did this?"

"Probably the same thug who caused Hailey's accident."

"That thug is dead," Lucas said. "He died last night. From what I understand, Colleen's accident happened hours later."

Judging from the startled look in Minton's eyes, he hadn't known that. Or else he was pretending not to have known. "Eric could be behind this," Minton added after a long pause.

Yes, he could be. Or Colleen. Or even Minton himself. Lucas kept his speculations to himself to see if Minton would continue. He did.

"Whoever did this had a chance to kill you that night," Minton reminded Hailey. "He might have had the same chance to kill Colleen. But he didn't take it." He paused. "Why?"

Hailey shook her head. "I don't know."

No more startled look in Minton's eyes, but the comment seemed to rile him. "There are rumors that you have some files. Files that could incriminate Eric. If you have something like that, it's illegal to withhold them."

Hailey didn't back down from the agent's suddenly lethal stare. "It's illegal only if I know about the files. I don't. Truth is, I have huge gaps in my memory."

Normally, Lucas hated lying and liars, but in this case, the lie was warranted. His gut told him to hold off on giving Minton anything until they'd sorted all of this out. The *sorting* began with Colleen.

"Once you get approval from the sheriff, I'll let you in to see her," Lucas said to Minton.

Minton protested, of course, but Josh blocked his way while Lucas ushered Hailey inside. Josh wouldn't let the agent in without a fight, but just in case that happened, Lucas stayed near the door. That meant letting go of Hailey while she stepped around him and turned toward her sister.

"Thank God you came," Colleen said.

Lucas had never met the woman, but he recognized her from the hospital surveillance tapes. Colleen was a blonde, and despite the fact that there were cuts and bruises on her face, she looked as if she'd recently combed her hair and put on some lipstick. That sent an uneasy feeling up his spine. People who'd just had a brush with death didn't usually think about their appearance.

Of course, maybe Colleen had faked the accident to make herself appear innocent.

"Laura, it's been so long," Colleen added.

"Hailey," she automatically corrected her. "I don't use Laura anymore." Hailey limped closer until she was finally able to catch onto the end of the bed for support. "Has anyone been in here who could have planted a bug in the room?"

Colleen's eyes widened, and then she shook her head. "Only the doctor and some nurses have come in to check on me. I would have noticed if they'd planted something."

Maybe, but just in case, Lucas took a look around. When he didn't find anything, he went back to his guarding duties.

"Did Minton leave?" Colleen asked, and it took Lucas a moment to realize she was talking to him. Since she hadn't asked for introductions, she likely knew who he was.

"He's still in the hall. The sheriff will stall him, but eventually he'll get in here to see you. Is that a problem?"

"Of course." Colleen didn't hesitate, either. "I don't trust any of the agents who helped put Preston behind bars."

Preston.

Interesting. Colleen certainly didn't say the man's name with the venom that Hailey did.

"Preston's dead," Colleen went on. "And Minton is one of the people responsible for that."

"Preston was killed in a prison fight," Lucas pointed out. "Are you saying that Minton arranged to have him killed?"

Colleen opened her mouth but then closed it just as quickly. "I don't know. But there was a lawman involved in the dirty stuff Preston was doing, and if I trust the wrong person, I could end up like Preston."

Yes, she could. So could Hailey, and it might happen even if she withheld that trust.

Hailey went a few more steps toward the bed and looked surprisingly steady. Maybe because she was trying to look strong for what was no doubt about to be a confrontation with her sister.

"Aren't you even going to ask me if I'm all right?" Colleen asked before Hailey could speak.

Hailey paused a long time. "Are you okay?"

"No," her sister snapped. "Someone tried to kill me." And she stared at Hailey as if she were somehow responsible for that.

"Are you going to ask me if I'm all right?" Hailey fired right back. Heck, she sounded stronger, too. "After all, I was in a coma, and not long after coming out of it, someone tried to kill me, too."

And she waited for Colleen to respond to that.

Lucas watched Colleen's expression and her body language, but the woman seemed clueless as to what was going on. Again though, she could have been playing dumb like the agent outside the door.

"The hospital surveillance footage," Lucas finally prompted her. "We saw you on it with the man who tried to kill Hailey."

Colleen gasped and pressed her fingers to her lips. "That man tried to kill my sister?"

"Not once but twice," Hailey confirmed.

Colleen gasped again and frantically shook her head. "He said he was a marshal, and he showed me a badge. It looked real."

"It was fake," Lucas told her. "And he was a hired gun. Any idea who he was working for?"

More head shaking from Colleen. "I honestly thought he was a marshal and that he was here to protect Hailey."

Hailey drew in a long, weary breath and sank down onto the foot of the bed. "Start from the beginning. We need to know everything about him, everything that he said to you."

There were tears shimmering in Colleen's eyes now, and while Lucas wasn't immune to those tears, he wasn't fully buying them just yet. The woman could be crying because she'd just gotten caught and could be arrested.

"The marshal called me yesterday," Colleen started. "He said his name was Donald Silverman."

"It was Darrin Sandmire," Lucas corrected her.

"Was?" Colleen questioned.

"He's dead. Killed in a shoot-out with one of my cousins while he was attempting to get to Hailey."

Colleen pressed her fingertips to her mouth for a moment. "I didn't know. I swear I didn't," she added, her attention shifting to Hailey.

Like Lucas, Hailey still didn't look convinced. "This man asked you to meet him at the hospital?"

She nodded. "He said you were in danger, and that he needed my permission to access your personal things, like your computer."

So that he could get those files that Hailey had hidden. Files that Lucas needed to know more about as soon as they were finished here with Colleen.

"I told him that I didn't know where the rest of your personal things were," Colleen went on. "That the only things I had were what was collected from the car the night of your accident."

"It wasn't an accident," Hailey said. "That man ran me off the road and put both my baby and me in grave danger."

Colleen blinked back the tears, and her expression changed a little. Not so much alarm on her face but concern. "You're not suggesting that I was working with this snake?"

Hailey stayed quiet a moment. "I only need to find out the truth. So we can keep Camden safe."

"Camden?" Colleen asked.

"My son. That's what Lucas named him, and I will make sure no one, including you, does anything to harm him."

That didn't do much to ease Colleen's alarm. "You think I was together with him on this," she concluded. "I'm your sister."

"Yes, but we haven't always seen eye to eye in the past. You refused to testify against Preston."

Colleen's alarm turned to something else, and Lucas was pretty sure that something else was anger. It flashed through her eyes. "Because as you well know, I didn't witness the crimes you said he did."

There it was. Not just her words but Colleen's tone. Yeah, there was bitterness. Maybe because Colleen had been personally involved with the man? Or maybe she'd been doing more than only IT work for him.

"Why would Darrin want you dead?" Colleen came out and asked Hailey.

Lucas hoped she wouldn't mention those files, and she didn't. Hailey only shook her head. "Is it possible he was working for Preston and that Preston left orders to have me killed?"

"No," Colleen answered. Way too fast. She was definitely in the defensive mode when it came to her former boss. "Preston wouldn't have done that."

"How do you know that?" Lucas snapped.

Colleen volleyed some annoyed glances between Hailey and him. "Because I visited Preston in jail a few times."

Lucas rolled his eyes, took out his phone. "If I call the prison, I can find out exactly how many visits you made."

Her mouth tightened. "I saw him every week. And I'm not going to apologize for that."

"You should," Lucas argued. "Because even from behind bars, Preston could have arranged for the attacks against Hailey."

"He didn't," Colleen practically yelled. It took her a moment to regain her composure, and then she shifted her gaze back to Hailey. "You always believed the worst about Preston, but I believe it was the dirty agent who set him up. The same agent who's been trying to get into this room. Probably to kill me. Maybe he's the one who wants to kill Camden and you."

That was entirely possible. "You have any proof that Agent Minton is dirty?" Lucas asked her.

"No, but since you're a lawman, you should be the one getting that proof. Because someone put me in this hospital bed, and the next time, he might succeed in putting me in the grave."

Because that was possible, too, Lucas decided it was time to have a more thorough chat with Minton. Of course, that meant Hailey spending a little more time in the room with her sister, but Lucas could chat with Minton in the doorway. That way, he could keep an eye on Hailey.

Lucas opened the door, expecting to come face-to-face with the riled agent, but Minton wasn't there. However, Josh wasn't alone. There was another man standing in front of him. A man that Lucas recognized from the research he'd done the night before.

Eric DeSalvo.

Like Minton, Eric was wearing a suit. But he sure wasn't scowling. The man was smiling. A slick kind of smile that reminded Lucas of a snake oil salesman.

"You're supposed to be at the sheriff's office for an interview," Lucas immediately reminded Eric.

"I'm on my way there, but I decided to make a detour." His smile widened. "Lucas Ryland, Texas Ranger," Eric greeted him. Obviously the man had done his research as well. "I understand you think I'm guilty of all sorts of assorted felonies."

"Are you?" Lucas growled.

"No, but I think I can help you solve this." He tipped his head to the end of the hall, where Lucas saw Minton walking away. "Arrange a plea deal for me, and I'll give you what you need to put Agent Minton behind bars."

Chapter Seven

Hailey hadn't wanted to make this trip to the Silver Creek Sheriff's Office. She'd wanted to be back at the ranch with her son. But these interviews could be critical to helping Lucas and her make sure that Camden stayed safe.

Well, there was one official interview anyway—with Eric.

But since Agent Minton had shown up, Grayson would be questioning him, as well. Of course, that didn't mean Minton would answer anything. Especially anything that could incriminate him, but maybe he would spill something that would be helpful. For that matter, maybe Eric would do the same, and this nightmare would stop right here, right now.

"They're about ready to start," Lucas said, joining her by the observation window of the interview room. He handed her a cup of much-needed coffee.

Eric was already seated at the gray metal table, an attorney on each side of him, and even though he couldn't see Hailey through the one-way glass, he occasionally looked in her direction. And he smiled again.

No doubt to unnerve her.

There was certainly no love lost between them, and

after his father had been convicted, Eric had issued plenty of veiled threats to get to her. Not because he'd wanted to defend Preston. He hadn't.

Eric hadn't had much love for his father, either, but he hadn't wanted Hailey to do anything that would include him in the charges against Preston. Father and son still had plenty of business ties. Ties that Preston would have gladly continued because from all accounts, he'd wanted to protect his son.

Hailey now understood the lengths a parent would go to to protect a child. Even when that child—Eric— had done everything to distance himself from his father.

"Where's Minton?" she asked.

Lucas hitched his thumb to the hall. "In the other interview room, where Dade will question him. Let's just say he's not happy about being questioned by a *local yokel* deputy sheriff, and he's on his phone to his boss to find out if he can get out of it."

Maybe his boss would side with Grayson. And even if he didn't, perhaps they could get the information some other way.

She glanced back at Eric when he smiled at her again. "Any idea what kind of plea deal he wants?"

Lucas shook his head. "After dropping the bombshell at the hospital, he clammed up, claimed he didn't want to say anything else without his attorneys present."

That didn't surprise her. "Eric always hides behind his attorneys. So did his father. Not the same attorneys, of course. Preston would have shared, but Eric never trusted his father enough to mix his personal stuff with the family business."

Lucas stared at her. "After this, you should be able to access those files. Too bad you can't do that before

Grayson talks to Eric, because there might be something he could use for leverage. Just how much jail time would Eric get with what you have?"

"Not nearly enough. It's an illegal sale of some land. He paid off some officials one county over and got the land rezoned so he could in turn sell it to one of his puppet companies. There's also a sale of confiscated weapons."

That got his attention. He moved even closer. So close that his arm brushed against hers. It was just a slight touch, but she felt it head to toe.

"How many weapons?" he asked.

"Not nearly enough," she repeated after she gathered the breath to speak. Mercy, she had to figure out how to stop these flutters when she was around Lucas. She also had to focus since this was an important conversation. "It's a felony, but since he's got a spotless record, he might not get more than a year."

Lucas's forehead bunched up. "Yet it was enough to keep his father from coming after you."

"Preston loved him. Despite everything."

"Exactly what is *everything*?" he asked.

Because he was looking her straight in the eyes and because he was so close to her, it took Hailey a moment to realize they were still talking about Eric. And not this attraction between them.

"I don't know all the details," Hailey explained, "but Preston was a widower since Eric was a little boy, and Eric always blamed his father for his mother's death."

"Was Preston to blame?"

"I don't know, but she did die in a car accident. The cops did investigate it. Nothing concrete turned up, though."

Lucas made a sound, one of skepticism. A sound that Hailey totally understood. "Three car wrecks, and I know mine wasn't an accident," she said. "Perhaps the others weren't, either."

"You think Colleen's telling the truth about that? About any of this?" he asked.

Hailey drew in a long breath. "I want to believe her. But things have sometimes been—well—tense between us. She was three when her father married my mother, and I think once I was born a couple of years later, she thought our parents doted on me more than her. And maybe they did when I was little. Then our mother died of breast cancer, and my father ended up abandoning us. Colleen blamed me for that, too."

She stopped and realized she'd never told anyone that. "Sorry," Hailey said. "Didn't mean to dump all of that on you."

"No. I wanted to hear it because it's motive. People have certainly killed for a lot less, and coupled with her disapproval over you testifying against Preston, maybe Colleen decided she'd had enough."

That turned Hailey's stomach. Because *enough* nearly cost her Camden.

"What happened to Colleen and you after your father left?" Lucas continued.

"Foster care. That's when we got closer. I think because we only had each other."

And now Colleen might be trying to kill her. Of course, her sister wasn't their main suspect. That person was sitting on the other side of the observation mirror, and Eric smiled again when Grayson finally came into the room.

Lucas reached over to turn on the audio so they could

hear the interview, and again his arm brushed against hers. The other time he hadn't noticed. Or at least, he'd pretended not to notice. But this time their gazes met.

And held.

He mumbled some profanity and looked away. "This isn't going to happen," he said, but she wasn't sure if he was trying to convince her or himself.

No way did he want to get involved with her. She totally understood that, but the attraction was undeniable. The heat was still just as strong as it had been the night she'd gone to his bed. Thankfully she didn't have to keep remembering it, because Grayson got her attention when he spoke.

"Tell me about this plea deal you want," Grayson demanded.

Eric looked directly into the mirror. "I've heard that Hailey might have something she believes could be incriminating about me. It'll be all fake, of course, but I need the chance to clear my name."

"You said you thought that Eric didn't know about those computer files," Lucas reminded her.

"I didn't think he did. The only one I personally told was Preston."

Lucas stayed quiet a couple of seconds. "Is it possible Preston told Colleen?"

Hailey sighed. Nodded. Yes, it was possible. "But why would Colleen have told Eric?"

Lucas didn't get a chance to answer because Grayson continued. "What kind of incriminating info?" Grayson pressed. He knew all about the computer files they'd soon be able to access, but he no doubt wanted to hear Eric's take on this.

"I'm not positive, but I think it's supposed to be about illegal arms. It could be anything since it's fake."

Grayson just stared at him. "And you think Hailey manufactured this?"

Eric shrugged. "Probably not her, but my father could have."

"From everything I've heard, your father cared about you. In fact, I heard he'd do pretty much anything to prevent you from going to jail."

"That's what he wanted everyone to believe, but as a lawman, you certainly know what he was capable of. It's not much of a stretch to think he'd come up with something to keep me in line."

Oh, mercy. Was it false evidence? "It looked real," she said to Lucas. "And besides, if it were fake, why wouldn't Preston have sent someone after me? He hated me for testifying against him."

"Maybe even Preston didn't have the stomach for murdering a woman in a coma. Still…the latest attacks didn't happen until after he was dead."

True. And that led them right back to Eric.

"All right," Grayson continued. "You want a look at these so-called files. What are you offering in exchange?"

"Some files of my own," Eric said without hesitation. "They won't be admissible in court, but they're recordings that my father made when people visited his office."

Judging from Eric's smug look, there was something critical on the recordings. Judging from Grayson's scowl, he wasn't pleased about it.

"Any reason you didn't turn these recordings over to

the authorities when the investigation was going on?" Grayson snapped.

Eric's smug look went up a notch. "Because I only recently found them. Yesterday, in fact."

Hailey groaned. He was lying. He'd probably had them all along. But why had he held on to them?

"Eric's up to something," Hailey mumbled.

Lucas made a sound of agreement, but before he could say anything, the door to the observation room opened, and she saw Dade and Minton standing there.

"I've played along with this fiasco long enough," Minton snarled. "I'm an FBI agent and won't be treated like this."

"Let me guess," Lucas said to his cousin. "The interview went well." His voice dripped with sarcasm.

"No, it didn't." Minton's tone was full of sarcasm, too. "I don't know anything that can help you end whatever the hell's happening to Hailey. And I won't know until you tell me everything that's going on." He glanced at the mirror. "Including what's going on with that piece of slime."

Hailey wanted to tune Minton out and focus on Eric's conversation, but Grayson, the lawyers and the DA had moved on to the details of the plea deal, and from what Hailey could tell, Eric was asking for immunity from prosecution.

Which meant there was likely something incriminating him on those recordings or in the files Hailey had.

Hailey hadn't intended to bring up anything to Minton about what Eric had just said, but Lucas obviously had something different in mind.

"Eric claims he has recordings that he got from his

father's office," Lucas tossed out there. "He's working out a plea deal now."

And Hailey soon knew why Lucas had done that. He pinned his attention to Minton, clearly looking for a reaction.

He got one.

Minton charged toward the window to have a closer look. "Any recordings come under the jurisdiction of the FBI."

Lucas huffed. "You seem to keep forgetting that this isn't an FBI matter. The recordings could be evidence in the recent attacks against Hailey. Attacks that happened right here in Silver Creek." He glanced at Dade. "Did anyone here in the sheriff's office request FBI assistance? Because that's the only way Minton could be involved in this."

Dade pretended to think about that. "Nope. No one here made a request like that. Grayson said if we needed help, we'd call in the Rangers. Of course, we won't have to call very loud since a Texas Ranger is standing right here in this room."

Minton's mouth tightened, but instead of verbal fire at any of the men, he turned toward Hailey. "I'm trying to keep you and your son alive." He nodded toward Eric. "You'll need all the help you can get with that piece of slime. He's dangerous. That's why you should give me copies of anything you have on him."

Lucas's huff was even louder this time. "This conversation is over." And he took Hailey by the arm and maneuvered her around Minton and Dade.

"It's not over," Minton insisted. "One way or another, I will get the evidence you have."

It sounded like a threat. Worse, it felt like one.

Hailey reminded herself that Minton could just be focused on the job, but if he was the dirty agent Preston had on his payroll, then she had two snakes to watch out for—Eric and Minton.

"I'll take you back to the ranch," Lucas said once they were out of earshot of Minton. "We'll wait there until you can get into the files. Maybe by then Grayson will have worked out something with Eric."

They went to the front where Lucas had left the cruiser, but before they reached the door, his phone buzzed. Hailey saw Josh's name on the screen. Since he was at the hospital, she instantly got a bad feeling.

Lucas obviously did, too, because he belted out some profanity under his breath. "A problem?" Lucas greeted his cousin.

"Yeah. Please tell me we have something to hold Colleen. Because if not, she's about to leave the hospital."

Hailey released the breath she'd been holding. She'd braced herself for something worse, like an attack. "Did the doctor say it was okay for her to go?"

"No. But she's leaving anyway unless we've got grounds to hold her."

"She was on the surveillance tape with a hit man," Hailey reminded Lucas.

But Lucas shook his head. "Not enough since she had an explanation for that, and there's no proof that she knew who he was. Can Colleen hear me talking right now?" he asked Josh.

"No," Josh repeated. "She's in her room getting dressed, and I'm in the hall."

"Good. Then let her leave, but I want a tail on her. Tell me where she goes and who she sees. Because if she's behind this, she might try to meet with her hired thugs."

True. Hailey hated to think Colleen would do that, but this might be a way to be sure.

"Will do," Josh said. "Hold on while I send a text to the reserve deputy who's in the parking lot. He's dressed in plain clothes."

Maybe Colleen wouldn't notice the man and would do whatever it was she was setting out to do. Part of Hailey wished, though, that her sister had had no part in any of this.

"Colleen's coming out of her room now," Josh added a moment later.

Josh said something else, something that Hailey didn't catch. Ditto for whatever her sister said to the deputy.

"Colleen just handed me a note that I'm supposed to give to Hailey," Josh finally explained.

"A note?" Hailey asked. "Why didn't she just talk to me?"

"Don't know. You want me to unfold it and read it to you?"

"Yes," she answered as fast as she could.

Hailey heard the rustling around on Josh's end, and a moment later he mumbled some of the same profanity that Lucas had just used. "It says, 'I'm sorry, Hailey. I know you'll never understand, but I did what I had to do.'"

Chapter Eight

"I did what I had to do."

Lucas hoped Colleen was referring to checking herself out of the hospital, but he had a bad feeling in the pit of his stomach.

It certainly hadn't helped when Colleen had managed to ditch the tail they had on her. Now she was in the wind. Could have been anywhere. Heck, she could have been out there planning another attack. Colleen had a lot of questions to answer, but first they had to find her and somehow force her to tell them the truth.

Of course, in addition to Colleen, Lucas had plenty of other things adding to that bad feeling. Minton, Eric.

And Hailey.

Hailey, though, was a bad feeling of a different kind.

Once again, he had no choice but to take her to his house at the ranch. It was either that or spend more time at the sheriff's office, and neither of them wanted that. In fact, Hailey had jumped to say yes when he suggested they go.

Hailey had *jumped* yet again when they'd arrived home and Tillie had offered to show her how to give Camden his bottle. Now Lucas was supervising that while he waited for updates on both the plea deal and Colleen.

"He really is a little miracle," Hailey said, smiling at Camden while she burped him.

Of course, Hailey was in heaven over doing something as simple as feeding and burping their son. "You might not call him a miracle when he wakes up every three hours," Lucas joked, because he thought they could use some levity.

At least, he could use it, anyway. His muscles were knotted so tight that his back and shoulders were hurting.

Hailey smiled, and he got a knot of a different kind. This one in his stomach. He remembered that smile. It was one of the first things that had attracted him to her, and even now it stalled his breath in his chest. Then she chuckled when Camden let out a burp that sounded as if it'd come from a grown man drinking beer. Lucas didn't join her on the chuckling, but he'd had the same reaction the first couple of times it had happened.

His phone dinged with a text from Josh.

Lucas glanced at his watch. "You should be able to get into the storage cloud to retrieve those files." That would get his mind off her smile and back to what he should have been focusing on.

She nodded, her forehead bunching up. Obviously she didn't want to let go of the baby just yet, but Lucas needed to see exactly what Hailey had against Eric.

Hailey kissed Camden, and she waited for Tillie to come and take the baby before she got up from the chair. She made her way to Lucas's office just up the hall. It seemed as if each hour she was walking a little better, but she still caught onto the wall to steady herself.

And she also caught onto him when she eased into the chair.

"Sorry," she said. No doubt because she felt his muscles tense. "I know it bothers you for me to touch you."

Yeah, it did. But not in the way she was thinking. It bothered him because it reminded him of things he shouldn't have been remembering. Instead of mentioning that, though, Lucas just motioned for her to get busy on the laptop.

She nodded, looked disappointed that he hadn't addressed the elephant in the room—the attraction. Something he had no plans to address.

"It'll take a couple of minutes for me to get through the passwords and security questions," she said just as his phone rang.

Since it was Grayson's name on the screen and no doubt a call about the investigation, Lucas answered it on speaker. That way Hailey wouldn't have to lean too close to him to hear.

"We worked out a plea deal with Eric," Grayson said. "A limited one for both of us. He'll get immunity only if there's something of evidentiary value on the recordings. The second condition is that the immunity will cover only one criminal count. A count that doesn't include murder or accessory to murder."

Lucas looked at Hailey. "Any chance of Eric having murdered someone?"

"Not that I know of," she answered. "From what I learned, the DeSalvo family crimes seemed to be limited to money laundering and the sale of illegal arms. Of course, it's possible someone was killed during those deals, but the deals I had knowledge of were mainly Preston's, not Eric's."

That didn't mean Eric didn't have any side deals of his own. But then, if he had, there was no way the man would give Grayson evidence to incriminate himself for murder.

"What did you mean about the deal being limited for both Eric and you?" Hailey wanted to know.

"The recordings are on old compact disks, and Preston set it up so they can't be copied. Eric wants the disks to stay here in the sheriff's office, and that means I'll have to tie up some manpower to listen to them."

Eric had probably added that into the deal to make sure Minton and the FBI didn't get their hands on them. Or maybe Eric had another reason for doing that.

"Did Eric give you any idea what was on the recordings?" Lucas asked Grayson.

"He says he hasn't listened to them all. Which I find hard to believe."

So did Lucas. Eric didn't seem like the sort to shoot himself in the foot by handing over anything that could be connected to him beyond the limits of the plea deal. Still, there might be something that Eric had missed.

"But what Eric did say," Grayson went on, "was that there are dozens of recorded conversations with his father and his business associates. Of course, he didn't get permission from any of these people. But there are names, he claims, that we can use to make some arrests if we can link those names to the crimes."

Yeah, because the recordings themselves probably wouldn't be admissible in court since Preston didn't get prior consent from at least one of the people he was recording. Then there was the problem of the tapes being in the hands of one of their suspects, one who could have doctored the conversations.

"I'll call you as soon as we have the recordings. Let me know what you find out from Hailey's files," Grayson added before he ended the call.

Lucas put away his phone and watched as Hailey accessed the site. Thankfully her fingers were working better than her legs. She had no trouble typing.

No trouble cursing, either.

That bad feeling in his stomach went up a couple of notches.

"The files are gone?" Lucas concluded, but he hoped he was wrong.

Hailey didn't answer him. She kept mumbling profanity. Kept searching through the storage cloud. Even though Lucas was far from a computer expert, he could see that all the files were empty.

Except one.

Hailey clicked on it, and when Lucas saw what was there, he was the one cursing. Not files to incriminate Eric. There was just a single document with one sentence written on it.

I did what I had to do.

It was the exact wording of the note Colleen had left with Josh, but in this case it didn't make sense.

"Why would Colleen want these files deleted?" Lucas asked. "From what I can tell, Colleen despises Eric."

Hailey groaned, obviously still dealing with the bombshell of what her sister had done. Or else what someone wanted them to believe Colleen had done.

"She does," Hailey confirmed. But then she shook

her head. "Or maybe that was all a pretense. I just don't know anymore."

Another groan, and she buried her face in her hands for a couple of seconds. When she lowered them, Lucas spotted the tears in her eyes.

Oh, man. Not tears. Not now. He was already feeling raw and exhausted, and he was a sucker for a woman's tears. Especially this woman. Because this was quickly turning into a very bad day for Hailey and this investigation.

She stood and looked around as if trying to decide what to do, but Lucas could see that there wasn't much fight left in her. "Colleen must hate me to side with a snake like Eric."

"Maybe she didn't have a choice. Maybe Eric has some dirt on her. Something that would send her to jail."

The tears continued. "Yes, but she knows those files are meant to protect Camden and me from Eric. Or from any of Preston's thugs who might be out there ready to carry out their late boss's dying wish to see me dead."

She was right. And Lucas had had enough of the tears. Before he could talk himself out of it, he reached out and pulled her into his arms. Of course, Hailey had been in his arms since she'd come out of the coma. It'd been necessary to keep her from falling.

This was different.

Lucas could feel it. And Hailey could feel it, too. She didn't go stiff as she had the other times they'd touched in the past twenty-four hours. She sort of melted against him.

"I'm just so scared," she admitted. "Not for me but for Camden and you. For your family."

"No one is going to hurt Camden or my family," he

assured her. Not that he was in a position to give that kind of assurance. Not with hired guns after them. Still, those hired guns would have to get past him, and since he was protecting his son, Lucas had no intention of making that easy for them.

Hailey looked up at him at the exact moment he looked down at her. Lucas silently said more of that profanity. He was so not ready for this. Well, his mind and heart weren't, anyway, but the rest of him seemed to think it was a good idea to kiss her or something.

Especially *something*.

The heat came. Memories, too. Vivid memories of Hailey naked and beneath him in his bed. The very bed that was just up the hall.

She didn't look away from him, and hell, he didn't look away, either. They just stood there with all those bad thoughts running through his head. Lucas was within a fraction of a second of acting on those bad thoughts by kissing her, but Hailey cleared her throat and stepped back.

"I'm sorry," Hailey said, rubbing her forehead and dodging his gaze. "I know that makes things worse."

It did, and Lucas didn't want her to clarify that. Or talk about it. Hell, he just wanted to concentrate on anything but this ache that was begging him to have sex with her right here, right now.

"You should try to call Colleen and ask her about this," he managed to say, and he handed her his phone.

Focus. He needed to deal with the problems of the investigation and not create new problems by having his body go rock hard with thoughts of Hailey.

She nodded. "I'm not sure if Colleen still has the same number. Until I came out of the coma, I hadn't been in touch with her since Preston's trial, and that was over eighteen months ago."

It was a long shot, but it was one that paid off. In a way. Colleen didn't answer, but when her voice mail greeting kicked in, Hailey and he got verification that her sister had kept the old number.

"Call me ASAP," Hailey said when she left the message, and there was a definite urgency in her tone.

But whether Colleen would phone her back was a different matter. After all, even though she'd been injured in that car accident, Colleen had still managed to elude the reserve deputy. Something Lucas wished he'd handled differently. He should have requested one of the regular deputies to follow her.

Hailey sank back down onto the chair and gave a heavy sigh. At least she wasn't crying, but this was obviously getting to her. Or rather, it was, until she looked up at him again, and there was something in her eyes. Not attraction this time.

"What if Colleen and Eric believe I have hard copies of everything that was in the online storage?" she asked.

It didn't take long, only a few seconds, for Lucas to figure out where this was going. And he shook his head. "You're talking about setting a trap. Definitely not a good idea, because it could send those hired killers after you again."

"The hired killers will come no matter what. I'm not sure why, but obviously the person behind this sees me as a threat. Or maybe the things that I know are what he or she considers the threat."

That was true, and it didn't rule out any of their suspects. Minton could want anything destroyed that could link him to being a dirty agent. Eric could be trying to save his butt from going to jail. And Colleen? Well, Lucas still didn't know why she was seemingly playing on Eric's side in this, but it was obvious she didn't want her sister to have any incriminating evidence about the man.

Or maybe the information in the file incriminated someone else? Like Colleen herself?

Too bad they didn't have the real files to examine.

"Just think this through," Hailey pressed. "We could leak that the computer files have been erased and that I'm getting the hard copies to give to Grayson. We could say that I'm getting them from a safe deposit box or something."

Lucas huffed. It would still put Hailey in immediate danger. Unless…

"Maybe we could get a cop to go in posing as you," Lucas said. "There's a reserve deputy, Kara Duggan, who has a similar height and build. We could arrange for there to be eyes on her and give her plenty of backup." But then he paused. "Of course, the gunmen might be expecting a trap and come here after you."

She pressed her lips together a moment. Clearly this thought had already occurred to her, but then Hailey's gaze drifted in the direction of the nursery. If the gunmen came here, Camden would be in danger.

"How about you and I go to the sheriff's office and then leak the info?" she suggested. "That way, if they do smell a trap, they'll go after me there and not come to the ranch."

Lucas went through all the things that could go wrong. And with hired killers, there was plenty that could go wrong.

"You know that none of our suspects will go after

the decoy, right?" he reminded her. "He or she will send a lackey."

Hailey nodded. "But if we have a lackey—alive—we might be able to find out who hired him."

True. Once they had the hired thug's name, then they could search for a paper trail or maybe work out a plea deal. Still, it wasn't without huge risks.

"You're sure you want to do this?" Lucas asked.

"I'm sure," Hailey said without hesitation.

Lucas hesitated, but he knew this was the only straw they had a chance to grab right now. He took out his phone, but it rang before he could call Grayson to set all of this up.

Dade's name popped up on the screen. "We got the recordings from Eric," Dade told Lucas. "They're actual disks. Dozens of them. He flagged one that we should listen to first. It's a conversation between Preston and Colleen." He paused. "I really think Hailey should hear what her sister had to say. Then we can figure out what we need to do."

Chapter Nine

Hailey didn't know what she was dreading more—this return trip to the sheriff's office to hear the recorded conversation that Dade had said she'd definitely want to hear, or leaving Camden.

Still, it was necessary. Not just for the recordings but also because they needed to work out the final details for the trap to lure out whoever was behind this. She hated that the reserve deputy would be in possible danger, but Hailey was hoping that Lucas would be able to set it all up so they could minimize the risks.

"Maybe this won't take long," Lucas said as they got into the cruiser.

They weren't alone. Josh and one of the armed ranch hands, Avery Joyner, were with them. Josh was behind the wheel with Avery riding shotgun. Lucas and she took the backseat.

"And I'm still not sure this is a good idea," Lucas added.

She'd lost count how many times he'd said a variation of that, and Hailey agreed with him. She wasn't sure it was a good idea, either, but at the moment they didn't have a lot of options as to how to put an end to the danger. Plus, she really did want to listen to those recordings. Of course, she could have had Dade play the conversations for her over the phone, but from the sound of it, there'd need to be some follow-up action when it came to her sister.

"Colleen or Preston must have said something bad for Dade to have called," Hailey remarked.

Lucas made a sound of agreement, but what he didn't do was take his attention off their surroundings. Like Avery and Josh, his gaze was firing all around them, watching for anyone who might attack them. "Not a surprise, though. After all, she's the one who likely deleted those computer files."

True. But there was something about it that didn't feel right. People with solid computer skills could have hacked their way in and then set up her sister to take the blame.

"What the hell?" Josh mumbled, and he slowed the cruiser.

Hailey followed his gaze to the end of the road, where someone had parked a black car. The road was barely a few yards off Ryland land, which was probably why the security system hadn't detected it, but there were also two ranch hands armed with rifles. They weren't pointing the rifles at their visitor, but Hailey figured they would if he tried to get on the ranch road.

"You know that man?" Avery asked Lucas.

And that's when Hailey spotted Minton stepping from the car.

"Yeah," Lucas answered. "That's FBI Agent Brian Minton."

Both Lucas and she groaned. She definitely didn't want to deal with the agent today. Especially since he was one of their suspects. But from the way Minton had parked, they wouldn't be able to get around him without speaking to the man. Judging from the way Lucas was cursing, the *speaking* wouldn't be friendly.

"Wait here, and I'll see what he wants," Lucas said to Hailey. He drew his gun, reached for the door but then glanced back at her. "And I mean it about waiting inside the cruiser. If Minton's behind the attacks, he could have snipers in the area."

That caused her heart to jump to her throat, and Hailey caught onto his arm. "If there are possible snipers, it's too risky for you to go out there."

"I won't be long," Lucas insisted, as if that made everything okay. Hailey wanted to remind him that it took only a split second for someone to gun him down, but he was out of the cruiser before she could even gather her breath.

Josh opened his door, as well. So did Avery. And they drew their guns while continuing to watch around them. Hailey tried to do the same, but it was hard not to focus on Minton and Lucas. Thankfully, with the front doors open, she could hear Minton when he *greeted* Lucas.

"These men wouldn't let me onto the ranch," Minton complained.

"Because they're smart and following orders. *My* orders. No one's getting onto the ranch unless you live or work here. Neither applies to you."

In addition to hearing them well enough, Hailey had no trouble seeing Minton's steely expression. "We're fellow peace officers. You'd think we could cooperate long enough to bring someone to justice. Especially since that someone is obviously after Hailey and now you since you're trying to protect her. They'll kill you to get to her."

"Cooperate? Right. You and I have a different notion about what that means. You want me to give this investigation to the FBI, and it's not mine to give. Sheriff Grayson Ryland is in charge."

"Well, he shouldn't be," Minton snapped. Every muscle in his face was tight, but he said something under his breath. Something she didn't catch. And then it appeared he was trying to rein in his temper. "I just need the information, that's all. I need to know what Hailey has. Eric, too. Especially Eric, because he could have altered those recordings." Minton paused. "I think Eric's trying to set me up."

"And how and why would he do that?" Lucas asked.

"I'm investigating him, and I think I'm close to giving him a dose of the justice he deserves. He'd obviously do anything to stop me, and that includes doctoring the tapes that he claims he just found. Eric's got the money and resources to do something like that."

Interesting. Maybe Minton was trying to do some damage control beforehand just in case there was anything in those conversations about him.

"Did you and Preston have conversations in his office?" Lucas pressed. He was still keeping watch around them, and while Hailey knew this chat could be important, she didn't want Lucas out there any longer.

Minton nodded. "A couple of them, in fact. Remember, I was investigating both Eric and him, and I interviewed Preston. Anything I said could be altered or taken out of context, and I just don't want my name sullied because of a snake like Eric."

"I get that, but it still doesn't mean you can listen to the recordings. Eric worked out a plea deal, and we have to abide by that." Lucas glanced around again. "If you want to keep up this little chat, then call the sheriff's office and make an appointment." With that, he headed back to the cruiser.

Obviously Minton didn't like being dismissed that way, because the flash of anger returned on his face. "Not cooperating with me is a huge mistake," the agent snarled, and he, too, turned back toward his car.

He didn't get far.

Because a shot slammed through the air and smashed right into the front end of Minton's car.

HELL.

Lucas had known right from the start that something like this could happen, but he'd hoped he would get lucky. Apparently not, though.

He was still a few yards from the cruiser and started to run so he could dive in, but the next shot stopped him. It didn't go toward Minton's car but right at Lucas. He had to drop to the ground, and it wasn't a second too soon.

Because if Lucas hadn't, the next shot would have hit him.

"Get in!" Hailey yelled.

He had no trouble hearing her and the fear in her voice, but Lucas hoped like the devil that she was staying down. The windows in the cruiser were bullet-resistant. That didn't mean, though, that these shots wouldn't eventually tear their way through the glass and reach her.

Another shot came.

This one landed near Minton again, and like Lucas, the agent had no choice but to go to the ground and use his car as cover. The ranch hands outside took cover, as well. They scrambled into the ditch.

Good.

Lucas didn't want them in the line of fire, but he also needed the attack to stop. Because they weren't the only ones in danger. Anyone else on the ranch could be hit if this idiot trying to kill them had a long enough range.

Judging from the sound of the shots, they were coming from a heavily treed area across the road. The oaks were huge there and would make the perfect catbird seat for a sniper. But that wasn't all that Lucas realized. There was more than one gunman.

"Can you see who's shooting?" Minton called out to him.

"No. But I think they're at your eleven and one o'clock."

Lucas only hoped there weren't more, but considering the other attacks, there was no telling how many the sick person behind this had sent after them.

The two gunmen were clearly working together to keep all five of them pinned down while also keeping watch on the cruiser. When Josh tried to open the door, no doubt to return fire, one of the gunmen sent a bullet his way. Definitely not good because it didn't stop with just one shot. A barrage of bullets went into the cruiser, each of them with the possibility of being deadly.

Lucas had to do something *now*.

"Minton, somehow you need to get in your car and move it," Lucas ordered.

Because until he did that, they wouldn't be able to move the cruiser forward and get the heck out of there. There was no way Lucas wanted to go in reverse and have these hired guns just follow them onto the ranch.

Minton did try to move. He made it a few inches

before the shots turned in his direction, and he had to scramble to the ground again.

By now, someone had called for backup, and even though there were several of his lawmen cousins on the grounds, they wouldn't be able to get to them right now without putting themselves in grave danger.

The shots shifted again. Some went in the direction of the ditch. No doubt because Avery had tried to fire. Since the hands were armed with rifles, they would stand a better chance of putting an end to this than Lucas would with his handgun. It was obvious, though, that the thugs weren't going to give the men a chance to shoot.

Lucas glanced over at the cruiser to make sure Hailey was staying put. She wasn't. She was by the door nearest him, and she was opening it as wide as it would go. Of course, that caused the gunmen to fire at her.

"Get down!" Lucas told her.

He didn't want her risking her life, but he was thankful about the door maneuver. It would make it easier for him to get back into the cruiser if he could just get a break from the gunmen. Even then, though, he'd still need Minton to get the devil out of the way.

"I'll create a diversion," Lucas said to Minton. He didn't shout and hoped his voice didn't carry so the gunmen would hear him. "When they start shooting at me, get to your car."

Minton nodded. Lucas had to admit that the man looked just as concerned about this as Lucas was. Maybe that meant Minton wasn't a dirty agent after all. But then, this could all be a ruse to make him look innocent, especially since no one had actually been shot. The gunmen would have had ample opportunity to do that when Minton and he had been talking out in the open.

Anything that Lucas did at this point was a risk, but doing nothing was even riskier, so he got into position the way a sprinter would at the start line, and after saying a quick prayer, he bolted toward the cruiser.

"No!" Hailey shouted when Lucas started moving.

But he was already doing that diversion that he hoped would work. It did. The shots started coming right at him, each of them smacking into the ground and kicking up bits of asphalt right at him. Still, Lucas didn't stop. He barreled to the cruiser and jumped inside.

"You shouldn't have done that," Hailey cried out. She grabbed him and pulled him into her arms.

Lucas could feel her shaking. Could feel the relief, too. Relief he understood because he was feeling it as well. But he couldn't think about that right now. Instead, using the cruiser door for cover, he took aim and started shooting in the direction of those gunmen. They were perhaps out of range, but it might distract them enough to buy Minton a little time.

Avery joined Lucas, and both of them fired. For the first time since this attack had begun, the gunmen stopped shooting. It was just enough time for Minton to dart around to the side of his car and get in.

"Put on your seat belt," Lucas told Hailey.

He didn't have to tell Josh to get ready to move because his cousin had already put the cruiser in gear. Thankfully it didn't take long for Minton to start his car engine, and as soon as he'd done that, he hit the accelerator.

Josh did the same.

Minton sped out onto the main road, turning toward

town. The majority of the bullets followed him, slamming into the back of his car. But some of the shots came at the cruiser, too.

"Don't go the same direction as Minton," Lucas instructed Josh.

His cousin didn't question that, probably because he already knew that Lucas considered Minton a suspect. Josh went in the opposite direction. That would also get them to town. Eventually. But it was a longer route. Still, as long as it got them out of the path of those shots, Lucas didn't mind the extra miles.

Well, provided he could keep Hailey safe by going that extra distance. Lucas didn't want to be near Minton, but he also hoped they weren't heading straight for another attack.

"I've already called Mason," Josh explained. "He heard the shots and was already putting the ranch on lockdown. Grayson's sending someone to find those snipers."

Lucas figured they wouldn't be easy to find. They'd probably had a darn good escape route mapped out before either of them ever pulled their triggers. Still, that didn't mean they wouldn't leave some kind of evidence behind.

"Is anyone following us?" Avery asked, looking around.

Lucas was looking, as well, but he didn't see anyone. Not at first, anyway. And then, just ahead, he spotted the black SUV that had pulled into an old ranch trail. Josh no doubt saw it, as well, because he muttered some profanity under his breath.

No way could it be the shooters because they wouldn't have had time to leave those trees and make it to this point. But Lucas doubted that it was a coincidence that someone happened to be on this rural stretch of the road at the same time someone had been trying to kill them.

"Turn around," Lucas said to Josh. He kept his attention pinned to the vehicle while he pushed Hailey down onto the seat. "Go back in the other direction."

It was dangerous, but he didn't want to risk driving past that SUV in case someone started shooting at them again. Best to get Hailey to safety, and then he could have the deputies go on the search for the SUV.

"Don't stop by the ranch," Lucas added. "Just keep driving to the sheriff's office."

Josh hit the brakes, and even though the road was barely wide enough to do a U-turn, his cousin managed it by using the gravel shoulder of the road. He got the cruiser headed in the other direction. But not before Lucas caught a glimpse of the people inside the SUV.

"No," Hailey said under her breath. And Lucas knew from her tone and her gasp that she'd seen them, too.

There was a man behind the wheel. Someone that Lucas didn't recognize, but he sure as heck knew the person in the front passenger seat.

Colleen.

Chapter Ten

One minute Hailey felt numb from the spent adrenaline, but the next minute she wanted to scream. Yet another attack could have killed them.

Attacks perhaps orchestrated by her own sister.

It turned her stomach to relive the image of Colleen in that SUV. Less than a half mile from those snipers at the ranch. Had she been sitting there, staying close to her hired thugs? Because she certainly didn't look like a hostage.

From the glimpse that Hailey had gotten of her, she'd seen no restraints on Colleen, but her sister had looked surprised to see her. Maybe because Colleen had figured they'd be heading toward town and not her direction.

The one good thing in all of this was that Camden and the rest of the people at the ranch were safe. Their attackers hadn't tried to get onto the grounds to continue their rampage there. Even more, Mason had sent additional armed ranch hands to guard Lucas's house. Of course, they wouldn't be able to go outside, but that was better than putting themselves in harm's way.

"Are you okay?" Lucas asked her.

Hailey didn't even try to pretend she was. She just

shook her head and hoped the truth didn't worry him too much. There was already enough worry on his face without her adding more.

Josh pulled to a stop directly in front of the sheriff's office, and Lucas quickly ushered her in. She'd already prepared herself that Minton would be there, and he was. He was also glaring at them.

"I blame you two for this," Minton snapped. "I could have been killed because of you."

Lucas returned the glare. "How do you figure that?"

"You should have already called in the FBI on this. Obviously this is too big an investigation for the locals to handle."

Now that got Grayson glaring, but it was Lucas who took up the argument with Minton.

"And by calling in the FBI, you mean *you*?" Lucas challenged the man. He huffed. "I didn't have a lot of reasons to trust you before this latest fiasco, and this didn't improve things."

"You think I had something to do with this?" Minton howled. He didn't wait for Lucas to answer. "I didn't, and because you're so stubborn about handling this yourself, you put Hailey right back in danger. Is that what you want, huh?"

"I've had enough of him," Hailey managed to whisper. She was barely hanging on by a thread, and she needed a moment to compose herself. Maybe during those moments she'd figure out how to put an end to all of this.

That's all she had to say to Lucas to get him moving. He still had his arm around her waist from when he'd ushered her in from the cruiser, and now he got her moving toward the hall, heading to the break room.

"I'm sorry," she added. "I should have just stood up to him—"

"No, and we shouldn't have stayed in the squad room for as long as we did. It could have been a ploy to keep us near the windows so that the snipers can finish us off."

Mercy. She hadn't even considered that, but she should have. She needed to be thinking clearer because the stakes were sky-high.

"I need to call Colleen again," she said, figuring that Lucas would hand her his phone to do that.

He didn't. He took her into the break room, had her sit on the sofa. "Grayson can talk to Colleen. In fact, he'll bring her in for questioning."

Yes, because her sister was more than just a person of interest. She'd been in the vicinity of a crime scene and had likely deleted those storage files. Grayson no doubt had lots of questions for her. Anything Colleen said at this point should be part of the official investigation. Still, Hailey needed to hear what her sister had to say, and if Grayson couldn't get her in soon, then she'd try again to call her.

Lucas handed her a bottle of water that he took from the fridge. "This will have to do for now, but you probably could use something stronger."

She could indeed use it. And she got it when Lucas dropped down next to her and pulled her into his arms. It was such an unexpected gesture that Hailey went stiff for a moment. Lucas noticed, too.

He eased back a little, glanced down at her. "I know. This isn't a smart thing for me to be doing, but you look ready to drop."

"I am," she admitted. "And you're right about it not being a smart thing."

It brought back the memories of when they'd been lovers, and Hailey didn't have the energy to fend off those old images. Or the heat, which wasn't old at all. Anytime she was around Lucas, that heat flared up with a vengeance. Now was no different.

"I'm also scared," she admitted. "For Camden. For you. For all of us."

He didn't try to dismiss those fears. He couldn't. Because they were real. The danger just kept coming at them.

Lucas made a sound of agreement and eased his hold on her a little. Hailey was certain he would just pull away. But he didn't. He stayed there right next to her, and he slowly turned his head to look at her again. Since she was already looking at him, their gazes met. Held.

The air was suddenly so still it felt as if everything was holding its breath, waiting. Hailey certainly was. She had no idea where Lucas was going to take this, but she knew what she wanted.

She wanted him.

Hailey saw that want in Lucas's eyes. Saw the storm that was brewing there, too. He hadn't forgiven her for what she'd done. Probably didn't completely trust her, either, but that didn't stop this attraction.

He cursed. His voice hardly had any sound. And she saw the storm get much stronger as he lowered his head and touched his mouth to hers. It was barely a kiss, but it caused that fire inside her to blaze out of control. A simple kiss from Lucas could do that.

And then he did more. Much, much more. His mouth

came to hers again, and this time it was for more than just a touch. He kissed her. Really kissed her.

His taste was a reminder of all those memories and images she'd been battling since she'd come out of the coma. A battle she was losing because the memories came flooding back and mixed with this new firestorm that the kiss was creating.

A sound rumbled in his chest. Definitely not one of agreement this time. It was one of protest and a reminder of a different sort. He didn't want to be doing this, but like her, he seemed helpless to stop it.

The kiss lingered on a moment. Then two. And just when Hailey was ready to pull him even closer Lucas stopped.

"I think I've complicated things enough for one day," he grumbled.

That made her smile even though there wasn't anything to smile about. What he'd said was the truth. The kiss had complicated things. Heck, being together upped the complications, as well, but until they found a way to put an end to the danger, they were joined at the hip.

And afterward…well, Hailey wasn't ready to go there just yet, though she knew a future without danger also meant a future in which Lucas and she had to work out a custody arrangement for Camden.

There was a knock at the door, and a moment later Grayson opened it. He stared at them, and even though he didn't say anything about how close they were sitting, he probably noticed that they looked as if they'd just been doing something they shouldn't have been doing.

"Everything okay?" Grayson asked.

"I was about to ask you the same thing." Lucas got to his feet. "Bad news?"

Grayson lifted his shoulder. "Josh filled me in on the details of the attack. Two of the deputies just arrived in the area where those snipers were. They're not there, of course, but there are tire tracks. It's a long shot, but CSI might be able to get a match from them if they were driving a custom vehicle. The gunmen might have left prints or trace evidence behind as well."

That seemed like such a long shot, but everything was at this point. "What about the black SUV?" Hailey asked.

Grayson shook his head. "No sign of it, either. I don't guess either of you got the license plate numbers?"

"No," Lucas and she said in unison.

Hailey added a sigh. Again, she wasn't thinking straight. The shock of seeing her sister had prevented her from looking at the plates. Plus, Josh had been so fast at turning the cruiser around that she'd barely managed a glimpse of Colleen, much less any specifics about the SUV.

"Any luck getting in touch with my sister?" Hailey wanted to know.

"No. I've left her a message, and San Antonio PD will go out to her place and see if she's there."

She wouldn't be. In fact, Colleen was likely on the run right now, and there was no telling when she'd surface.

"Minton finally left," Grayson went on. "But we haven't seen the last of him."

"No, we haven't," Lucas agreed. "Either he's the most persistent FBI agent in the state or else he's dirty."

Yes, too bad they didn't know which. Because if

Minton was clean, then he might truly be able to help them with this investigation.

"I know you wanted to lure out the person who's doing all of this, but we'll have to put the trap on hold for a little while," Grayson added. "I need all the reserve deputies out looking for that SUV and dealing with the snipers."

Understandable. He had a new crime scene to process.

"Is Eric still here?" Lucas asked.

"No. He's at the DA's office getting a copy of the plea deal." Grayson paused, looked at Hailey. "If you're feeling up to it, you need to come to my office. We have Preston's recordings set up in there, and we listened to something else that you should hear."

LUCAS CERTAINLY HADN'T forgotten about the recordings that Eric had given Grayson. After all, that was one of the reasons Hailey and he had been on their way to the sheriff's office.

The other reason they had come was to set that trap that was now on hold. No way did Grayson have enough manpower to cover protecting the reserve deputy, and there'd been enough people put at risk today without adding that.

"You're sure you're steady enough to do this now?" Lucas asked her as they made their way to Grayson's office.

She nodded, didn't stop walking. He suspected Hailey was nowhere near *steady*. Not so soon after nearly being killed. But it was clear she was going to steel herself up and listen to what he hoped would give them information they could actually use. As opposed to information that would just make Hailey feel worse than she already did.

Grayson had two laptops in his office, and Josh was listening to one with headphones. Since there were hours of recordings, there was no telling how long it would take to go through them all.

"I've loaded the recordings into audio files that we can access from several computers," Grayson explained, and he hit the play button, motioning for Hailey and Lucas to sit. "This is the first conversation that's connected to you," he added, looking at Hailey. "It was recorded about two weeks before the start of Preston's trial."

It didn't take long before Lucas heard a man's voice. Preston, no doubt. "We need to do something about your sister," he said.

"I could talk to Laura." It was Colleen who responded. Lucas recognized her voice from the phone conversation she'd had with Hailey.

"Talking won't help," Preston snapped. "She could send me away for life. Is that what you want?"

"No. Of course not." Colleen paused for several seconds. "What do you want me to do?"

Preston, however, didn't hesitate. "Find something I can use against her, something to neutralize her."

"There wasn't anything to find," Colleen insisted. "Nothing illegal, anyway."

"Then make Laura believe that I'll hurt you if she doesn't back off. She loves you. She'll protect you. If that doesn't work, plant something that'll get her to stop."

"Plant what?" Colleen asked.

"Anything illegal. I don't care what, just something

to make the cops think she's trying to cover up her own crimes by pinning them on me. You're a whiz with the computer, so hack into hers and see what you can do."

Grayson hit the pause button and turned to Hailey. "I'm guessing this is the first you're hearing of any of this?"

Hailey nodded. "I knew Colleen didn't want me to testify against Preston, but she never said anything about this false threat of making me think he would hurt her."

"Maybe because Colleen thought something like that wouldn't work with you?" Grayson pressed.

"No. It might have worked." Then Hailey groaned softly. "But I wouldn't have just stopped pursuing Preston. I would have just figured out a way to keep Colleen safe."

Lucas hoped Hailey would have done that by going to the cops. She didn't know him then. They hadn't met until after Preston's trial and after she'd entered WITSEC, but she'd obviously been working with some cops that she'd trusted.

"As far as I know," Hailey continued, "Colleen didn't plant anything illegal on my computer." She took a deep breath as if to steady her nerves. This was no doubt only adding salt to the wounds, but Lucas knew this wasn't the last of the things she probably wouldn't want to hear.

"Preston and Colleen sound *friendly*," Lucas commented. "Just how friendly were they?"

"I don't know for sure, but since Colleen didn't do what Preston wanted her to do—I mean, by planting something to frame me—then maybe they weren't as friendly as Preston seems to think they were."

Lucas latched right onto that. "You think Colleen was afraid of him?"

Another headshake from Hailey. Then a shrug. "Maybe, but Colleen never gave any indication of that."

"Of course, we haven't had a chance to listen to all the recordings," Grayson said. "But so far there's nothing about Colleen being afraid. Nothing about the specific nature of Colleen and Preston's relationship, either." He paused. "In fact, I'm betting that the recordings have been edited with parts cut out."

"You think Eric did that?" Lucas asked.

"Maybe. But it could have just as well been Colleen or Preston. The CSI lab is analyzing the originals to see if there have been any alterations. If not, it makes the second recording—well—all the more interesting. It's the last one, made the final day of Preston's trial. He was out on bond, but since he was convicted just a few hours later and put in jail, he didn't have a chance to go home again."

Grayson pressed the play button again, and like on the other recording, Lucas immediately heard Colleen's voice. "It's true. Hailey does have something incriminating on Eric. I'm not sure exactly what, but she won't use it against him. She wants to hold it over your head to make sure you don't go after her."

Preston cursed. "If I end up behind bars, you need to fix that for me. Swear that you will."

"I will," Colleen answered without hesitation.

"You'll also need to pay your sister back for what she's doing to me," Preston continued. "Understand?"

Again, Colleen didn't hesitate. "I understand."

Even though Hailey didn't make a sound, Lucas could see her body tense, and he put his hand over hers.

It must have felt like a punch to the gut to hear her sister basically say that she would get revenge for Preston. Was that what the attacks were all about? Payback?

Colleen didn't say anything else because Preston's phone rang. "I need you to step out while I take this call," he told her. He didn't continue for several seconds, probably until Colleen had left. "How's my favorite FBI agent?" Preston said to the caller. There was plenty of sarcasm in his voice. "Have you tied up the loose ends for me?"

Lucas moved closer to the computer so that he wouldn't miss a word. This had to be the dirty agent.

"Please tell me that Preston gives us a name during this conversation," Lucas said to Grayson.

"Sorry, there's no mention of a name, but there's other info that might be able to help us ID him."

Good. Lucas kept listening.

"If the worst happens and I'm convicted," Preston continued, "go to my bank in San Antonio and destroy everything in the safe deposit box."

Too bad they couldn't hear how the agent responded to that, but Lucas knew what Grayson meant about that *other info*. "You're getting surveillance footage from Preston's bank?"

Grayson nodded. "It'll take a while, though, because I need a court order." Which he would get for something like this. Eric might have been telling the truth when he said the recordings could help them arrest Minton.

"One final thing," Preston said to the caller. "If Colleen doesn't take care of the situation, I want you to kill Laura."

Lucas didn't think it was his imagination that Hailey became even paler than she already was, and he did more than hold her hand this time. He slipped his arm around her. Yes, she already knew someone was trying to kill her, but it was hard to hear it spelled out like that. But Hailey eased out of his grip and reached for the phone.

"I'm calling my sister," she insisted, snatching up Grayson's desk phone and putting it on speaker.

No one stopped her, mainly because Lucas didn't expect Colleen to answer. But she did. She answered on the first ring.

"I just heard proof that Preston asked you to kill me," Hailey said without issuing a greeting. "Don't bother to deny it. What I want to know is if you're carrying through on his wishes."

"No." Colleen's voice was shaky, and she didn't jump right into an explanation. She took several moments. "I couldn't go through with it."

"You're sure about that?" Lucas snapped. "You were near the ranch today when there was another attack."

"I was lured there." Colleen paused again. A long time. "I thought I was meeting someone who could give me information. But it turned out to be a hoax."

"What kind of information?" Hailey demanded.

More hesitation. "About this nightmare that's happening. Hailey, I'm so sorry, but I'm not behind the attacks. Things haven't always been good between you and me, but I'm not a killer."

"Then who is?" Hailey pressed. "Who's the dirty agent who was working for Preston? Is it Minton?"

"Maybe." Colleen gave a heavy sigh. "I wish I could say it's him, but I'm not sure there is an agent. Not a real one, anyway. I think it could have been one of Eric's henchmen posing as an agent."

Interesting. This was the first Lucas was hearing of this possibility. "Why would you say that?"

"Some things just aren't adding up, and I think Eric duped Preston into believing he had an agent on the take. I also believe Eric might have used that fake agent to spy on his father. I'm so sorry," Colleen repeated. Lucas heard something in her voice. Guilt maybe. Maybe fear.

It wasn't fear, though, that he saw on Hailey's face. It was pure frustration. Something he felt as well. Because Colleen was stalling, and he wanted to know why.

"Why did you erase the files that Hailey had on Eric?" Lucas demanded.

"I swear, I didn't have a choice."

Lucas huffed. "That's not an answer. Why did you do it?"

Colleen hesitated again before a hoarse sob tore from her mouth. "Because it was part of the ransom demand."

Lucas looked at Hailey to see if she knew what the heck Colleen was talking about. Clearly she didn't.

"A ransom?" Hailey questioned.

Colleen sobbed again. "For my baby with Preston."

And with that, Colleen ended the call.

Chapter Eleven

A baby.

Hailey sat there for a moment, stunned with the news her sister had just dropped on them, and then she pressed Redial. Colleen didn't answer. The call went straight to voice mail.

"Colleen could be lying," Lucas pointed out.

Yes. This could all be some kind of ploy to make them believe that her sister was being manipulated into doing these things. But it was also possible.

"Preston and she could have had an affair." Hailey was talking more to herself than anyone specific, but it prompted Grayson to take out his phone.

"I'll have someone run a search of birth certificates," Grayson explained. "Any idea how old a baby would be if it exists?"

Even though the thoughts were racing in Hailey's head, she forced herself to think. "Preston went to prison eighteen months ago, so unless he had conjugal visits, the baby would have to be at least nine months old. But possibly older. Colleen never said anything about being pregnant, though."

Not exactly surprising, because Colleen and she

hadn't been on the best terms when Hailey had entered WITSEC.

"If there really is a baby, then Eric could have kidnapped it to get Colleen to cooperate," Lucas suggested. "*If*," he emphasized.

Yes, that was a big if. But even if Colleen did have a child, that didn't mean it was Preston's. She could have gotten pregnant by someone else after he went to prison.

Grayson was still on the phone, but Hailey heard a familiar voice coming from the squad room. And she groaned. It was Minton, and she didn't want to go another round with him today. Obviously, though, that's what was going to happen, because he was demanding to see Lucas and her.

"I'll handle this," Lucas said, getting to his feet.

It was tempting to let him do just that, but Hailey got up as well so she could see what had prompted this latest visit from one of their suspects. Of course, he was no longer at the top of her list because Colleen was now in that particular spot.

"I'm getting a court order for those recordings," Minton informed them the moment he caught sight of them. "My boss will be here any minute with it. You need to turn over copies of those recordings Eric gave you along with the files you have on Eric. And I want them now."

"We'll just wait for that court order if you don't mind," Lucas answered. "Even if you do mind, we'll wait."

Hailey had no idea if there really was a court order or if this was a bluff on Minton's part. But she could clear up one thing for him now. "My sister hacked into my online storage and erased the info I had on Eric."

Minton's eyes were already narrowed, and they stayed that way. "You expect me to believe that?"

She lifted her shoulder. "I don't care what you believe, but it's the truth."

Now Minton cursed. "No way would Colleen help Eric."

Not voluntarily. But Hailey had to rethink that, too. With all the possible lies being bantered about, Hailey had no idea if Colleen even despised Eric.

"Why would Colleen have done something like that?" Minton pressed.

Hailey looked at Lucas to see if he had an opinion on how much or how little she should say, and he took the lead from there.

"Colleen perhaps had a child who's been kidnapped. You know anything about that?" Lucas asked.

Hailey carefully watched Minton's reaction, and now his eyes widened in disbelief. Or perhaps he was faking that response. Because if someone had indeed taken Colleen's child, it could have been Minton. Yes, Eric had a stronger motive, but Minton could have done it to force Colleen to do whatever was necessary to make sure his crimes weren't revealed.

Anything, including those attacks to murder Hailey.

"This is the first I'm hearing of a child," Minton answered. "It's true?"

"We're trying to confirm it now," Lucas assured him.

Minton took out his phone. "I want to talk to Colleen. Where is she?"

Hailey shook her head. "Your guess is as good as mine."

It didn't surprise her that Minton had Colleen's number in his phone. After all, her sister was part of the investigation into Preston. And now Eric. It also didn't surprise her when Colleen didn't answer.

"I'll have someone from the bureau look for her," Minton said, and he fired off a text.

Finding Colleen still wasn't within the FBI's jurisdiction, but at this point Hailey just wanted her sister found so she could be brought in for questioning. She only hoped that whoever Minton had contacted wasn't as dirty as he possibly could be.

"What do you know about this so-called kidnapping?" Minton continued when he'd finished the text.

"Not much." Lucas took out his own phone. "But let me talk to someone who might know."

Hailey wasn't sure who he was going to call. When Lucas put the phone on speaker, though, the DA's office answered, and he asked to speak to Eric.

"Tell me about Colleen's baby," Lucas said the moment Eric came on the line.

"What baby?" Eric snapped.

He seemed as surprised as Minton had been. Of course, it was possible neither man had had much personal contact with her sister, so their reactions might have been genuine.

"Colleen claims someone kidnapped her baby with Preston," Lucas explained. "Was it you?"

Eric's profanity was even worse than Minton's had been earlier. "She's lying. She's doing this to get money from Preston's estate. Well, it won't work. He left everything to me in his will."

Hailey figured that was true, and maybe that was her sister's motive for this. Of course, if Colleen truly had been having an affair with Preston, then he'd probably arranged to have her receive some money before he was killed in prison. At least Hailey hoped that was the case. No way, though, would Eric want Colleen or anyone else, for that matter, to have a dime of his father's money. Eric hated Preston, but he loved the big bucks and trust fund that came with the family name.

"I want to talk to Colleen," Eric practically shouted.

"Welcome to the club," Lucas grumbled, and without even saying goodbye, he ended the call.

Minton jabbed his finger toward Lucas's phone. "That doesn't prove Eric's innocent. No way would he admit to kidnapping his half sibling. If a baby really exists, that is."

"A baby does exist," Grayson said as he came out of his office. For four little words, he got everyone's attention. He came into the squad room before he continued. "According to Texas Vital Statistics, Colleen gave birth to a daughter eleven months ago. Her name is Isabel."

The emotions flooded through Hailey. She had a niece. Colleen had been telling the truth. About that, anyway.

"And the father?" Hailey asked.

Grayson shook his head. "No name's on the birth certificate. In Texas, Colleen would have needed written consent to include the father's name."

Maybe because it would have been too much trouble to get the consent with Preston in jail. Or perhaps Preston wasn't the father after all.

"So, where's the baby?" Minton asked, his attention volleying among Grayson, Lucas and Hailey.

None of them had an answer. Only Colleen could give them that information, and they had to find her first. But if her niece had indeed been kidnapped, Hailey wanted to help. Especially now that she was a mother herself, she couldn't stomach the thought of a baby being taken.

"I'm sorry," Lucas said to her, his voice a soothing whisper. So was the slight touch on her arm.

She looked up at him, their gazes connecting, and the look he gave her was comforting, as well. For a second or two. Then he must have remembered that it wouldn't take much for the comforting to turn to something more.

The fire.

No, it wouldn't take much at all, and now wasn't the time for that. Maybe there'd never be time. Because, like now, Lucas would continue to fight this attraction. No way did he want to go another emotional round with her, especially since she wasn't in any position to renew a relationship.

Hailey cleared her throat, hoping that would clear her head, as well. "I'll try to call Colleen again. If she doesn't answer, I can leave a voice mail so she'll know I found out I have a niece."

She turned to go back into Grayson's office to do that, but the sound of the door opening stopped her. Hailey braced herself for another visit from Eric, but it was a bulky, dark-haired man she didn't recognize. Apparently neither did Lucas, because he instantly stepped in front of her and drew his gun.

But their visitor had a gun, too. And a badge.

"You can put your weapon away," Minton insisted. "This is FBI Agent Derrick Wendell."

Judging from the now smug look on Minton's face, this was someone he wanted to see, and it didn't take Hailey long to figure out why.

"Sheriff Ryland?" Agent Wendell asked, looking at Grayson. When Grayson nodded, Wendell took a paper from his pocket. "This is a court order. You're to turn over the recordings and all evidence that's connected to Eric DeSalvo."

Grayson mumbled some profanity under his breath and took the court order to read through it. However, Hailey figured it was legit.

"The FBI has been conducting a long-time investigation into Eric and his business operations," Wendell continued. "We have reason to believe some of these operations have crossed into other states, making it a federal case."

Lucas looked at her, and even though he didn't say anything, Hailey knew what he wanted to ask her. Did she know about any of Eric's illegal interstate deals? She didn't.

But that didn't mean there weren't any.

She shook her head and was about to tell Minton and Wendell that, but Wendell's attention went to her next. "Hailey Darrow." He didn't wait for her to confirm that. "I'm here to take you into custody."

"WHAT THE HELL do you mean by that?" Lucas growled.

Even though Lucas glared at the agent, Wendell only shrugged as if the answer were obvious. It wasn't. Not to Lucas, anyway.

"Miss Darrow is a material witness in this federal investigation. Plus, someone's trying to kill her. One of Eric's henchmen, no doubt. The FBI intends to put her in custody and keep her safe so she can testify against him."

"She's already in protective custody—mine," Lucas argued. No way was he letting Hailey go with this clown. "There's proof on the recordings that Preston was dealing with a dirty agent. How do I know that agent isn't you? Or him?" he added, tipping his head to Minton.

Judging from the way Minton's face went red, he didn't appreciate that. Apparently neither did Wendell, because he scowled. But it was going to take a lot more than riled FBI agents to get Lucas to hand her over.

"I'm not dirty," Wendell insisted. "And you haven't done a good job of protecting Hailey so far."

"I'm alive." She stepped out from behind Lucas. "I'd say that's a good job, considering that someone's been trying to kill me from practically the moment I came out of a coma."

No, he hadn't done a good job. Because if he had, Lucas would have already found the person responsible for the attacks. Though he did appreciate Hailey standing up for him. But part of him didn't like it, either.

Hell. They were on the same side of this argument, and that was tearing down more barriers between them. Barriers that Lucas wanted in place until he'd worked out a whole lot of things with Hailey. Including her intentions for custody of Camden.

"Hailey can't go with you," Grayson told the agents. "I haven't even interviewed her about the attacks."

"Again, our jurisdiction," Minton argued right back.

"Possibly," Grayson said. "But the attacks might not even be related to Eric. Or the dirty agent. This could be connected to some other things that went on in Silver Creek prior to Hailey's coma."

"What things?" Wendell challenged.

"I'm not at liberty to discuss that with you right now. But it's not federal."

Grayson was sticking up for them. Sticking his neck

out, too, since he could be hit with obstruction of justice if the agents could prove he was stonewalling them. Which Grayson was. But he was also buying Hailey some time. She'd already been through hell and back and definitely didn't need to be around someone who might be trying to kill her.

Minton huffed, put his hands on his hips. "Then go ahead. Interview her. Do what you need to do, but she'll be coming with us when you're done."

Grayson shook his head. "Not anytime soon." He glanced at the court order. "This applies only to the recordings, which you can have. But there's no mention of Hailey being forced to be in your *safekeeping.*" There was plenty of sarcasm on that last word.

The muscles in Minton's jaw stirred, and he turned toward his fellow agent. "Get the paperwork for Hailey. I'll get the recordings."

Wendell didn't jump to leave. He glanced at all of them as if trying to figure out how to resolve this without attempting to convince a judge that it was a necessity for him to take Hailey into forced custody. But he must have realized this wasn't an argument he could win with the Ryland lawmen, because he issued a terse "I'll be back" and headed out.

"Give me the recordings now," Minton said the moment Wendell was gone. "But Hailey doesn't leave the building until Wendell gets back."

Grayson nodded, headed to his office to get them. Giving up the recordings was no big deal since Grayson had made copies of them, but Lucas needed to make sure that Wendell didn't find a judge to do Minton and Wendell's bidding. He took Hailey by the arm and led her to the break room.

Lucas called one of his fellow Rangers and asked him to keep an eye on Wendell for him, and once he'd done that, he saw to Hailey. Who was obviously even more shaken up.

"Please don't let him take me," she said, her voice with hardly any sound.

"I won't." But Lucas only hoped it didn't come to a legal showdown between them and the FBI.

He sat on the sofa next to her, and because he thought they could both use it, he made a FaceTime call to the nanny. It was something he did often while away on business so he'd be able to see his son—if not in person, then at least on the screen.

"Is everything okay?" Tillie asked the moment she answered.

"Fine," Lucas lied. Of course, Tillie must have known it was a lie, but she managed a smile.

"Camden's sleeping," she said, whispering, "but I'll carry the phone to the nursery so you can get a peek."

Hailey moved closer to him, her attention glued to the screen, and she was holding her breath. A breath she released when Camden came into view.

The baby was sleeping, all right. He was on his side, a blue blanket draped over him. Tillie moved the phone closer to his face so they could have a better look.

Hailey touched her fingers to her lips for a moment. "I wish I were there to hold him."

Yeah. So did Lucas. Being away from his son created a horrible ache in his chest. "Maybe soon," Lucas told Hailey, and he hoped that was true. He didn't want this mess with the FBI to drag on so they'd be stuck here in the sheriff's office.

Even though Camden wasn't moving and certainly

nowhere near being awake, Hailey and he continued to watch him for several minutes.

Lucas thanked Tillie before he ended the call. "We'll check in again with her in a couple of hours, when Camden will be awake," he added to Hailey.

She nodded, and he figured she was trying to look a lot braver than she felt. "You're being nice to me," she said.

He wasn't sure how to respond to that, so Lucas didn't say anything. Big mistake. Because his silence caused Hailey to look up at him. Normally her looking at him wouldn't be a big deal, but they were close. Side by side. Arms touching. With their emotions running sky-high, something as simple as a look could become a trigger for this attraction.

And it was.

Lucas felt the slam of heat go through him, and before he could remind himself that kissing Hailey would be a dumber-than-dirt sort of thing to do, he lowered his head and put his mouth to hers.

He'd thought that the attraction between them couldn't get any hotter, but he had been wrong. It did, and along with the fire came the need. A need that his body remembered only a couple of seconds into the kiss. That fire and need were what had started this whole ordeal with Hailey. Apparently the ordeal was going to continue, too. Because he certainly didn't stop kissing her.

Hailey didn't stop, either. In fact, a soft sound rumbled in her throat. A sound filled with the same need and heat that Lucas was feeling. She slipped her hand around the back of his neck, pulled him closer. Not that he needed much encouragement for that, because Lucas was already moving in on her.

He deepened the kiss, took hold of her shoulder and dragged her against him. Great. Now they were body to body with the kiss raging on and on until finally he had to stop just so they could catch their breaths.

She looked at him again, silently questioning whether this was a good idea. It wasn't. But that didn't stop Lucas from going back for a second kiss. It didn't help, of course. But this time he stopped not because of air. If he didn't stop, he was going to drag her upstairs. There was an apartment up there. With a bed.

Definitely not good.

Kissing had already added too many complications to this mix, and sex would spin those complications out of control.

He was about to apologize to her, but Grayson opened the door to the break room. Hell. One look at his face and Lucas knew something was wrong.

"The FBI isn't taking Hailey," Lucas jumped to say.

Grayson shook his head. "Not yet, anyway. No, this is about Colleen."

Hailey slowly got to her feet. "What happened?"

"There's something you need to see." Grayson motioned for them to follow him, and he led them to his office.

Thankfully, Minton wasn't there. He was still across the hall in the squad room, pacing, and judging from his expression, he was riled about something other than not getting his way about taking Hailey.

"If that's something that pertains to the FBI's investigation," Minton called out, "then I want to see it."

"It's not about the investigation," Grayson assured

him. "This is a family matter." Once Hailey, Lucas and he were inside the office, Grayson locked the door, no doubt to stop the agent from barging in.

Josh was no longer in the room listening to those recordings. Or rather, the copies of the recordings. Grayson had no doubt put him in one of the interview rooms.

"What's going on?" Lucas asked, but he was almost afraid to hear the answer.

Grayson tipped his head to his desk. There was a padded envelope, opened, along with several papers. "This just arrived by courier," he explained. "There's no name on it, but I've already called the courier's office and asked them to tell me who sent it."

Lucas went closer, Hailey following right behind him, and he saw the first piece of paper. It appeared to be test results.

"DNA," Grayson supplied. "According to the person who sent it, this proves that Isabel is Colleen's baby."

"Does the test really prove it?" Hailey immediately asked.

Grayson lifted his shoulder. "This sort of thing can be faked, but it looks real. It has both the baby's DNA and a sample apparently retrieved from Colleen. Josh is calling the lab to verify." He wore a plastic glove when he moved aside the test results to show them what was beneath.

A photo.

Of a baby girl.

Hailey leaned in even closer, her gaze combing over the picture. She nodded. "The baby definitely resembles Colleen."

Of course, they'd known Colleen had a child, but Lucas figured all of this was leading to something bad.

It was.

"This was the final thing in the envelope," Grayson said, showing them another piece of paper. "It's a ransom demand—for a quarter of a million. But there's another demand. The kidnappers say if Hailey doesn't personally turn over everything she has on the De-Salvo investigation, then Colleen will never see the child again."

Chapter Twelve

Hailey heard every word of what Grayson said. Saw it, too, written in the ransom demand. But it still took a moment to sink in.

Mercy.

If this was real, then her niece could be in grave danger. It didn't matter that she'd never seen the child. Hailey still loved her and wanted to protect her.

"No," Lucas said before Hailey could speak. "You're not going to do this."

Since she was about to tell him that she would indeed do it, he'd obviously known what she was thinking. "I have the money in savings. It's from my father's life insurance. I've never spent any of it, and it's in a bank in San Antonio."

"The money's not the problem," Lucas argued.

Yes, she knew what he meant. It was the *personally* part of the demand. Someone wanted her dead, and this could be a trap to lure her out into the open.

"But we can't just let them disappear with the baby," she snapped. What she felt was pure frustration because Lucas and she were both right. She couldn't go out to deliver anything, but she also couldn't just give up on getting back the baby.

"Just sit," Grayson suggested to her. "We'll work this out somehow."

His phone buzzed, and he lifted his finger in a wait-a-second gesture. Since the caller had gotten Grayson's full attention, Hailey figured it had to be about the kidnapping.

"Eric or Minton could have taken the baby," Hailey tossed out there.

Lucas nodded. "Or this could be something Colleen concocted. We don't know what her real motives are."

True, but it sickened her to think that her sister might be using her own child to do whatever it was she was trying to do. Plain and simple, maybe this was about the money.

"Even though my mother adopted Colleen, she didn't leave Colleen any money from her life insurance," Hailey told Lucas. "She and my mother were on the outs at the time of her death, and she left it solely to me. I offered to share it with Colleen, but she was so angry at being cut out of the will that she refused."

"Was Colleen angry enough to do something like pretending to kidnap her own daughter?"

Hailey had to shrug. "Colleen was always angry about a lot of things. Still…this doesn't feel like something she'd do."

Of course, she'd been wrong about Colleen before. She hadn't thought her sister would delete those files she'd stashed away about Eric. Which was a reminder that she didn't have a key part of what the kidnappers were demanding.

"If we can work out a deal with the kidnappers so I don't personally have to deliver their demands, I'll need to put together some fake files to give them."

Lucas didn't give her his opinion on that because Grayson finished his call and turned to them. "That was the agency for the courier who delivered the package. The person paid in cash, and according to his driver's license, his name is Eldon Silverton. It's fake," Grayson quickly added.

Hailey didn't even bother to groan because it had been such a long shot, anyway. She seriously doubted that the kidnappers would have used someone who could be identified and therefore linked back to them. Or rather, linked back to the person who'd orchestrated all of this.

"What about security cameras?" Lucas asked. "Does the courier agency have them?"

Grayson shook his head. "I think we've struck out with the courier. With the lab, too, because it was Darrin Sandmire who ordered the lab results."

Darrin was the man who'd tried to kill her the night she'd been put in a coma. According to Colleen, he'd been behind the attack shortly after Hailey left the hospital.

Darrin was also dead.

So, yes, that meant they had indeed struck out since they couldn't question Darrin about it. But something about that didn't make sense.

"Why would the person behind the kidnapping use Darrin for this?" she asked. "Why not just use someone with a fake ID?"

"It was to convince us that this is real," Lucas answered, and it prompted Grayson to nod. Thankfully, Lucas continued with his explanation, because Hailey wasn't following this. "We know Darrin's a thug. *Was* a thug. The kidnappers wanted us to understand that a thug like this was involved. That way, we could be sure the baby was truly in danger."

All of that made sense, but it also tightened the knot in her stomach. Because if a snake like Darrin had been involved, there was no telling who had the baby now.

"Let me take care of Minton," Grayson said. "And then we'll try to contact Colleen again. From now on, any conversation with her needs to be recorded."

And Hailey knew why. Her sister might be involved in this crime in some way, and anything Colleen said might lead them to the truth.

When Grayson unlocked the door and threw it open, Minton was standing right there. It was possible he'd heard some or even all of what they'd said, and he clearly wasn't happy about being excluded.

"You need to leave," Grayson ordered him before Minton could get out a word. Lucas went to his cousin's side. "Until you have papers putting Hailey in FBI custody, you have no right to be here," Grayson added.

Minton had never been a happy-looking person, and Grayson's words only made it worse. "I'm an FBI agent."

"Which gives you no right to be here. This is the sheriff's office, and last I checked, I'm the sheriff. You're leaving, and that's not a request. You can come back when and only when you have something to convince me to turn over Hailey to you."

Minton still didn't budge. He threw glances at all of them, his glare lingering on Hailey for a few long moments.

"You'll regret this," Minton said, and it sounded like a threat. He turned and stormed out.

Grayson and Lucas stood in the doorway and

watched the man leave, and they didn't move until Hailey heard the front door slam.

"Make sure he doesn't come back," Grayson told one of the deputies.

He returned to his desk, handed Hailey the phone and put the recorder right next to it. Hailey pressed in the number, and it rang. And rang.

Her heart dropped when it went to voice mail.

"Colleen, I need to talk to you right away," Hailey said once she was able to leave a message. "We got a ransom demand from the kidnappers of your baby. Please call me back ASAP."

She was about to put the phone away, but it rang before she could do it. Hailey answered it as soon as Grayson hit the record button again, and she immediately heard her sister's voice.

"The kidnappers got in touch with you?" Colleen asked. "How? When?" She certainly sounded like a mother who'd had her child taken.

"A package was delivered to the Silver Creek Sheriff's Office," Lucas answered. "There's a demand for a quarter of a million and any info Hailey has on the DeSalvo family. They want her to deliver everything to them herself. Now, who's behind the kidnapping?"

"I don't know. I swear, I don't. But I'll pay them whatever it takes to get back my baby. Where and when do they want Hailey to make the drop?"

Colleen made this sound as if it were a done deal, that Hailey would indeed be involved in the exchange, but Hailey figured no way would Lucas let that happen.

"We'll go over all the details with you," Lucas said. "But only if you come here to the sheriff's office. I have some questions for you."

Hailey guessed that Colleen would come up with an excuse as to why that couldn't happen. After all, she'd stonewalled them practically from the start of this nightmare. And her sister did hesitate for a couple of seconds.

"All right," Colleen answered. "I'm just up the street and can be there in a few minutes. But please come out and watch for me. Draw your gun, too. Because when I come out in the open, they'll try to kill me."

"Who's trying to kill you and why?" Lucas snapped. But he was talking to himself, because Colleen had already hung up.

Hell. It didn't make sense that someone was trying to kill Colleen. Especially not the kidnappers. They'd probably want her alive so she would push Hailey to pay the ransom.

Maybe.

And maybe the idea was to kill Hailey when she delivered the money and files. Then, also murder Colleen so that anything the sisters had learned about the DeSalvo family would die with them. Of course, that theory worked only if Colleen was innocent. The jury was out on that. Still, Lucas couldn't risk her being gunned down if she was truly out to rescue her child.

"Wait here," Lucas warned Hailey.

She took hold of his arm. "It's too risky for you to go out there." The very thing she'd said to him when he was meeting Minton at the ranch.

That hadn't turned out so well, but Hailey must have realized they didn't have much of a choice about this, because her grip melted off him. "Just be careful," she added.

There was plenty of emotion in her voice, and Lucas didn't think all that emotion was related only to what was about to happen. No. That kiss was playing into this. It had deepened things between them. Had upped the stakes. And that wasn't good, because they were both already distracted enough without adding higher stakes.

"I mean it," Lucas warned her. "Stay put."

He headed toward the front door with Grayson following right behind him. Both drew their weapons. However, they didn't actually go outside. They stayed in the doorway, Lucas looking up one side of the street and Grayson the other. One of the deputies hurried to the window. All of them preparing for what might be another attack right on Main Street.

But there was no sound of shots. No sign of Colleen, either. Not at first, anyway, but then Lucas spotted someone on the sidewalk just two buildings up from the sheriff's office. Not Colleen, though.

Eric.

Lucas didn't like the timing of the man's arrival, and apparently Eric didn't like it much, either, when he spotted Grayson's and Lucas's weapons. He cursed as he got closer.

"Are the guns really necessary?" Eric asked.

"They're not for you," Lucas assured him. "There might be gunmen in the area."

That put plenty of alarm on Eric's face. Alarm that he could have been faking, but it still got him running toward them. Lucas considered not letting him in, but if Colleen was innocent and she saw Eric out front, that might send her back into hiding.

"Frisk him," Lucas told the deputy when Eric went into the reception area.

Lucas barely spared Eric a glance. Instead he kept his attention on Main Street, and he finally saw more movement. It was in the same area where Eric had just been. But the person wasn't on the sidewalk but rather peering around the corner of a shop.

Definitely Colleen.

Lucas motioned for her to come to them. She didn't. Not right away. She kept looking around. Not just up and down the streets but also on the rooftops. Colleen definitely seemed concerned about being gunned down. Lucas was concerned about that, as well, but if she was in danger, then that alley wasn't a safe place. Heck, nowhere out in the open was safe.

Colleen finally came out and raced toward them. She was limping, maybe an injury from her car accident, and judging from her expression, she wasn't just afraid but also in pain. The moment she reached the door, Grayson pulled her inside.

"What's he doing here?" she snarled, looking at Eric.

"I could ask you the same thing," Eric countered.

"Take Eric to an interview room," Grayson told the deputy who was still in the process of frisking the man.

"I don't want to be put away in an interview room," Eric protested. "I need to talk to Colleen."

Lucas was about to tell him, "Tough." But Colleen spoke first. "Did you kidnap my baby?"

Her voice was shaking. So was she. And that was no doubt what prompted Hailey to come out of Grayson's office and go to her sister. Something Lucas definitely didn't want her to do. Especially when Eric stepped in front of her. Eric wasn't facing Hailey, though, but rather Colleen.

"You really had a baby?" he demanded.

"Yes," Colleen snapped, "and someone took her. Was it you?"

Eric stared at her as if trying to sort all of this out. Of course, maybe he already had it sorted out if he'd been the one to kidnap the child.

"No. I didn't. Is there DNA proof?" Eric pressed. "Real DNA proof that hasn't been faked by you?"

"There is proof," Grayson verified. "Now, let's all move away from the windows." He pointed to Eric. "You either leave or go in the interview room."

Eric's chin came up. "I'm not leaving until I see solid evidence that I have a half sibling."

"Arrest him," Grayson told the deputy without hesitation. "He's obstructing justice."

Eric howled out a protest, moved out of the deputy's grip. He glared at all of them before he stormed out of the sheriff's office. Good. One less pain to deal with.

"What did the kidnappers send you?" Colleen asked the moment Eric was gone.

But Lucas didn't get a chance to show her. That's because his phone rang, and he saw Unknown Caller on the screen.

Usually not a good sign.

"Record it," Grayson said, and Josh hurried to get a recorder from his desk so that Lucas could do that.

Grayson's phone rang, too, and he stepped into the hall to take it. He motioned for Lucas to go ahead and answer his call. Lucas did, and he put it on speaker.

"Are you ready to talk?" the caller immediately said.

It was a man, but Lucas didn't recognize the voice. "About what?"

"The kids, of course. You want to get them back, right?"

Every muscle in Lucas's body tightened. "Kids?"

"Yeah. Colleen's girl and your boy. We have them both."

Chapter Thirteen

The panic slammed through Hailey so fast that she couldn't speak, couldn't breathe. But she could feel, and what she was feeling was the sheer terror after learning that someone had taken her son.

Lucas didn't respond to the caller. He looked at Grayson, and Hailey could tell from his expression that something had gone wrong.

Oh, God.

"The ranch is under attack," Grayson said, confirming her fears.

"Do they really have Camden?" Lucas asked.

Grayson shook his head, then cursed. "They're sorting that out now. An SUV armed with gunmen broke through the gate. Mason and the others responded, but it's chaos there."

"Told you," the caller taunted.

"They might not have him," Lucas tried to assure her. But he didn't look convinced of that any more than she was.

Hailey wanted to know how in the world this had happened. She wanted to scream, run outside, find the nearest vehicle and hurry to the ranch. Lucas must have known what was going through her mind, because he took hold of her arm and had her sit at the desk next to Josh. No way could she stay put, though. She got up and started pacing.

"Let's just wait for a report from Mason," Lucas told her. He motioned to Josh who was at his desk, and Lucas mouthed, "Try to trace the call."

"Yeah, and Mason will soon tell you that we have the boy," the caller added. "And now it's time to talk about how you get both kids back."

"Prove to me that you've got him first," Lucas insisted. "You sent a picture of the girl, but I don't have anything to convince me that you truly have my son."

"Soon. I'll give you proof before our little exchange happens, and if you do what you're told, I'll give you the kids."

"I swear we'll do whatever you ask," Colleen blurted out. "Just please don't hurt them."

"Nobody will get hurt if you follow my instructions to a T."

Hailey didn't put much trust in a snake who would kidnap babies, but she moved closer to the phone so that she wouldn't miss a word of those instructions. It was so hard to focus, though, with the tornado of bad thoughts going on in her head.

"The price is now a half million," the man said. "All because there are two of them now. Go ahead and start gathering the money. I'll give you an hour—"

"That's not enough time," Lucas interrupted. He was almost certainly stalling the kidnapper to give Josh more time to trace the call. "The money has to come from a bank in San Antonio. It'll take a while for them to pull together that kind of cash."

"All right, you have until morning. And no, don't ask

for more time than that, because it's all you're going to get. Along with the money, Hailey's got to give us the files she has on the DeSalvos."

Files that she didn't have. Because Colleen had deleted them. Colleen opened her mouth, maybe to tell the kidnapper just that, but Hailey shook her head, stopping her. If this man learned that the files were gone, it might compromise the ransom and rescue. Hailey would just come up with some fake files to give them.

But there was something about this particular kidnapper's request that didn't make sense.

Hailey had assumed that Colleen had deleted the files to appease the person who'd kidnapped her baby. If she'd done that, though, then this man wouldn't be demanding them now, because he would know the files no longer existed.

"Hailey won't be delivering anything to you," Lucas argued. "You'll get the money and the files, but someone else will be doing the drop."

The kidnapper paused for several heart-stopping moments. If this man insisted she deliver the goods, she'd have to do it, of course. But it would be a suicide mission. Still, she'd go through with it if it meant Camden and her niece were safe.

"All right," the kidnapper finally said. "Not Hailey."

Hailey's breath swooshed out, but she certainly didn't feel any relief. She waited for the other shoe to drop, and it didn't take long.

"You and Eric DeSalvo will bring the money and the files." The kidnapper's words hung in the air.

Grayson and Lucas exchanged a glance, but she could see Lucas's answer in his eyes before he even spoke. "Why Eric?" he asked.

"Let's just say Eric will be bringing some cash of his own. For those files."

So Eric was being blackmailed. Or at least, according to this man he was.

Lucas huffed. "I'll have to work it out with Eric—"

"Just do it," the kidnapper snapped. "I'll call you back with the drop-off point. Have everything ready to go."

"I got the kidnapper's location from the cell tower," Josh said the moment the man ended the call. "It's coming from Sweetwater Springs. I'll get the sheriff to send someone out there."

Hailey latched onto that like a lifeline. Maybe the sheriff could find them and put an end to this.

While Josh contacted the Sweetwater Springs sheriff, Hailey went to Grayson to see if he'd heard anything about what was happening at the ranch. He had the phone pressed to his ear, and while she could hear someone talking on the other end of the line, she couldn't make out what the person was saying.

Lucas came closer to her, and he slipped his arm around her waist. Waiting. And no doubt praying, as Hailey was doing.

"I'll wait to talk to Eric," Lucas explained.

Yes, but it would have to be done. Well, it would unless they managed to end this kidnapping. But Eric would still have to be brought in to answer questions about whether or not he was being blackmailed about those blasted files.

"I didn't know you two were back together," Colleen said.

Hailey glanced at her sister, ready to explain that it wasn't like that between Lucas and her, but she didn't want to waste the energy. Besides, it seemed a strange observation to make when their children could be in grave danger.

Grayson pressed the end call button, his attention going straight to Lucas and Hailey. "Mason and the ranch hands are closing in on the trespassers. There are three of them. And we still don't know if they took Camden. It shouldn't be long, though, before Mason calls back."

A second was too long, and Hailey's legs suddenly felt ready to give way.

Josh finished his call and joined them just outside Grayson's office. "I know the timing for this is bad, but I found out something about that surveillance footage from the bank."

Hailey certainly hadn't forgotten about that. It was the security feed that was supposed to show the dirty agent Preston had sent to destroy whatever was in his safe deposit box.

"It was Eric," Josh said.

It took Hailey a moment to get what he was saying. "Eric?" she asked. "Why would he be on that footage?"

Josh shrugged. "He'll have to answer that. Have to answer, too, what was in the box, since there's no security footage for that."

Hailey tuned out the rest of what Josh was saying when Grayson's phone rang. The sound shot through the room, shot through her, too, and Grayson answered it as fast as he could. What he didn't do was put the call on speaker. Probably because he wanted to buffer any bad news that he got. But that wasn't a bad news kind of look on his face. He blew out a quick breath.

"Camden's safe," Grayson relayed.

Suddenly she was in Lucas's arms. This time, though, not because of a kiss but because they were both overcome with relief. Relief that Colleen wasn't sharing. She went back into the squad room and sank down into one of the chairs. Hailey hoped she was having that reaction simply because she was still terrified for her daughter and not because her sister had planned this failed kidnapping.

"Is everyone okay?" Lucas asked Grayson.

"Yes. The attackers didn't get into your house. Tillie's shaken up, of course, but she said Camden's too little to know what was going on. She hid with him in the bathroom."

Good. That was probably the safest place for her to have been, but it ripped at Hailey's heart to know that her precious son, the nanny and everyone at the ranch had been put in that kind of danger.

"One of the attackers is dead," Grayson went on. "The other two escaped, but Mason called in help to look for them."

She figured the men were long gone by now, but if they could get an ID on the dead one, it might lead them back to who'd hired him.

"I need to see Camden," Hailey insisted.

Lucas didn't even argue with that. He looked at Grayson. "Can you spare a deputy to go with us?"

"Josh can do it." Grayson didn't get to add more because Lucas's phone rang.

Unknown Caller was on the screen again. Lucas waited until Grayson turned on the recorder before he answered it.

"So, we didn't get your boy," the kidnapper said. It

was the same man who'd called earlier. "Not this time, anyway. But there's always tomorrow."

The muscles tightened in Lucas's jaw, and Hailey could tell he wanted to go through the phone lines and rip this guy to pieces. Hailey did, too. But more than anything, she just wanted to hold her baby and make sure he truly was safe.

"You'll still pay the ransom if you want your sister's kid back," the kidnapper insisted. "Get that money together. Those files, too, and I'll be in touch." And he ended the call.

"I'll have the call analyzed," Grayson volunteered. "To see if he's still in Sweetwater Springs. The three of you go ahead and leave."

"But what about my daughter?" Colleen asked, getting to her feet. "You can't just leave while that monster has her."

"Staying here won't help her," Lucas answered. He hooked his arm around Hailey, and along with Josh, they started toward the door. "When the kidnapper calls with drop-off instructions, I'll come back."

Hailey hoped not. Maybe they could work out a different deal. One that didn't include Lucas, her or anyone in his family. Perhaps Eric could do this solo.

There was a cruiser parked out front, and the three of them hurried to get in it. Josh took the wheel. She thought Lucas would ride in the front, but he got in the backseat with her. He brushed a quick kiss on her forehead. A kiss no doubt of relief, and he kept watch around them. So did Josh.

There was a storm moving in, and the sky was already getting dark, but Hailey hoped the rain would hold off until they made it to the ranch. She didn't want anything to slow them down.

Josh certainly wasn't moving slowly. He was speeding through town, and like Lucas, he was also keeping watch.

"You think Colleen could have been the one to arrange this attack?" Lucas asked. It was a question that hadn't been far from her mind.

"It's possible. But even if she wasn't the mastermind, she could have known about it. Getting Camden could have been part of the kidnappers' demands to her."

Of course, Colleen hadn't said a thing about a demand like that, but it still could have happened. If Colleen was truly desperate to get her daughter back, then she might be willing to do anything. That could include having Camden taken.

Because if the kidnappers had him, they had the ultimate bargaining tool to get Lucas and her to cooperate.

Josh had just made it out of town when Lucas's phone rang again. Hailey hoped it wasn't the kidnapper calling to give them an immediate drop for the ransom. But it was Grayson. Hailey felt a new slam of fear and prayed that nothing else had gone wrong at the ranch.

"Pull over and check the cruiser," Grayson said the moment Lucas answered the call.

"What's wrong?" Josh and Lucas asked in unison.

"It might be nothing, but a waitress from the diner across the street said about thirty minutes ago she saw somebody walking by the cruiser. A man she didn't recognize. She said at one point the guy appeared to drop something, and he stooped down out of sight for a couple of seconds."

"Hell." Lucas added some more profanity as Josh

pulled to the shoulder of the road. "Why didn't she tell you this sooner?"

"She got busy with some customers and just now got a break. Like I said, it might be nothing. I just want to be sure."

Judging from Lucas's and Josh's reactions, though, it could be some kind of tracking device. Or worse.

"I didn't see anyone around the cruiser," Hailey said.

But then, they'd had plenty of distractions with Minton, Eric and Colleen all there. Plus there'd been the calls from the ranch about the attack and those from the kidnapper.

"Stay inside the cruiser until I check it out," Lucas told Josh and her.

She hated that he was going out there again, but Grayson was right. They had to be certain no one had tampered with the vehicle.

Lucas already had his gun drawn, and he stepped out. Josh opened his door, too, no doubt in case this became an ambush. But there really was no place for attackers to hide on this particular stretch of the road. There were no trees, just flat pasture, and the ditches weren't particularly deep. She also couldn't see any vehicles either ahead of or behind them.

Hailey held her breath, waiting as Lucas went around the cruiser. He was moving quickly. Until he got to the rear of the vehicle. Because she was watching him so closely, she saw the instant alarm on his face.

"Get out now!" Lucas shouted. "There's a bomb."

LUCAS FELT HIS heart slam against his chest.

He didn't take the time to kick himself for not checking out the cruiser before hurrying Hailey into it. He should have gone over every inch of it before they left the sheriff's office. But they'd been so eager to get to the ranch and check on Camden, so he hadn't done it.

Now it might cost them their lives.

Josh was out of the vehicle within seconds, mainly because his door was already open, but Hailey was struggling with hers. Lucas threw it open for her, dragging her out, and he started running with her in tow. But they weren't moving nearly fast enough. They had to put some distance between them and the car, so he scooped her into his arms and raced toward the pasture.

They made it only a few yards past the ditch, though.

The blast ripped through the air, throwing them forward and onto the ground. Lucas scrambled to cover Hailey's body with his and hoped that the flying debris didn't kill them.

Chunks of the cruiser came crashing down. Most of the pieces were in flames, and the other jagged shards fell into the pasture all around them.

"Josh?" she said, no doubt checking to make sure he'd gotten out.

He had. Lucas's cousin was on the ground only about two yards away, and from what he could see of him, he didn't have any injuries. In fact, he was already calling for backup.

"Josh is okay," Lucas assured her.

But Hailey was a different matter. When she looked up at him, he saw the two small cuts on her forehead. Probably from the fall. Maybe she hadn't broken any bones or suffered any internal injuries.

He glanced back at the cruiser. What was left of it, anyway. It was now a fireball, and if they'd been inside when that bomb had gone off, they'd all be dead.

"We need to get into the ditch," Lucas told them.

The sound of the blast was still causing his ears to ring, and it was hard to think. However, he didn't need to think hard to know they shouldn't stay out in the open like this. Someone could be coming to finish them off.

He helped Hailey to her feet, and despite the ringing noise, he still heard the grunt of pain she made. She'd need to be checked out by a doctor. First, though, they needed to get out of here.

"Grayson's on the way," Josh relayed.

Good. They were so close to town that it wouldn't take him long to get there, but trouble could arrive ahead of him. Lucas figured whoever had planted that bomb was probably nearby so they could finish them off.

And he was right.

Within seconds after having that thought, he saw the SUV coming up the road from the direction of the town, and Lucas knew they didn't have much time. They had to take cover now. He ran toward the ditch, dropping down into it. It was shallow, too shallow, but it was the only thing they had right now.

"Stay down as far as you can get," he warned Hailey, and both Josh and he got into crouching positions so they could return fire if necessary.

The SUV screeched to a stop just about twenty feet from them. It was hard to see just how many were inside, though, because of the black smoke coming from the cruiser. The gas tank was already gone, so there probably wouldn't be a secondary explosion, but Lucas wanted Hailey to stay down just in case. That's why he cursed when he felt her put her hand in the waist of his jeans and take his backup weapon from his slide holster.

"You might need an extra hand," she insisted.

He didn't have time to argue with her. Didn't want to turn his attention from that SUV for even a second, but he hoped like the devil that she didn't do anything to get herself hurt worse than she already was.

"Can you see how many of them there are?" Lucas asked Josh.

His cousin shook his head and then scurried down the ditch, no doubt to get a better angle. While Josh was still in motion, though, the front passenger door of the SUV flew open. The barrel of a gun appeared.

And the shot came.

Like the explosion, it ripped through the air, and the bullet slammed into the asphalt just a few inches from Lucas and Hailey. He shoved Hailey back down, took aim and returned fire. His shot smacked against the door and sent the gunman ducking back inside the SUV.

But not for long.

The driver lowered his window and started shooting. Not just one shot, either. These came at them. A barrage of bullets that tore right through the mud and dirt in the ditch. Soon it would tear into them, too, if Lucas didn't do something.

He couldn't lift his head for long. Too risky. And if these thugs managed to kill him, then Hailey would be left as easy prey. So Lucas glanced up just long enough to get his aim. Then he lowered his head.

And he fired.

Lucas could tell from the pinging sound of the shots that he was hitting the SUV. Ideally he was hitting the gunmen, as well, but if so, that didn't stop them from continuing to fire.

"Grayson," Hailey said.

It took Lucas a moment to pick through all the noise from the gunshots to hear a welcome sound. A siren. Grayson certainly wasn't making a quiet approach, and Lucas was thankful for it. Thankful because the gunmen stopped firing.

But that wasn't the only thing they did.

Almost immediately, the driver threw the SUV into Reverse and hit the accelerator hard. He sped backward until he reached the dirt path at the edge of the pasture and then spun the SUV around so that it was heading in the opposite direction.

Lucas came out of the ditch and started firing, hoping to shoot out the tires. Just up from him, Josh did the same. But they were too late.

The gunmen were getting away.

Chapter Fourteen

Hailey held Camden close while he slept in her arms. She wasn't sure she would ever want to let go of him again. Lucas and she had come so close to losing him.

So close to making him an orphan, too.

But Hailey didn't want to think about that. She only wanted this time with her son. Of course, Lucas wanted time with him, as well, but he was on the phone, pacing and trying to get more information from Grayson about the attack. Especially more information about who'd been in that SUV.

Since they'd gotten back to his place, Lucas had learned that the camera at the bank on Main Street had captured some footage of the SUV used in the attack. The footage wasn't clear, but the CSI lab might be able to enhance it enough so they could see the license plate number or even their attackers' faces.

Outside, the storm was finally moving in, and the rain was starting to spatter against the windows. The air felt heavy and thick, almost as if it were bearing down on them. It didn't help that the house was nearly dark, too. Lucas had turned off all the lights when they'd gotten in. Probably so anyone watching them wouldn't be able to see their shadows and know where to aim.

Lucas finished his latest call and went to her, sinking down on the sofa next to her. He didn't say anything. He just looked at her. Or rather, he looked at the cuts on her face. Tillie had tended them after Hailey had showered and changed her clothes, but they were no doubt a clear reminder of what'd happened to them.

"I'm sorry this happened," Lucas finally said.

Hailey shook her head. "It's not your fault. Remember, we're in danger because of me."

Admitting it put a lump in her throat. Brought tears to her eyes, too. She blinked them back because it wouldn't do either of them any good for her to break down and cry. Still, she lost the battle fighting it, and tears spilled down her cheeks.

Lucas cursed under his breath, pulled her to him and kissed her forehead. She was almost positive he didn't want her in his arms. Or so she thought. Until their gazes connected again. Yes, he did want it. Even though he knew it was only breaking down more of those barriers between them.

"What about Colleen's baby?" she asked. "Have the kidnappers called back yet with the drop-off point?"

"No, but I suspect we won't hear from them until morning. I hope it's not sooner, because Grayson still hasn't convinced Eric to do the drop with me."

Hailey hoped the kidnappers changed their minds about that. She didn't want Lucas out there where he could be gunned down, and she especially didn't want him out there with Eric. If Eric was the person behind everything, then he could lead Lucas right into a trap and then use Lucas to draw her out.

And it would work.

No way would Hailey hide herself away and let Lucas be hurt or killed just to protect her.

"Grayson said there's no sign of the gunmen," Lucas continued after he looked away from her and stared at Camden. He touched his fingers to the baby's toes peeking out from the blanket.

She hadn't expected there would be, and Hailey already knew it would take the crime lab a while to get to the camera footage from the cruiser, especially since they had so many other things to process from this investigation. Which was a reminder about Eric showing up on the security footage from the bank.

"Has Grayson had a chance to talk to Eric yet?" she asked. It'd been a couple of hours since the attack. Maybe more than a couple since she hadn't been keeping up with the time. But she figured Grayson would make that a priority.

Lucas nodded. "Eric claims the only reason he went to the bank was that he listened to the recordings and wanted to get to the safe deposit box before one of his father's lackeys did."

It could be true. Could. But this was Eric, so there was no telling. "What was in the box?"

"According to Eric, nothing much. Just some records of illegal land deals and such that Preston had done over the years. He says he destroyed them since those were his father's last wishes."

Since Eric hated his father, she seriously doubted he would care a flying fig about carrying out Preston's wishes. "There must have been something in the box to incriminate Eric."

Lucas made a sound of agreement. There was no way to prove that, though. Maybe Grayson could go after

Eric for destroying possible evidence, but with every-thing else he and his deputies had on their plates, that probably wouldn't happen soon, either.

"Minton came by the sheriff's office again," Lucas continued. "Of course, he says this latest attack is yet another reason for you to be in his protective custody." He paused. "If that's what you want—"

"No." And Hailey didn't even have to think about it. "I want to be here with Camden and you."

Lucas stayed quiet a moment, just long enough for her to know something was wrong. It was also plenty long enough for the feeling of panic to start spreading through her.

"Please tell me I don't have to go with Minton," she said.

"No. Well, not unless he manages to get a court order, which hasn't happened. Even then, I think we could fight it."

Good. But something else was obviously wrong, be-cause his forehead bunched up. "Grayson and I talked about Camden, and we don't think it's a good idea for him to be here. Those attackers could try to come after him again. The ranch is secure, but he'd be better off at the main house."

The place where Mason and his family now lived. It was in the center of the ranch, which would make it harder for kidnappers to get to Camden. Still, there was a problem.

"If the kidnappers have us under surveillance, they might see that we're taking him there," Hailey pointed out.

Lucas nodded. Hesitated again. "The kidnappers want Camden only to use him to get to you."

Because Hailey was fighting the spent adrenaline and the new wave of panic, it took her a moment to figure out what he was saying. "You don't want me to be with Camden."

Another nod.

Oh, mercy. That felt like a punch to the stomach, and it caused a fresh round of tears to fill her eyes. It broke her heart to think of not having Camden close to her.

But Lucas was right.

Her baby was much safer without her around. Plus, Lucas's house was close to the main road. Too close. It would be the first place that gunmen reached if they stormed the ranch.

"How soon would Camden have to leave?" she asked.

"Soon," Lucas said. "Now would be better. I already talked to Tillie about it when you were in the shower, so she's ready. Sawyer and two ranch hands are outside patrolling, but they'll drive Tillie and Camden to the house."

That punch felt even harder, and she saw Tillie peer out from the kitchen, where she was almost certainly waiting for Lucas to break the news. The nanny gave her a sympathetic look, but Tillie was probably ready to put some distance between her and Hailey. After all, Tillie was in danger, too, simply by being around her.

"I'll take good care of him," Tillie assured her.

Hailey knew she would, but it was still hard to let go of the baby. She gave him a kiss on the cheek. Added several more. And she handed him to Lucas so he could take him to Tillie. Once he'd done that, he sent a text. No doubt to Sawyer or one of the hands, because it wasn't long before Hailey heard the sound of a vehicle pulling directly in front of the house.

"We'll come up in the morning to see him," Lucas told the nanny.

When visibility would be better, and it would be easier to spot any attackers who were trying to get close to the ranch. Of course, the visibility wasn't that good right now, which only made her fears skyrocket.

"What if they start shooting when Tillie and Camden go outside?" Hailey asked.

"There's nothing to be gained from them hurting Camden," Lucas assured her. "They want to take him, but they can't do that if he's at the main house."

It felt like a horrible loss to have these next hours taken away. But maybe Lucas and she could use that time to figure out a way to put an end to the danger. They could still set the trap using the reserve deputy to try to lure out the culprit with the promise of getting those files that Colleen had deleted.

"Stand back," Lucas told her. "I don't want you by the door when it's opened."

Yes, because it might prompt the gunmen to fire shots at her. That would put everyone, including the baby, in harm's way.

Hailey tried to hold it together but failed miserably when Lucas disarmed the security system so he could get Tillie and Camden out of the house. They didn't spend but just a couple of seconds out in the open before Sawyer got them in a cruiser. He took off with them as soon as they were inside.

Two other ranch hands stayed behind, no doubt to keep guard. Lucas did his part in keeping them safe, as well. He locked the door and reset the security system.

As fast as she could, Hailey went to the windows

on the same side of the house as the road and opened the curtains. She watched as Sawyer sped out of sight.

"That's not a safe place to stand," Lucas said. He not only moved her back but also closed the curtains again. Shut off the lights, too. "You should try to get some rest," he added. "I'll call Grayson and see if there are any updates."

Hailey had every intention of moving toward the guest room where she'd been staying, but her feet suddenly seemed anchored to the floor. Her eyes seemed out of her control, too, because she started to cry again. She hated the tears. They wouldn't help anything, and in fact, they clearly made Lucas uncomfortable, because his forehead bunched up.

Lucas gave a heavy sigh and went to her. He pulled her into his arms. "It's just temporary," he reminded her.

She got the feeling he was talking about more than just Camden. He probably meant her being here in his house.

In his arms.

They stood there in the darkness with only the sound of the rain and their breaths. She could feel his heartbeat since his chest was against hers. At the moment Hailey could feel everything about him. Feel everything about herself, too.

Especially the heat.

It came, of course. It always came when she was anywhere near Lucas. It was especially there now because they were coming down from the nightmare of the attack and having to be separated from Camden.

"I'm okay," she told him, giving him an out so he could back away.

But Lucas didn't budge. "I always swore that I'd never go another round with you."

That stung, but it was exactly what she expected him to say. "Understandable. I made mistakes with you. Not the sex," Hailey quickly added. "That wasn't a mistake because we got Camden. But I messed up pretty much everything else."

A sound that could have meant anything rumbled in his chest. "I still don't think it's a good idea for us to get involved. Not like this." He glanced at the close contact between them.

Because she thought they could use some levity, she smiled. "Are you trying to convince yourself?"

"Yeah," he admitted.

The levity vanished. So did what was left of her smile. Now, that was not what she'd expected him to say. Lucas was the sort of man who kept his feelings, and his pain, close to the vest. She'd hurt him by not trusting him, and it would take him a long time to get over that.

Or maybe not.

"I'm not doing a good job of convincing myself," he added. "In fact, I'm sinking fast here. I'm trying to come up with a damn good reason why I shouldn't just strip you naked and take you to my bed."

That robbed her of what little breath she had. And it fired up every inch of her.

"I hope you can't think of a reason," she whispered.

There. She'd given him the green light that he probably didn't want. Probably wouldn't take, either.

But she was wrong.

He lowered his head, kissed her. Not a gentle I'm-still-thinking-about-this kind of kiss. It was the real deal. Long and deep. It didn't do anything to cool down her body. Just the opposite.

The kiss went on for so long that Hailey staggered a little because she couldn't breathe. Lucas caught her, tightening his grip around her, and he pulled back so they could take in some air.

He also cursed himself. And he looked down at her. Despite the darkness, she could still see a storm of a different kind brewing in his eyes. Fire mixed with the bitterness of the past.

The fire won out.

Because Lucas scooped her up in his arms, kissed her again and headed in the direction of his bedroom. He stopped along the way to kiss her again. Maybe to make one last-ditch effort at rethinking this, but they were obviously past the point of no return.

Later there'd be consequences.

But Hailey didn't want to think about those now.

She wanted only to feel, wanted to let Lucas take her to the only place she wanted to go. A place with no tears, no gunmen. It was just the two of them, giving in to the heat that had been blazing since they'd first met.

He carried her to the bed, eased her onto the mattress. He was being too gentle with her. Probably because she didn't have her full strength, but she didn't want gentle. Not with this ache starting to throb inside her.

Hailey caught onto him, dragging him closer, and ideally letting him know that she wasn't fragile. Also letting him know that there was already a need to finish what they'd started. In case he didn't get the message, she put her hand over the front of his jeans.

Yes, he got the message, all right.

He lowered the kisses to her neck. Foreplay. Definitely not overrated when it came to Lucas, though there really was no need to fan these flames any higher.

She was wearing a loaner dress that had been in a stash that some of the Ryland wives had sent over. It was loose, so Lucas had no trouble pushing it up, and she felt his hand on her bare skin. His mouth, too, when he took those kisses to her breasts. Then her stomach. He lingered there a moment before he stripped off her bra and panties.

And he kept kissing her.

Hailey didn't want to be the only one naked, though, so she went after his shirt. Not an easy task, though, since Lucas was still wearing a holster. He had to put the kisses on hold to help her with that, and the battle started up again. Hailey wanted his clothes off *now*, but Lucas was back to the kisses.

Which kept going lower.

If they continued in that direction, he was going to make her climax. Something she desperately wanted. But not like this. She wanted him inside her.

Hailey caught onto him, pulling him back up. The movement created an incredible sensation with his body sliding over hers. That made her reach for his zipper. She fumbled around and cursed, causing Lucas to smile. As he'd done with the shirt, he helped her get off the rest of his clothes.

But then he stopped. And moved away from her.

She could have sworn her heart stopped, too, but then she realized he was only getting a condom from the nightstand drawer. It brought back the memories of the other time they'd been together.

The memories got a whole lot better, though.

Lucas came back to her, and once he had on the condom, he gathered her into his arms again. Kissed her. And entered her slowly, easing into the heat of her body. Hailey hadn't thought she'd wanted gentle and easy, but this was working just fine for her. He took his time, building the fire even hotter.

It didn't last.

Couldn't.

The need soon took over, and slow and easy was done. Now it was all about finishing this. And he did. Lucas moved in her, the pace as frantic and deep as the need. Until both of them went flying right over the edge.

Chapter Fifteen

Lucas tried to get some sleep. Hard to do, though, with a naked Hailey right next to him. Especially hard to do with the thoughts racing through his head. Thoughts of tomorrow's ransom drop and of the danger to his son.

Thoughts, too, of what'd happened between Hailey and him.

He figured he should regret the sex. And in some ways he did. It was a distraction that he didn't need at a time when he should have been focused on the investigation. Still, it was hard to regret something that'd been damn good.

At least she was sleeping now. That was good. But he figured her body hadn't given her much of a choice about that. Hailey had been running on adrenaline since coming out of the coma, and she needed to rest. Because tomorrow would be a hellish day for her, as well.

Lucas only hoped he could get back Colleen's baby without anyone getting hurt or killed. While he was hoping, he added that Eric would cooperate and do the drop with him. So far, he hadn't agreed, which meant Lucas would have to convince him or else renegotiate with the kidnappers.

Maybe Colleen wouldn't do something stupid before then.

Shortly after Hailey had fallen asleep, Lucas had gotten a text from Grayson telling him that Colleen had refused to stay at the sheriff's office any longer. Grayson hadn't had any grounds to hold her, and even though he'd reminded her that the kidnappers could be watching the place, Colleen had left anyway. At best, she was just going somewhere else to wait for the ransom drop. At worst, she was in grave danger. And Grayson didn't have the manpower to send someone out to make sure she didn't get herself into trouble.

Right now, the Rylands had enough trouble on their hands.

Lucas glanced at the laptop that he'd brought into the bedroom after Hailey had fallen asleep. It was on the nightstand next to him, and it showed the feed from the security cameras positioned all around the ranch. No doubt several of his cousins were watching the cameras, too, as was the head ranch hand. All of them looking to make sure someone didn't try to sneak onto the grounds.

So far, so good.

It was a bad night, though, for any kind of sneaking around outside. The rain was steady and heavy, and there was the occasional jag of lightning in the sky. Maybe the storm would be enough to keep the thugs from another attempt to take Camden or Hailey.

With a few strokes on the laptop keyboard, Lucas pulled up the feed from another camera. This one was in the nursery at the main house. Tillie had set up the camera so that they could see Camden. And there he was, sleeping in a crib. He was sharing the room with Mason's son, Max. Tillie was in the guest room just up the hall and would no doubt have a baby monitor next to her bed so she'd be able to hear the babies if they woke up.

As if she'd sensed what Lucas was doing, Hailey stirred, her eyes opening and her attention going straight to the screen. She smiled. Sat up.

"It's not the same as having him here with us, but it's still nice to see him," she said.

Yeah. It was. But the *us* gave Lucas some hesitation. She'd said it so easily, as if it were normal. It wasn't. And Hailey must have realized her slip, because she muttered an apology under her breath.

Lucas hated that she felt the need to apologize. Hated even more that he felt as if he should have one. Because despite the fact that she was in his bed, they were a long way from getting to the *us* stage.

Once he'd taken care of the danger, they could start working on that. And Lucas refused to believe he couldn't put an end to the attacks, because if he couldn't, it would mean Hailey and Camden going to a safe house. Or her even returning to WITSEC, but this time she would have to take Camden with her since as long as he was out there, the snake behind this could use the baby to get to Hailey.

"Colleen left the sheriff's office," Lucas told her. "Grayson couldn't talk her out of it."

Hailey gave a heavy sigh. "No, he wouldn't have been able to do that. Did Colleen say where she was going?"

Lucas shook his head. "But unless she manages to get her hands on the money, she can't do the ransom exchange." And he hoped she didn't even attempt it.

She looked at Camden again. Then Lucas. "You're

no doubt thinking we messed things up big-time," she said. "And yes, I'm talking about the sex."

He let that hang in the air for a couple of seconds. Then lifted his shoulder. "Well, yeah, when I mess up, I aim for big."

She laughed, but it wasn't exactly from humor. More nerves. Something he understood. Reality was quickly settling in, and there was no way they could go back to where they'd been just hours earlier. There was no such thing as casual sex when it came to Hailey.

The silence settled between them. And it wasn't exactly comfortable. Hailey fixed her attention to the laptop and on Camden. As much as he wanted to continue looking at their son, though, he had to switch the camera back so he could help watch the security feed. That didn't do much to ease the discomfort between them.

"Just how bad do you think it'll get tomorrow?" she asked.

He considered lying and saying "not bad at all," but he couldn't make that kind of guarantee. He looked at her, though. Saw the worry on her face again, so Lucas decided to go with a half guarantee.

"I'll make it work," he assured her and brushed a kiss on her cheek.

Of course, that sparked the attraction again, along with sparking another kiss. This time not on the cheek but her mouth. Hailey moved right into the kiss, too, sliding closer and touching him.

Not good since they were naked.

That didn't stop him, though, from deepening the kiss and hauling her right against him. However, then something stopped Lucas.

It was just a soft beep, barely audible because he

had the sound turned down on the laptop, but it was a sound that went through him like the lightning bolt that slashed outside.

Because it meant something or someone had triggered one of the dozens of sensors positioned all around the ranch.

The laptop was showing six different cameras, the ones positioned on the most vulnerable points of the ranch. The fence lines and the road. He looked at each of them but didn't see anything.

"Does that sound mean what I think it means?" Hailey asked. She moved away from him, her attention back on the screen.

"It could be nothing," Lucas tried to assure her. "Sometimes animals trigger the sensors. The storm could, too, if the wind knocked down a tree branch or something."

Lucas held on to that hope, but it was hard not to think the worst. Hard to stave off the knot that was already tightening in his gut. A knot that got even tighter when his phone buzzed, and he saw Mason's name on the screen.

"Any idea why the alarm went off?" Lucas immediately asked him.

"No. I'm looking through the camera feeds now, all of them, and I don't see anything. You?"

"Nothing." Lucas put the phone on speaker so he could get dressed, but he also tapped the keyboard to scroll through some of the other security feeds. "But I'll keep watching."

"Yeah, be ready just in case," Mason said, ending the call.

That sent Hailey scrambling from the bed. There

were no signs of the heat and attraction on her face now. Just the fear as she grabbed her clothes and started putting them on. Fear that Lucas needed to rein in right now, because this could be a long wait to find out if anything was truly wrong.

"No one can get near the main house," he reminded her. "Not without going through a dozen ranch hands and plenty of other houses."

Since those places all had lawmen inside them, Lucas was pretty sure Camden was safe. But "pretty sure" didn't ease the knot in his stomach. He wanted a hundred percent guarantee when it came to his son, and it didn't matter where Camden was. He wouldn't have that guarantee until the person responsible for the attacks was dead or behind bars.

Hailey finished dressing—obviously she was preparing herself in case they had to go outside, but Lucas was hoping that didn't happen.

Lucas put back on both his weapons, and even though it was hard to force himself to sit down, he did for Hailey's sake. So that she'd sit, too. She did, right beside him, and they both watched the screen as he scrolled through all the feeds.

She shook her head. "I still don't see anything."

Neither did he, but it was dark, and even with the security lights, there were still plenty of shadows. Plenty of places for someone to hide, too, what with all the fences, trees and outbuildings. But if someone was out there and that person moved, then the sensors would pick him up, and the alarm would ding again.

The seconds crawled by, turning into minutes, and just when Lucas was ready to try to level his breathing, he saw something. Movement not near the fence line but near the road. It was just a blur of motion, barely in camera range and not actually on ranch land.

"What?" Hailey asked. She'd obviously noticed that he'd tensed.

"Maybe nothing," he repeated.

Lucas clicked on that specific screen, enlarged it and zoomed in on the area where he'd seen the motion. He was hoping it was a deer or an illusion caused by the rain.

But it wasn't.

It was a man dressed all in black. And he had a rifle aimed right at Lucas's house.

HAILEY COULDN'T STOP herself from gasping when she saw the man. He was lurking behind one of the trees directly across the road from the ranch.

"Oh, God," she said, and she scrambled to get the gun from Lucas's nightstand.

He took hold of her hand and had her sit next to him again. He also adjusted the view of the camera so that she could see the truck that was parked at the end of the road. Unlike the man with the rifle, the truck was actually on the ranch.

"Two of the hands are in the truck," Lucas explained, and he took out his phone and fired off a text. No doubt to warn them that there was definitely a problem.

Lucas went back to the camera angle so they could see the man, and Hailey realized he wasn't alone. There was another armed guy directly behind him.

The skin crawled on the back of her neck. Because she knew what those men wanted.

They wanted her.

And they'd try to use Camden to get her.

"Get down on the floor," Lucas instructed.

She did as he said, and he grabbed the laptop to bring it to the floor with him. The difference was he had her lie all the way down while he stayed in a sitting position. Probably so he'd be better able to respond if things turned bad in a hurry.

Hailey tried not to panic. Hard to do, though, when all she could feel was the panic and fear. Both went up a significant notch when she saw the headlights of an approaching car on the screen. The vehicle no doubt carried more thugs arriving to launch a full-scale attack.

Both the hands in the truck opened their doors, and they put out their rifles. Ready to return fire.

She gasped again when the dinging sound shot through the room. But it wasn't a security alarm. It was Lucas's phone to let him know he had a text. She saw Mason's name on the screen.

"Mason's on the line with the hands at the road," Lucas said when he read the text. "He's sending them backup right away." He cursed. "But I need to stay here."

She knew the profanity wasn't for her but the situation. He wanted to be down there helping the hands, but all of this could be designed to have him do just that. So that she'd be alone and an easy prey.

The car came to a stop directly in front of where the hands were parked. Hailey saw another vehicle, too. A cruiser barreling down the ranch road toward the hands, the two armed men and the newly arrived vehicle. A moment later, another cruiser followed the first. So there were plenty of lawmen responding to what was no doubt about to become the scene of another attack.

"What the hell?" Lucas said, moving closer to the laptop screen.

Hailey watched as the driver of the car got out. Colleen. And her sister lifted her hands into the air as if surrendering. Colleen said something to the ranch hands, but since there was no audio, Hailey had no idea what.

But this couldn't be good.

Either her sister was part of the oncoming attack, or else she was going to be right in the middle of it.

Even though it was pouring rain, Colleen stayed outside the car, and after a very short conversation with the hands, she took out her phone. A moment later, Lucas's own phone rang. He answered it and put it on speaker.

"Hailey?" Colleen asked. Her voice was frantic. As was her expression. "You have to tell these men to let me onto the ranch."

Hailey debated how to answer that. But Lucas had no such debate with himself. "Did you bring those gunmen with you?" he asked.

"What gunmen?" Colleen's gaze began to slash all around her.

"The ones across the road."

A sob tore from Colleen's mouth, and she ducked back into the car. "No, I didn't bring them, but I think they want me dead."

"If they wanted that, you already would be," Lucas pointed out. "They had a clean shot and didn't take it."

And it wasn't as if the men had left. Hailey could still see them on the corner of the screen. Could see the approaching cruisers, too. They pulled to a stop behind the ranch hands' truck. The doors opened, and four of Lucas's cousins—Dade, Sawyer, Josh and Gage—all took aim at the gunmen while they used the doors of the cruisers for cover.

"You're just going to let me stay out here?" Colleen protested.

Hailey was torn about what to do. Her instincts were screaming for her to protect her sister, but her instincts were even stronger to keep Camden safe.

"Answer me!" Colleen practically shouted.

"I can't let you near my son," Hailey said. "Leave and go to the sheriff's office. You'll be safe there."

That brought out some vicious profanity from Colleen. "I stopped Preston from having you killed. You owe me!"

That chilled her to the bone, but then Hailey reminded herself that it might not even be true. It could be Colleen who wanted her dead. Or even Colleen just carrying through on Preston's old wishes.

Colleen added some more profanity, but Hailey shut her out when Lucas's phone dinged, indicating he had an incoming call.

Unknown Caller popped up on the screen.

"I have to put you on hold," Lucas said to her sister, and he answered the other call.

"I know I said I'd be in touch in the morning," the man said by way of greeting, "but I just couldn't wait." It was the kidnapper, the same one who'd been communicating with them.

"Where are you?" Lucas asked.

"Nearby but out of range of all those pesky cameras you got all around the ranch. You might be able to see a couple of the fellas I brought with me, though."

"I do, and you probably see that there are six men with guns aimed right back at them."

"Yeah, they know. None of us want a gunfight. Especially not Hailey and you. Not with your boy and all those Ryland kids and babies so close. Somebody might get hurt."

Instead of ice in Hailey's blood, that sent some hot rage through her body. How dare this snake threaten not only her son but also everyone else on the ranch? She nearly yelled at him and wanted to use some of those same curse words that her sister just had, but Lucas spoke before she could say anything.

"If you don't want a gunfight, what do you want?" Lucas asked the man.

"I thought you'd like to see who's with me," he said, obviously not answering Lucas's question. "I'm sending you a pretty picture now."

Almost immediately, Lucas's phone dinged with a text. Again from Unknown Caller, and it did indeed have a picture attached. It took a moment to load.

Hailey's heart went to her knees.

Because it was a picture of Colleen's baby. Not alone. Minton was holding her in the crook of his arm.

And there was what appeared to be a bomb strapped to Minton's chest.

Chapter Sixteen

Hailey snapped to a sitting position, and she practically snatched the phone from his hand so she could get a closer look of the photo that the kidnapper had just sent them.

But Lucas didn't need a closer look. He'd already seen more than enough.

"It could be fake," Lucas reminded Hailey. "Minton could be their boss, and he could have set all of this up."

She gave a shaky nod, repeated that last part. But he wasn't sure she was buying it. Her breathing was already way too fast, and she was no doubt having to battle the panic that had to be crawling through her. Lucas felt some of that same panic, too, but he had to rein it in so he could focus on what exactly he was seeing.

And how to fix it.

"Let me speak to Minton," Lucas told the kidnapper.

"Thought you'd want to do that. I'll put him on the line, but for just a few seconds. After that, you and I will have a little chat about what you need to do for this to turn out good for all of us."

Lucas didn't have to wait long before he heard Minton's voice. "They hit me with a stun gun when I was going into my office," Minton said, his voice a snarl.

His expression in the photo matched the snarl, as well. Either he was one unhappy camper or he was pretending to be one. "Now I have a bomb on me, right next to the baby."

"Yes, I saw the photo. Is it real?" Lucas came out and asked.

"Hell, yes, it's real!" Minton's shout must have startled the baby, because she began to cry.

Not good. Hailey's nerves were clearly already frayed enough, and the baby's cries only added to the urgency of this situation.

"How do you know the bomb is real?" Lucas pressed. "Do you have personal knowledge of explosive devices?"

"Yes, I do, but not in the way you're insinuating. I didn't put this bomb on myself. These idiots did after they kidnapped me. And I don't know who they're working for, but if you don't do as they say, they're going to start the timer. After that, I'd have only two minutes before this kid and I get blown to bits."

Lucas glanced at the photo again, at the placement of Minton's hands, and he saw that they were literally tied around the baby. Two minutes probably wouldn't be enough time to get out of those ropes and remove the bomb. Especially since it was possible the kidnappers were also holding Minton at gunpoint and wouldn't give him a chance to escape.

"Well?" the kidnapper said, coming back on the line. Lucas could still hear the baby crying, so obviously the little girl and Minton weren't too far away. "Convinced that we mean business?"

"I was convinced of that before you put an innocent

baby in danger. Get the baby away from that bomb and then we'll talk."

"We'll talk now," the man snapped.

"All right," Lucas snapped right back. "You want the baby alive to collect the ransom. Well, you're risking a half million dollars by keeping her that close to the explosive."

"There's no real threat to her," the kidnapper said. "Not at this moment, anyhow. You gotta do something, though, to keep it that way. You can have the baby in exchange for Hailey. And before you go all cowboy cop on me, this isn't your decision. It's Hailey's. I'll give her five minutes to decide."

Lucas was about to tell him that he didn't need a second of that five minutes, that the answer was no. But the kidnapper hung up.

"You're not going out there," Lucas insisted.

She moved as if ready to get up, but he caught her arm to force her to sit back down. He needed to convince her to stay put, but he also had to keep watch on the security screens in case those gunmen started firing.

"These men want you dead," Lucas reminded her. "And along with two of our suspects, Colleen and Minton, there are gunmen. Going to meet them won't get the baby rescued. It will only get you killed."

She stopped struggling to get away from him, and even in the darkness, Lucas saw the tears shimmer in her eyes. "I have to do something to help that baby. She's my niece."

Lucas got that. Hell, he had a niece, and he would have done anything to keep her safe. But a suicide mission wasn't the way to go, especially since it was possible the child wasn't even in any real danger.

"So, what do we do?" Hailey asked.

He looked at the screen again. Still no movement from the gunmen. Lucas panned around, trying to get a glimpse of the vehicle holding Minton and the baby, but he didn't see anything.

Hell.

The kidnappers could have the baby anywhere, including out of the state.

"Let me see first if Colleen stayed on hold," he said.

Though Lucas wasn't sure what to tell Hailey's sister. It didn't seem a good idea to mention the bomb. However, it turned out he didn't have to make that decision, because Colleen was no longer on the line. Her car was still at the end of the road, though.

But it didn't stay there.

Colleen backed out the car, turned onto the main road and hit the accelerator. Lucas thought she had decided to leave, and he adjusted the camera angle to see if she was heading back to town.

She wasn't.

Colleen turned her car directly at the white wooden fence that fronted the ranch, and she bashed right through it. Her car went straight into the pasture. Too close to Lucas's house.

Hailey gasped. "What is she doing?" she said under her breath.

Lucas hated to think the worst, but he did. Colleen could be coming to kill them.

Dade and Gage got back into their cruiser and went in pursuit. Mason was no doubt sending someone, too, but there wasn't a lot of help to send. Most of the men were already tied up guarding the houses and the other fences, especially the back, where it would be easier for someone to launch an attack.

Colleen's car didn't make it far, though. The rain had obviously soaked the pasture, and she made it only about a hundred yards before her tires bogged down in the mud and grass. That didn't stop her, though. She barreled out of the vehicle and started running.

Directly toward Lucas's house.

He hadn't even been sure that Colleen knew which house was his, but she must have done her homework, because she was headed their way on foot.

And not alone, either.

Before Dade could get the cruiser turned around, another vehicle came up the road. A black SUV. And it looked like the same one with the attackers who'd tried to kill Hailey, Josh and him after the bombing.

"Those men are after Colleen?" Hailey asked.

Lucas didn't know the answer. Not at first, anyway. But he soon got one. The SUV didn't go after Colleen. Nor did it bog down. The driver came to a stop, and his passenger opened his door.

And the guy aimed something at Lucas's house.

It was too big to be a regular firearm, and Lucas had to zoom in on it to figure out what it was. A tear gas gun. At least, he hoped it was that and not a grenade launcher. Either way, Hailey and he had to get the heck out of there now.

Lucas closed the laptop, tucking it under his arm, and he took hold of Hailey to get her moving. It was chilly and raining, but Lucas was pretty sure there wouldn't be enough time to grab any raincoats or umbrellas.

And he was right.

There was a crashing sound of breaking glass in the

living room, the side of the house that faced those thugs. Followed by another sound of the canister plinking to the floor. A couple of moments later, another canister came flying into the house.

"We have to hurry," Lucas warned her. He handed her the laptop so he could draw his gun.

Time was up, because tear gas started to spew through the entire house. Lucas ran with her to the back door and prayed he wasn't carrying Hailey right into an ambush.

HAILEY WAS MOVING as fast as she could, but it wasn't fast enough. The tear gas was on them before Lucas and she could get to the back door.

She started to cough, the gas cutting off her breath along with burning her throat and eyes. It was no doubt doing the same thing to Lucas, but he still managed to get the door open. He already had his weapon drawn when he stepped out onto the porch and looked around. He must not have seen anyone because he pulled her out of the house.

"We can't stay here," he said.

A moment later, she realized why. Another canister came bashing into the house. Then another. It wouldn't be long before the tear gas was so thick back here that they would be coughing too hard to run.

But where?

If they ran outside, they could be gunned down.

She could see Lucas's gaze darting around while he was trying to figure that out. They had a couple of choices. They could try to make it to the side of the house where he'd parked his truck. The problem with that was it was also the side where those canister-shooting thugs were positioned.

It was where she'd last seen Colleen, too.

So that probably wasn't a good direction to go. That left the barn, a detached garage and a storage building. Beyond that was open pasture, where one of those riflemen would be able to pick them off.

"We'll run to the garage," Lucas told her. "I have another truck there we can use to escape. Stay as low as you can and move fast."

Hailey wasn't sure she could go fast. Not with her legs so wobbly, and now that she couldn't breathe so well, it would be even harder. Still, they didn't have much of a choice.

Lucas took her hand and led her off the porch and down the steps. When they reached the yard, there was no more awning, so the rain and wind came right at them. Even though Hailey had on the hoodie, it wasn't nearly thick enough, and it didn't take long before she started to shiver. Still, she ran until Lucas pulled them behind a large oak.

Not a second too soon, either.

A shot blasted through the air and slammed right into the tree.

It wasn't just the rain that was raw and bitter. Suddenly the fear was, too. Not because the shot had come so close to hitting Lucas and her, but because she didn't want bullets being fired anywhere near Camden and the others.

More shots came, but these didn't slam into the tree. That only made the fear worse because Hailey couldn't immediately figure out where those men were shooting.

Then she realized they were aiming at the cruiser that Dade and Gage were trying to get closer.

Mercy.

The shooters were no doubt doing that to stop Lucas's cousins from helping them. At least the cruiser was bullet-resistant, but she figured sooner or later, either Dade or Gage would step out so they could return fire.

Hailey considered taking out the laptop to see if she could check the security cameras, but she needed to be ready to move. Plus, she didn't want to risk getting it wet. Right now, it was still under her arm where it was semiprotected. Once they were in the garage, then she could check and make sure none of these hired killers were heading for the main house. Maybe she'd also be able to find her sister. If Colleen was innocent, then she was in grave danger out in the open with those bullets flying.

Lucas's phone buzzed, and he took it from his pocket and handed it to her. Probably so he could keep his hands free. When Hailey saw Mason's name on the screen, she answered it right away.

"Is everyone all right?" she immediately asked.

"Fine for now. I want to keep it that way. Dade told me about the bomb, the baby and Minton. As soon as Dade can, he'll move in to help. In the meantime, our other cousins, Nate and Landon, are trying to work their way to the pasture. If they get a clean shot, they'll stop the gunmen."

That was good. Hailey hoped that would happen. It wouldn't get back her niece, but it would end the immediate danger. At least, it would if these men didn't set off that explosive. But she figured they were going to use Colleen's baby as the ultimate bargaining tool to get to her.

"What about my sister?" Hailey asked. "Where is she?"

"I lost sight of her, but the last I saw her, she was moving in the direction of Lucas's barn."

Then that was all the more reason for Lucas and her not to go in there. "What about the car with Minton and the baby?"

"Still nothing on that. Grayson's coming in from town, and he'll look along the way."

Maybe they'd get lucky and could spot it. Of course, in the dark and rain, it would be hard to do.

"I can see Lucas and you," Mason went on a moment later. "Make your way to the main house when you can. You're too damn close to these dirtbags."

Yes, they were. And while Hailey desperately wanted to see Camden, she was also terrified of having these men shoot at them if they went in that direction. Plus, Lucas and she had to get to the garage first.

"I'll have the ranch hands fire at the dirtbags," Mason added. "That should keep them occupied a couple of seconds so that you and Lucas can get moving."

"But what about the shots going to the main house?" she asked.

"The ranch hands are positioning themselves so that won't happen," he assured her.

She thanked him and added, "Just keep Camden and everyone else safe." Maybe Mason and the others would be able to do that.

She relayed the information Mason had given her to Lucas, but before she even finished, Hailey heard the shots. These weren't coming from the hired killers but rather from the ranch hands. As Mason had said, it created a distraction because the gunmen were now shooting at the hands.

"Let's move," Lucas told her.

They started running. There weren't any trees or anything else right by they could use for cover, so Hailey held her breath while they were out in the open. It seemed to take an eternity to go the fifteen or so yards. The rain certainly didn't help, either, and her shoes sank down into the boggy ground.

The moment they reached the garage, Lucas took her to the side door and threw it open. He stepped in first, his gaze slashing from one side to the other. What he didn't do was turn on the lights. Probably because it would alert the gunmen to their position. Maybe the men had been so involved with the gunfight distraction that they hadn't seen Lucas and her make their way there.

"Stay right next to me," he warned her.

She did, and while he continued to look around them, he inched his way to a truck parked at the front of the garage. The back was a workshop and storage area and was filled with shelves, tables and equipment. It would give someone places to hide. Not exactly a reminder to soothe her already raw nerves.

"I need to check and make sure no one tampered with the truck," Lucas added. "Keep watch around us."

That didn't help her nerves, either. Hailey just wanted to get out of there, but after what'd happened with the cruiser, they had to take precautions.

Lucas stooped down, and using the light from his phone, he began to make his way around the truck. She followed him while keeping watch, but Hailey didn't see anyone, thank goodness.

But she heard something.

Lucas must have, too, because he quickly stood and moved in front of her. They waited, listening. Hard to hear, though, what with the shots continuing outside, but Hailey was almost certain she'd heard something move. Or maybe it was just the wind and rain.

No, it wasn't.

There was another sound, and this time Hailey was able to pinpoint it.

Someone was in the truck.

Chapter Seventeen

Hell. What now?

Lucas pivoted and took aim in the direction of the truck cab. He didn't see anyone, but he was positive someone was in there.

He had known it was a risk to come into the garage, but it would have also been a risk for them to stay in the yard with heaven knew how many hired thugs now on the ranch. However, they might have gone from the frying pan right into the fire.

"Come out or I'll shoot," Lucas warned the person. But it was a warning he hoped like the devil that he didn't have to carry out. Because he didn't want to shoot in cramped quarters with Hailey.

Definitely didn't want to start a gunfight.

And he also didn't want to alert the armed thugs that Hailey and he were in the garage. That would only cause them to open fire. Or maybe launch another tear gas grenade.

"It's me," someone said.

Colleen.

Lucas groaned and definitely didn't lower his gun. "Put your hands where I can see them," he ordered.

"I'm not the one trying to kill you." Colleen added a sob. "When will you believe me?"

"I might start to believe you when you get out of the truck, hands up."

Other than another sob, Colleen didn't respond, and the seconds crawled by before she finally lifted her head. Lucas could see then that she'd been down on the seat. She lifted her hands, too.

"Satisfied?" Colleen snapped.

"Not yet. Step out, keep your hands in the air and don't make any sudden moves. Get behind me," he added to Hailey. "And try to keep watch around us in case she's not alone."

Because Hailey's arm was right against his, he felt her tense even more. He hated that he was having to put her through this, but they couldn't get in the truck until Lucas figured out what the heck Colleen was up to.

Colleen stepped from the truck, and Lucas could see she didn't have anything in her hands. She also didn't appear to be carrying a weapon. Like Hailey, Colleen wasn't wearing a coat. The rain had soaked her jeans and top, and they were clinging to her. Still, Lucas motioned for her to turn around, and when she did, he made sure she didn't have a weapon tucked in the back waist of her jeans.

She didn't.

"I told you I wasn't trying to kill you," Colleen said.

Just because she wasn't armed didn't mean she wasn't behind this attack. "Why are you in here? *How* are you in here?" Lucas amended.

"I just started running when my car got stuck. This was the first place I reached. I knew I needed to try to get to my baby, but I couldn't find the truck keys."

They were on a hook on the wall, but since Colleen hadn't turned on the lights, either, she would have had trouble spotting them.

"Do you know where the baby is?" Lucas asked.

"No." Colleen winced when there was another round of loud gunfire. "But I have to find her. I have to save her." She made a loud sob. "Is there anything you can do to make them stop shooting? Can you try to negotiate with them or something?"

Her fear seemed genuine enough, but after the hell Hailey and he had been through, Lucas planned on hanging on to his skepticism a while longer.

"I don't have any control over those gunmen," he told her. "But there are armed ranch hands out there, and they might get them to stop soon."

Colleen looked at Hailey. "Please help me get my daughter back. Please. Just think if it were your son and how hard this would be for you."

"I have thought about it," Hailey answered. "Those kidnappers want me in exchange for the baby."

"Then do it." Colleen didn't hesitate even a second, either. Maybe because she knew there was no danger for her. But there'd be plenty for Hailey. "I'd go if they would let me."

"Really?" Lucas pressed.

"Of course."

Then he was about to put that to the test. Without taking his gun off the woman, he passed his phone back to Hailey. "Hit Redial and see if the kidnapper will answer."

Colleen's eyes widened. "What are you going to do?"

Lucas didn't actually expect the kidnapper to answer

and was surprised when he heard the man's voice. "Are you ready to send out Hailey?" the man asked.

"No, but Colleen is here, and she's willing to meet with you."

And Lucas carefully watched Colleen's reaction. She didn't look annoyed or afraid. "Yes," she said. "I'll come right now. Just tell me where I need to go so I can get my baby."

"Guess Lucas told you about our little explosive device, huh?" the kidnapper taunted.

Colleen's gaze slashed to Lucas. "What is he talking about?"

"So he didn't tell you," the kidnapper continued before Lucas could speak. "Minton and your baby girl are real close to a bomb right now."

Colleen gasped. "Oh, God. Is it true? Is there actually a bomb?"

"There is. A bomb set to go off with just a flip of a switch. And if you want that to change, then convince your sister to come out and chat with us. You come, too. In fact, I insist both of you come."

Even though Colleen looked on the verge of a panic attack, Lucas blocked Hailey from going closer to her. If Colleen was truly innocent, then he'd owe her a huge apology, but for now his priority had to be keeping Hailey safe.

"What exactly do you want from the women?" Lucas asked the kidnapper.

"Any and all files they have about the DeSalvo family," he answered without hesitation.

"And then what?" Hailey added.

"Then, tomorrow morning you'll get that ransom money, and you'll get both the women and the kid."

Lucas seriously doubted it. Judging from the sound she made, so did Hailey. Colleen was the only one of them who was clearly eager to do this.

"Let me know if the women are coming out," the kidnapper said. "Once they do, the shots will stop on our part. You'll have to make sure the Rylands and the ranch hands stop, too." And he ended the call.

"Call him back," Colleen insisted. "Have him tell me where Hailey and I need to go to get my baby."

"That's not going to happen," Lucas assured her. "Not on Hailey's part anyway."

But what was his next move?

He wanted to get Hailey to the main house, where she'd be safer and with Camden. However, he couldn't just leave Colleen here, either.

"Call Mason," Lucas told Hailey. "Let him know that Colleen is here, and I'm trying to figure out what to do with her. I also want to know if the road is clear between my house and his."

"You don't need to figure out what to do with me," Colleen shrieked. "We have to get the baby." She snapped toward Hailey. "This is all your fault, anyway. You probably have all sorts of information stashed away on Preston and Eric. Information that could send me to jail, too."

"Are you admitting to some crimes?" Lucas immediately asked her.

"No! But Hailey always had it in for Preston. I figure Eric, too. And if she hadn't been so hell-bent on putting them in jail, none of this would be happening."

Maybe that was true, but in this case, being hell-bent was the right thing to do. "Preston was a criminal. He deserved to be behind bars." And that was all the breath he was going to waste on Colleen. "Call Mason," he repeated to Hailey.

"I really am innocent," Colleen continued while Hailey located the number. "Darrin forced me to go to the hospital. He said it was the only way to get my baby. But he lied. And then he tried to kill me when he ran me off the road."

If that was true, then it was another reason Lucas was glad that Darrin was out of the picture. Hailey made a sound of agreement, probably because she felt the same, and she finished making the call to Mason. She also put it on speaker.

"What's the latest on the gunmen?" Lucas asked the moment his cousin answered.

"Pinned down, for now. But they're not budging, and I can't have the hands, Dade or the others go in any closer."

So they were at a stalemate. Well, in a way. Hailey was still in danger.

"Grayson called," Mason went on. "He spotted a vehicle just up the road from the ranch, and he's going to do a quiet approach to see if Minton and the baby are there. One of the deputies is with him."

"Tell the sheriff to be careful," Colleen blurted out.

"Who the hell is that?" Mason asked.

"Colleen. I'm in my garage with Hailey and her. Colleen was hiding in here."

Mason cursed. "And your plans?"

"Still debating that. How safe would it be for me to drive Hailey to the main house and then come back here to wait with Colleen?" That was just in case she was innocent and therefore in danger.

But Hailey was shaking her head before Lucas even

finished his question to Mason. "That's too risky for you," she insisted.

"Hailey's right," Mason agreed. "When the gunmen spot your truck, I figure they'll start shooting at it."

Lucas wasn't giving up just yet on this particular plan. He wanted some distance between Colleen and Hailey. Between Hailey and those shooters, too. "Maybe the hands could continue keeping them occupied?"

"They could, but why don't you stay there for a couple more minutes. That'll give me time to hear from Grayson. If the baby is in that vehicle, I'll need to send him some help. Plus, I'd rather the gunmen not have any reason to get to the main house."

No way could Lucas disagree with any of that, but he definitely didn't like the idea of staying put, either. Maybe he tempted fate with that thought, because he heard a sound. Not one of the normal gunshots. This was more of a blast. One that he'd heard four other times before.

It was the sound of another gas canister being fired.

And this time it didn't smash into the house. It hit the garage door, and from what he could tell, it bashed into the wooden part of the door and not the glass inserts just above it. However, that didn't stop the gas from spewing in around the sides and bottom.

Mercy. Lucas definitely hadn't wanted things to go this way, but they had to move. That was especially true when the next canister came crashing through the glass.

"In the truck, now," he told Hailey and Colleen. He grabbed the keys from the wall hook.

They were already starting in that direction anyway. First Colleen. Then Hailey, who got in the middle. They were already coughing, too, and he hoped the tear gas didn't water his eyes so much that he wouldn't be able to see.

The moment Lucas started the engine, he hit the remote control to open the door, and once he had enough clear space to get out, he gunned the engine.

Driving right into that cloud of tear gas.

But that was just the start of their troubles. Because the gunmen started shooting at them.

HAILEY TRIED TO clear her eyes and throat so she could help Lucas get them to safety. If that was possible. The shots were coming at them so fast that it was like being trapped in a hailstorm.

The bullets tore through the windshield, and Hailey took hold of Colleen and pushed her lower on the seat. She got lower, as well, but Lucas couldn't while driving.

Lucas cursed. "Hell, they shot into the radiator."

No doubt to disable the vehicle. But how had they even known Lucas, Colleen and she were in the garage in the first place? Hailey hoped it was a guess on their part and they didn't have some insider information from Colleen. Her sister could have called or sent those thugs a text when she saw them come into the garage.

"Where are we going?" Hailey managed to ask Lucas even though she was having to fight for every breath. And she was shaking from the wet and cold. She had such a tight grip on the laptop and Lucas's phone that she was afraid they might shatter.

"Away from those shots. Away from the main house, too."

Good. As much as she wanted to get to safety, it was too risky to go in that direction. Too risky to stay put, too, and Lucas didn't speed toward the road but rather across the backyard and to the side of his own house. That put an instant buffer between them and the gunmen. What it didn't do was get rid of the lingering tear gas.

Probably because the thugs sent two more canisters their way.

The gunmen were trying to flush them out, trying to force them out into the open, where they'd be easier targets.

"Watch Colleen," Lucas said to her. A reminder that he didn't trust her sister. Neither did she, and her alarm went up a significant notch when Colleen threw open the glove compartment.

"I need a gun," her sister insisted.

Hailey wanted that, too, but she hoped there wasn't one for Colleen to find. There wasn't. But Lucas took out his backup weapon, and when he handed it to Hailey, she had to shift the laptop under her arm so she could take it. Hailey put it in her pocket.

Giving her the gun earned Lucas and her a glare from Colleen, but Hailey didn't care. She preferred not to be in a closed vehicle with one of their armed suspects.

She lifted her head enough so she could adjust and pull out the laptop. She opened it and prayed the Wi-Fi signal was strong enough outside the house.

It was.

She pulled up the security camera screens so she could help Lucas keep watch. After all, the gunmen could sneak around the front of the house and attack. Hard to see much of anything, though, with the darkness, the tear gas and the rain, but at least the rain was washing away some of the gas. That should make it easier for them to breathe and see.

Despite the nightmare going on around them, Lucas's gaze met hers. For just a couple of seconds. She wanted to tell him how sorry she was that this had happened again.

She wanted to say a lot of things to him.

But since it wasn't the time or the place, Hailey went back to keeping watch. Right now, that was the best thing she could do for all of them. Too bad she didn't see something on the screens that would help Dade and the others close in on the gunmen. She switched the angle.

Nothing.

Then she switched it again, and that's when Hailey saw the movement. With the thick rain, it was just a blur, but someone had definitely moved up behind the two gunmen.

Another man dressed all in black. This one, though, was also wearing rain gear—a coat with a hood.

Hailey wasn't sure how he'd gotten there, but it was possible he'd come from the vehicle that had crashed through the fence. That SUV was only yards away from the other thugs.

"There's a third gunman," she relayed to Lucas.

And it made her wonder if there were others in the SUV. It tightened her stomach even more to think that there could be enough of them to overrun the ranch. Plus, there were the two across the road with the sniper rifles who had pinned down Josh and Sawyer.

"If any of the gunmen move," Lucas said, "let me know."

The words had no sooner left his mouth when the newcomer did move. He hurried behind a tree.

Coming closer to the ranch.

Closer to Lucas's house.

More movement caught her eye, and when she adjusted the camera angle, she saw the guy aim the tear gas launcher. No, not again. But he fired. Not one but two canisters.

Except these were different.

The gas coming from them was thicker, and it was milky white.

Hailey turned the laptop so that Lucas could see it, and he cursed. "Smoke bombs."

Hailey knew the reason for his profanity. As bad as the tear gas was—and it was *bad*—the smoke bombs could be worse. Because they could conceal the gunmen trying to move closer to the house.

And that's exactly what was happening.

The smoke began to spread, and it continued when the men fired off several more.

"Keep watch as best you can," Lucas advised her.

She would, but it was next to impossible to keep track of the men now. Maybe the rain, though, would work in their favor and quickly wash the smoke away as it was dissipating the tear gas.

A buzzing sound shot through the truck, and Hailey's heart jumped to her throat. At first she thought it was their attackers, but it was only Lucas's phone. With all the chaos going on, she'd forgotten that she was still holding it.

"It's Grayson," she relayed, looking at the phone screen. She answered it right away and put it on speaker.

"Please tell me you found my baby," Colleen jumped to say.

"No, but I'm close enough to the car to see inside.

There are two men in the front seat and an infant carrier in the back. The person I don't see is Minton. Any idea where he is?"

Hailey quickly scanned through all the camera angles. Even with the smoke, she could see Dade and the others pinned down. She couldn't see the gunmen, though, who'd been shooting and launching that tear gas and the smoke bombs.

But there was no sign of Minton.

"I don't know," Hailey told Grayson. "According to what the kidnapper showed us, he was in the car with the baby earlier."

"Yeah, but he's not there now, or if he is, he's down on the floor where I can't see him."

"Does that mean the bomb isn't there, either?" Colleen blurted out.

"I can't tell. But I'm going closer as soon as I have the backup that Mason's sending." Grayson paused. "Do I want to know how bad things are at the ranch?"

"The gunmen haven't gotten to the houses," Lucas answered.

What Lucas didn't say was—they hadn't, *not yet*. But there was always the possibility that they would unless the Rylands and ranch hands figured out a way to stop them.

"I'll call you back when I can," Grayson said before he hung up.

Hailey hoped he could get the baby out of there. That would be one less worry on their minds. Because even if Colleen was guilty, Hailey still wanted her niece far away from this dangerous situation.

"Where's the third gunman you saw?" Lucas asked her.

That sent Hailey's attention back to the computer

screen. As she'd done before, she panned around the camera angles, looking at the tree where she'd last spotted him. But even when the smoke cleared a little in that area, there was no sign of him now.

Sweet heaven.

Because she'd gotten so preoccupied with Grayson's call, Hailey had lost sight of him. That could turn out to be a fatal mistake. Especially considering the gunman could be hiding in one of those smoke clouds that were drifting toward Lucas's house.

"Any chance the third gunman could be Minton?" Lucas added.

Hailey went back through what she'd seen of the man, but she had to shake her head. "I never saw him standing fully upright, so it's hard to know how tall he is. Plus he was wearing a hood, so I couldn't see any part of his face. But it's possible it's Minton. Or Eric."

However, it was just as likely that it was another thug who'd been hired to kill her.

"Grayson has to get to my baby," Colleen said.

Obviously she wasn't thinking about the third gunman. Maybe not even thinking about who was responsible for this. Her focus seemed to be solely on the baby. And she was crying.

Hailey was definitely affected by those tears, and it tore at her heart to think how much her sister could be suffering right now. She slid her hand over Colleen's, causing her sister to flinch. At first. Then Colleen gave her hand a gentle squeeze.

"No matter what happens," Colleen said, "I'm sorry for the way things have turned out."

Hailey was about to ask her exactly what she meant by that. But she didn't get a chance to say anything.

Chapter Eighteen

Lucas whipped his gun in Colleen's direction. But it was too late. The man already had her before Lucas could do anything to stop it.

However, Lucas could do something to keep Hailey safe. He crawled over her, putting himself in front of her. He didn't lower his weapon. He kept it aimed at the guy. He also watched Colleen's reaction.

She called out for help, tried to get away, but the man only jammed the gun harder against her head. It seemed convincing.

Seemed.

But Lucas reminded himself that this could all be part of the ploy to get to Hailey. A ploy he hadn't been able to prevent because he hadn't seen the guy sneaking up on the truck.

Behind him, he could hear Hailey's breath gusting, and he knew she had to be scared. Lucas hoped, though, that she would continue to keep watch around them, because heaven knew how many hired guns could be coming at them.

"Let Colleen go," Lucas demanded, though he figured this would get zero results.

And it didn't.

The guy laughed. He was wearing a tear gas mask that covered the lower part of his face, but Lucas could see enough of him to know that this wasn't Minton or Eric. He was likely just another hired gun.

"Sorry, can't let her go," the man finally said. "Got my orders, and I'm to keep this gun on her."

"Who's giving those orders?" Lucas snapped.

"It's not my place to tell, but you'll know soon enough. The boss is on the way. He should be here any minute now, and then things will get real…interesting."

Hell. Lucas had figured as much, but it was gut-tightening to hear it spelled out for him.

"Keep an eye on the security feed," Lucas told Hailey, but he wasn't even sure there was enough room for her to maneuver the laptop around so she could look. There hadn't been a lot of time when he'd moved in front of her, and she was literally jammed against him, the steering wheel and the door.

"Don't let him kill me," Colleen begged while she stared at Lucas. "*Please.* I don't want my daughter to be an orphan."

Neither did he, but Lucas wasn't sure yet how to put a stop to this. Especially when the guy shifted the gun and took aim at him. Hailey must have seen that, because she came over his back, putting her head in front of his.

Lucas cursed at her, tried to get her to move back, but she fought him.

"He won't kill me," Hailey insisted. "Not until he's sure I've given him everything I have on the DeSalvo family. But he'll kill you."

"The little lady's right," the gunman verified. "And since I can't risk a bullet going straight through you and into her, then I have to settle for just telling you to toss out that gun."

One of the last things Lucas wanted to do was surrender his gun. But he didn't want to risk Colleen and Hailey being shot, either. So he tried to reason with this guy.

"Whatever you're getting paid, I'll double it," Lucas offered. "I can make the call now and have the funds transferred to your bank."

"That sounds real nice." The sarcasm dripped from his voice. "But doing something like that would get me killed. Besides, I'm getting paid pretty good for this. Now, throw out that gun."

Lucas felt something against his back. Hailey's hand. And it wasn't empty. She had hold of his backup weapon, no doubt a reminder that he could use that. But the problem was that once Lucas didn't have a visible weapon, this thug might change his mind about shooting.

And yes, the bullet could go through him and kill Hailey.

Even if it didn't, it could kill him, and then this thug would be able to do whatever he wanted with Colleen and Hailey.

"Time's up," the guy said without warning.

The shot blasted through the air.

Followed by Colleen's piercing scream.

Lucas felt as if someone had slugged him, and he had to fight his instincts to move away from Hailey and leave her unprotected. But it also sickened him to hear Colleen make sharp sounds of pain.

And to see the blood.

"Oh, God," Hailey said, and she would have come over Lucas if the thug hadn't pointed his weapon right at her. She stopped, freezing, but she kept repeating, "Oh, God."

"I only shot her in the arm," the man said as if that was some huge concession. Which, in a way, it was. Because he could have just as easily killed her.

The blood spread quickly across Colleen's arm, and she looked at Lucas, silently begging him to help her. He'd wanted proof that Colleen was innocent in all of this, and the gunshot was it. He seriously doubted that she would have agreed to a henchman shooting her as part of the deal.

In the distance, Lucas heard another blast from the launcher. More smoke bombs, no doubt.

"No more warnings," the gunman said to Lucas. "Toss out the gun or I shoot her again. This time I might not be so careful where I aim."

He wasn't bluffing, so Lucas had no choice but to throw his gun out of the open truck door. Now he only hoped he could get to his backup weapon when he needed it. And he would need it. He was certain of that.

"Now what?" Lucas snapped.

"We wait." The guy glanced at the back of the house, where the smoke was still the thickest. He also peeled off his gas mask. Probably because the rain had rid them of the tear gas. Lucas's eyes were still burning, but the sensation wasn't nearly as bad as it had been.

Hailey still had his phone, and Lucas heard it buzz. Mason or Grayson was probably calling. But the thug shook his head. "Let that go to voice mail."

Hailey did, and she eased the backup weapon to Lucas's side. Ideally the gunman didn't see what was going on, but he had his attention nailed to them.

"Help me," Colleen said. She was shaking now.

Maybe going into shock. And she needed medical attention. However, the only way she was going to get that was for Lucas to get rid of his thug so they could call for an ambulance.

"When I move, get down," Lucas whispered to Hailey.

He felt the muscles in her body tense. Clearly, she didn't like the idea of him moving. Probably because she knew what the outcome could be. But thankfully Hailey didn't argue with him.

Lucas got ready to launch himself at the gunman. Maybe he'd be able to knock both him and his gun to the ground. Of course, Colleen would be in the middle, and Lucas prayed she didn't get hurt any worse than she already was, but if he didn't do something fast, they'd all be dead.

His phone buzzed again, distracting him for a moment. Something bad was probably going on. Maybe that bad thing didn't include Camden, but even if it did, Lucas had to put it out of his mind and try to finish this.

He didn't get far.

Lucas hadn't even started moving when he saw something out of the corner of his eye. Someone was coming toward the back of the truck. Maybe one of his brothers or a Ryland cousin.

But it wasn't.

The gunman smiled, and while he still had hold of Colleen, he moved away from the truck door, making room for their visitor.

"Told you it wouldn't be long," the gunman taunted. "The boss is here."

LUCAS SHIFTED HIS body so that it was hard for Hailey to see. He did that so he could reach the gun she was trying to give him, but it also meant she didn't know who had just arrived. She had no trouble recognizing his voice, though.

"Finally," he said.

Eric.

She hadn't known which of their suspects would be coming at them through the smoke, but Eric certainly wasn't a surprise. But was he working with Minton? Or had he come up with this all on his own?

Whatever *this* was.

"Can we leave now?" the thug asked Eric.

Eric shook his head. "Soon, though. I'm getting another vehicle up here since your idiot comrades shot out the radiator of Lucas's truck. Not very smart, and they'll pay for that."

So Eric was planning on using it to escape. But she doubted that he and his hired gun would be leaving alone. No.

Eric would try to take Colleen and her with him, and that meant Lucas would try to stop it. He could be hurt or killed in the process.

Hailey put aside the laptop so her hands would be free in case things were about to get worse than they already were. Lucas took the gun, but there was no way he could lift it without causing Eric and the thug to shoot first. Both had their weapons aimed at Hailey and him.

"You bastard," Colleen spat out. "You took my daughter, and now you had your hired gun shoot me. And why? I erased all those files. I did everything you told me to do."

"You knew it was Eric?" Lucas asked, and he didn't sound pleased that Colleen might have withheld that from them.

Colleen shook her head. "No. But I suspected it. He knew Preston had left me money, and taking my baby was the only way to get it back."

Eric lifted his shoulder. "You didn't deserve a penny of DeSalvo money just because you slept with my father."

"I had his child!" Colleen practically shouted, but the outburst combined with the blood loss must have drained her, because she sagged against the gunman holding her. He shoved her back up, jamming the gun against her head again.

"You think that matters to me?" Eric didn't wait for her to answer. "Because it doesn't."

Hailey saw the anger rise on Eric's face and knew she couldn't let his short fuse and horrible temper come into play here. "Why did you do all of this?"

"Isn't it obvious? I don't want to die in jail like my father. You have files and information that could put me behind bars."

True, but it wasn't for anything serious.

"You made the deal with the DA," Lucas reminded him.

"It included only the recordings from my father's office." He glanced around, no doubt looking for the vehicle that was coming for them.

Lucas's phone buzzed again. The third time someone had tried to call them in the past couple of minutes. It was no doubt important. Maybe even about Camden. But Hailey didn't answer it.

"When the FBI, CSIs or some other agency with initials analyzes the voice on those tapes, they might be able to identify Melvin here." He tipped his head to the gunman. "Melvin has worked for me for years. He has a record, and it wouldn't take much to connect him to me if they were able to match his voice."

"There was no dirty agent," Lucas concluded. "But you let your father believe there was."

"You'd be surprised what I learned from the old man when he thought he was talking to an actual agent. I made lots of money on deals where my father gave the fake guy some insider information. Of course, I had to share some of that cash with Daddy to make him think he was running things."

Yes, but Preston wouldn't have known his own son was working behind the scenes to milk him of family funds. It was all so senseless since Eric would have inherited most of it anyway.

At least, he would have, unless there'd been another child.

Oh, mercy.

"What are you going to do with your half sister?" Hailey blurted out.

That put some new alarm in Colleen's face. Probably because she'd pieced it together, as well. Eric wouldn't want any competition for the DeSalvo estate, and it was possible that the baby—and therefore Colleen—would have a claim.

"Yes," Eric said, looking at Hailey. He'd obviously seen the realization in her eyes. "And of course, you have to go, too. You know too much. Plus, I'm betting you have some dirt on me squirreled away."

Hailey was about to say that she didn't have anything else now that Colleen had deleted the files. But she changed her mind and went with something that might save them.

"If anything happens to me, the files I have will be sent to every news agency in the state," she lied.

Eric laughed, but the laughter stopped just as quickly as it'd started. "Where are the files?" he snapped. His temper was definitely showing again.

"I'm not telling you. Not until you get Colleen an ambulance and you and your hired killers are off Ryland land."

Eric's mouth tightened. "Nice try. But you're all dying. Including him." His glare slashed to Lucas. "Thanks to Hailey including you in this, she's signed your death warrant."

"Hailey didn't involve me," Lucas said, his voice low and dangerous. "*You* involved me when you tried to kill her and put my son in danger. How the hell do you possibly think you're going to get away with this?"

"Easy. I plan on pinning all of this on Minton. He's an idiot. And soon he'll be dead like the rest of you."

Sweet heaven. If Minton was anywhere near the baby, then she could be hurt, too. Or worse.

Hailey heard the sound of a car approaching from the back of the house. A moment later she saw the black SUV, the one that had brought in the gunmen. Had no doubt brought Eric, too.

"All of you will come with me," Eric insisted. "And that way I'll have some leverage to make sure Hailey gives me everything that she possibly has on me."

By leverage he meant they would become his hostages.

Eric would no doubt torture Lucas and Colleen to get Hailey to give him something she didn't have. Once he figured that out, he would indeed kill all of them. Probably Minton, too.

"Let's move," Eric said, and he used his gun to motion toward the approaching SUV.

Hailey knew that time was up. They had to do something now even though Lucas didn't have a clean shot. Eric was staying behind Colleen and his hired gun.

And Lucas did something, all right.

He sprang from the seat, barreling out of the truck, and he crashed into Colleen, Eric and the gunman.

They all went to the ground.

But the only sound Hailey heard was the shot that one of them fired.

THE SHOT WAS DEAFENING, but Lucas prayed that it hadn't hit Hailey, Colleen or him. It was hard to tell because the impact of slamming into the ground had knocked the breath out of him, and the pain spiked through him when his jaw collided with the hired gun's Glock.

Lucas hadn't wanted things to play out this way, but Eric hadn't given him much of a choice. If they'd gotten into that SUV with him and his hired killers, Colleen, Hailey and he would have soon been dead.

Colleen screamed when they fell, but Lucas still didn't know if she'd been shot again. That's because the fight started almost immediately. The thug slammed his gun against Lucas's head so hard that it probably gave him a concussion.

That didn't stop Lucas from fighting, though. The stakes were too high for him to lose. He still had hold of his gun, but it was too risky to get a shot off now. He had to get Colleen out of the way first, and that wouldn't be easy since she was trapped between Eric and him.

Eric spewed out a string of profanity, and for a guy who didn't work with his hands, he was fighting hard.

He was also trying to shoot Lucas. Eric brought up his gun, but Lucas managed to knock it away in the nick of time.

Eric's shot blasted into the ground right next to Lucas.

Hailey yelled out something. Something that Lucas didn't catch, but he hoped she would stay back.

She didn't.

He saw her out of the corner of his eye. She had gotten out of the truck and had picked up his gun. The one he'd thrown out of the truck. She was trying to take aim, but there was no way she'd have a clean shot.

But Eric did.

The goon was punching Lucas, but he still managed to see Eric lift his gun again. And this time he aimed it at Hailey.

"Get down!" Lucas shouted to her.

He wasn't sure if she did—not in time, anyway—before Eric pulled the trigger again. Lucas didn't look to see where the shot had gone. Instead he shifted his weight, shoving Colleen out of the way so that he could pin down Eric.

Melvin was obviously looking out for his boss, because he walloped Lucas in the head again. More than anything, Lucas wanted to shoot the guy, but he couldn't let go of Eric to do that.

Someone fired, though.

Hailey.

She'd shot into the ground. Maybe to distract Eric and Melvin. If so, it worked in a bad way. Melvin looked at Hailey.

And he took aim.

That meant Lucas had to release Eric so he could

dive at Melvin. Melvin still managed to pull the trigger, but Lucas was able to throw Melvin enough off balance that he didn't shoot Hailey. But Melvin had come darn close to doing just that.

Too close.

Lucas couldn't tell her that now because he was fighting for their lives, but later he wanted her to know that she should never take a risk like that again. Because she could have been killed. He could have lost her.

Colleen scurried away from them, and while she was holding her injured arm, she ran to Hailey. Maybe because Hailey didn't see it coming, Colleen wrenched the gun from her hand. Colleen pointed it at the men.

"Give me back my daughter, Eric," Colleen shouted. "Or so help me, I'll kill you right now."

Lucas prayed she didn't shoot, because the way she was shaking, there was no telling who Colleen might hit. His cousins were likely nearby, and a stray shot could kill one of them. It also caused his heart to slam against his chest when he saw that Hailey was trying to get the gun back from her sister. No way did he want Hailey in a struggle—any kind of struggle—where there was a gun involved.

Since every second this went on was another second when someone could get killed, Lucas threw his own gun aside so he could latch onto Melvin's. Of course, Eric took full advantage of that. He tried to take aim again, but Lucas stopped him by slamming his elbow into Eric's jaw. Eric howled in pain and dropped back down to the ground.

A shot cracked through the air.

Lucas's breath stopped, and despite being in a fist-fight with Melvin, he glanced at Hailey to make sure she was all right. She wasn't. She was seemingly frozen with both Colleen's and her hands on the gun.

Melvin cursed, and he froze as well.

Lucas looked on the ground beside him and saw Eric. Bleeding. The shot that Colleen had fired had hit him in the stomach.

"You're gonna pay for that!" Melvin yelled, and he tried to turn his gun on Colleen.

Lucas didn't let that happen. He used the new surge of adrenaline that he got to grab Melvin's gun. Of course, Melvin didn't just give it up. He kept trying to aim it at Colleen. But instead, Lucas turned the gun on the hired killer.

Just as Melvin pulled the trigger.

The bullet went into his chest. Since the shot was at point-blank range, Melvin didn't even draw another breath. It killed him instantly.

Lucas didn't waste a second on the gunman. Instead, he took the guy's weapon and aimed it at Eric. He also kicked Eric's gun from his hand and took aim at him in case he tried to move. He did, but it was only to clutch his stomach and his chest.

And he laughed.

"You think this is over," Eric said, looking at Colleen and Hailey. "It's not."

That's when Lucas realized that Eric wasn't just holding his hand to his gunshot wound. He pressed something on his chest. A small box that resembled a remote control on a garage.

A split second later, Lucas heard a sound he definitely didn't want to hear.

An explosion.

Chapter Nineteen

"No!" Colleen yelled.

Lucas didn't yell, but he frantically looked around to see if he could find the source of the explosion. It hadn't come from the area where the tear gas had been launched. No. This was further away. Just up the road from the ranch.

In the same area where Grayson had said he'd spotted the kidnapper's vehicle.

Colleen must have realized that, too, because despite her injury, she turned and started to run in that direction.

"Stop her," Lucas told Hailey. Though he hated to give an order like that since Colleen was still armed. It was obvious she was hysterical, and there was no telling what she might do.

Lucas checked first to make sure there were no weapons near Eric. He was bleeding, maybe dying, but that didn't mean he wouldn't be able to shoot them. It would be the ultimate way to get his revenge.

Hailey hooked her arm around Colleen's waist but didn't have a solid enough footing and her sister slung her to the ground. That meant a change of plan. Lucas scooped up one of the guns and handed it to Hailey.

"Make sure Eric doesn't get up," he told her, and he took off running after Colleen. There were possibly some of Eric's hired guns still in the area, and he didn't want Colleen shot for a second time tonight. The next bullet just might kill her.

Might kill him, too.

Lucas only hoped they didn't get caught in the middle of a gunfight.

He had to tackle Colleen, dragging them both to the ground again. This couldn't be good for her injury since she was still bleeding. But despite that injury, she fought like a wildcat.

"I have to get to my baby!" she shouted.

Yeah, Lucas understood that, but he shook his head and got in her face. "You can't go down there. It's a good quarter of a mile away, and you'll be killed."

Logic wasn't going to work here, so he just pinned her to the ground with his body and wrenched the gun from her hand. Colleen kept fighting him, punching his chest with her fists, and Lucas just let her do it while he kept watch to make sure they weren't about to be ambushed.

He looked back at Hailey. Even from a distance he could see that she was shaking, but she still had the gun aimed at Eric. Eric wasn't saying anything, wasn't moving, either. Lucas had rarely wished someone dead, but he hoped in this case that Eric was so that he would no longer be a threat to Hailey and Colleen.

But there were other threats out there.

Colleen finally quit fighting, her hands dropping to the ground, and she sobbed. The tears came, mixed with the rain on her face, but Lucas could deal with the tears as long as she didn't run out into the path of those possible gunmen. Now that he knew Colleen was innocent in all of this, he definitely wanted to make sure he kept Hailey's sister alive.

He got up, pulling Colleen to her feet, and he took her to the truck, pushing her into the middle so Hailey could get in, as well. He wouldn't be able to drive the truck, but at least being inside it was better than having them stay in the open.

Hailey had such a fierce grip on the gun and her muscles were so rigid that it took Lucas a moment to get her moving. When he finally did, she sagged against him.

"The baby," she said.

Lucas figured she was praying that her niece was okay. He was doing the same and adding some extra prayers for Camden and the rest of his family.

"Both of you stay down," Lucas told them once he had Hailey in the cab of the truck.

She nodded, took out his phone and showed him the screen with the missed calls. All three were from Mason. Lucas certainly hadn't forgotten about them, but he wanted to keep his hands, and his attention, free in case they were attacked again.

Hailey must have understood that, because she hit the redial button and put it on speaker. Mason answered on the first ring.

"What the hell was that explosion?" Mason immediately asked.

"I'm not sure." Lucas didn't want to spell out his worst fears. "Have you talked to Grayson?"

"He's not answering his phone, and he's nowhere near any of the security cameras. Please tell me he wasn't near that bomb when it went off."

Lucas didn't know, and again he didn't want to guess.

Grayson was smart, so maybe he'd made it out of there with the baby.

"The reason I called you earlier was to warn you about Eric," Mason went on. "I saw him on one of the cameras. Is he dead?"

"Not yet. Can you call an ambulance for Colleen and him?" Lucas asked.

"Already done, and they're on the way. Dade and the others have cleared the gunmen so the medics can get through. I'll send a cruiser down to pick up Colleen, Hailey and you. Colleen is innocent, right?"

Lucas glanced back at her. "Yeah." Innocent and shaken to the core. Also still losing some blood. Hailey had peeled off her hoodie and was using it as a make-shift tourniquet.

"Good," Mason answered. "Then the three of you can come here. I'll have Dade or someone wait with Eric. Let me know the moment you hear anything from Grayson."

"I will." Lucas looked around the yard again. "Are you sure the gunmen are all out of commission?"

"All the ones on the ranch grounds. The ones across the road, too." He paused. "Don't know about Minton, though."

Yes. Lucas hadn't forgotten about him, either. Eric had claimed there was no dirty agent, and that should clear Minton's name. If Eric was telling the truth.

Lucas heard the sound of an approaching car coming from the main part of the ranch, and he automatically pivoted in that direction with his gun aimed and ready. But it wasn't one of Eric's thugs. It was Sawyer and Josh. Josh hurried out of the cruiser toward them.

"I drew the short straw," Josh said. "Go ahead with Sawyer. I'll make sure Eric doesn't go anywhere."

Lucas hated to put this on his cousin, but one look at Hailey and Colleen and he knew he had to get them out of there. He thanked Josh, and because he didn't want the women out in the open any longer than necessary, he scooped up Colleen and took her to the cruiser. He would have gone back and done the same for Hailey, but she was already trailing along behind him. He put Colleen in the front seat. Hailey and he took the back.

"I'm okay," Hailey said to him.

It was almost certainly a lie, but Lucas latched onto it. He also latched onto her. He pulled her into his arms, probably with a lot harder grip than either of them had been expecting.

The relief came. She was alive and in one piece. No thanks to Eric. That fight could have played out a dozen different ways, and in any one of the scenarios, Hailey could have been hurt or worse.

Colleen, however, wasn't faring as well. She was sobbing now, hunched over and probably in a lot of pain. Maybe it wouldn't be long before the ambulance arrived, though Lucas was worried that she might not go to the hospital until they got news about the baby.

It wasn't a long trip to the main house, but it certainly felt like one. Lucas kept watch the whole way, but thankfully he didn't see any signs of danger.

Only the aftermath.

He spotted one of the gunmen, dead, in the pasture. Not far from where they'd launched the smoke bombs and the tear gas. The goon and his fellow hired thugs had turned the Silver Creek Ranch into a war zone.

That twisted at Lucas's gut. But it was also something he had to push aside.

For Hailey's sake.

Heck, for his own peace of mind.

Because he thought they could both use it, he brushed a kiss on Hailey's forehead. Then her cheek. Yes, they both needed that. Needed the real kiss that followed, too. It wasn't nearly long enough, but Lucas figured he could do better later. Later, he wanted to do a lot of things. Like tell Hailey that he had died a thousand times tonight worrying about her, and that it had driven home to him just how important she was to him.

"I'm in love with you," Hailey blurted out.

Judging from the startled look in her eyes, she hadn't intended to say that. Nor did she have time to add more, because Sawyer pulled to a stop directly in front of the main house, and that was their cue to get moving. Sawyer helped with Colleen, but before they even made it up the steps, Lucas heard two welcome sounds.

The ambulance sirens.

And his son.

Camden was fussing, and while it was obvious he wasn't happy about something, just hearing him eased the knot in Lucas's stomach.

Despite her limp, Hailey hurried in ahead of them. And Lucas let her. She looked around the massive foyer. No sign of Camden there, but he was in the adjacent family room with Tillie and Mason's wife, Abbie. Tillie was pacing while rocking Camden, obviously trying to get him to sleep. Hailey went to him and pulled him into her arms.

Camden stopped fussing right away and studied her face. Hailey was still pretty much a stranger to him, but that didn't stop his boy from smiling. He smiled even more when he looked in Lucas's direction.

Everything suddenly seemed all right with the world.

Well, almost everything. His phone buzzed, and when he saw Grayson's name on the screen, Lucas knew this was a call he had to take.

"Is it about the baby?" Colleen asked. Sawyer was trying to get her to sit, but she batted away his hands and went to Lucas.

Lucas figured it was indeed about the baby, but he wasn't sure it would be good news. No way to buffer it from Colleen, though, since she was right next to him. Because she would probably be able to hear every word anyway, he went ahead and put it on speaker.

"I have the baby," Grayson immediately said.

Lucas could feel the relief go through the room, and Hailey went to her sister to give her a hug. Colleen broke down again, crying, but Lucas figured these were happy tears.

"Is she okay? Was she hurt?" Colleen blurted out.

"She's fine," Grayson answered. "I'm bringing her to the ranch right now. The ambulance is ahead of me."

Which meant Colleen wouldn't have much time with her daughter before being whisked away to the hospital. She wouldn't care much for that, but Colleen needed medical attention ASAP. She also clearly needed to see her daughter right away, because she started toward the door and would have hurried out, no doubt to watch for Grayson. But Lucas stopped her. He didn't want any one of them outside just yet.

"What about the explosion?" Hailey asked.

"The bomb detonated after the baby was already out of the car," Grayson answered. "Minton killed the kidnapper, but he couldn't disarm the bomb, so he took the baby and ran. When I'd looked in the SUV earlier with the binoculars, I thought she was still in the vehicle, but it was only her car seat that I saw."

Good. Lucas hated that the baby had even had to go through a nightmare like that, but at least she wasn't near the blast.

Thanks to Minton.

"Where is Minton?" Lucas pressed.

"With me."

Lucas felt no regret about that whatsoever and hoped all of Eric's hired thugs were dead or arrested. And speaking of Eric, he needed to give Grayson an update on the idiot who'd done his best to make their lives a living hell.

"Minton won't be staying," Grayson continued. "He wants to borrow a vehicle to get him back to his office, so once I'm at the house, I'll let him use my truck."

Even though Minton was innocent and had helped them by saving the baby, Lucas could understand why the agent didn't want to hang around. He hadn't exactly been friendly to Hailey and the rest of them. Plus, like Grayson, he probably had reports to write up about the attack.

"If Eric's still alive, he'll need to go to the hospital, too," Lucas said.

"Yeah. I got a call from Dade. Eric died a couple of minutes ago. The ME will come out and take care of the body. The bodies of the other gunmen, as well."

Lucas thanked him. He definitely didn't want any of his cousins or their families waking up to a giant crime scene, so maybe the bodies and the debris could be cleared out by morning.

Grayson had been right about the ambulance, because Lucas heard the siren as it made the turn toward the main house. He wished he could talk Hailey into going to the hospital, too, to be checked out, but judging from the grip she had on Camden, that wasn't going to happen.

"Maybe I can ride with the baby and Colleen in the ambulance?" Tillie suggested. Lucas wanted to kiss the woman for making the offer. "Unless Hailey and you need me here for Camden, that is."

"No," Hailey and Lucas said in unison. They'd be just fine now that the danger had passed.

Well, maybe it had passed.

"Are we sure there are no more hired killers?" Lucas asked Grayson.

"The hands and deputies are doing a final search now, but there's no one shooting. Just in case one's hiding, Sawyer and Josh are going to do a sweep with infrared. Mason's still in his office checking the security cameras."

Hailey closed her eyes a moment, nodded. She was obviously thankful for these extra security measures. It would help everyone get some sleep for what was left of the night. Everyone except Colleen. But he figured she wouldn't mind. She was alive, and her baby had been rescued.

Grayson ended the call just as the ambulance pulled to a stop in front of the house, and this time Lucas wasn't able to hold Colleen back. That's because Grayson had said he was right behind the medics. And he was. He didn't waste any time getting out and bringing the baby to Colleen.

There were more tears, of course, and Colleen

hugged her daughter as tightly as Hailey was hugging Camden.

"You should go," Grayson prompted Colleen. Apparently he'd already given his keys to Minton, because the agent drove away.

Colleen managed a shaky nod, but despite the fact she was bleeding, she carried the baby toward the ambulance. Tillie was right behind her.

"Call me when you can," Hailey told her sister. "And if the doctors keep you at the hospital overnight, I'll be there first thing in the morning."

Despite everything that had gone on, Colleen managed a weak smile and a thank-you. Maybe this was the start of a better relationship between the sisters.

"Tell Mason I'm taking his cruiser," Grayson said to Abbie. "If anyone needs me, I'll be with the ME and then at the office."

Lucas felt guilty since Grayson had a long stretch of work ahead of him. And he'd help. But not tonight. Tonight he needed to be with Hailey and Camden.

"Do you want me to take Camden?" Abbie asked.

Lucas certainly hadn't forgotten about Mason's wife being there, but he didn't understand her question. No way did he want Camden out of his sight. But Lucas looked at Hailey. Then himself. They were soaking wet, covered in mud, blood and heaven knew what else.

"You can use the showers in the guest rooms," Abbie suggested.

"In just a couple of minutes." Hailey kissed Camden's cheek, and despite the fact that he was right up against her wet clothes, he didn't seem to mind.

Abbie must have decided they needed some alone

time, because she disappeared down the hall. Probably to check on her own sons.

Hailey got a few more kisses and then passed Camden to Lucas so he could do the same. It was pure magic. Somehow, just holding his son could melt away most of the misery from the past couple of days.

But misery wasn't the only thing that'd happened tonight.

"You said you were in love with me," Lucas reminded Hailey.

She made a soft sound of surprise. "Yes, *that*." Then she dodged his gaze and opened her mouth to say something that Lucas realized he might not want to hear.

"You can't take it back," he growled, and then frowned when he heard the tone of his own voice. He hadn't meant to make it sound like an order. "Please don't take it back," he amended.

Hailey didn't make another sound of surprise, but judging from the way her eyes widened, she certainly hadn't been expecting that from him. Well, Lucas hadn't expected it, either. Nor was he sure when he'd wanted Hailey's "I'm in love with you," but he definitely wanted it.

With Camden in the crook of his left arm, Lucas slid his right hand around Hailey's waist and pulled her closer. He kissed her. Not some gentle, everything-will-be-all-right kind of kiss, either. This was long and deep. Just the way he liked his kisses when it came to Hailey.

The kiss stirred the heat between them, but it did more than that. It made things crystal clear for Lucas.

"I fell in love with you shortly after we met," he said with his lips still against hers. "That hasn't changed.

Never will. I want you in my bed…my life. Our lives," he added, glancing down at Camden.

And Lucas pulled back so he could see her reaction. He expected her to be stunned. Maybe even have a run-for-the-hills kind of look in her eyes.

She didn't.

Hailey smiled, slow and easy. A smile that lit up her whole face, and she pulled him right back to her for another kiss. "Good. And you can't take it back."

Lucas had no intentions of ever taking it back. Ever. He gathered Hailey and his son into his arms and held on.

* * * * *

There's much more to come from
Delores Fossen in 2017.
Don't miss BRANDED AS TROUBLE
on sale in July from e-Book (HQN).

He leaned over and silenced her with a kiss as he pulled her tight against him.

She could feel his arousal pushing against her and all she wanted was to give every ounce of passion she had to him. But this wasn't the place, not here on a plane with their client only yards away from them. It couldn't happen and she wanted so badly for it to happen.

Her heart pounded and something deep inside wanted only to melt into him. Her mind screamed to pull away. It couldn't be—this was the wrong time, the wrong place, the wrong man. And yet, her body felt differently.

She put her hands on his shoulder, creating a suggestion of distance between them.

"Jade."

"No." She shook her head. For as much as she wanted him against her, as much as she wanted his lips ravishing hers, as much as she wanted all of it and more, she couldn't.

She was a professional agent and she refused to sleep with her boss. No matter how good she knew it would be.

SHEIKH'S RESCUE

BY
RYSHIA KENNIE

MILLS & BOON

First Published in Great Britain 2017
By Mills & Boon, an imprint of HarperCollins*Publishers*
1 London Bridge Street, London, SE1 9GF

© 2017 Patricia Detta

ISBN: 978-0-263-92882-2

46-0517

Our policy is to use papers that are natural, renewable and recyclable products and made from wood grown in sustainable forests. The logging and manufacturing processes conform to the legal environmental regulations of the country of origin.

Printed and bound in Spain
by CPI, Barcelona

Chapter One

The howl of a lone wolf cut through the gray Wyoming sky, shattering the valley's early-morning silence. The howl echoed across the sharp lines of the Teton mountain range, which rose in a jagged line against the horizon. The raw cry broke through the unseasonably late April snow as it drifted down in a freezing veil that covered the prairie grass surrounding Nassar Security.

On his office balcony just outside Jackson, Wyoming, Vice President Zafir Al-Nassar took a deep breath. A sense of foreboding ran through him. Normally he would have enjoyed the reflective stillness of the late-spring snowfall, but now his thoughts were elsewhere. He wasn't sure what he was looking for. There was nothing disturbing the area except the blanket of snow that covered everything. It seemed to mock his unease as it powdered the nearby landscape and the roofs of the distant houses. It was Hollywood snow, big white flakes coming down in a gentle curtain beneath a still sky. It was the kind of weather that the film industry sometimes chased through the northern states and Canada. His thoughts were broken as, in the distance, he saw a dirt bike buzzing along the road that ran along the interstate.

He rubbed his temple. He'd had a low-grade head-ache all morning. He'd been up too late last night trying out the limits of an online game his brother Faisal had shown him a few days earlier. They'd played it a number of times while he'd been in Marrakech and Faisal had been here in Wyoming. He'd been looking forward to playing it with him in person when he arrived in Wyoming. He'd been disappointed to find Faisal was on assignment on the East Coast, departing just before his arrival. He'd just arrived with his sister, Tara, from Marrakech, Morocco, via New York, only thirty-five hours ago. Yesterday afternoon he'd seen her off on the last leg of her return journey to the university via the company jet. The travel, the online game, all of it combined into too many days with too little sleep. He stuffed his hand into the pocket of his low-rise jeans.

"Idiot," he muttered as he watched the motorcycle. Driving a bike in this kind of weather was, across the board, a bad idea. He shook his head and would have lost interest, except for the fact that minutes later, the bike turned into his parking lot.

"What the…" His mouth was set in a grim line. Could this be one of the employees from the Wyoming branch of Nassar? Who else would come out here on a Saturday? They didn't hire risk-adverse individuals, but they didn't hire thrill-seekers, either. Both personality types came with their own set of problems. He stayed where he was, intrigued by whom it might be as the bike swerved in a wide arc and pulled in beside his rental. Minutes passed. The rider seemed to be fiddling with something on the bike. It was an older model dirt bike—even worse as far as handling on slick roads. The driver might be a teenager.

He shook his head. That was an ageist thought, but he couldn't imagine who else would be crazy enough to chance riding such a vehicle in this weather. With the driver's back to him it was hard to tell. What he could tell was that he wasn't very big; at least, he had no bulk to him. It looked like he was tall but other than…

The man pulled off the helmet. Black hair fell to his shoulders. He turned around. The gray bomber jacket was half zipped, and it was now clear that this was no man. She held a helmet by its straps as she threaded her fingers through her hair and stopped as her eyes locked with his.

Jade Van Everett. The face and the picture on the file snapped together in his mind like an errant jigsaw puzzle. She was the agent assigned to their latest case. He wasn't familiar with her, at least not in person. She'd been with the agency only a little over a year, and both times he'd been here, she'd been either on a case or on vacation. But he was very familiar with who she was on paper. Twenty-nine to his thirty-one, her track record was impressive and the fact that she was easy on the eye, a bonus. Again, all of it had only been on paper. Yet he knew in his gut that Jade was different.

Jade… He felt that he knew her so much deeper than he should. She'd fascinated him before he'd ever physically laid eyes on her. But it was her accomplishments in the field that really impressed him, not her picture in the file. He'd studied every angle of the cases she'd been assigned with Nassar and was familiar with her past record with the agency. He knew her like he knew no other agent, and he refused to let himself consider why that might be.

The case she was assigned to now was the same one that had found him at the office this early in the morning. He'd been making sure that everything, as low-key as it was, went off without a hitch. As a family operation, Nassar Security depended on him to manage either the Morocco or Wyoming office at a moment's notice.

This case involved a Moroccan prince. In fact, it had been Moroccan royalty who had hired the company to provide security for the minor royal, who was visiting Wyoming. The client was a cousin too many times removed from the current king of Morocco to ever attain power, and he wasn't wealthy. That eliminated two factors that might threaten his safety. Except for the weak link to royalty, there was nothing special about the man. Thus, only one agent, Jade Van Everett, had been assigned.

In the file picture her hair had been lighter, shorter—her expression more serious. She was an extraordinarily good-looking woman even on file, but the paper copy didn't reflect the vibrant beauty that the real woman possessed. It was hard not to stare, for he was caught by surprise.

Now that she'd finished with the bike, she wasted no time in striding across the small lot, her attention focused on him with a look that hinted at trouble. This was clearly a woman with an issue, and as he was the only person here, he could only assume that the issue was with him.

So much for quietly sliding into the pulse of the business, he thought.

She had trouble branded on the tight line of her full red lips and in the frown that cut between her delicate, well-defined dark brows.

While he felt the chill in her azure eyes slice through him as she came closer, he couldn't help but admire her figure. He pulled his gaze up from her full bust and met her slightly sarcastic look as she stood on the bottom step looking up.

"Have you seen enough?" she drawled. Her voice was surprisingly relaxed despite the flashing accusation in her look.

She had spunk to go along with her success.

"Maybe," he replied easily, while at the same time he was fully aware that he deserved every ounce of her sarcasm. The accusation in her eyes faded, and he could tell from the softening of her lips that she'd decided to not push the issue. He admired her for that.

"I'm Zafir," he began, taking a step forward.

"I know," she said in her husky voice, and came up a few more steps. "You're why I'm here. I wanted to meet you in person before I picked up the client."

Her eyes raked over him as if she, too, had studied him through his work. He imagined that if she was as good as her file suggested, then that was the case. One didn't come in blind to anything, not a Nassar agent. They were all good, but to be in the top few meant that you left nothing to chance.

Professional, he thought, despite the bike. She smiled and threaded her fingers through her hair, pushing the shining black curtain up and away from her face. She came up another step. They were only a few feet apart.

She put one hand on the railing and held out the other to him. He took it and was caught in a firm grip that held no hesitation.

"What I'd like to know is why Prince Sadiq el Eloua is flying here alone on a commercial airline," she said as she let go of his hand. She was referring to the client. The one she was assigned to. "I know it's too late to do anything about it but really, even if there's no identified threat, at the least he should have been accompanied."

"There's apparently never been a security issue—he has no money or status," he said, realizing that she'd mirrored many of his first doubts. "It appears more for ego that we were hired."

"Seems like there should be more to this, otherwise there's no need to hire us."

He shrugged. "Overkill on Prince Rashad's part," he said, referring to the crown prince next in line to rule Morocco. "An easy assignment for you."

There was something in her eyes and the way she looked at him that, if he were a vain man, he would have called admiration. Instead, it struck him how much the agency had grown, and how often, despite being vice president, he was faced with this situation— where he didn't know the people in his employ. Not that he was complaining; his youngest brother Faisal ran this branch and had done so more than competently.

Jade brushed past him and headed toward the entrance to his office. She pulled the door open and walked in as if it were hers. "While I'm here I want to check the file one last time before I pick him up," she said over her shoulder.

He followed her inside, closing the door behind him as a drift of snow skimmed the heated cork floor and immediately began to melt. He walked over to where she stood by his desk.

"You've had it out?" she asked as she picked up the only file on his desk. She did so without hesitation. But that was how Faisal's office ran, with casual efficiency. While the Marrakech office had gone completely digital, Faisal still insisted on paper files. He loved all things retro. Retro had never appealed to Zafir. He'd take the latest smartphone over the century-old wooden file cabinet that stood in a corner of the office.

He watched her review the file. He assumed that she was going over details that she'd seen before. They were details that he'd just familiarized himself with. His mind reviewed what he knew of the client. The man was an amateur photographer. He was months short of his fortieth birthday and attached to nothing, not family, career, not even a stable home. He was rather like a man a decade or two younger. The majority of his income came from a life insurance policy that he'd received after the death of his parents. He supplemented that by occasionally selling his photos to magazines. That was why he was here, to take outdoor pictures of the Jackson Hole valley. It was the one thing he had in common with the client: they both felt the allure of Wyoming's wild beauty. The file lay open where Jade had dropped it. He looked down and a chubby-cheeked man smiled back at him.

"Twenty-fifth in line to the throne," Jade's voice

interrupted his private assessment. "My instinct says that's important."

Instinct, he couldn't dispute that. It was what separated the good agent from the excellent.

She went to the window and stood there as snow hit, melted and slid down the glass. He took the file from the desk, closed it and put it back into the cabinet.

"He arrives in under two hours." She glanced at her watch as she turned around. "I just can't get over it. I mean, he's a royal, I'm to make sure he's safe, and yet he's flying halfway across the world alone." She shrugged. "That's why his lineage was grating on me. But even twenty-fifth, with zero chance of ever attaining the throne... There's safety in numbers, in having someone trained to watch out for you. Someone who pays attention to the surroundings to..." She trailed off. But he could see her frustration. Her blue eyes were alight with passion and concern.

"I'm not sure how it went down. He shouldn't be flying either alone or commercial. What I know is that Prince Rashad isn't happy about it. I wouldn't be surprised if it's our client's doing." He shrugged. "Anyway, he isn't our problem. At least, not until he lands..."

She frowned. "Despite what I just said, it's a low-key case. Let's just hope he gets here safely." She paused, her attention not on him but on a point somewhere outside the office.

"There's nothing we can do about it."

"You're right," she said. "Our job begins as soon as they have wheels on the ground." She looked at her watch. "I should get moving."

"What's with the dirt bike?" He couldn't help but ask.

She shrugged and looked slightly sheepish. "My pickup wouldn't start this morning. I'm going to get a rental on the way to the airport."

"I'll give you a lift."

"No." She shook her head. "The rental agency is only a few miles up the road. Besides, I love riding the bike in fresh snow," she said. "I'd take it to the airport but I doubt Prince Sadiq would like riding on the back."

From what he'd seen of Jade, he doubted that Prince Sadiq would mind at all.

"I'm not looking forward to it." She paused. "Didn't you find it strange—the name he prefers?" It was the name that neither of them had yet used.

"A bit old-fashioned." He slid a hand into his pocket and rubbed an American penny he always carried between his thumb and forefinger. A long time ago his father had given it to him for luck. His father had been a very logical man, but he believed in talismans and luck. His parents had died tragically three days after his father had so casually tossed him the coin. Now he withdrew his hand, curious at her take.

"Stanley?" Her frown deepened. "What Moroccan royal is named Stanley? I mean even as a nickname." Her eyes crinkled as if she were holding back a laugh. "He uses the name exclusively."

"Royalty. Good chance he has an attitude, which will be a challenge," he said, knowing that he should try to be helpful instead of goading her when they both knew that she was stuck with a dull case.

"I'm betting you're right." She pulled a quarter from her pocket. "Want to flip for odds? Heads he's a challenge."

"Tails, I lose," he finished.

She flipped the coin and looked up with a smile. "Heads. Doesn't change the fact that I've got myself a code white."

He smiled at both the tone of her voice and her lighthearted approach that led them to betting on a case. That was a first, but he didn't doubt that Jade was full of surprises—crazy little firsts.

"Code white." She shook her head, her brow furrowed as if the thought of it pained her.

He empathized with her pain. The agency had codes for assignments. They ranged from the least dangerous, white, to the most, red. There wasn't an agent at Nassar who didn't dread a code white. They were well-paid assignments that were the bread and butter of the agency. But they were also, as in this case, ten days of guaranteed boredom.

She waved as she turned to leave.

"Take a good book," he called after her.

She gave him a look that would have torched a lesser man.

He only laughed.

Jade van Everett had been a pleasant surprise.

Three days earlier

THE SMALL STONE house had stood on the edge of the massive estate outside Rabat, Morocco, for generations. It had survived two world wars. Now, an explosion rattled the windows of the main house and blew the roof off the small stone house. The outer walls held for seconds after the initial explosion before the shock rippled through the structure and caused the small building to fall inward. The resulting fire licked quickly through the old wood and paper within the building. The smoke curled easily into the still air. It wasn't until the building was engulfed in flames and the last wall had collapsed that sirens could be heard. By then, it was too late. It was exactly as he had planned. Time would take care of the rest.

His jaw tensed as he looked around in the dim light of the plane's cabin. A young woman stood up two rows ahead of him and stretched. Behind him someone coughed. He covered his mouth and nose with the back of his hand. He hated flying, hated the people, the tight space, the snotty flight attendants. He hated all of it. He pushed his seat into an upright position and tried to stretch, but one foot was trapped by the seat in front of him. He was stuffed and cramped like he, too, was one of them, like the other nothings on this plane. But he was nothing like any of them—he didn't belong here, and soon they would know it.

He'd like to hurt someone right now. He knew that would make him feel better, but he couldn't do that for obvious reasons. Instead, he relaxed his features and tried to keep a pleasant look on his face. The last thing he needed was to act suspicious so that when they landed he was pulled aside by security. That would have his entry into the States delayed or worse, denied.

Calm down, he told himself. There was no reason for any of that to happen. But it wasn't over. His fingernails dug into the armrest. He looked down and forced himself to relax. He'd learned years ago as a child that one must relax to gain control. A strap against bare skin was easier to take if one was relaxed rather than tense. It was a tough but useful life skill. He looked furtively around him. But there was nothing unusual. The lights dimmed, and ahead of him a reading light clicked on. To his left was an empty seat and beside that was an elderly woman who'd been snoring off and on since takeoff.

He closed his eyes even as he knew that he couldn't sleep. Minutes passed. He opened his eyes, and his thoughts went back to where they had never left, to all that had transpired. The explosion that was the first step in completing the job he'd been hired for. It was unfortunate that he'd only seen his handiwork from afar, that he couldn't have stayed to hear the man's dying screams. Instead, he'd had to leave, catching the explosion from a distance, seeing the lick of flames and knowing he was one death away from the cash prize.

Across the aisle, a middle-aged man snored, lurched forward and shook himself awake.

He looked away. To any of the other passengers he was unmemorable. A swarthy man with a tired expression in the aisle seat of the Boeing 737. He feigned reading a newspaper. His left ankle was crossed over his right. He ran a hand along the seam of his pant leg. He scowled and then glanced at the watch on his right wrist. He moved the silver band back and forth as if that would adjust the time, but no matter how he looked at it, there were still hours before they landed.

He shoved the paper into the flap in the seat in front of him and looked up. He smiled at the passing flight attendant and thought how he'd like to twist her slim neck until it snapped. He forced his eyes closed, and smiled for the first time since he'd gotten the news. For it was in Jackson, Wyoming, where he'd finally finish what had begun so long ago.

Chapter Two

Take a good book.

It was a lighthearted statement. At least that's what she had thought at the time. Now Zafir's comment held new meaning. At the airport, the client's round, olive-toned face had lit up at the sight of her as if she were a prize in a game of chance. But an hour later, she would have preferred the company of a good book to the client's chatter and fawning eyes.

She remembered trying to lead him through the airport. He'd been distracted by everything. He'd stopped to stare out a window, claiming that he hadn't seen anything so beautiful as that particular view of the Teton Mountains. And when she finally got his attention again, he'd asked that she call him Stanley and then followed her to collect his luggage. She'd had to nudge the duffel under his arm as she gathered his bags. She'd updated him on his living arrangements as she ushered him to the rental vehicle, but she wasn't sure if he heard a word of it.

At the van, she'd slid the door shut after wrestling his bags into the backseat. Stanley had dropped the duffel by the back door and taken his seat without asking whether she needed help with his luggage.

On the way into Jackson, she asked him about the obviously expensive Nikon camera that he pulled out of its case shortly after they left the terminal. That's when she'd found out that Stanley was a talker, at least about his passion—photography.

"How much farther?" His voice would have been average except for the slightly nasal whine.

"Five minutes," she said shortly. She could feel his gaze on her but kept her attention on the snowy, and now icy, road. Her knuckles were white, and it wasn't because of the driving conditions. She knew admiration when she saw it, but she knew it could also turn into something worse. Stanley kept glancing at her in a way she didn't like. She wasn't sure how she was going to make it through an assignment that would be not only a bore but annoying, as well.

"We're here," she said minutes later as she parked the van. It was the only vehicle the rental agency had left that served her purpose. She would upgrade it tomorrow. Once that was done, she could take Stanley to the places he'd identified were perfect for a photo shoot.

"I'd like to take your picture, too, if…"

"No," she bit out. "I'm sorry. That was rather abrupt but no, I'm here to facilitate your trip." An interesting way to put it, she thought. "Not be a subject for your photography," she finished. "I'm sure we'll find more than you can imagine as far as scenery and wildlife to photograph. You don't need me."

"You're beautiful and…"

"No," she repeated. "Enough. This is business, nothing more."

"I'm sorry," he said, looking rather abashed and completely out of his element.

But this time she was sorry, sorry for so many different reasons than he might think. Sorry for making him uncomfortable, sorry for taking this assignment. Although she had to admit that there was no choice in the latter. It hadn't been voluntary.

Her attention went to the building in front of her. This was her headquarters for the duration of Stanley's stay. The three-story red cedar apartment building was small but perfectly situated. She didn't expect anything less. Leslie, Nassar's relocation expert, had scouted the city and located this building. It had all the amenities the client requested as well as being easy to secure. The street was quiet, part residential and part business. Even now, mid-morning on a Saturday, there was little noise other than the soft drone of traffic on nearby roads. Stanley's apartment was located on the second floor. The apartment above was vacant, as was the one below it. Combined with its small size, its low occupancy made the building even more perfect. She'd been briefed on the other occupants. All ten were trouble-free; none of them had criminal records. They ranged from two senior citizens to a professor currently on sabbatical overseas. The ground-floor apartment was assigned to Jade. The location was perfect for her to stay close for the duration of the client's visit.

"Let's go," she said as she unbuckled her seat belt and opened the van door.

No response.

She looked over at Stanley. He wasn't looking at her but rather chewing his lower lip, almost like he hadn't heard her. Maybe he needed a moment, she thought. But her other thought was that the man was a bit odd.

She thought of Zafir. It was hard not to make the comparison between the two men. She had just recently met them both, and they were so completely different. Sinfully good-looking, cocky Zafir, she thought. She shouldn't be thinking of him like that. But it was like she knew him. She'd studied every case he'd worked and heard stories of his exploits from his brother Faisal. In person, Zafir was more gorgeous and sure of himself than a man outside the pages of a men's magazine should be, and yet there was something down to earth about him, too. He'd put her off balance, off her game. As a result, her first reaction was to snap at him.

Stop it, she told herself. He was her boss on this case and not a man to be lusted after. Besides, looks weren't everything. She'd learned that the hard way. Give her a homely man with a great personality any day, or better yet, no man. At least not at the moment. She was enjoying her job too much, current assignment aside.

"This is it," she said to Stanley, who hadn't moved.

He had a slight smile on his face and a glow in his eyes as if excited by the idea, yet he hesitated to open his door.

"What's wrong?"

"Nothing, I…"

He was looking uncertain, as if he had made a bad choice. Fine time to think of that now, she thought, now that he was here. Despite the thought, she was concerned. As long he was in the States he was her problem, and the last thing she needed was for him to fall apart.

His hands shook slightly as he fumbled with the seat belt. "Nothing at all."

"You're sure?"

"Yes. I always react like this after a flight. Kind of a delayed reaction."

An outright lie, she thought, noticing how his voice sounded thinner and he wouldn't look at her. With any luck it was a temporary case of fear of the unknown. "Let's get you settled," she said. She got out and slid open the back door to get his luggage.

"The photography will be amazing," Stanley said from just behind her. Now his voice sounded normal, as if the last few minutes hadn't happened. There was nothing but anticipation in his tone. It was like he was trying too hard to hide his unease. "I can't wait."

"Wyoming is known for that, scenery. A photographer's dream," she agreed as she tried not to let her prejudice for all things Wyoming show. She supposed she'd already failed at that mission with her last sentence.

She went to step back and was stopped by Stanley. "Give me a bit of room," she said as she leaned in and pulled his too-heavy suitcase from the backseat. Too heavy for anyone visiting for only ten days.

"Stanley," she bit out as she backed up and her elbow bumped his soft midsection. "Move."

A few minutes later, she slipped the key in the lock to the apartment door. She could almost feel him breathing. She swung around.

"Look, Stanley." She hesitated, almost stumbling on the name. "If you want me to do my job properly,

I need some space." She wondered how many times she'd have to repeat that phrase.

He took a step back. He looked puzzled and anxious. It was becoming like a dance with two mismatched partners. She took a deep breath. As soon as she got his luggage inside, it was a dance that was going to end.

"In fact, wait here. Hold this." She slipped the handle of the suitcase into his hand and turned to push the apartment door open. She was only mildly amused to hear the suitcase thump onto the floor.

"Having trouble?" she asked. She glanced over her shoulder. He was fumbling with his vintage suitcase. It had no wheels and a worn faux-leather cover. It was an oddity. Like Stanley, she thought.

Her hand dropped to her Colt. She had just purchased it. The gun had replaced her old standby Glock that had seen her through her training and first year. The Colt was an exciting purchase. She could hardly wait to see action with this in her hand. But so far, other than target practice, she had yet to use it.

She moved past the entrance, noting everything. White laminate floors, gray walls, a couch to the left, table to the right. There was nothing else. She had to be sure. Stanley and his suitcase were forgotten. This was business. There was nothing but silence and the ticking of... She pulled the Colt, reveling in the feel of it in her hand. Other women loved new clothes. She loved guns. The thought made her smile. Something clicked. She swung, pointing the Colt in the direction of the sound. It was nothing but a wall clock in the kitchen. Someone had plugged it in since the last time she'd been here.

"Is this necessary?" Stanley's frightened voice came from the hallway.

She held up a hand to him, motioning him to be quiet. On another assignment, in a different place, ticking had meant something so much more sinister. This wasn't such a case, she reminded herself. Still, she needed to make sure. No matter the high probability that there was no threat. If there was, she needed to eliminate it. After all, someone had paid her to do just that.

The kitchen and living area gleamed as if they'd been recently cleaned and infrequently used. She took a step in and then two—she did a visual sweep of the area. It was overkill, she knew that, but one could never be too safe. She'd learned that through her arduous FBI training. The experience had been put into practice during the last year with Nassar.

A minute, two—she went through the small one-bedroom apartment. All clear, exactly as it should be. She went to the hallway and gave Stanley what she hoped would be interpreted as a friendly smile. One more come-hither look from him and she might punch him, she thought, knowing that of course she wouldn't. She was too professional for that, but…the thought was out there.

"Let me take that," she said. She lifted his duffel bag and set it on the coffee table. "You might want to take the suitcase into the bedroom."

"Fine," he said, looking slightly bewildered.

She opened the blinds that masked the balcony, letting in a stream of feeble sunlight. The snowstorm was on its last legs. The snowfall was a thin curtain, unlike the thick flakes that had blanketed the area in a layer of white earlier in the day.

"You'll have a good view, and I'll be just downstairs while you're here."

"Living?" he asked in a puzzled voice.

"Yes. As long as you're here, I will be, too." Exactly ten days, she wanted to say, no more.

His face lit up at that like she'd told him she'd be his best friend. And she supposed that in a way, for a time, she would be.

"There's a beautiful view of the mountains," she said as she slid the glass patio door open. She could smell his aftershave as he approached. She'd first become aware of the scent at the airport terminal, where it had preceded him as he'd disembarked in a cloud that was as pleasant as the lingering smell of cooked fish. She'd felt some sympathy for his seatmates on the flight and even those who might have been sitting nearby. Stanley wasn't one to slide into the background; everything about him was distinctive.

She turned her attention to the street. A vacant lot was directly across from them. Beside it there was a parking lot with only a few snow-shrouded cars. The lot was blanketed in snow and shadowed by the stark branches of winter-dead trees. She frowned. The trees and shrubs blocked her view. She could see nothing between the parking lot and the low-rise brick building beside it.

"This place is small," Stanley said as he came up too close beside her.

She moved one step over and thought again how this game was getting very old. She glanced at him, but he was looking not at the view but behind her, at the apartment. She turned back to the street.

"That's because it's temporary."

And because they were staying away from the luxury homes and condos that would be harder to secure. She pressed a finger to her temple. She could feel the beginnings of a headache.

He wasn't going away. She needed to deal. She turned to face the only headache she had—Stanley.

"Often the hunters and skiers use this same lodging, but there aren't many around this time of year. Right now there are a few permanents, or longer stays, I guess you'd call them, and you. But you won't spend much time in the apartment."

"I suppose." He turned his attention back to the apartment. "What channels do I get?"

"No idea," she said, not caring if she was abrupt. She watched as he went back inside. That was one thing no one had checked, television channels. She knew there would be something wrong with them. Stanley was a complainer. Since the airport, he'd had a list of minor complaints. They ranged from the length of time it took for the luggage pickup, to the hard seats in the rental van. The apartment was no different. It was too small, too little light, too… He was in the kitchen now, running a finger along the counter.

"What's around here? To do, I mean," Stanley said a few minutes later as he came up beside her. "Other than great scenery."

"You didn't research before you came?" She supposed he'd want to do something other than take pictures, but that wasn't her problem.

"Yes, but…I thought you might…" He smiled a

slightly slick smile, obviously another ploy for her attention.

That was it.

"Have a seat," she said pushing him toward the couch just off the kitchen. She picked up a couple of brochures she'd seen resting in a small squat bookcase and tossed them at him. "Looks like you have some reading to do."

The way he didn't look at them. The way he dangled the brochures between his thumb and forefinger like they were tainted. All of it told her everything.

"You weren't really needing that information, were you?"

"No," he said, and blushed.

It was apparent that he'd only wanted a topic of conversation to connect with her. She didn't have time for conversation. That wasn't her job.

She turned and went back to the balcony, but made the mistake of looking over her shoulder. She sighed, feeling sorry for him and his rather hangdog expression. "Come here. Check out the view."

He stood a foot away from her. Unlike last time, this time he looked at the scenery. There was an expression of awe on his face and she wasn't sure how he could have been so wrapped up in the apartment's conveniences, or lack thereof, to miss the extraordinary view the first time he'd stood on the balcony. But Stanley appeared to be a man with a one-track mind. He was no multitasker. Now he gazed out at the snow-covered plains and mountains that swept around the city limits seemingly transfixed, like he'd just realized all of this was here. He lifted his camera and snapped a picture then two, three… She lost count. Stanley was finally in his element and she was forgotten. Ten minutes later he put the camera down with a small smile on his face.

"Thank you," he said. "For picking me up. And putting up with me."

"It's what I'm paid for," she said, trying to inject a touch of humor into the words.

"I suppose."

"So what's with the name? Stanley, I mean," she asked.

He looked at her; his hazel eyes were awash in innocent confusion. At five-eight she almost looked eye to eye with him.

"I mean, it's a nickname obviously. How'd you get it? Did your parents come up with the name?" She wasn't overly interested. But it might serve to get to know the man she was supposed to protect just a bit better. Actually, it would help her get to know the man she would be chauffeuring around Wyoming. That was probably a more apt statement.

"No." He shook his head. "It was a name my older brother gave me. It's after a cartoon character. I don't suppose you have the program here. Anyway, I got the name when I was two. The show hasn't played in years. But at the time, he thought that I looked like the main character." He shrugged. "Of course, when he gave me the nickname, he was little more than a kid himself."

She wasn't sure what to say. How could they have missed the existence of a brother? The file listed no siblings. In fact, the closest relatives listed were an uncle and two first cousins. Then there were only distant relatives listed in order of succession. It was a major oversight, and it had her immediately concerned. "I didn't know you had a brother."

"I don't," he said rather sadly. "Not anymore. He died a few years before my mother." He cleared his throat. "Accident," he said with a rasp to his voice. "His death destroyed my parents."

For the first time, her heart went out to him. It was tragic, and he said it so nonchalantly. The hurt in his eyes told her that wasn't how he felt about the tragedy.

It was interesting how she'd had to tweak the profile she'd established for him. He was annoying but he wasn't arrogant; instead he had expectations. He was socially awkward, especially around the opposite sex. She wasn't sure if that was just her. The most surprising had been his compassion. There was a lot she still didn't know, as the file hadn't spoken to personality. But what she did know was that he was basically a good egg.

"Don't hit it!" he'd yelled when she'd swerved for an elk on the way from the airport.

"Oh my goodness," he'd said after the animal had dodged into the bush. "I'm so glad you did that. That you were able to swerve like that." He'd taken a slightly strangled breath as if he'd been holding it. "That he lived."

In that moment, she could have forgiven most of Stanley's annoying behaviors, at least the ones she'd recently suffered through, when he displayed that kind of compassion for a wild animal. Add in that he was the client, and they were never wrong, and he was in a pretty good place. For the first time she relaxed and smiled at him.

"I'm sorry," she said in reference to his brother.

According to the file, his mother had died twenty-two years ago. His father had died a few years after that of a heart attack. She wondered what else the file might have missed.

"Don't be," he said softly. "He had a good life. Just short."

She looked at him with a frown. It was an odd thing to say about losing a brother, as far as she knew, his only sibling. Since it was accidental, she imagined it had been tragic—definitely sudden. She had questions, but she asked none of them. None of it was relevant to the case.

Instead she mulled over the strangeness of Stanley's response. Everyone dealt with grief differently, but she was curious. She started to say something and then stopped.

Before she could consider the matter further, there was a movement to her right. Her attention immediately focused on the cluster of stark, leafless trees on the edge of the parking lot. They were across the road, and her mind quickly calibrated the distance. Approximately one hundred feet to the right—shooting distance. She tensed, but her eyes never left that location.

"Go inside," she said over her shoulder. She wasn't taking any chances, code white or not. She could hear him breathing behind her. He wasn't listening, as usual. It was strange that they had a *usual* in the short time she'd known him. That was the one intriguing thing about him, despite his oddness—it was easy to develop a rapport with him. She shoved the thoughts back.

She focused on the change across the street, the potential threat. She doubted it was anything. But she wasn't taking the chance. She needed to focus on one thing, and that was keeping Stanley safe.

Something flashed across the street, like sunlight on metal. She looked up. There was a break in the cloudy sky and a glimmer of sunlight.

With her Colt in her right hand, she moved close to Stanley, pushing him back with her left.

One sparrow, then two flew out of a low-lying bush that edged the parking lot. They flew diagonally down the street, the two joined by two more, as if they'd been disturbed.

"Get inside. Keep down," she commanded.

He looked at her, puzzled, his mouth working as if he were about to protest. She gave him another little shove when he continued to stand there.

It could be nothing. But she'd rather overreact and have Stanley safe. The other option wasn't worth considering. For that meant failure, and she'd never failed... The thought trailed off. Now all senses were on alert.

Something was off.

She peered over the balcony. The snow was lessening, but the wind was picking up. A stray fast-food wrapper was tagged by the wind. It seemed to skip across the street. She watched as it tumbled in the direction where, if she were to pinpoint trouble, she'd point there. But there was no evidence of anything. Just the same superficial signs and now nothing. The only noise was that created by the wind. The break in the clouds disappeared, and everything seemed dimmer.

She might have imagined it. The possibility was high. She wasn't sure if there was trouble or not. What she did know was that her instincts screamed that something wasn't right. It was hard to pinpoint what had been the defining moment that had triggered her full attention. But now she was on and ready for action.

Seconds ticked by.

"What are you listening for?" There was a demand in his voice; it carried the edge of expectation, like someone who had always gotten his way.

A shot rang out, cutting off anything else he might have wanted to say. The glint of something, a glimpse of blue-black, a gun—or maybe that was just her imagination. The shot had been real. It seemed to come from exactly the spot she'd mentally marked as a potential problem area.

"Get down!" she shouted as Stanley let out a noise that sounded like a cross between a yip and a shriek. She hurled herself down and back so she was within range to take him down by force if necessary.

"What's going…" he began as she had him by the arm, taking him down, too.

"Shut up! Stay there!"

She got up in a half crouch while giving him a bit of a push on his chest to remind him to stay down. She turned her back to him, moving toward the railing. Cement, she thought with disgust. The railing was a solid block of cement. Great protection and lousy visual. The only way to find the perp was to make herself vulnerable and lift her head over the edge.

Another shot.

Seconds ticked by. A minute, then two.

A rush of movement to her right and a crash directly below her.

She was blinded by the balcony. She looked to her

right. The ceramic planter that had sat on the railing had been taken out. It had crashed into the parking lot. Hit by gunfire, she was sure, considering everything that had happened in the last few minutes. But the sound had been muted and the only real alert was what had followed, the noise of pottery shattering. She bet that whoever was shooting at them was now using a silencer. Why hadn't he used it for the first shot or even the second? That was a mystery she might never have the answer to. Unnecessary question, unnecessary information, she told herself. But the shadow that flitted from one dead tree to the next and where the last shot had come from wasn't. This might be her only chance. She took aim and fired.

She glanced back. Stanley was on his knees in a position that in yoga was called a prayer position. The only difference was that his hands were covering his head.

She turned back to the balcony. She scanned the street. She doubted she'd hit anything. There'd been no evidence of her taking out anything more than the bark of a tree.

Whoever was out there would not want the attention of the sheriff. She had to assume that they would shoot only when they spotted a target, that they would not fire needlessly and create extra noise and, potentially, undue attention. She moved slowly, trying to find a place to see and not be seen.

Her Colt was clutched in both hands as she considered the next move. Everything had changed. The white-coded, dull little assignment had just been upgraded.

To code red.

Chapter Three

"Why are they shooting at us?" Stanley looked at her as if the answer to that question would spin back the clock, as if this had never happened.

There was no time to ask who and why. No time for the volley of questions that answering that one question could turn into.

She looked over her shoulder. Stanley was crawling toward her. His face was white, but he wasn't stopping.

"Get back," Jade said, and waved him back toward the safety of the apartment. She should have known that there was a time limit on how long he'd follow instructions. She rose slowly to peer over the concrete railing. There was another movement to her right. A flash, and she dived down, glancing over her shoulder as she did so. Stanley hadn't moved.

"Stay down," she commanded in a whisper. "Stay there."

She shifted her attention away from Stanley. The assailant might be across the street, but she had no idea if he was alone. She rose up on one knee. "This sucker's not done with us," she muttered as she peered over the balcony. Everything was quiet except for an odd shuffling sound behind her. She turned and found herself face-to-face with Stanley. "Down," she repeated, and he nodded, flattening himself to the balcony floor.

She hunched down, her eyes meeting his. Panic was in his eyes and in the tense line of his lips. "There's nothing you can do. This is why I was hired," Jade said patiently as if more words would somehow calm him. "You're unarmed," she reminded him, betting that he didn't even realize that important fact. She saw the fear in his eyes as she delivered the clinching words. "I'm not."

This time he seemed to get it as his frightened eyes met hers.

Jade turned, rising to her knees to peer over the balcony as she scanned the street for further trouble.

Silence.

To the left of the parking lot was a two-story plain brick building. Its main floor was boarded up. She looked away. Whoever had fired at them had done so from the right. That meant that they were close to the low-rise building. It was an office building, closed on the weekends. Nothing had changed from the last time she'd looked. She glanced back at Stanley. She breathed a sigh of relief to see that he had retreated inside. Her attention went back to the street. Her Colt was in both hands. There was no sound from the other apartments. Her mind went over the last few minutes.

Two shots.

Three if you counted the one with the silencer. That shot had been muted and mostly unheard by those inside, living in the vicinity, but it appeared, so had the others. Gunshots were out of the norm. They were sounds that many people might consider part of their imagination. Television programs, online games, the clamor of day-to-day living masked all sorts of noise, including that which was unanticipated and unfamiliar, gunfire. It would be easily discounted as part of the noise of a television program. Now there was nothing but a strange silence. Was the gunman still out there? And if he wasn't, where was he?

She slid down with her back to the concrete balcony railing. She debated whether now was the time to report in that her assignment had taken a critical turn.

One more check.

She pushed up over the balcony, looking left and right down the street. A movement to her left; she watched with bated breath. It was nothing but a jackrabbit that had made its way into the city. The hare took its time. It seemed to lope, hopping this way and that, stopping to sniff the air. Finally, it disappeared between two buildings. The street was again empty.

She sank below the railing as she put the Colt down and pulled her phone out of her pocket.

"Zafir," he answered with a concerned tone, for this number was never used except in case of emergency.

"Code red," she said simply. "I'm pinned down at the client's apartment. Shots from across the street at the client's balcony. The client's secure."

"Last count?"

"Unknown shooter. Three shots fired. Four, if you count mine. He has a silencer." She looked where the planter used to stand. "It's been quiet for over five minutes."

"Did you see…"

"Nothing," she interrupted. "No visual. Like I said, I got one shot in, that was it. I never had a clear shot and on a public street, well, that just made it difficult."

"I can imagine," he said. "Keep it contained if you can. I'll be there in five."

The call disconnected as abruptly as it had begun.

Keep it contained if you can.

With gritted teeth, she shoved the phone into her pocket. For a second she really wished that she could shove it somewhere else.

THE SNOW WOULDN'T stop falling. The man wiped perspiration and melted snow off his upper lip and swore as a car came down the street. Until now, it had been deserted.

He should have taken him out. Except he'd never had a clear shot. The woman had placed herself between him and his target. The plan was to take him out in a maximum of two shots and then get out before the authorities showed up. He'd already shot three. He couldn't fire any more. Even with his silencer, it was too dangerous. The woman was shooting back. Her gun didn't have a silencer. The cops could be alerted at any moment. His opportunity had slipped through his fingers, and Stanley had moved off the balcony. There was nothing to be done.

He looked at the handgun with disdain. It had failed him. The silencer didn't work as easily as he'd been told. He'd fumbled with it. As a result, he hadn't used it on the first two shots. The owner of the gun store had assured him that it was a "never fail." He'd said that it was easy to use. He had lied. If he were home, he'd go back and let him know what he thought of his lie. He couldn't. He was in a foreign country and he had to abide by its rules. If he stepped afoul of the law in any way other than planned, he had a greater chance of getting caught. That would destroy his chances at what was most important. But it was clear that taking someone out wasn't his forte. He needed help. He would find someone else, someone who could do the job for him.

He'd been stupid to think that he could remain anonymous and complete the job. He needed the money. He hadn't come all the way here to fail.

He considered the fact that he required assistance. He wasn't sure why his cousin had hired him. Except that wasn't true. He knew why. Besides his lies and exaggerations and the fact that he really had killed before, he was disposable. He always had been. He grimaced.

Maybe a hit man was what he needed, someone more skilled at killing than him. He'd killed only two people in his life—one who had invaded his home and another who'd invaded his life. That hardly made him an expert, not like a hit man. He'd read of them and seen shows, American productions. Those shows had been fiction. Still, he knew that such people existed. They just did not advertise their wares in a storefront that was easily found.

He looked at the watch on his right wrist. He fiddled with the silver bracelet. It wasn't quite noon. He pulled out his phone and thumbed over the screen. There was one man who would know where to look. One man he could rely on to dig deep into the dregs of society and find someone who could do the job. The unfortunate thing of it was that it would not come cheap, and he needed every penny that had been offered him to get this job done.

Panic ran through him. He didn't have time to

waste. He wasn't willing to give up on the money yet. He shoved the phone into his back pocket. He'd have to do it himself until, or unless, he found someone who was better. In the meantime, he was on his own, and he had less time than he'd anticipated.

His left leg ached from the cold and from having to scrunch into a cramped position for too long. The leg had plagued him since he was a child. It had been the result of what everyone had called an accident. He'd always known that it was no accident. Nothing that happened to him was accidental. The world was against him and always had been.

He rubbed his free hand along his calf as if that slight movement would dispel the bone-deep ache. His cousin needed to die, and he needed to do it soon. And if that meant he took out others with him, it didn't matter. What mattered was getting this job done and getting back to Morocco as soon as possible.

Chapter Four

Zafir grabbed his keys, his go-bag and an extra magazine for his Glock and headed out the door. He hadn't expected to back anyone up. But every agent in the Wyoming office was busy and already assigned to a case. So there was no choice. He'd be stepping into the role of backup to Jade's lead. It was an exceptional situation, but it was also policy. He and Emir had hammered out the guidelines for Nassar Security a little less than a decade ago. Those guidelines had always included the brothers' full involvement. Action was what they loved. They'd vowed never to have that love drowned because of leadership duties and responsibility. They'd promised they'd be in the field whenever possible. Unfortunately, "whenever possible" had too often given way to days of tiring office duties. He was more than ready to move into action.

His hand brushed the gun. The solid feel of it seemed to connect with his hand in a way that was more an extension of him than the tool that it was. There was nothing more exciting than a new gun. Not even a glimpse of a spectacular woman or the chance to caress the sleek lines of the latest woman could compare—it was how he rolled. He didn't expect any of that would ever change.

Romance was short-term fun and long-term trouble. He'd grown up with parents in a loving marriage. Yet no matter how much he liked his future sister-in-law, Kate, he recoiled at the thought of his brother Emir marrying her. In case after case, he'd seen what jealousy and anger could do. Marriage and long-term relationships could be the perfect breeding ground for both those emotions. He wanted none of it, and he'd told himself that a long time ago.

He started the rental Nissan Pathfinder and was about to pop it into Reverse when his phone beeped. His hand dropped from the gearshift and he reached for it. Only a few numbers weren't screened out. He had two admin assistants to handle those calls that he didn't answer.

Emir's name showed on the screen. It wasn't a surprise. It wasn't uncommon for his twin to connect like this—unexpectedly. And as always, instinct had told him who it was before the first beep had finished.

"Yeah," he said, knowing he sounded rushed and hurried. This was a call he knew he couldn't miss, and even knowing that, the delay grated on him. Something was up; Emir wouldn't have phoned otherwise. His twin didn't phone for social chats—never had, especially now, when their agency was overwhelmed and understaffed. It was something they'd have to address soon. His grip on the phone tightened.

"What's going on, Em?" he asked, trying to keep the edge from his voice. He knew that whatever information Emir had, it was going to put an additional crimp in his day.

"The code on your latest case just flipped to red," Emir said. Red meant that either the client's life was in imminent danger or there was a threat to an agent.

"I could have told you that five minutes ago," Zafir said, and his lips tightened. He didn't have a lot of time.

"What happened?" Emir asked.

"There were shots fired at the apartment we rented for the client. It's under control now. Jade held them off. Just one shooter that we know of. We're getting the client out of the area. Jade's waiting for me now." He dropped his hand from the steering wheel and rolled down the window an inch. A spatter of fresh snow hit his face. It was oddly calming. He loved the smell of fresh snow, but he was more anxious to get moving and make sure everything was secure.

"There's more to this than we were led to believe," Emir said. "It's making me uneasy."

The tension since he'd first answered the call retreated. He and Emir, as usual, were on the same page. But it had been the sudden change in status that he knew had really set him on edge. Moving into action always smoothed things over. "I'm at loose ends so I'll back Jade on this. What else do you have?"

"An explosion on an estate near Rabat belonging to your client's uncle." He paused. "The explosion was intentional. It was a homemade explosive device and it killed one of the estate's employees."

"Any idea who…"

"Of the bomber, nothing," Emir cut him off. "We believe he was acting alone. There was nothing left near the scene to even get a fingerprint. But even if there were," he mused, "whoever did it would have to have a criminal record for them to be of any use. One thing to consider, the uncle is old and very wealthy. I'd start digging into the details of that, but I'm buried in a case we have going here."

"I heard," Zafir said. "We're shorthanded with Faisal on the East Coast, and there's five other cases on the active roster. But we'll get it done. We always do."

He disconnected the call and looked at his watch. He debated getting in touch with Jade. Was the new information something that would change things for her in the next few minutes? He doubted that it would. But things could also change on a dime.

WITHOUT BACKUP, THE only thing Jade could do was keep Stanley safe and wait for Zafir to arrive. But one agent couldn't be in two places at once. They needed to get their client to a safe place. That was the priority.

She looked at her watch. They had to get moving and to find out who was after Stanley, and why.

She did a final sweep of the area. The street was silent. It had been like that for the last few minutes. She needed to make sure Stanley was safe. She stepped back into the apartment. She had to secure both him and the apartment before she went out and scouted a wider area. It was clear they needed to move him and for that they had to find a safe place. That wasn't her job. Her job was to protect him in whatever safe house was decided.

But when she stepped past the patio doors, the silence was heavy. She took a deep breath, trying to control her over-stressed breathing. The apartment was ominously silent except for the clock measuring off time; the steady beat made her want to yank it from the wall and chuck it over the balcony.

"Stanley!" Her gun was in both hands, aimed—ready. She took one step, moving left, her arms moving with her body, keeping the gun in front, ready. There was nothing to be ready for. The apartment was empty, and all that she could think was that it wasn't possible. She'd protected him, held off the sniper and made him safe, and now Stanley should be here waiting for her. As she moved through the small apartment she became more tense. It was clear that Stanley was gone, even his luggage was missing.

Outside a car door slammed.

She ran to the balcony, gripping the cold cement as she looked over the railing. The street was dreary, falling snow the only movement. She went to the other side, to the edge of the balcony that hugged the perimeter of the building. There, she could see into the parking lot and also see that the stall that her rental van had occupied was empty.

"Unbelievable," she said through clenched teeth. "Un-frickin-believable," she muttered. Nothing like this had ever happened to her. Until now, she could never have imagined it happening. So far she'd had a stellar, if short, career with Nassar—until now.

What had gone wrong?

How had this happened?

She'd handled the attack on the balcony smoothly only to lose the client. This didn't sit well with her, and it wasn't going to sit well with the agency. But it wasn't the agency she was thinking of, but rather the sinfully good-looking Zafir. She gritted her teeth. Instead of impressing him, which would up her chances of success and status with the company, she looked like amateur hour.

"Damn, Stanley," she gritted. "You're not making it easy to like you."

Chapter Five

Jade headed out the door without a backwards glance. The apartment door banged behind her. She never checked if it was locked or not. It didn't matter. She wouldn't be back.

Irrelevant.

They needed to get moving. She had to brief Zafir. They needed to get wheels on the road and find Stanley.

As she stepped back into the parking lot ten minutes later, Zafir pulled up in an arctic-blue Pathfinder. Top of the line. She wouldn't have expected less. The metallic paint gleamed in the dull light. She'd had to wait for him, but she hadn't wasted any of that time. She'd gathered what evidence she could in the ten minutes it took Zafir to get here.

What she knew was that Stanley had been in a hurry. The evidence of that was a cover for one of his precious camera lenses, lying where the van had been parked. He was frightened, panicked even, but considering what had happened, she couldn't fault him. She ran the lens cover between her fingers.

Zafir stepped out.

"Stanley's gone," Jade said grimly.

He closed the driver's door. His gaze never left her face, and his eyes told her what he didn't. That he was waiting for her to fill him in.

"He took off while I was securing the balcony. No more than fifteen minutes ago." There was no sugar-coating the information. There was just getting it out and getting moving. "Took everything but his camera lens with him." She held it up with a look of irony. "He'll miss that." She stuffed it into her pocket.

"I don't believe this," Zafir said. A dark brow arched and his chiseled lips were flat, disapproving, as if this had all been her fault. "Foul play?"

"No. At least, I don't think so."

Silence beat between them, and with it, so many implications. Had she watched him closer, would this still have happened? Had she kept the keys for the van out of his reach, had she...

She met Zafir's troubled gaze. "There was no sign of scuffle. In fact, only one set of footsteps in the snow, and those are disappearing fast." She wiped snow-flakes from her brow with the back of an ungloved hand. "Tire tracks indicate he was heading west. They disappeared within fifty feet of his first turn."

Jade glanced to the street as if the van would mi-raculously appear. But there was nothing, no worn white van. If they didn't find him quickly, it would be too late. She knew that as surely as she knew that she'd had cereal for breakfast. Her stomach grumbled.

Her body was obviously not on the same page as her head. Now—there was no time for food. They had to get moving.

"I was on the balcony. He was in the apartment,

or so I thought. He took the van while I was securing the area." She brushed a strand of hair off her face.

"He couldn't have gone far. There wasn't enough time," Zafir said. There was no inflection in his voice. There was no judgment, either. Somehow that made it all worse.

"You're right, and there's a chance he might return on his own. He's more than likely only frightened and has taken off to get away. Maybe he's thinking of taking some photographs. An hour or two in the countryside to calm his nerves." She shook her head. "Not going to happen," she said.

"It already has," he said, his lips compressed.

Now she could see the disapproval in his eyes.

She ignored that. It was true. Stanley had disappeared on her watch. But it was also true that she'd get him back, and then they'd move on to the next step, securing Stanley in another location. "Look, he's familiar with me. I can take your Pathfinder and retrieve him. You stay here in case he returns."

"No."

"No?"

"We'll go after him. Together."

"We?" Dread dropped into the pit of her stomach. That hadn't been what she planned even when she'd reported the code red. Somehow, she'd thought that she'd continue on in the case. Alone. That she'd keep Zafir informed as it progressed. That he'd assign another agent as backup.

"There's no one else available," he said as if reading her mind. There was a hard inflection in his voice that clearly told her this was nonnegotiable.

She took a breath. She was on edge, and it wasn't

the situation. Zafir on paper was intimidating enough but in reality, even more so. She'd admired him for too long. Now she was scared that he was the one man who had the ability to pull her off her game. She took a deep breath. There were more important things to think of than her admiration for one of her employers.

She had to remember who he really was. He was a man like any other despite his legendary status with Nassar. She struggled with that, with staying focused on the job and not on him. But to her he was like no ordinary man. The cases he'd closed amazed her. She'd been in awe of what he had done, what he had faced and how he'd succeeded. She had to bring her adoration down to earth. Working with him had to be like working with any other man. She had no idea how to make that happen.

She took a breath and felt his dark eyes on her; the passion and intelligence in them was hot and commanding. She turned away. This was no time for such thoughts, and yet she had to allow them before she could discard them.

She had to remember that he was a womanizer, if office rumors were to be believed. For even now, he was looking at her with more heat than one would look at someone who was only a business partner. Worse, she wasn't immune.

Darn him, she thought.

"WHAT'S YOUR TAKE on Stanley?" His eyes drilled into hers and he knew that he probably seemed focused on her response like it was all that he had on his mind. He knew that it was all he should have on his mind. He needed to get his head in the game, for he found everything about Jade to be distracting. Her photograph, as he'd thought earlier, on first meeting her, hadn't done her justice. A photograph couldn't reveal biting intelligence or a body that was meant for...

Outrageous, his internal monitor roared at him. She was a gorgeous woman but more important, she was a business associate. The reminder wasn't much help.

His eyes went to her face. That was a safe place to remain except for the fact that her eyes—her eyes were hypnotic, and her lips... She was muddying the waters of his normally clear mind worse than a sandstorm in the Sahara.

"He didn't seem to know how to act with a woman. I mean, he acted rather like a starstruck teenage boy rather than the middle-aged man he is. It was rather strange. Manageable, but strange." She looked at him and then followed everything she had said with a contradiction. "At least it was manageable, until now. I can't believe he's gone. I would never have expected that of him. He didn't appear to have that much initiative."

"He's frightened. Fear causes unexpected reactions." He felt nothing but empathy for the missing Stanley. He was probably intimidated by Jade's presence and likely knocked off his feet by her beauty. He bet that their client had been a mess before one shot had been fired.

He looked at Jade. Questions hung between them as well as the recently obtained intel that he needed to share. The rest of what happened, the explosion in Rabat, had the potential to impact this case. But it was information that would have to wait. First they needed to find Stanley. Then he'd tell Jade, and they could make some sense of it. He hadn't begun to analyze it himself. At this point, he had no idea if it impacted Stanley's presence here in the States or their ability to keep him safe.

"I should have remembered that. Fear," she repeated softly. "If I had, I might have prevented him from running," she said. "I should have checked on him before…"

"You didn't have time," he interrupted. "You were handling a potential assassin, which, by the way, was exceptional work."

"He got away."

"He didn't kill Stanley," he said. "That was your doing." He paused and scanned the street, which was empty, deserted as if the storm had confined everyone to their homes. "Was there a reason for anyone to try to take you out?" He was pretty sure of the answer to that even as he asked it, but he needed her to verify it.

"None," she said. "The shots stopped soon after I got Stanley out of sight."

"The threat was assessed wrong from the beginning," he said with a scowl, hating to admit any of that. He was on his phone punching numbers even as he talked. But that was how he ran things. His siblings joked about his ability to take multitasking to the next level.

"I've already called the rental agency," she said. "I mean, if that's what you're doing." Aggravation was thick in her voice. "They're activating the location device on the vehicle so that I'll have access."

Another sign that none of the glowing praise of her abilities had been wrong. The client had slipped away, but he was sure from the evidence presented, and what he knew of Jade, that it was through no fault of hers. His gut told him that nothing short of tying him down could have prevented it. But instead of telling her that, he scowled at her. Then he asked in a voice that would have suited any interrogation room, "You're sure he's planning to leave town?"

She nodded. "He's seriously into photography. As we knew from the file. But what we didn't know is how passionate he is. I don't think anything would stop him from taking the landscape pictures he came for. He's already made that clear. Add to the fact that he had a frightening experience, and that experience was in the city." She paused. "I suppose terrifying for someone unused to guns. He's comfortable in the countryside. He spends a lot of time there in Morocco."

She frowned.

"What is it?"

"You know, on the way here he asked me where the nearest international airport was. I told him that Casper was the largest and closest airport but you required a transfer for anything international. I didn't even get a chance to explain how limited the flight choice was. The whole topic was dropped because of the elk on the road. I managed to miss it and then we moved on to other topics."

"You think that's where he might be headed, Casper?" he said.

"No, at least not to hop a flight." She shook her head. "Despite the fact that someone tried to kill him, I don't think it was enough to have him heading home, at least not yet. For all his gaucheness, he has a stubbornness about him. Plus, he loves the States. He told me that this was the trip of a lifetime for him. I don't think he's apt to give up so soon. No, I think it's the opposite. Because of the extreme nature of the experience, he now thinks it's over. He thinks that he's safe. They tried and failed." She looked at him, her eyes seeming to graze his face with the passion of her commitment to this case. "Is that crazy?"

"Nothing at this point is crazy," he replied. "We've got to hit all angles, as you know."

"He mentioned Casper on more than one occasion as a drive he might like to take while he's here. There's some great photography between here and there."

"You don't..."

"I think—" she cut him off "—that he's taking that drive just a little earlier than planned." She shook her head. "I hope he's licensed and doesn't hurt himself in these conditions."

"We'll find him before that happens," Zafir said with gravel in his voice.

"I hope so," she said as she glanced at her phone messages. Her brow furrowed as her right hand ran through her hair. "The rental agency is having trouble with the app," she said. She put the phone down. "It could be anywhere from a few minutes to an hour before they get it working." She frowned. "At least that's what the tech guesstimated in his message. In the meantime, they've pinpointed his last location, so that's hopeful."

There was something in the way that she looked at him that held some sort of warning. Yet his attention was fixated on her lips.

Pouty. It was an interesting and decidedly delicious feature, and it was completely distracting. He looked away.

"We don't have a lot of time. He's got a head start, and I don't trust him on his own. He could get himself killed left to his own devices for any length of time." There was an edge to her voice. "It's been too long."

"It only seems that way," he said calmly. It had only been minutes since his arrival, less than four to be exact.

He opened the driver's door of the Pathfinder as she got in the passenger side. As he shut the door, he went over what he knew. When he'd arrived, she hadn't looked directly at him. An admission of guilt. She believed the missing client was her fault. Now she met his look with the determination of a drill sergeant, raking over him, assessing. She'd accepted what she believed was her part in the situation and had moved on. She knew exactly what she was about and wasn't expecting any less from him.

Each case she'd been on, for one reason or another, had been the talk of the office on both sides of the ocean. They only hired the best. All their agents were cutting edge, yet in case after case her skills had shone above the others. In the fourteen months she'd been with the agency, she'd closed a record number of cases. She'd been lauded by two different municipalities and a women's group.

She pulled her Colt. She stroked the barrel like it was cherished and loved. But the way her focus remained on him sent a sensual shiver through him even when he realized that she was unaware of either the gesture or the suggestion loaded in it. She slid the weapon back into the holster at her waist.

He put the vehicle in gear.

"And what weapon are you going to use to contain

Stanley when you find him?" he asked. He was curious about her, but prodding her for a reaction was a poor way to get information. He knew that, but it had slipped out, a question poorly timed and poorly formed.

"Excuse me?" She frowned, clearly unsure of what he was referring to.

"Got a peek at airport security footage. He's more of a handful than you're admitting." He shrugged as her frown deepened. "Of course, I did all that before you reported in. Just wanted to make sure everything was going all right."

"You were checking up?" Her face flushed, and the words were tight, controlled, as if he had been doubting her abilities.

Her file mentioned a temper. It was information obtained from her psychiatric evaluation, required screening for all Nassar agents. In her interview, she'd admitted to an impoverished blue-collar, single-parent upbringing. As a result of that, she'd declared she had high goals and expectations for herself. She'd proven that ambition and ability again and again in the field. It was only her quick temper that might cause her to stumble along the way. So far it had proven to be well controlled. She'd mastered even that.

"Actually, at the time I was just briefing myself, in case you needed backup. Which…" His eyes met hers, stormy blue and almost accusatory. "Turns out you do. The case is upgraded and the client has disappeared, has he not?" They were harsh words that held none of his admiration. Instead they were fighting words. He needed any doubts she felt to be replaced by a driving will to succeed.

Silence hung between them for a second, two.

"It could have happened to anyone," she said with an edge to her voice.

"Right," he agreed. "But it happened to you." He couldn't help pushing the envelope, seeing what her reaction would be.

He knew she was annoyed. His last comments were uncalled for, insensitive if you didn't know where he was going with them. He might have pushed her too far; he reined it in. "I'm sorry."

Her lips were compressed and the look in her eyes suggested she'd rather see him in hell than here, and she wasn't much interested in his apology.

"Look, on this case I'm no one's boss. I'm sorry for giving that impression or for laying blame when none should be." He cleared his throat. He needed to eat crow to make this case go smoothly. "I was a jerk."

"Agreed," Jade said with a hint of a smile. "Let's go," she said. "We need to find Stanley."

Chapter Six

"We've got a location," Jade, said looking up from her phone.

"Still moving?" He turned the corner.

"Yes…no. Unbelievable!" She shook her head.

"What's going on?"

"I've lost the feed." She turned the rental's locating app off and then back on. She smacked her palm against the dash. "Off-line again. I can't believe it. What are the odds of that?"

Neon lights glared to her right. A convenience store. Ahead of them, a Jeep turned off a side street. There was no sign of the white van, nothing that said Stanley had even been here.

"Exactly," Zafir said with a small laugh.

"Slow down," she said, and instead he seemed to speed up as her shoulder hit the door and the seat belt tightened, easing the impact as he took a curve in the road too fast and the vehicle slid.

He glanced at her with a look of apology and slightly raised eyebrows, as if he were hinting that it might be a joke. This was no time…

The thought was broken. A siren flashed and bleeped, once, twice. Zafir slowed down and pulled over.

"Unbelievable," she muttered. There'd been enough delays. Stanley could be in any kind of danger by now. There was the possibility that they weren't the only ones on Stanley's tail. The earlier assailant could be tracking him, too.

"We'll make this quick," Zafir replied. "It's Jake," he said as he glanced in the rearview mirror.

"This case just won't catch us a break," she said as they waited for Jake to approach. The agency had a silent agreement in place with local law enforcement. It allowed them reasonable leeway to operate—the occasional bout of speeds slightly over the limit were usually overlooked. With any luck, they'd be on their way in minutes. Still, minutes were minutes.

She looked back at the police unit and down at the app, which was now showing Stanley's progress. "He's moving," she said. Of all times to be pulled over, just when the rental agency had fixed its software glitch. She looked at her watch and back at the app. "He's got a ten-mile lead on us."

"Jake," Zafir said, acknowledging the sheriff as he came up to the window.

"We're on the lookout for your sniper," Jake said with a curious look inside the vehicle.

Jade frowned. She was unsure how the sheriff would have learned of the incident so quickly. There were no witnesses that she knew of and she hadn't reported it. No witnesses—was that a false assumption?

"I would think that if you leave town, he'll leave with you," Jake said. He glanced past Zafir and took her in with an appreciative sweep of hazel eyes.

Jade tensed and bit back what she thought of the sheriff's unspoken admiration. It wasn't the first time she'd met up with the man and not the first time he'd offered that type of response. It was unprofessional and made her want to smack him, both times. She bit back the words, and her right hand reached for her Colt. The smooth feel and the power it promised were always soothing, no matter what the emotion.

"There's a weather warning. Travel isn't advised," Jake said drily.

"We don't have much choice," Zafir replied.

Snow fell on the windshield. The wipers beat a slow dance. The snow, the wipers, Jake's slow mannerism, all of it beat like the ticking of a clock, reminding them that they were wasting time.

Jade looked out the passenger window. *Hurry up*, she thought.

Jake wasn't the most ambitious sheriff they'd ever had. He was probably thanking the stars or the universe or both that the case was out of his hands. That attitude often made things easy for the agency, but it didn't give any of them a reason to respect the man.

"I suppose you don't," Jake agreed. "I'll keep my eyes peeled here."

Jade grimaced at his words and at the second almost-lecherous look he gave her.

"Thanks," Zafir said, and glanced at her with a smile that said he knew her pain.

She offered him a weak smile.

Zafir nodded and put the Pathfinder in Drive, pulling away from the curb and away from Jake. The police car sat where they had been pulled over, the emergency lights still flashing.

All in all, they'd wasted less than five minutes.

"There's a coffee shop just around the corner. I'd put

odds on Jake making an appearance there now that his services aren't needed." He shook his head. "Remind me if I need to cloud an issue with Jake to send you in."

"That wasn't even funny," she said with a smile.

"No, I suppose it wasn't."

"He's the most laid-back sheriff we've ever had. Guaranteed to do nothing," she said. "He's not even interested in the issue. Just how he can get out of work."

Zafir laughed. It was a low, almost sexy growl that curled down her spine with a seductive caress. "Good thing there isn't too much going on in Jackson."

"Yeah, not too much at all," she said with irony in her voice. She thought of the earlier sniper and of all the cases that Nassar had quietly worked under the nose of local law enforcement. It had been different once, the law more involved, or so her colleagues told her. That had all been before her time.

Five minutes later they hit the city limits. Her finger ran along the route indicated on the app. "Where the heck is he going?" Jade muttered. "He's traveling back roads, keeping off the interstate. But there's miles to go on that road before there's a more trafficked road." She ticked off the miles on her fingers. "Too many miles of vulnerability. What is he thinking?"

"I'd assume, from what I know, a lot of panic," Zafir said. "I really don't think it's about photographs at this point."

"Whatever his reasons, this is crazy." She shook her head. "We've got no idea what or who else is out there."

Zafir gunned the Pathfinder as they left the city limits. But this wasn't the interstate, and it wasn't made for fast travel. The highway was slick, narrow and plagued by antelope straying onto the road. The animals unexpectedly crossed the highway during the dawn and dusk hours, and sometimes in between. It was all unpredictable.

"You might want to slow down," she said. "We don't want to die like…" She stopped. Motor vehicle tragedies, death—loss, all of it—the possibility that life could be short. All Nassar employees had been brutally reminded in a recent case. The case exposed a decade-long cover-up.

"In an accident," she finished lamely. "Could you slow down? Just a bit. The antelope, the snow… It takes one misstep…"

"Do you want Stan to live or die," he growled.

He gripped the wheel and looked at her with anger in his dark eyes.

She realized then that he'd known what she had been referring to. He recognized exactly what she'd been backtracking over—his parents' fatal accident.

"I'm sorry," she said.

"Don't be," he said. "It was a long time ago."

He gripped the wheel. But the look he gave her seemed like a challenge. There was a charge in the air, an awareness of each other that was different, more pronounced, than it had been before.

Her phone beeped. It was nothing more than a reminder of the passing of time.

"DANG IT!" STANLEY MUTTERED as the van slipped into a skid and he wrestled with the wheel. The vehicle didn't respond. The slide continued as if the van wanted to fling itself sideways on purpose. It was unstoppable.

He gritted his teeth and hit the brakes. The van

rocked as its tires spun, and the slide seemed to in-
crease in speed rather than decrease. He was heading
for the ditch and there was no stopping it.

He turned the wheel—nothing. The van was on a
mission of its own. This shouldn't be happening. He
knew what to do; at least he thought he had. Snow in
the mountains of Morocco wasn't an uncommon occurrence, but he'd never driven in it. In fact, he'd never
driven in Morocco, period.

He vaguely remembered that hitting the brakes
wasn't a good idea. He tried to steer, but which way?
Into or out of the slide. The advice he'd read was lost.

His heart pounded. Coming here had been a bad
idea, and he'd known it would be from the beginning.
It was a feeling he'd had on the flight over. Now the
feeling was a reality. It had been a mistake. All of it,
coming here—running from Morocco, running from
Jade. He wasn't sure where to begin, where to un-
ravel it to make it all right. He gripped the wheel. He
remembered something about turning into the skid.
Was that right?

He turned the wheel, but even if it made any difference at all, he was too late. The van rocked and
then slid off the road, wobbling like it would tip over
before it lurched to a stop in the ditch, stopped by a
bank of snow.

Stanley stayed where he'd been thrown. His chest
was pressed against the steering wheel. He took a
breath and then another. He was still alive, and as
he became more aware, he realized that a horn was
honking.

It was his horn.

He leaned back. The honking stopped.

He put the van into Reverse, and the tires spun. The van didn't move even as the engine revved. He put it into Drive. The same thing.

Nothing.

"What were you trying to do?" he muttered to himself. He'd wanted peace and quiet. Jade had flustered him, and the attack had terrified him. He hadn't planned to be gone long. In fact, he'd only wanted to take a few pictures. When he'd come here, to Wyoming, all he'd wanted was peace. Instead, he'd been saddled with a gorgeous type-A-personality woman. She made him jittery. She reminded him of a time when he'd almost had a nervous breakdown. He'd been a child, but the feelings had been real. He'd hated his life, his home. It wasn't like that anymore.

Home. He wanted to go home. This had been a mistake.

He'd told Prince Rashad that protection on his trip was unnecessary. He'd insisted on it. He'd been wrong.

He didn't know why anyone would threaten him. He'd done nothing, had nothing. That was all going to change, but it wasn't enough for someone to kill him. The trust fund would end if he died. So why would someone shoot at him?

His phone beeped as if it had been listening, as if it somehow had the answer. He pulled it out and checked the text message, praying that it was Jade. Except it couldn't be, for she didn't have the number, didn't even know of the phone.

His hands shook, praying for salvation. But the words he read were some of the most terrifying of his life. He was reading the words of a ghost, a demon who was, and always had been, out to get him.

He held the phone clutched against his sweaty palm. He couldn't let it go. He was mesmerized. There should be no text. No one had the number except for his uncle. He'd left the information for him on a table in the small cottage on his uncle's estate. It was the cottage where they'd spent many pleasant afternoons playing rummy and drinking tea. He'd bought the phone solely for this trip so that he could keep in touch with the animal rescue that was his passion, and his uncle, who was his responsibility. Until now, it was unused.

For a minute, two—he couldn't move. He thought about what was on that phone. Nothing. They were meaningless words. He took a deep breath. It was a lie. They weren't meaningless words; they were the words that foreshadowed every nightmare he'd had as a child.

He gripped the wheel. He needed help, and there was no help here. He was on his own. He had to save himself.

He took a deep breath. He should never have run, but he'd also needed time to get himself together.

"So, get it together," he muttered through gritted teeth as he dropped his hands into his lap. He was in a bad situation, and it was his own stupid fault. Now he had to get himself out. He just wasn't sure how or what he needed to do. Should he lie low for a while? If this was a scene from one of his favorite movies, that's exactly what the actors would do.

He stroked his camera and shrugged his jacket on. Despite his thoughts, he didn't know what he was going to do. Everything had changed with that text. He wasn't sure what it meant, and he knew he didn't want to think about it. He looked at the map he'd lifted from the apartment. There was a small community five miles north of the last intersection. He could disappear into the wilds of Wyoming for a while, until he figured out what to do.

He slipped out of the van. Snow had stopped falling but still the drifts were high enough for snow to fall over the tops of his sneakers. Too late, he realized that he should have listened to Jade and purchased boots. Of course, even if he had listened, there had been no time to shop. He turned around and grabbed his camera, ignoring the cold trickle that ran down his ankles. He'd have to endure that discomfort.

He pulled the phone out of his pocket. He looked at the message again. He couldn't help it. No matter how disconcerting it was, he felt like none of it was real. The dead didn't come back to life, but the message suggested they did.

No one ever said those words. For they were strange words that no one would say or had said in the context of most communication. No one but his brother had used those same words to torment him and to torment the animals he loved so well. But his brother was dead.

He shivered, unsure of what it all meant.

He looked at the message one more time before he threw the phone. He watched as it sank into the snow-covered ditch. He was left with only a memory and the knowledge that the dead really can come back to life.

For the first time since he'd last seen his brother, he felt the urge to hit something. But violence wouldn't fix anything; he'd learned that a long time ago.

He walked, or more aptly, he slogged through the snow. He kept going long past where the van had been left. Finally, at the edge of the ditch, he bent down to crawl through the barbed-wire fence. He headed across the field. It was the shortest distance to the town on the map that he'd just stuffed into his pocket.

He felt oddly exhilarated. The horror was behind him. He was taking charge of his own life.

Everything was so silent, so still and so white. It was pristine, gloriously wild and untouched. He took a deep breath of air so clean that it made him shiver and want to hug himself with joy. This was how the world should be—innocent, beautiful and safe. He raised his camera to create a memory of the moment. He took one picture, then two. The camera click was the only sound in the pristine silence.

Minutes passed.

Leaving had been right, he was sure of it now as he aimed and clicked—repeating over and over...

The first gunshot had Stanley diving face-first into the snow. Minutes ticked by. Gingerly he lifted his head. He was five yards away from a shanty. It wasn't much. The weather-softened gray wood looked like it might tumble down with a slight breeze. He had been intrigued by it only seconds earlier. He already had a half dozen photos of it. Right now it was all that stood between him and imminent death.

Jade was gone.

Prince Rashad had been right. He needed protection. It wasn't safe anywhere. He'd been right, but he'd been right for all the wrong reasons.

He could do this. He had to do this; there was no one else but himself to depend on, to get away from the madman who was trying to kill him.

Another shot sheared a drift of snow only ten feet away from him.

A man shouted. The words were as indistinguishable as they were angry and threatening.

Bile rose in his gut, and he fought to keep from throwing up. He couldn't think about the past or about what the future might bring. He had to deal with the now. He had to stay alive.

He crawled the remaining feet to the shanty. Then he stood up and bolted through the doorway, pulling the broken door closed behind him. He couldn't move another step. Instead, he dropped to his knees. Huddled in a ball, his camera dangling around his neck, he considered how he could escape from this new insanity.

Chapter Seven

"The van's not moving," Jade said with a scowl. She shook the phone as if that would change what the app was telling her. "I thought the app had stalled out again. But that's clearly not the case. The van just isn't moving." She paused and looked at him. Her delicate brows were drawn together. "I don't think it's on the road, either, but I can't bring up a real-time photo."

"What are we looking at?"

"Eight miles," she said. "So less than ten minutes and we'll have our answer."

"With any luck," he said drily.

They drove in silence. The snow had finally stopped falling. Here and there, gold shocks of prairie grass burst through the snow. A herd of antelope grazed a half mile to their right, halfway between the foothills and the road. Snow-capped mountains were visible in the distance. At another time, under other conditions, it would have been a scenic route.

"There's either a problem or it's as simple as he stopped to take pictures." She squinted as if that would somehow bring their client into view. "It makes sense. He probably isn't feeling threatened. He feels safer out here. Like he left all the danger behind." She paused. "I'm just speculating, but from what I know of him…"

"He's impulsive."

"Big-time." She looked out the window and back down at the app. The van still hadn't moved. She wondered if Stanley was still with the vehicle. She hoped so. "We might find the van, but there's no guarantee that he's still with it."

That possibility hung between them. Neither of them mentioned the other possibility, that Stanley was already dead. It was an option of which they were both aware but one that neither of them was willing to entertain.

"This case isn't going to be like any other we've had." He broke the silence as he glanced at her. "It's the first to become transcontinental."

"What do you mean?"

"Emir called just before we left." He navigated an icy patch on the road before looking her way again. "I would have told you immediately, but as you know, we were short of time and we had other priorities."

"What do you have?" she said, and couldn't stop the hint of impatience in her voice.

Hot air blew in from the vents, and snow dusted and swept across the road in seemingly chaotic swirls.

The highway was becoming even more treacherous as the snow that had melted on the pavement turned to ice when the temperature plummeted.

"There was an incident reported in Rabat, Morocco, three days ago. A cottage on the grounds of an estate was blown up. A gardener died."

"Wow," she muttered. "How is that tied…" She broke off before her thought could even become a full question. Her gut told her that the case was about to be turned on its head.

"What was destroyed was a cottage that Stanley apparently likes to retreat to. He often spends time there with his uncle playing cards." He looked over at her. "The estate belongs to his uncle."

"You're kidding me," she said, and she couldn't keep the edge out of her voice. She shook her head. "No, obviously you're not. I can't believe this."

He glanced at her, a frown on his face. "We didn't hear anything until early this morning."

"And it took this long to tell me? And the case wasn't upgraded," she said. She was beginning to fume. Not only had the code not been changed until they'd been shot at, but she hadn't been told earlier.

"It was reported to Emir," he said, mentioning his twin and head of the Marrakech branch. "The connection with Stanley wasn't made until just before I left to meet you."

The Pathfinder skated for a moment over a patch of black ice. A minute passed and then two before he spoke again.

"The results of the explosion didn't even make Moroccan news. Stanley's uncle has pull."

"How'd Emir find out?" Her hand relaxed and dropped from her waistband where her gun was concealed. It was an instinctive reaction to danger, perceived or otherwise.

"Our family's employee grapevine."

"Your employees? The ones who work on the family estate?"

"Exactly. The Marrakech estate employees are sometimes our strongest communication device for homegrown cases. This time, one of our maids had a sister whose friend worked at Stanley's uncle's estate."

He offered her a lopsided smile. "Emir went to the mansion as soon as he heard and interrogated the uncle. According to Emir—to quote him, 'he's old, but a crusty bugger.' Apparently, he's an army vet and wasn't intimidated by much, but Emir has a knack about him. If there's information to be had, send in Emir. He's the human bulldozer."

The news of the explosion was unexpected, and she knew, with the connection to Stanley, that it had the potential to change everything they'd thought about this case. She waited for him to continue.

"We're swamped. There's not an available agent on either side of the Atlantic. Emir could only do so much with his time constraints. It's our case, so he's left the rest up to us."

"Anything else?" She thought of the implications, of the possibility that this might end overseas. She swallowed back the exciting challenge of an overseas case.

"The gardener who died in the blast was a new hire. He had no connections to the family. His credit rating was clear—no debt, no grudges that could be found."

"No threat to anyone. Wrong place, wrong time." It was such a common occurrence as to be trite, almost clichéd. Expect the Unexpected was a motto that few people lived by and more should. It was a motto that was almost a religion to her.

"Exactly. But so far we're basing everything on assumption. But it did flush something else out. The uncle obviously has money, and he's a widower. More importantly, he's just updated his will. The new beneficiary is none other than Stanley."

"Stanley?"

He nodded. "It's so recent and been kept so quiet that even Stanley may not know."

"This is crazy," she said. "So Stanley stands to inherit what I assume may be a fortune."

"That's what we have for now. But…"

"You think there's more," she interrupted. This was going south fast.

"Yes." He looked at her with a hint of admiration with an overtone of surprise. "As you know, we've continued a low-key investigation in Morocco into Stanley's background. It's been hampered by a lack of resources. My sister, Tara, will be helping out part-time with the online investigation."

"Computer science is her major," she said. "Perfect fit."

She smiled hearing what he wasn't saying—that Tara's involvement in the business was safe. Tara was Zafir's youngest sibling and only sister. Only months ago she'd been the victim of a kidnapping. Since then, her brothers wanted to keep her safe by sheltering her. But their sister's formidable will was well known throughout the agency. It looked like that will had won out. Jade thought, from everything she knew of Tara, that she'd make a fantastic agent once she finished her schooling. She was smart enough to know not to mention such an idea to Zafir.

"So, Stanley's inheritance, how much are we talking—enough to put his life in danger?"

"More than enough. Around fifty million or so American dollars. That's what Stanley's uncle admitted to Emir," Zafir said. "From what Emir told me of the estate, he's probably not exaggerating."

She shook her head.

"And Stanley..."

"Like I said, Emir was fairly certain that Stanley was in the dark about the whole matter."

"If he knew, I don't know if he could keep it a secret long." Or could he, she thought, thinking of the Stanley who had stolen her rental and bolted. He wasn't as open or as naive as he liked to portray. "So who wins if Stanley is taken out?"

"That's the burning question," he said. "Is it enough motivation to take him out?"

"It's fifty million," she said with disbelief in her voice. "I don't know about your world, but in mine that's a crazy amount of money."

"Which means it's enough to kill for."

"Exactly. Can you step it up a notch?" She heard the edge in her voice. "I know, first I tell you slow down and now I'm telling you to speed up. Kind of contradictory."

"You think?" he asked.

"I know it's slick." She shook her head. "I know— weather conditions. Of all times to get a late storm. Hopefully, Stanley manages these roads. Last thing we need..."

Her words dropped off, for they both knew the other concern. Accidents on days like this were not uncommon. Toss in a traumatized foreigner and the odds just skyrocketed.

Zafir glanced at her with a smile and a slight arch of his dark brow. "We'll get this case roped in and under control," he said. "Weather, assassin, whatever we have to tackle. We've both seen worse."

"We need to know the wording of that will," she

said. Her mind was already moving ahead to other issues. "And next of kin, including those not listed."

She looked at him with a half smile, but she clutched the door handle and squinted into the horizon. She saw what they'd both been looking for—the white flash of metal paint. They'd found the van. But it was also what they were hoping not to see, for the van was in the ditch and from this distance there was only the van in sight. So where was Stanley?

Chapter Eight

Zafir hit the brake and brought the Pathfinder to a stop on the edge of the highway. The sun had broken through minutes earlier and the snow had stopped over ten minutes before that.

Jade had her Colt in both hands. She'd put a bulletproof vest on before they stopped. Now, like her, he made a visual scan of the area before approaching the van.

He adjusted the vest, shifted his grip on his gun and moved in just behind Jade. Big mistake. She had a butt more attractive than any agent's should be. He pulled his gaze back to the perimeter around the van. He crept up beside her. The side of the van nearest the field was sunk lower than the rest, the hood dipping into the ditch. The right front tire was flat. The driver's door was half open as if the driver had exited in a rush. They split up, Jade approaching that side while he moved to the passenger door and pulled it open. It took a good heave to do it. He frowned. The van was old. It should have been moved off the lot rather than rented. Yet in an odd way it had been the perfect vehicle. Plain and unobtrusive, it blended.

The van was empty except for the Wyoming tourism magazine that lay open to a page with a map of Wyoming. A half-eaten candy bar lay beside it and in the back was Stanley's suitcase, duffel and his camera bag.

"He ran," Jade said with that soft-as-butter tone to her voice. She straightened, looking across the field as if seeing immediate danger there. But there was nothing. "Let's hope he didn't get far." Her lips pinched as she looked at the van and back again at the landscape.

She looked down.

"What the…" She moved a few feet from the van and reached down to pick up a disposable phone. It was the kind bought in convenience stores for short-term use.

She flipped it open. "I don't think it's ever been used," she said after she scanned through the call history. "Wait, no, there's a text. Number isn't registering." She frowned. "Doesn't make much sense."

She handed it to him.

"'By your ears.'" He frowned. The phrase was odd and she was right, made absolutely no sense. "I'm not sure what the hell that's supposed to mean if anything." He handed it back to her, and she shoved it into her pocket.

"It's too strange not to mean something," she said with a frown.

"We'll take a closer look at it later. We don't have time to speculate."

He moved along the road, a few feet from the van. He was searching for evidence that there'd been any other vehicle involved. There was nothing. Everything seemed to end here, with the van.

He bent down, his ungloved hand sweeping across the snow as he looked at the footprints.

"Sneakers."

"It was what he was wearing when I picked him up at the airport," she said.

He looked back at her and saw she was squinting. The sun was overly bright against the snow. He'd grabbed his sunglasses before they'd left the vehicle. She lowered her sunglasses, which had been perched on top of her head.

"He must have been terrified," she muttered.

And without explanation, he knew that she was revisiting that earlier moment on the balcony of the first safe house.

"I should have been on him immediately. Instead, I gave him a window," she said with a touch of self-recrimination.

"You were securing the perimeter. Critical work. You couldn't have been two places at once."

"And Stanley disappears on my watch," she said grimly. She held up a hand. "Don't say anything more. The results are the same. It was my watch. You can't deny that." She looked around, scanning the area. "I need to take responsibility so I can fix what didn't work. So I can make sure it doesn't happen again."

"It could have happened to any one of us," Zafir said.

"Doesn't make me feel any better," she said.

"You wouldn't be as good as you are if it did."

He looked along the ditch, following the sneaker prints as far as he could from where he stood. "Let's go," he said.

She took the lead. He followed as she walked

along the ditch, following Stanley's footprints. They'd walked for about a quarter of a mile before the footprints veered into the field.

"No trespassing," she muttered as they approached a metal sign attached to the fence. "Great."

They ducked under the barbed-wire fence and headed into the field, disobeying the sign, following Stanley.

"Look," she said a few minutes later.

In the distance there was a dilapidated small building.

"A homesteader's cabin?" she asked.

"Possibly."

They walked in silence for another few minutes. In other circumstances, it would have been a beautiful walk. Another minute passed and then two as they made their way through the isolated ranch land.

The rotting remains of a shanty that looked like nothing more than one room stood about another half mile ahead of them.

"Do you think he's there?"

He shook his head. "We couldn't be that lucky."

Scrub brush to their left was laden with snow. Silence seemed to wrap around them.

Despite what he'd said, the footprints seemed to be leading directly to the shanty.

"Where is he going?" Jade muttered. "He could take pictures anywhere around here if that's what he wants."

His gaze swept over the land immediately around them. The ground was frozen, but the promise of spring seemed to burst through the snow. A stalk of

wild barley here, a green bud there. It was all beautiful and oddly surreal.

"If he's there, we're close enough for him to hear
us," Jade said. "I'll call him."

Before she could act on it, there was a flash to their
right.

They looked at each other. Ahead of them and just
to the right of the shanty there was a dip in the land
before it rose into foothills. It was the perfect place
for an ambush.

Gunfire echoed through the valley and had them
flat on their bellies.

Jade turned her head, her cheek to the ground.
"What the hell?" she murmured. "I didn't expect that."

"Leave me alone!" came a voice from just ahead of
them, very near, if not in, the shanty.

"Stanley," she mouthed.

"Son of a…" Zafir said through clenched teeth as
Stanley screamed something incomprehensible. "Is
there any way we can get him to quiet down before
he gets himself killed?"

"Or us," she muttered.

Another shot ricocheted off a stand of barren pop-
lars that clustered on the south side of the little structure. This time they could judge the position of the
shots. They originated from somewhere behind and
to the right of the shanty.

Jade motioned to her left. There was another grove
of trees there.

He nodded. It was best if they came in from two
different angles.

"If I head for the trees, I can divert him, maybe get
a look at what we're dealing with."

"Keep low," he whispered. "For whatever reason he's not shooting directly at us. Yet he had to have seen us." He wondered at that.

"We're trespassing. He just wants to frighten us. It could be as simple as that," she whispered.

He nodded. "Don't shoot unless necessary," he whispered. "Let's try to get a handle on what's going on. If it's a rancher, we don't want to appear aggressive and get Stanley killed."

She nodded and moved away, almost doubled over as she kept low to the ground.

He knew that Jade would come in on the shanty from the left. She would work her way through the dips and hollows in the land. He was sure of her ability to keep herself out of the sniper's line of vision. There was plenty of brush now that they were almost into the foothills that she could use for cover. He was going straight in, using the rockier, hilly face ahead of him. He wasn't sure how they were getting Stanley out. But a gunfight was the last option.

Another shot.

He moved forward and saw red plastic sticking out of the snow. A shotgun shell.

Was it possible that they were being shot at by someone armed with a shotgun? Or was the shell just the remnants of an earlier hunting party and nothing to do with their current situation.

Who was shooting and why? The earlier shots in town had been from a handgun, at least that's what they had assumed. A shotgun wasn't easily hidden and not usually the weapon of choice in an urban environment.

He pushed the thoughts away. Now wasn't the time

to build the profile, rework what little they had or think about it at all. He needed to keep Jade safe and then ensure Stanley was protected. He didn't think much about the fact that he'd just put the client last in his priorities.

He looked to his left. There was nothing. Everything was still. His heart stopped. Had she been hit? Was she hurt? He began to move closer to the shanty. He was on his knees and elbows, trying to keep his Glock out of the snow and his head down.

Jade had slipped out of his line of vision. He didn't like not knowing exactly where she was.

He scanned the landscape looking for movement. There was nothing, only silence.

The door to the shanty creaked open.

His grip on his gun tightened and his teeth gritted. Stanley needed to close the door, and if thoughts could direct him to do so, he'd do it now. Amazingly, the door closed.

Zafir's attention veered as a movement to his right stole his attention. A shot, then two. Snow and dirt kicked up near him.

Cease-fire was off. Whoever was out there was now directly shooting at them. Threatening them with deadly harm.

He fired in the direction the shots had come from. But he still had no visual. There was a shout from the shanty, or it could have been a shriek. He wasn't concerned. From the information he had on Stanley it might be fear. He doubted that Stanley was injured, because none of the shots had hit the shanty.

Jade slipped down beside him.

"I had a visual. Just a glimpse. Male—wearing a green-and-brown hunting cap, and he has a shotgun."

"Local?"

"Possibly," she said. "I can't see a sniper using a shotgun."

He nodded. She was right about that. He'd thought the same when he'd found the shell.

"Who are you?" he shouted.

"Get the hell off my land!" came the low, gravelly voice.

"Jade!" This time the frightened voice was Stanley.

"Stay there, Stanley!" Jade shouted as she glanced at Zafir.

Another shot echoed through the valley, seeming to bounce off the hills.

"Cease-fire!" Zafir shouted. "We'll move off, but our friend needs help. Let me get him and we'll be gone."

His request was met by silence.

Zafir moved forward, using a bush a few feet ahead of his previous position for cover. Now he could see the green-and-brown low-brimmed hat poking over a boulder forty feet to his right.

"Nassar Security," Zafir yelled. "Our client is an amateur photographer. He just wanted to get some pictures. He didn't know he was trespassing."

"This is private land!" the man shouted back, as if that was all that mattered and any explanation was null and void.

"He's Moroccan, a foreigner. He didn't know to read the signs," Zafir yelled back. There was a time when property was the most valuable thing a man owned on these windswept plains. That need to protect it was still very much alive. Stanley had unsuspectingly stepped from one bad situation into another.

"He isn't fluent in English. It isn't his first language," he added as if that might make any difference. It was a lie, but it served a purpose in their current situation. He knew Stanley could read, write and speak English perfectly, as well as Arabic and French. It wasn't uncommon for educated Moroccans to be multilingual. He could only guess which one was his primary language.

He waited.

Silence.

He looked back at Jade. Her lips were tight, and she looked worried.

A minute passed, and then two.

"Drop your weapons and put your hands up!" the throaty voice demanded.

The command was unprecedented. The situation was unexpected. None of it was fitting anything that had transpired before in any other case.

"I'll put my gun away," Zafir said to Jade as he slid his gun into his holster and nodded to Jade to stay where she was. He wasn't going to put both of them at risk. He was fairly certain that they'd been cornered by an enraged rancher. With any luck, his compliance would diffuse the situation.

He put his hands up.

"The client is unarmed," he said. "I'm from Nassar Security," he repeated. "I'm an investigator. State licensed," he added, in case that hadn't been clear, and in case the man hadn't heard of them or their reputation. "I'm hired to protect the man in your shanty." He repeated the fact as if it explained everything: "He's unarmed."

He was taking a risk, but now he was almost certain the risk was minimal. He had a gun in the back of his belt that he could reach, and Jade had him covered.

"If you're who you say you are…"

"I am," Zafir assured him. "I just want to get our client back to the city where he'll be safe and won't be trespassing on anyone's land."

"All right…" There was a brief pause. "Your client…" A glint of a shotgun barrel flashed in the sun. "The idiot in the shack," came the now-amused throaty voice. "Get him off my land—I'll give you five minutes."

Zafir moved cautiously from behind the bare bush. It had been the snow that clung to its branches that had offered any real cover. He was surprised that the rancher didn't demand Jade's visual, as well. He had to know she was there. He'd already motioned to Jade to move back toward the road.

"Stanley," he called. He walked slowly as he headed to the shanty. His hands were in the air. There was a glint to his right as the rancher's shotgun winked in the sunlight.

The rancher was standing in full view with his shotgun trained on him, but with the sun at his back and in Zafir's face, he could make out little. He'd raised his sunglasses to appear less threatening, but that also made him more vulnerable as he couldn't see through the sun's glare. The man could shoot him now and say they'd been trespassing, that he'd been justified. And he was right. They were trespassing.

He approached the shanty slowly, as if it, too, were

rigged with an armed attacker rather than just a frightened royal. "Stanley," he said. "Let's get you out of here.

The beaten shanty was only one room, but a closer look told him that it had held up amazingly well through the years. It looked like it was still used. The stone chimney was intact and had soot clinging to it as if someone had recently used it. As he observed that, the broken plank door swung open.

His first look at their client didn't surprise him. He was everything he'd expected and what the photo in his file had portrayed. He was an average-sized man by Moroccan standards. His camera hung around his neck and rested on the top of his belly. His round face was flushed, and his eyes were panicked.

It was always strange, Zafir thought, to see a client for the first time. Who they were on paper was often different from in person. In Stanley's case he was surprised to feel sympathy. He couldn't imagine what this might have been like for him. Hearing gunfire around him, being stuck in a weather-worn, one-room building—having that as his only protection. The man had more than likely never been near firearms, never been this deep into the wilderness. He broke off his thoughts and focused his full attention on getting Stanley the hell out of there.

"I'm Jade's boss," he said, although the truth was that he was Jade's partner, at least in this case. But he guessed that *boss* would have the most clout, get the client out of here without a dispute delaying that. "We're going to get you out of this, Stan," he said. He slipped into the nickname easily. Stan was a man's name; Stanley—somehow that name just grated.

Stanley was shaking slightly. "This is crazy."

"Maybe. But he was justified."

"Justified?"

"You were on his land without permission."

"That's why he was shooting at me?"

"Let's get out of here." He watched behind him to make sure the man was following his instructions. "Follow me. I'll keep you covered."

"He almost killed…" Stanley said as he stopped as if he couldn't take another step. He looked over his shoulder. "Where's Jade?"

"She'll meet us," Zafir said. "C'mon, keep moving." He doubted the rancher's patience was going to stretch much further. "Follow me. Let's get you out of here." He moved ahead of Stanley until they were past the rancher's position, then he moved behind. That made it difficult for the rancher to get a clear shot of Stanley. While the bulletproof vest wasn't a guarantee of protection, it was more than Stanley had.

"Hurry it up," the rancher bellowed. "I'm not going to shoot you if that's what you're afraid of. Unless, of course, you don't get moving faster than you are."

"Let's go, Stan," Zafir said. He looked to his right and could see a flash of movement—Jade. "Walk in front of me and head for the road. I'm right behind you."

He looked over his shoulder. The rancher was still standing, watching them. His shotgun was in both hands but pointed slightly down. In that moment, he realized that the threat was very close to over.

"Keep quiet and keep moving," Zafir said. "We're not out of the woods yet."

"He won't shoot?" Stanley asked.

Zafir prodded him with the palm of his hand. "Hurry up!" he snapped. He wasn't sure how this assignment was going to get better from here. He was scared it might continue to go south. Only a minute into a face-to-face meeting and already he was losing patience.

Ahead he could see the brush where Jade was now concealed. He moved away from her and toward the road, knowing that she'd follow and keep out of sight for as long as possible as she did so. It wasn't anything they'd discussed, just something he knew in his gut. There were moments where he'd just known what she was thinking, where nothing needed to be said. He'd never experienced anything like that before. And it made him uncomfortable, to say the least. But there was something else. She made him feel like no woman ever had. He'd admit that to no one.

He didn't believe in such things—that one could instantly fall for a person. That was hokey garbage. He'd told Emir that many times. But his twin had his own reasons for believing—his fiancée, Kate. Zafir liked playing the field far too much. There were too many fish in the sea to ever settle for one.

He wouldn't be thinking these things if he thought they were still in crisis. But the rancher appeared satisfied, and the drama appeared to be over. This time when he turned around, he saw Jade just behind him. He motioned ahead of him, so that he could stand between her and the last remnants of danger.

He didn't think about what that might mean. It meant nothing. His need to protect her—his fear for her, placing himself between her and danger—it was only what a good man did. But thinking that and believing it were becoming two completely different things.

Chapter Nine

"What is wrong with you people?" Stanley demanded five minutes later as he hurried to keep up.

Neither Jade nor Zafir slowed their pace despite their client's plea. At this juncture they preferred to get on the other side of the fence, to the road and safety. They'd left the rancher well behind them, and the road was in sight. But until they reached the highway, neither of them would feel comfortable.

"Is this country all like this?" he demanded. "Are you all crazy?"

"This isn't the normal way of things, Stan, but property is a big deal in Wyoming. You can't just step onto someone's land," Zafir said calmly and without slowing his stride. But Stanley was testing his patience in a way no other client ever had. He had to remember, Stanley was Moroccan. He'd never been to the States before. According to the file, he'd never been anywhere. He was in a culture that was unfamiliar to him. "He has rights as a landowner. You've got to remember that while you're here. Especially if you plan to take pictures in the countryside."

"He could have asked me to leave," Stanley said.

"That would have been the civil thing to do. There was no reason to try to kill me."

"He could have killed you, Stan. He didn't."

"He has a point, Zafir," Jade said. "I have to say that threatening to shoot him was a little over the top."

"A little?" Stanley asked, his voice an octave higher than normal. He opened the back door of the Pathfinder. "It was craziness. This wouldn't have happened at home. This…"

"You're wrong there, Stan," Zafir said, thinking of the many cases he'd handled at home, in Morocco. He looked at Jade, and she smiled as if she was completely aware of where his thoughts had gone.

"Don't bolt like that again, Stan. We can't protect you if we don't know where you are."

"You don't know the country…" Jade began.

"You're not kidding," Stanley muttered. "This would never happen in Morocco," he repeated, obviously set in what he believed no matter what Zafir said to the contrary.

"Never." Jade smiled as she looked at Zafir, because they both knew it could happen anywhere and had. She might not have worked a case in Morocco, but she'd certainly read the files. "I believe this is yours." She tossed the lens cap to Stanley who caught it with one hand and put it in his pocket without a word of thanks.

"Another thing, Stan," Zafir said. "You can only take pictures of land where you have permission or on land that's not privately owned."

"You're kidding me," Stanley muttered.

Zafir was turning onto the highway before anyone spoke again.

"Is there something you're not telling us, Stanley?"

Jade asked. "The rancher's aggression is extreme, depending how you view such things, but explainable. But what happened earlier, the shooting at the apartment, that's not. Is there a reason that someone would want to shoot you?"

"No," he said almost too sharply, too abruptly. "I don't want to think about that."

"That won't make it go away," Jade said.

"Why do you think I left? I couldn't deal. No one has ever shot at me. And now it's happened twice. This is craziness. You should report that man. The rancher, I mean. I bet we could look up…"

"You were at fault, Stan," Zafir interrupted him.

"From what you've said, Stanley, this incident aside, whoever was shooting at you in Jackson has no motive that we know of. Is that what you're saying?"

Zafir hoped the tact Jade was taking, of feigning ignorance of the inheritance, might lead Stan to reveal anything he knew.

"I'm not important enough for someone to want to kill." Stanley's voice began to shake.

"What do you have that someone else wants?"

"Nothing!"

Zafir looked in the rearview mirror and saw that Stanley was looking out the window; his lips were tight and one hand clutched the door handle as if he were prepared to flee. Again.

"It's all been crazy," he muttered. But his left hand was clenched in a fist and he was chewing his bottom lip.

Zafir was certain that he knew something about the earlier attack. Maybe he knew who or why—possibly both. Somehow they were going to have to get him to trust them enough to tell them. It was only then that they'd be able to protect him.

"I thought this was the countryside. You know, untouched—safe, full of friendly farmer types." Stanley scowled. "Bucolic, like Heidi land."

"Heidi land," Zafir mouthed the words, an amused smile on his face.

"It was misrepresented. Nothing like the brochure said it was," Stanley said.

"You can't just appear on someone's land and expect to be welcomed," Jade said.

"So I'm learning," Stanley said rather sardonically and nodded. "The locals aren't friendly at all." He paused for breath, looking out the window with a grim expression. "He would have killed me."

Zafir met Jade's look. They both knew that Stanley was overwhelmed by the back-to-back experiences with firearms. It was a logical assumption. What layman wouldn't be if faced with the same situation?

For a minute there was silence.

"Insanity," Stanley muttered. He was stuck in a track he just couldn't seem to clear.

"You might be right, Stan, but right doesn't make you safe. We do. So in the future, I don't care what you think," Zafir said. "As long as we're protecting you, when we give an order we need you to follow it. No more taking off."

"Orders?"

Zafir glanced in the rearview mirror. The tone of their client's voice had changed. His eyes had narrowed and his nostrils flared. He'd just acquired major attitude. In fact, Stanley was now sitting up straight and there was a look about him that was very clearly royal. The look in his eyes was unleashed outrage, like they were minions who had failed him. "There weren't any orders, and even if there were, I'm…"

"Suggestions, Stanley," Jade said, cutting him off.

Zafir's mouth quirked as he glanced at Jade. She smiled. It seemed their client with the wallflower personality actually had some backbone. Of course, that backbone had almost gotten him killed.

"I hired you, not the other way around," he muttered before slumping back in his seat. "And you people are crazy. I'm not sure I want to listen to any of you."

"I assume you mean the man shooting at you, not us," Zafir said. "You were trespassing. Trespassing is an offense, it means you were on property…"

"I know what it means," he interrupted with an edge to his voice. "I have an excellent command of the English language."

"And yet you failed to read the no trespassing sign?" Jade asked.

"No, I saw it and the no hunting sign," Stanley added. "But I thought as long as I wasn't hunting, it was okay." He took a breath. "Besides, I was clearly unarmed, yet he shot at me anyway. I'm not sure what he thought. He couldn't miss the camera. It was really unforgivable," he said with a hard edge to his voice. He seemed to be determined to ignore everything they had said including what Jade had just told him about taking photos. "He wanted to kill me for stepping on his scrub excuse for a field." His voice rose two octaves, as if that would put emphasis on the outrage he felt.

"It doesn't matter what you think of his property, Stanley." Frustration was clear in Jade's voice.

"So, here's the deal. We're here to protect you. We

already know from the attack in Jackson that there's a very real possibility that someone wants you dead," Zafir said. "The best way to ensure that happens is to leave our protection. The best way not to…"

"I've got it," Stanley interrupted. "You're right." He ran a hand through his thinning dark curly hair. "But I'm not going back to Jackson." He dropped his hand. "I don't think it's safe. I'd like to go to Casper. I've read good things about it, and there are some good photography spots."

"Agreed," Zafir said.

Stanley had fallen into a plan that was already in the works. Their relocation specialist, Leslie, was at this moment getting that option together. It was the best-case scenario all around. But what Stanley didn't know was that it was also temporary.

"Caspar, Wyoming, it is," Zafir said with a look at Jade. "Do you know what I'm thinking, Stan?" He didn't wait for the man to reply. "I think that there's a little more to this than a photographic vacation."

Jade glanced at him. The real reason that their company was hired had been kept secret from them when Nassar has been contracted. That secret had propelled a gunman to go after Stanley this morning. Stanley wasn't the easy, risk-free tourist he'd been portrayed as—not even close.

"Everything you can tell us will help us do our job." Jade turned to look at him. "Stanley?" she asked softly, ready to use her wiles if that's what it took.

"You have everything you need to know," he said as he looked out the window. His lips were taut and his expression troubled. It was obvious that he had no more to say.

Jade frowned. Obviously her wiles had an expiration date. She looked at Zafir, and when he glanced at her, his dark eyes were filled with amusement. But it was the twitch of his lips and the dimple that she hadn't seen before that almost had her laughing. His humor was contagious. She smiled. If the situation wasn't so troubling she might have outright laughed.

Silence filled the vehicle as the miles disappeared behind them.

A hawk swooped low, its shadow dipping over the highway, paralleling their progress before it swept up and away.

They were alone with one indignant client and more questions than answers.

Chapter Ten

Stanley fell asleep fifteen minutes into the drive to Casper.

"This hasn't ended. Whoever was after him in Jackson is still on the loose, still after him," Jade said quietly despite the fact that Stanley was out cold.

"At least we were able to get a safe house in Casper arranged. With any luck we can get a quiet night, some rest, and get a plan together before any more trouble hits. In the meantime, we're going to have to lay down the law with Stan," Zafir said.

"Who would try to shoot him?" she mused. "Is it all about this inheritance or is there something else?"

Zafir didn't reply. He was concentrating on the road, which was still treacherous.

"You should have let me drive," Jade said with a smile. "I have more experience with winter driving." His driving had been fine, but she'd felt like something needed to be said, something mundane to take their minds out of high gear.

"Are you telling me that I'm driving too slow? First it's too fast, then..." He chuckled. "I think you like to be in control. You don't like being in the passenger seat." He glanced over at her with a half smile. He looked at the speedometer. "All right, you have a point. Once the heat was off and we had Stanley, I slowed down a bit."

"A bit," she said with a laugh.

"Unlike a certain motorcycle rider…" He let the rest trail.

"Look, I'm not usually that risky of a driver." She wasn't sure why she was explaining it to him, but he made her want to justify herself, or maybe the truth was, to prove herself. "It wasn't a normal occurrence—the motorcycle, I mean. I was desperate. Running out of time and…"

"A cab wasn't a consideration," he interrupted with a smile.

"Never," she said with a laugh. "Too far for one."

They smiled at each other. It was a relief to switch the conversation to a lighter topic. It gave them a chance to recharge and open their minds to other possibilities and angles of the case. Angles that they might not have considered in the heat of the back-to-back crises they'd just experienced.

Time passed. It was getting dark. The temperature began to drop as the sun began to slip below the horizon. The highway was rapidly becoming even more slick than it had been before. Now it was a sheet of ice, making driving, even on the interstate, treacherous. With the small city of Casper visible in the distance, Stanley stirred and stretched.

"Casper," Stanley said as he came fully awake and saw the highway sign. "Will it be safe?"

"We'll make it safe," Jade assured him. "I think we've had more than enough excitement for one day."

THEY STOOD OUTSIDE the west unit of a small duplex near the outskirts of Casper. The other unit was empty. The duplex was monitored by a camera that had been placed there during another assignment and kept the perimeter of the building secure.

"We're set up and the area is clear," Jade said to Zafir an hour later. Leslie had let them know that the office was swamped, and although a more permanent place would be found, for now, they weren't at the top of the list. That was one thing that Jade loved about Nassar—none of the brothers who headed the branches of the agency pulled rank unless absolutely necessary. Every employee's area of expertise was respected.

"This case started out as one thing and morphed into another. Everything so far has been out of the norm. I feel like I might have missed something," Jade said with a frown. She folded her arms beneath her breasts, holding back a shiver. The sun had set, and with the wind and the snow cover there was a winter chill to the air despite the fact that it was late April.

"The area's clear. You determined that five minutes before you did the second check." He looked at her, a frown on his face. "Don't question yourself."

She smiled, but the gesture seemed forced; her lips felt stiff.

"You've got it covered," he said with a note of finality.

He was right. The street and the surrounding area were as benign and quiet as it appeared the previous times that she had checked. Other than a sparrow flitting from one bare branch to another, there was nothing except a few parked cars and a shroud of snow.

They'd stopped for takeout on their way into the

city. Now it was only a matter of making a plan and getting some rest.

They went up four wooden steps that led to the front door. In the entranceway, there were two doors, an exterior screen and an interior security door with a dead bolt.

"While you were checking the outside perimeter, I hooked Stan up with an online game. Keeps his mind off doing anything stupid like running again, at least in the short term," Zafir said as he closed the doors behind them.

"I think his 'adventure' cured him of that. At least for now."

They entered a small hallway that led to a minuscule storage area to the left and ran eight feet beyond that to open into a one-bedroom suite.

"Brilliant," she said as she glanced over at the couch where Stanley was completely focused on a game.

"Space Odds?" she asked, guessing that it would be the game Zafir had mentioned earlier that he had been playing online with Faisal a few days ago. She glanced back at Zafir and then wished she hadn't. His eyes were too hot, dark and intense, and inescapable. She looked away, her gaze shifting around the room. She would have looked at anything but him to regain her equilibrium.

"Intriguing name for a game. I'll have to give it a go one day." She couldn't think of another thing to say. She knew it was a game of many levels that involved taking over interplanetary colonies. She knew, too, that Zafir wasn't much of a gamer. That was Faisal's department. She guessed from that and what had already been said that it was an easy way for the brothers to stay in contact even when separated by cases and continents.

She drifted into the small kitchen that was open to the living area and separated only by a miniscule counter. She was at a loss as to what to do. Earlier, it had been different. There had been danger. Danger had allowed her to go into action with a natural surety and no thought to anything but protecting the client. Now she was facing what she considered a legend in the agency. With nothing to distract her, there was nothing to buffer his proximity. There wasn't an unsub threatening them or even a client needing attention. They were trapped in a shoe box of an apartment, and she was more aware of him than she wanted or needed to be. She couldn't explain the why of it, but he'd always intrigued her in a way his twin, Emir, never had.

She'd admired his skill and had studied him since she'd first signed on with Nassar. She'd followed each of his cases, going through the details to hone her own skills. She'd learned from one of the best, and in the process, she had to admit, she'd become infatuated with the idea of him. But Zafir in a cold two-dimensional file was not the three-dimensional man filling this small space. In person, he was so much more.

"Hey Stanley, made the high score yet?" she asked with absolutely no clue what the high score might be. She'd never played an online game in her life and wasn't sure how Zafir had immediately realized that Stanley had. It definitely wasn't in the file, but there appeared to be a few things that weren't in the file.

"Exceeded it," he said with a quiet smile.

"That's great," she said with little enthusiasm as

she glanced around the kitchen area and saw a coffeemaker along with coffee on the counter, a toaster and a microwave. She opened the fridge. Someone had made sure that there was milk, bread, a small jar of jam, and eggs. She closed the door.

An hour passed and Stanley had put the game aside. He stood up, yawning.

"You can have the bedroom, Stanley," she said. "You must be exhausted."

He smiled at her with a look of irony. "Considering everything," he said. "I am and I'll take it." He glanced at the Murphy bed that hadn't been opened. "The two of you will have to fight for that," he said now looking at the Murphy bed with disdain before he went into the bedroom and closed the door.

"We need a plan," Jade said to Zafir. "Stanley seems to think he'll be safe here for the next ten days while he takes pictures in and around the city." She shrugged, knowing that they were on the same page with this, seeing the truth in his eyes, knowing his words before he spoke. "I didn't tell him that it wasn't a good idea. In fact, I didn't say anything. So he thinks that's what's going to happen. But staying in Casper…"

"Not going to happen," he interrupted.

"We're both agreed on that. Whoever is after Stanley may or may not track us here. We can't take the chance that they do, so there's an expiration date on this location."

It was dark, but neither considered turning on another light. It was as if the soft glow from one small reading lamp was enough, as if anything brighter might prove a distraction. She glanced across the room to the Murphy bed that hadn't been pulled down. She imagined that they would toss a coin to see who would use it, or maybe she would give it to him. Jade doubted she would sleep much at all that night; it was always like that after an adrenaline rush. It took her hours to come down and this time even longer, thanks to the presence of Zafir.

She didn't want to admit how he made her feel, not even to herself. She didn't believe in falling in love at first sight. But having him in the same room, for her to feign any kind of sleep when he was warm and hot and hard...

Holy Hannah, this was ridiculous. She'd never felt like this, and she sure as hell shouldn't feel like this now. Besides, her job was too important. Yet the attraction had been immediate and only fueled by her fascination with him for the last year. Ever since she was hired by Nassar she had followed his cases. She'd been drawn to him and she wasn't sure why except there was something in the way that he presented himself. It was strange to think that of a man she hadn't officially met. But it had started from the first moment she'd seen a picture hanging on the office wall of all the brothers. And it was also in the way Faisal had spoken about him. All of it culminated into that one time that she'd participated in an online video meeting that had brought together staff from both the Wyoming and the Moroccan office. She'd watched his mannerisms, listened to his thoughts and said little in that meeting. She'd been overwhelmed with how being in the same time and space as him, even virtually, had made her feel.

Not that that should be a surprise; hard and fast, it was how she ran her life. Everything turned on a dime, from her assignments to her vacations. She'd been known to organize a trip to South America and been on the plane within the space of forty-eight hours. It was not only how one got the best flight deals—last-minute hands down, every time—it was also more exciting. It was why she did what she did and ran her private life as she had. It was also how one made huge mistakes—her last relationship, for one.

She took a deep breath. That was the biggest lie she had ever told herself. Every one of her past relationships had been a mistake. They'd been based on what her body had told her rather than her head, and they'd all turned out badly. Only trips and assignments such as these seemed to work by turning on a dime. Based on past experience, she needed to ignore how she felt about Zafir. Her position at Nassar could hang in the balance. Getting it on with the man who was, in any other situation, her boss was a bad idea. Getting it on with a man who had a reputation for loving and leaving was not smart. But the voice of reason didn't seem to have any power over the feelings that had sprung to life from the first moment she'd laid eyes on him.

She watched as he moved to the window. He stood there silently looking at the street. His thoughts were as silent as his presence.

In the bedroom, Stanley's snores were rhythmic and so consistent that they were almost background noise. She imagined he was sleeping through the trauma, dream-free. He'd had enough trauma for a lifetime. The poor man had had a rough introduction to the United States of America.

Minutes ticked by. She made a pot of coffee and offered Zafir a cup.

She sat down on the opposite end of the couch from him.

"We can keep him safe here, in the States. Yet the danger looks more pervasive than that. We'll know more, hopefully soon," he said, and took a sip of coffee. "I've never liked the waiting game."

"What about Morocco? Can he be kept safe there?" she asked. It had to be considered. "Eventually, he has to go home."

Jade's phone beeped. She pulled it out and answered. "That was Colette," she said a few minutes later. Colette headed all administrative functions including supervising three other office staff. She was the heart of their office, and nothing happened there without her say so. "There was one Moroccan who cleared customs at JFK the day before Stanley and from there went on to Casper via Salt Lake City and from there on to Jackson." She frowned. "He didn't ring any alarms going through security. The only heads-up anyone had was my query. By then he was already long gone." She paused. "His name is Mohammed Jadid."

"So who is Mohammed Jadid?" Zafir asked.

"As in his relationship to Stanley, or if there is one?" she asked. "They've found nothing yet. But there's someone on it," she said. "In the meantime, Mohammed flew out of Rabat's international airport." Her gaze locked on his, and she knew that they were still on the same page. "How many Moroccans flew out of Rabat to Jackson, Wyoming, in the last few days? Two," she said, answering her own question.

"It's still a shaky theory," Zafir said.

"True. But it gets more interesting. After Jackson there's no paper trail on this guy. No vehicles rented, no hotel rooms, nothing."

Zafir looked thoughtful. "It is suspicious. The key question would be what's his relationship to Stan, if there is one?"

"That's what we don't know. Maybe there's nothing, but it's not like Moroccan tourists have been beating a path to Jackson in what is normally off season for skiers. Unless, like Stanley, they're into photographing wildlife. This snow was unexpected and won't stay on the ground long."

"So he leaves no trail. But arrives in Jackson and drops immediately out of sight."

"Does he know Stanley or…"

"Is he a hit man hired to take Stan out?"

She bit her lip.

"Worst-case scenario," Zafir said darkly.

"And Stanley doesn't stand a chance," Jade finished.

"The odds that he's not our sniper aren't great."

"The office is on it. I don't know how soon we'll get anything."

She went to the window as if there were answers there.

"I've been in contact with Emir. He's going to see about getting the contract extended past the original ten days." He looked tired. "If it comes to that…"

They both knew that they'd do what they had to do to successfully close this case and return the client safely to Morocco. Whether they had to escort him or not, they'd get him there. But for now that wasn't an issue. For now, the issue was keeping him alive, and to do that they needed to pin down the threat against him.

"There's something we can't put our finger on. I know you sense it, too. Like Stanley's…"

"Keeping secrets. Knows more than he's telling," he said. "That's a given. We both know that. I think we need to have a long talk with the man."

Another snore rocked the room, and despite the new twist in the case or maybe because of that, they smiled at each other. Stanley was like no other client. It was becoming a very quirky case.

"He's a challenge," she said, but her smile slipped as she met Zafir's eyes, which seemed to smoke with passion. It was a strange state of affairs. She hadn't been with him long enough to know him. Yet she knew him like she didn't know many people in her life. And that frightened her for it could change everything because she'd never wanted a man more.

Chapter Eleven

"He's not giving us anything," Jade whispered, and they both knew that she referred to Stanley. "At least not voluntarily."

It was still dark as they headed into the early hours of the second day that they'd been on this case. It looked like they'd be staying in Casper rather than moving on. The Wyoming office was stretched thin, as a family emergency had one of their office staff on leave and the others even more overwhelmed with priority demands. As there was no sign that their accommodations had been jeopardized, they prioritized the needs of yet another case over immediately finding a safe house for them. They were uncomfortably crowded but safe. It could be another day before they would move again. In the meantime, they would wait it out.

The streetlamp glinted, sending tendrils of light across the short expanse of counter and providing a muted glow in the kitchen. The rest of the small area remained dark. She flicked on the table light beside the sofa and sat down just to rest for a minute.

She must have fallen asleep, because the next thing she heard was her text alert. She looked at her phone.

She'd been sleeping for two hours. The message was
from Colette in the Jackson office warning her that
she'd be phoning in the next minute.

Zafir stood by the sink looking out the window, as
if he could see into the night.

He turned around.

"You're awake," he said.

"Stanley?" she asked.

"Sleeping."

Her phone rang and she answered. A few minutes
later she disconnected.

"We've got our answer about our second Moroccan," she said to Zafir.

"Who is he?"

"Mohammed Jadid is Stanley's first cousin. They're
relatively close in age."

"Let me guess, he stands to inherit should something happen to Stanley," Zafir said.

"Actually, that's the strange thing. No. He's a cousin
on the maternal side, while Stanley's uncle is his father's brother. All inheritance goes through the paternal side. This cousin is out of the loop as he's related
on the wrong side to have a chance at the inheritance."

"Yet he arrived in Wyoming, we assume, following
Stan. Interesting. I don't know what to think."

"I think we need to ask Stanley," she said as she got
up and moved to the small kitchen area that openly
adjoined the other living area.

"You're right, but timing is everything. We both
know that it won't take much to have him heading
home. He's on edge and depending on what the deal
is with this cousin…"

"Agreed. I'll try to gently lead him." She threaded

her fingers through her hair and then dropped her hands to the counter. "There's something else. I'd forgotten. You know when we were in Jackson? It was right after we arrived. I was just playing at getting to know him. You know, asking superficial questions."

"Before the code changed?"

"Exactly. I don't know if it's important or not but..." She shook her head. "No, that's wrong. It could be very important..."

It had been forgotten in the rumble of all that had happened. Yesterday had gone by in a blur as they'd secured the unit and made Stanley comfortable.

"What?" Zafir cut her off as he came over and sat down on a small straight-backed in the living area only a few feet from the kitchen counter where she stood.

"Stanley told me that he got his nickname from his brother."

"Brother? That wasn't in the file. I assumed he was an only child."

"The file didn't speak to the issue one way or the other."

"Prince Rashad would have known," he said. "He obviously didn't think it was important."

"Maybe it isn't." She shrugged. "But we have to cover all angles."

"The case began low-key. The file wasn't detailed as a result," he said thoughtfully. He looked at her, waiting for her to fill him in.

"According to Stanley, his brother has been dead for years. He was older than Stanley. His brother gave him the nickname based on a cartoon character. Apparently his brother told him he looked like the character called Stanley and he's been called that ever since."

"And as a grown man continues to go by that name," Zafir said. "Interesting. So is the information on the brother. What was the cause of death?"

"I don't know. Stanley only said it was an accident," she said, knowing that cause of death could reveal more things sometimes than a living being ever could. "He died twenty-five years ago, according to Stanley. So, since Stanley's thirty-nine now, he was only a child when his brother died." She shrugged. "There was no time to ask more questions. We were shot at not long after the subject came up."

"Considering how this case has changed, we need to find out how his brother died—his parents, too. Although their deaths were a few years later. At least that part was in the file." He glanced over at the bedroom. "Let's not mention any of this to Stan. For now, we'll get the official record. Later, we'll get the unofficial report from Stan. Like I said before, I think if we push him now we chance frightening him, having him insisting on going back to Morocco. I'd like to have a clearer understanding of the threat before that happens."

"I'll contact the office," Jade said. "I have his parents' given names and approximate ages. I was hoping to confirm the information the file has."

"Good plan," he agreed. "Let's make sure that what is there is accurate."

Silence drifted between them and she pulled out her phone and began an internet search. She was looking for information on Stanley's brother. But other than a dry layout of lineage to the Moroccan throne, there was no mention of a sibling.

"I just did an online search while I was sitting here.

Nothing." She frowned as she looked up at him, her fingers poised as if contemplating entering another search. "Interesting. So, we don't have much on his brother, not even a given name."

She frowned. They'd hoped that while they lay low, Stanley would feel safe and tell them what he knew. Interrogation, they feared, would cause him to withdraw. But giving him rope hadn't given them any more information, either.

Early-morning light drifted into the room. It reminded them that they were quickly losing the luxury of time.

"I'll make coffee," Zafir said.

"Great," she said, and returned his smile with a look of appreciation as she picked up her phone, texting her request to Colette in the main office.

"Colette," she said to Zafir five minutes later, "wanted you to know that the new admin is working out splendidly. I believe those were her exact words. We were afraid that training would complicate the shortage of support staff but it looks like she's going to help not hinder."

"She moved faster than I expected on hiring help. In fact, I didn't know the new hire was already in the office being trained." He shrugged. "Bonus, she's a quick learner and should take the edge off our shortage of staff."

"That's not all Colette's done since we last spoke. She's followed up on our case, as well. She checked with Moroccan authorities. They couldn't find confirmation of Stanley's brother's death, either. They found his birth records and we have a name, Chasi el Eloua, and a year of birth but nothing else. He's eight years older than Stanley. It's interesting that the mother's death record is registered twenty-two years ago and his father's twenty years ago. They both died of natural causes. That is if you call dying before you hit sixty natural." She sighed. "I know it's off topic, but that frightens me."

"What?"

"Dying in a hospital of sickness—heart disease, cancer or...I'd rather die in the field with my boots on." She shook her head as if dispersing the morose thoughts.

"Wouldn't we all?" he said with an easy smile, and switched the topic back to the case. "So, his brother was dead before his parents died. That leaves Stan the sole survivor and beneficiary of his parents' life insurance."

"Exactly. That's what he's been living on. But, there's more."

He waited expectantly.

"So far everything is adding up just as it should. Except..." She paused. "We're really stumbling on confirming Chasi el Eloua's death." She took a cup of black coffee from Zafir. "Thanks." She wasn't sure when he'd learned how she drank her coffee. Personal preferences seemed to blur into the background of the case.

"Depending what year he died, the record might not be online."

"Colette checked that. The year Stanley claims Chasi died, records were entered into a manual system that was transferred later to computer. Usually that's just straight data entry. It could have been as simple a mistake as the data entry clerk turned two pages instead of one. That was our initial thought. But we've just discovered that wasn't the case. There is no paper record, either." She ran a hand through her hair. "But I know what you mean. He died in an institution, mistakes, papers not being filed—rare, but it happens."

"Exactly," he agreed. "Twenty-five years ago when Chasi supposedly died, the internet was in its infancy. It may take a bit more digging." He pulled out his phone. "I'll get Tara on it. Colette has enough to do with training and dealing with what we've got going on already."

"I might have a suspicious mind, but in the meantime let's just keep this search as well between the two of us." She looked up and gave a rather forced smile at the sight of Stanley standing tentatively in the bedroom doorway. Her mind went back over what she had said, and she hoped that he hadn't heard their whispered conversation.

"I can't sleep. I'll try to nap later," he said as if his sleep patterns were on everyone's mind.

He hadn't dressed and seemed unfocused in his saggy white boxers and a ratty T-shirt. The minimal dress showed off a bit of a belly and hairy legs.

"Get dressed, man," Zafir growled. "There's a lady present."

"I'm sorry." He looked slightly befuddled. "I'm not used to having company. I usually— I live alone…" He stammered as if that explained everything. His voice trailed off as his face reddened and he turned away, heading back into the bedroom.

"I think the stress of it all, being cooped up with us for so long, is getting to him." She stood up and carried the coffee cups to the sink. When she turned around, Zafir was on his phone.

"The van hasn't been moved yet," Zafir said after he ended the call.

"You're kidding me. I didn't give it a thought…just assumed." She clenched her fist. Mistake.

"I just spoke to Destiny," he said, referring to another of their office staff. "She says the app is still active and the rental claims they've been overwhelmed and understaffed."

"Sounds familiar," Jade said with a laugh.

"I'm going back. See if I can find anything we might have missed." Zafir offered one of his rare smiles and revealed a second dimple that she hadn't known existed. "I should have gone back yesterday."

"It was dark by the time we set up here," she reminded him.

"True, but that's never stopped…"

"A Nassar agent," she interrupted him with a smile. "Nothing you can do about it now. But speaking of yesterday, Stanley said something last night. He said there was something odd about the steering right from the outset. I thought nothing of it with the weather conditions as they were. I thought…"

"Inexperienced winter-condition driver," Zafir finished.

"Exactly."

There was silence as they both contemplated what that might mean.

"Did Stanley end up in the ditch because of poor driving or…"

"You're saying that someone knew that I would rent

it, that I was picking him up." She frowned. "So did they want to hurt me or Stanley?"

"Maybe neither. Maybe it's a crazy theory." His fingers trailed over his chin, and for a moment he ran a thumb and forefinger on either side before dropping his hand. "Why did they rent you something like that, a vehicle that I would almost say was too old to be rented out?" His eyes met hers, probing, seeking answers. "Were there other vehicles available?"

"Of course there were but none of them were appropriate. I wanted something that could hold all his luggage and…" She paused. "I wanted an SUV." She considered the possibilities. "Actually, there was an SUV on the lot. They said it was rented. I never thought about it. I was running late." She pulled her hair back and away from her face. "You're suggesting that there was something wrong with the van? That they wanted me to take it knowing it would break down?"

"Possibly?" Zafir rubbed a hand along the dark shadow on his chin. "I'm no mechanic. But I'm thinking more along the line of other clues. Something we might have missed. We didn't go over the van that closely. Destiny is checking into who rented that last SUV."

"We didn't think there was…"

"Tampering? It's probably a long shot but something we shouldn't discount."

"I didn't think of that… I should have thought of some of this right at the time of rental."

"There was no need to think about it at the time," Zafir said. "It was a simple case then. If I remember right, I told you to take a good book."

"You did," she said with a slight smile, grateful for his attempt at humor.

"I've got a text and a name," he said as he looked at his phone. "The SUV was rented to a group of college students. They took it up to the resort."

"No threat."

"Exactly," he agreed.

"Look, I'll go back. You stay here with Stan. You're better with him," he said before she could protest. "Shock him a little. Push him like we haven't done yet."

"You mean tell him about Morocco? Is that wise?"

"Yes. But don't tell him about the will. See what he knows, what he might volunteer himself."

"When he hears, he may want to go back, or worse, run again."

"He might," Zafir replied. "But I doubt if he'll get by you twice."

Jade could feel color rise in her cheeks at the compliment. But another thought had her more concerned. "I don't know if I can stop him if he decides he's going back."

"Let's do everything in our power to make sure that doesn't happen."

UNLIKE HIS COUSIN STANLEY, Mohammed would never be a prince and it was all because of his parents, but he blamed his mother most. The stupid hag had birthed him and left him and the latter was the only good thing she'd ever done. He'd been screwed from the beginning. The royal lineage came down through the paternal side and was how Stanley became part of the in crowd and why he, Mohammed, did not. As a result, he despised his entire family. He was only the cousin of a minor prince, nothing more, and that had reflected negatively on him his entire life, or at least that was how he felt. Taking Stanley out would be easy; he'd anticipated he'd have it wrapped up in a matter of days.

But Stanley had surprised him. He hadn't expected him to have protection—someone who would shoot back. It wouldn't happen again. Trust Stanley to get a woman to defend him. He would take her out as easily as he'd take Stanley out. She'd only won the first round because of the element of surprise.

Stanley.

The name sent an unpleasant shiver that snaked through him like a bitter tonic. He'd had no use for him as a child, and he doubted he'd become any more impressive since. He hadn't seen him in a long time, and it was only when he'd been approached about this job that he had realized there was even a problem. He couldn't say no. The reward was too high. But it was strange. The whole thing had made him uneasy, brought back childhood memories that he'd thought were long forgotten. He'd never liked Stanley. He'd liked Stanley's crazy brother much better even though he had frightened him. Despite that, he felt no regret about saying yes to taking out Whining Stanley. There'd been better names for him, taunts that had him in tears.

It had all been so easy.

In the beginning.

Now it had all fallen apart.

"Where the hell has he gone?" he snarled through gritted teeth. His heart pounded with the thought that he'd lost his prey, that he was gone, swallowed up in the vastness of the United States. He needed to get home. He hated it here. But first he needed to kill Stanley and collect what was owed him.

Time was running out.

Already his contractor was placing unrealistic expectations on him. Unless something changed, he had forty-eight hours to get the job done. After that, either he delivered evidence of success, or it was not just Stanley who would be on the run.

He looked at the rental agency's locating app. He'd finally been able to hack it and at least now he knew where to start. He could see exactly where the vehicle was. The question remained whether Stanley was with it or not. Anything could have happened, and he wasn't privy to any of that information. What disturbed him was that the vehicle wasn't moving. After being attacked, surely the woman would have advised that taking photographs in the wilderness was a bad idea. So if they weren't taking photographs, what was Stanley doing?

Thirty minutes later he was standing by the white rental van. The sun was just coming up. He turned his flashlight on. The footprints around the van looked like they belonged to at least three people. That was a surprise. Was Stanley traveling with more than just the woman? And if so, who? But the footprints were a confused muddle in the snow, blurring over one another. They were unclear, and even if they weren't, they wouldn't be much help. He was no tracker. It didn't matter; he'd take out whoever was necessary to get to Stanley.

He opened the van door and saw the tourism magazine. He picked it up and flipped the pages. Two pages turned together, one stuck to the other by some type of sticky residue. He pulled the two pages apart and they opened to an overview of the city of Casper, Wyoming, and beside the page title there was a small black mark made by a pen. It was clearly marked for a reason, as if Stanley had decided that was where he would go next. It made sense. There was an airport there. It would be what he would do if he were Stanley—frightened and alone. Have an escape hatch ready to fly home at a moment's notice. If he hadn't gotten away from him already, he'd make darn good and sure that he wouldn't fly home—not unless he was going there in a body bag. His heart sang at the thought of that. Stanley dead meant that he would have succeeded.

His whole body seemed to relax now that failure didn't seem so imminent. Now he had a place. But there were almost sixty thousand people in Casper and no firm evidence that Stanley was there, too. Small by city standards, but a lot of ground to cover to find one man who may or may not be there. That wouldn't stop him. Especially with this much money on the line. Someone knew something, and they would talk.

"Bingo," he said with not even an inflection of a smile. He had to believe that's where he was. He had no other clues. He dug through his pockets and hauled out a half-smoked cigarette and a pack of matches. He lit the cigarette and tossed the match onto the seat, not caring if it burned or snuffed out. He stepped out and slammed the van door, taking pleasure in imagining that that was the gunshot that left the fatal wound in Stanley's head.

"Bang," he said with a laugh. "You're dead."

Chapter Twelve

It was past noon when Zafir made a U-turn and pulled in beside the white van that listed in the ditch exactly where they'd left it. Snow still coated the van's windshield and piled two inches high on the roof. He got out of the Pathfinder and walked over to the ditch. He stopped ten feet behind the van. There he crouched down for a better look at the footprints leading up to the van. There were so many, more than just what the three of them had left behind. But it was hard to tell, because they were inlaid in the snow over and around one another, becoming almost a collage of prints.

It hadn't snowed since just before they'd found Stanley yesterday although the weather forecast had threatened more snowfall. He moved closer to the van, bent down and saw what he assumed from the size and depth was a man's print. He lifted his foot, looked at the sole of his shoe and identified the print as his. Then there was a larger print, a sneaker print, Stan's; and a woman's, smaller, lighter—Jade. But there was another set of prints, ones that didn't match the other three. They were lost at points in the jumble of other prints, but the fourth set never seemed to stray farther than the perimeter of the van. They weren't clear, but what was clear was that someone else had been here. It could have been the rancher, but there were no footprints leading across the field from where the rancher had shot at them. It was possible that he'd come in by road and pulled over, coming to look at the van. That was likely, but his gut was telling him that that wasn't what happened.

There was another option. Actually, he thought as he ran through the possibilities, there were several of them. Whoever was here could be a random stranger. He didn't think that was the best theory. The odds of someone stopping because of an abandoned vehicle, unless they were law enforcement, was slim. Police would have had the van towed. The fact that it was still here made that unlikely.

But there was a third option that troubled him more than any of the others. It all led back to that earlier attack on Jade and Stanley. The person who had shot at them had never been identified as male or female, as American or foreign, and they were now missing. They'd assumed that it could be Stanley's cousin, the Moroccan who had arrived at the Jackson airport and then vanished. But there was no motivation. There were only questions. Why had he arrived and disappeared? Who was Mohammed hiding from? But those questions only led to others.

Who had followed them here? Had the unsub been able to track the van hours later in the same manner they had—through the rental locating device? The answer was yes—the information was there for anyone who was a capable hacker.

He looked beyond the van and could see Ski-Doo tracks. He assumed that was the rancher checking out the situation. That also explained another set of boot prints, smaller than the other's but bigger than Jade's.

He went over to the van and opened the driver's side door.

His phone rang. He looked at the number and frowned. It was Jake. What was the sheriff of Jackson calling him for?

"Yeah, Jake," he answered.

"Zafir. Look, I know that you're mid-case but I thought you might want to know this. Don't know if it has any connection, but we had a car theft late yesterday afternoon. A silver compact," he said, and then went on to give make and year details. "Maybe your guy, may not, but suffice it to say he was heading in your direction. At least that's what the witness had to say."

"You don't get many thefts…"

"Exactly," Jake cut him off. "My reason for calling you. A shooting and a car theft in that short a time frame. I'd say there's a good chance that they're connected. But unfortunately, the car theft is out of my jurisdiction now."

"Unfortunately," Zafir said with a hint of irony in his voice. He thought of the Jackson sheriff's lethargy and willingness to not get too worked up about most of the minor crimes that happened within city boundaries. The sheriff's response could have been easily predicted. "Any chance I could…"

"Speak to the witness," Jake finished. "Not a chance. He's already heading home to L.A."

Zafir clenched his fist. He'd expected as much of Jake but still… "Did he get a good description?"

"Nothing much we can go on," Jake said. "Thirties, male and tanned with dark hair. Foreign, too, I believe he said."

Moroccan, possibly, Zafir thought considering the way that things were going.

"This changes things," he muttered to himself as he pocketed his phone. His theory about what may or may not have happened at the rental agency was beginning to fall apart. Unless there was more than one unsub, but there was no evidence supporting that theory.

He looked once again into the van. He leaned far in and saw the brochure still lying on the front seat, but this time it was turned to information on Casper, Wyoming. The pages hadn't been turned there before. Jade had closed the magazine when they'd left. He'd watched her do it.

"Damn," he muttered through clenched teeth. Beside the brochure there was something else, a match. He picked it up. The end was charred. He spun it thoughtfully around between his fingers. Stan didn't smoke.

Someone else had been here. He looked long and hard into the distance. He could see the little shanty. There was nothing else. No sign of the rancher, no sign of movement of any kind. He pulled out his binoculars. He rolled his finger along the adjustment knob, focusing on the little building. There was nothing except a lone deer grazing nearby.

He had suspicions and needed answers. He glanced to his left and beyond the shanty. He'd seen a glimpse of it earlier, a rough country road that more than likely led to the rancher's home.

He strode back to the Pathfinder and put it into gear.

It was time to get those answers.

ZAFIR HAD BEEN gone over three hours, and it felt like six. There was little to watch on television. Earlier there had been no news coverage of what had happened in Jackson and now, all these hours later, it was old news. There was nothing to read and no one to talk to. She hated these kinds of lulls. She shut off the television after only a few minutes, not interested in hearing any of it.

She doubted that Zafir would find anything. What they had discussed earlier were possibilities, no more. She also knew that he would be in communication only if there was an emergent need. Communications could be intercepted. While there was no identified danger of that, they didn't plan to risk it. Chances were that she would not know anything until he returned sometime later this afternoon or early this evening.

They were still waiting for another safe house. Right now, the only thing that she knew for certain was that the new safe house wouldn't be in either Casper or Jackson, but it would be in Wyoming.

Her phone buzzed, and she took the call from their Marrakech office. When she disconnected, she was more confused than ever. There was a record of Stanley's brother's time at an institution and a notation that he had died. The death had supposedly occurred in a psychiatric hospital in Marrakech twenty-five years ago. He'd committed suicide, according to one of their senior employees. The administrator stated that all they had was the chart information in a hospital file. But there was no copy of a signed record of death. It was all incredibly puzzling. It might mean nothing at all, but it could mean everything.

She turned as she heard Stanley come out of the

bedroom. He'd lain down for a nap a few hours after Zafir left. She imagined that the trauma and jet lag combined were doing him in. Few people were prepared for that kind of adrenaline rush. She imagined it would tire most people, but then neither she nor Zafir was "most people." They lived for that rush.

"Coffee?" she asked.

"Please," he replied. "Sugar. One heaping."

She poured him a cup from the pot she'd made only a few minutes ago. She put in the heaping teaspoon of sugar, dropping a spoon into the unstirred mix.

She carried the coffee over to where he was sitting on the couch. He took it in both hands with a smile and a nod.

"There's something I need to tell you," she began.

Stanley's full lips thinned and his dark eyes looked troubled, frightened even as if he were already anticipating the worst. Cynically, she thought he should be afraid because since the attack in Jackson, they'd allowed him to coast. Admittedly he'd suffered traumas the likes of which most civilians were never asked to go through. Still, they'd given him time. They'd given him an evening to think, a night to sleep and recoup. It was more than time to push Stanley.

"My uncle's okay?" he asked when she'd finished the short version of the explosion on his uncle's estate.

She nodded.

"No one died?" He put the coffee down unstirred.

"Your uncle's fine," she repeated.

Relief seemed to push Stanley back against the couch. He eased his death grip on his coffee cup, but he still looked at her with worry.

"You're close to your Uncle Khaled?"

He nodded and took a sip of coffee.

"Why don't we know about him?" she asked softly. "Why wasn't your relationship in the file?"

"There was no need…" His frown deepened.

"You lived with him for a few years after your father died."

"So?"

"Why didn't you at least tell us?"

"It had no relevance and it was a long time ago. I mean, he's my uncle and we're in contact, but when I lived with him I wasn't twenty yet."

She walked a short distance away before turning to face him. It was a tactic that she'd used before when a client had been unwilling to reveal information. Not asking the most relevant questions first to put them slightly off guard.

"He's your father's brother?" She'd posed the question that way because she wanted as much as possible for the information to come from Stanley. Maybe then he'd learn to trust her just a bit more.

"Yes." He folded his arms. "Where are you going with this?"

"The authorities are fairly certain that the explosion wasn't an accident."

Stanley sank into the couch as if he wanted to disappear. Then he straightened up and leaned forward. The eyes that met hers would have been steely determination in another man, but somehow it was hard to attribute that trait to Stanley. "Was anyone hurt?"

"A gardening assistant was killed," Jade said. "That's not public news."

"What do you mean?"

"Just that the authorities are still investigating."

Darn, she thought, she shouldn't have said as much as she had. Stanley didn't need to know that the outcome from the explosion had been kept under wraps.

Silence sifted through the room. Stanley seemed immersed in his own thoughts. Minutes passed. Finally, he leaned forward and looked at her with new determination on his face. "I've got to go back. Make sure my uncle is taken care of. He's not young. He…" He stopped, his lips were pressed tightly together, and his face was flushed.

There was no doubt in his voice, no compromise, and Jade felt her stomach sink. She'd never met this side of Stanley, and she only hoped that it was controllable. The last thing they needed to do now was to go back to Morocco, to the heart of danger. It was why she'd held back on the questions and on what she told him for as long as she had.

"Aren't there other relatives your uncle is close to?" Jade asked. "One of your cousins, perhaps. They could check on him."

He skated right over that suggestion, his breathing coming fast, almost panicked. "My uncle. He needs my help. I should never have left. Not only that, but the rescue…" His voice trailed off.

"Rescue?"

"I work with a local dog rescue. I organized more than one fund-raiser for them," he said. "I had three fosters before I left. They've been adopted since," he said with quiet pride. "The rescue pays me a small salary. I bring in for them twice that through promotions. That's the deal. I wish it could be more. That I could take less from them, but until now I had no other income."

"What do you mean until now?"

"Nothing. I...I had life insurance from my parents but there was no adjustment for inflation." He shrugged rather pathetically. "In today's world, it's not enough to live on."

She didn't push the point. She was too surprised at this side of him, a charitable Stanley, passionate, if his voice was any indication, about a cause.

She changed the subject. It was something to remember for the future, but nothing she needed now. They had more important, immediate considerations. "Do you know any reason someone would have wanted to kill..."

"Was it the old stone cottage on the southeast corner?" Stanley interrupted in a slightly shaky voice.

"It was. What do you know about it, Stanley?"

"My uncle loved to read there in the afternoon."

"So there was a good chance he should have been there that afternoon?" A thought came to her. "What about you, Stanley? Have you ever been in that cottage?"

"A few times."

The way he said it, the way his eyes didn't meet hers, if she were to guess, she would say he was underplaying his answer.

"Were they trying to kill my uncle?"

"I don't know, Stanley. Do you know anything about his finances?"

"What are you implying?" Stanley asked, with outrage tingeing his words and a flush to his pale face. "Are you saying that I helped him for his money?" He took an outraged breath. "That wasn't the case. I wasn't there for his money." He repeated. "I wasn't."

It was becoming clear that whatever allowance his uncle had made for his death, Stanley knew nothing about it.

"Money changes a lot of things, Stanley." She wasn't quite ready to give up.

"I'm not his beneficiary. He would have told me if I were. Uncle is too organized and efficient to keep anything like that secret, so don't even imply it."

"I didn't imply anything."

"You had that look, Jade," he said. "We might not have known each other long, but sometimes what you think reads on your face."

She took a mental step back. She hadn't expected that, because she'd made a conscious effort to appear as bland-faced as possible.

He shook his head. "But you're right."

"About what, Stanley?"

"Money—not the will. Seriously, I don't know anything about one. I do know he'd talked about leaving his money to charity." He shook his head and his lips were pressed together even tighter than they had been before, as if something else was bothering him. "But we did have an agreement. It was between the two of us. Uncle needs help." His voice was muted as if they were not alone in the room. "A trust—a living wage that would begin when I return. In exchange for taking care of him. He had it drawn up just before I left."

"You should have told us that, Stanley—about the trust. It makes it fairly difficult to protect you when we don't have all the facts."

"It wasn't relevant." Color flared in his cheeks; contrary to what she knew of him, his passiveness, his fists knotted as if he wanted to hit something or someone. "I need to go back." He stood up, striding across the short space to the window over the sink. There was purpose and, for the first time, arrogance to his walk. He stood there for a moment before turning to face her. "There's no choice. I can't stay here." His right fist remained clenched. "Book me a flight, immediately."

"Stanley…"

"If you don't—" he cut her off "—then I will."

"No," Jade said, standing up.

"This isn't working."

"We'll make it work, Stanley. But it takes some give on both sides." She moved over to where he was sitting. "It would be a mistake to go now."

"A mistake?" He looked at her with troubled eyes.

"Wait. Give it some time."

"Time?"

"We need to talk about this. Come up with a plan," she said in a gentler tone. She put a hand on his shoulder, hoping to calm him. She knew that she had to change her approach, curb her impatience and her need to ask him the questions that were nagging at her. Instead she swallowed all that back. As she and Zafir had agreed, pushing him too soon could have exactly the opposite effect. He would only become more determined to do what they didn't want him to do right now—return home.

"Are you even sure my uncle is under protection?"

"Yes. It was verified by our Marrakech office. He's in good hands, Stanley."

"You're sure?"

"I'm sure," she replied. "I'm also sure that there's nothing you could do besides endanger yourself if you left right now. Don't forget that you're still a target. Someone has shot at you here. Tried to kill you. Do you want to lead that danger to your uncle?"

His cheeks paled, and she was glad that he'd sat down.

"Without knowing who they are or who else is involved, we would be flying into the unknown and potentially place you in even greater danger than you were in Jackson. And," she drew out the last bit, hoping to give it emphasis, "you could endanger your uncle."

"Uncle isn't as strong as he used to be. This kind of stress…" He broke off, his voice shaky, his face red. "I know what you said, the danger…all of that. I get it."

He stood up and then sat back down as if his legs wouldn't hold him.

"But the truth is that I can't stay here for the amount of time I planned. I can hold off a day, even two, but eventually I'm going home." He gazed at her with a dark look in his eyes. "With or without you. I've got responsibilities." He shook his head. "It was wrong of me to leave. I don't know what I was thinking. I should have known."

She thought of what she knew, of his cousin. Of the law of averages that said the probability of both Stanley and his cousin being here at the same time for different purposes unrelated to each other was highly improbable. It wasn't even a coincidence.

"Let us get you to a safe place, identify who is after you. Contain that threat. Then we'll escort you home."

He didn't disagree.

"That's a promise."

She knew what a weight it could be to worry about

an elder. She had seen her mother care for her failing grandmother when she'd been a preteen. With only one parent, she worried about that sometimes. Worried about her mother's old age. For now, that concern was eased by the fact that her mother was a vibrant middle-aged woman living her own life, and should it come to that, she had siblings to fill in any gaps.

The thoughts changed her perception of his situation. She looked at Stanley with new respect.

"I feel better knowing that," Stanley said. His eyes met hers, and she could see the worry in them. "I know that he's under protection, but I want to be there for him."

"He has protection 24/7, and if necessary he'll be removed to a safe house." She put a hand on Stanley's shoulder. "He'll be fine. Now all you need to do is stay with us and keep safe so that eventually you can be there for your uncle. Promise me."

They talked for another ten minutes, and it was only after that that she was able to nudge a reluctant agreement out of him.

She hoped that the handshake held meaning for Stanley, that he was a man of his word. For right now it was only the strength of a handshake that was holding him to a rather shaky promise.

Chapter Thirteen

Zafir got out of the Pathfinder and walked up the road past the no-trespassing sign. The air was crisp, the wind had wound down, and everything appeared still. Yet he knew that he was being watched. He could sense it in a way that could not be disputed. It just was.

"Hello," he shouted. "Anyone here?" His words echoed across the snow-covered silence.

He walked another ten feet. "Nassar Security," he shouted as if the owner of this isolated piece of land would know who or what that meant. But at least they might know that he was no threat, willing to cooperate.

Nothing.

He walked, pacing himself. He looked from right to left as he checked for danger. It had felt silly to shout who he was when it was clear that no one was here. But his gut told him that wasn't true. Someone was here.

Everything was still. As before, the prairie grass was covered with a layer of snow, brown stalks peeking through and awaiting the greening brush of spring. Somewhere in the midst of all this he knew the owner patrolled. It was just a matter of where. Would he have a sixth sense and know someone had breached his land? Would he be on a distant acre unaware? He kept walking.

"I have a few questions." His words echoed and fell unanswered. He felt rather silly, but he wasn't deterred. "Hello!" Something seemed to move to his right. He wasn't sure if it was real or his imagination. Again, he identified himself with the hope that the words of warning would be enough and the bulletproof vest adequate backup. There was no shelter nearby, only a boulder more than fifteen yards away and halfway up the slope. Too far to get to in an ambush.

The roar of an engine had him swinging around. A snowmobile was almost on top of him. It was so close that he could only assume that the rancher had been lurking behind a stand of brush not far off the road. It was close enough that he would have heard every word.

"You've got some nerve!" the rancher yelled as he swerved in an arc, his rifle slung across his back, the machine spraying snow around him.

That was a relief, Zafir thought as he noted the position of the rifle. This time, for whatever reason, the rancher wasn't feeling threatened. Maybe his shouted introduction had had the hoped-for result, or maybe walking on the road instead of across his land had done it, or maybe it was a combination of both.

The man turned off the engine and got off the snowmobile. He spat, pulled his rifle off his back and strode toward him. The rifle, which replaced yesterday's shotgun, remained pointing harmlessly away from him.

The man wasn't very intimidating up close. He was small and wiry, his skin was wizened and browned by the sun, his hair was thinning, and only the edges held any remains of his former color, brown. He waved his rifle, using it more as a pointer than a weapon. "Didn't I tell you not to come back yesterday? Don't you know any English?"

"I'm with Nassar Security," he repeated, ignoring the questions and the intended slur. "The man you were threatening yesterday was my client."

"So?"

"A Moroccan royal," he said, as if that mattered, but sometimes more information soothed turbulent water.

"Bloody foreigner," the rancher snarled. "Send them back. Send them all back." He squinted at Zafir as if he'd just realized that he, too, might be foreign.

"Look," Zafir said through gritted teeth. It was an effort to not grab the sun-wizened sack of offal by the collar of his weather-faded jacket and haul him off the ground and give him a good fright. Instead he said with chill frosting his words, "I see you checked out the van. Find anything of interest?"

"Like what?" the rancher spat with an attempt at disdain, but despite the rifle, he'd taken a step back from Zafir.

"Any activity?"

"Another one like you." The rancher jabbed a thumb at Zafir, but he kept the rifle pointed at the ground. This time, though, his finger was on the trigger. It seemed an odd compromise.

"Like me? You mean Moroccan?"

"Yeah, whatever." He spat again.

"When?"

"Why would I tell you?" The rancher glared at him.

"Because I'll rid you of your problem once and for

all," Zafir said in a low, confident voice. "He won't be showing up here again. Neither will I."

The rancher looked at him and seemed to consider whether there was any truth to that before he nodded.

"This morning. He was up to no good. In fact, he was gone as soon as he saw me."

"No good. What do you mean?"

"Nothing." The rancher spat. It seemed that he couldn't say more than a sentence or two before clearing his throat. "He left his trash." He pulled out a pack of matches and tossed them at Zafir. "Here. I have no use for them."

Zafir caught the pack one-handed and turned it over. The cover was embossed with the name of a well-known hotel in Rabat, Morocco. "Thanks for your time," he said with all the poise acquired through family pedigree and an Ivy League education.

"Don't forget you're still trespassing. I'll be watching." The rancher got on his snowmobile. He glared at Zafir and revved the engine. A minute later he shot across the road, heading toward the hills without a backward glance.

Zafir turned around with a thoughtful expression as he looked at the matches in his palm. "A Moroccan." He thought over that possibility, which now looked like it might be a probability. There were other Moroccans in Wyoming, like himself, he thought wryly, and two who had arrived recently. They knew where one was and it appeared that the other may have followed them here. It would be interesting to hear what Jade thought of it all and even more interesting to hear what she might have learned from Stan.

It was looking more and more likely that Stan

had been followed by Mohammed Jadid from Rabat, Morocco, and then his cousin had attempted to kill him on foreign soil. He didn't believe in coincidence. It was unlikely that the explosion on Stan's uncle's estate and the attack on him here were unrelated. With the pieces of the case increasing, it looked more and more likely that they'd soon solve the puzzle. They had to, because without knowing the overall picture, they were shooting in the dark when it came to protecting their client. The drive back to Casper held an urgency that he hadn't felt since the case had been upgraded to code red.

Chapter Fourteen

Jade was restless. She longed for action.

Behind her, Stanley sat at the table, a photography magazine in his hand.

"What do we do now?" he asked. He looked up at her as if he didn't have an opinion at all. "I mean where do we go from here?" He turned a page of his magazine.

"We can't stay here," she said. "You know that."

"I do," he replied. "I don't care what I promised. I can't stop thinking about going home." He turned another page of his magazine without looking at her.

"We talked about that," she said. "You agreed…"

"I know, but waiting isn't easy. I'd rather end this and go home."

"You could jeopardize your uncle by showing up out of the blue."

"How so?"

"There's someone after you here," she said, repeating what she'd told him earlier. Maybe it was stress, but he kept going back to the same need—to go home. "You're safe here, Stanley, in this place." She wasn't sure for how long, but they would be gone long before that ever became a problem. "They could follow you back to Morocco." She wasn't sure why she said *they*. There was only one person doing the shooting in Jackson; she imagined should they be followed, it would be one person again. The question was, who was that person?

"I never thought of that." He shook his head.

Even though she'd told him before, he hadn't remembered, hadn't heard—she wasn't sure which.

"Why does it have to be so complicated?"

"Money complicates," she said, thinking of the will. "Most of the time."

"I won't, just so you know," he replied. "Take off on you, and go to Morocco, I mean. But even saying that makes me want to jump on the first plane."

He turned to look at her, and she could see his frustration. He'd been confined to this small space for too long. She didn't give any thought to the fact that she had been stuck in this space, too, because it wasn't something that bothered her. She missed the adrenaline rush of the action, but she'd been in worse places, smaller places, on different assignments. It was a matter of distraction, taking your mind off the discomfort, which could turn into claustrophobia. Her own apartment was barely over four hundred square feet.

"On a completely different topic, if I'm not going immediately back to Morocco, then I'd like to take some pictures," Stanley said. "I mean when Zafir comes back, of course. Otherwise, we have no vehicle." His dark hair was mussed and he didn't look at her as she set a cup of coffee in front of him.

She'd scrambled eggs for him earlier, but if they were here much longer either she or Zafir was going to have to do a grocery run.

Rather than picking up his coffee, he stared rather morosely at it as if it were an alien entity.

"This hasn't turned out at all like I imagined."

She felt for him in that moment as his hazel eyes met hers, full of sadness and regret. For the first time she could totally relate to the man. Once, his worries had been about mundane issues; now he feared for his life and that of his uncle.

"I'm sorry you've had to face all this, Stanley. It's a little much for a layperson, but you've done fabulous." There was no point in mentioning the fact that he'd bolted and endangered himself further. That was in the past. "There's not many that would be shot at and remain as cool as you did."

He laughed. "I was scared to death and you know it."

She smiled back at him. "As far as taking pictures in the countryside, I'm not sure that it's safe. Whoever was trying to take us out in Jackson is still at large, and we have no identification on them."

"I know." He took a sip of coffee. "They're still out there. But we can't be squirreled away in here forever."

They didn't have a choice, because there were things he didn't know that he wasn't ready to know. She thought of his first cousin who was here and for only one reason that she could see: to kill Stanley. It was a guess and not confirmed by fact, yet. But she strongly felt that it was only a matter of time before he followed Stanley here, to their new safe house.

"No," she agreed. "But when we leave Casper we'll be able to function more normally and you can take some pictures. I promise. We'll get it all set up so that everything happens as close to what you planned as possible."

He looked slightly mollified at that information.

This time when he met her gaze, there was a look of guilt in his. Her intuition told her that the intimacy of just the two of them, the time that had passed since it had all happened and the revelation about his uncle might be the catalyst for a confession. Instinct told her that he knew a lot more than he'd revealed so far.

"Do you have any idea who was shooting at us in Jackson, Stanley? Do you have any enemies, someone who might want you gone?" She didn't add anything she already knew or suspected. She wanted Stanley to make his own pronouncement to prove once and for all that he trusted them. For without his trust, they had no ability to protect him short of locking him up.

"It would help us keep you safe, Stanley, if you would trust me."

She sat down across from him and put her hand over his. He looked down and then sadly back at her. He pulled his hand away and gazed at her for the first time as a man in charge of his own destiny.

"All right," he said gravely. "But you might not like what you hear."

"Try me."

He folded his arms, his brow furrowed as he sat back and a minute passed, then two. Then he began to speak. But the story that he told her had her wishing that there was something stronger to put into their coffee—for both of them.

But that wasn't an option. The new reality cast a dangerous shadow and put an edge to their case that hadn't been there before.

"It will turn out all right," she said.

"Keep it between the two of us," he said. "Don't tell Zafir, please."

"Stanley. I can't promise…"

"I know, but I don't want to be pressured into something when the truth comes out."

She could see his point. Zafir was strong and opinionated and could easily influence Stanley.

"I'll make sure he doesn't pressure you. But he'll obviously have some thoughts on what can be done, as do I. We only mean to make sure you're safe, and your uncle, too. If that means going back to Morocco, then that's what we'll do. But I'm not completely convinced of that. Let's just agree not to do anything rash." She met his dark eyes. "And that you trust us."

"Fair enough," he agreed. "I can't ask for more."

She wasn't sure if any of them could.

HE WAS BLOOD, and blood mattered. He'd believed that once, a long time ago. Now he knew that was a lie.

All that mattered now were the connections it afforded him so that he could go places and do things. For that, he needed money. Family connections were about to provide that for him, too. Best of all, family was going to allow him to play the ultimate childhood game. He'd get to torture Stanley one more time.

Stanley was nothing if not predictable. At least he'd been predictable until he'd come to the United States and hooked himself up with people paid to protect him. They'd been in Casper two days, and it had taken Mohammed that same amount of time to find them. Confined to that small apartment duplex, two of them and Stanley, who was used to living on his own and on his own terms; he couldn't imagine it. He would be going crazy by now rather like a rat in a cage.

He remembered how he and Stanley's brother had tormented him as a child. He remembered how they'd used his soft nature, his love of animals, to their advantage. But it was Stanley's brother who had taken that tormenting one step further. "By the ears," he'd say before he'd kick Stanley or better yet, a stray dog, for that was always guaranteed to set Stanley off more so even than his own pain. It was the first sign that things weren't quite right with Stanley's brother. But they got worse, much worse, and it was other, more brutal acts that finally had Stanley's brother locked up.

Time in what in those days had been called an asylum had only made Stanley's brother angrier. But it had made him no less violent. When the family had received the news notifying them of Chasi's death, he knew that it had been a grievous time for his aunt and uncle, but it had also been a relief. They'd been willing to believe anything that would relieve their pain.

Now, everything was working as planned; all he had to do was come through to get his promised share. One down and one to go.

He smiled. Now, with his uncle dead in the explosion in Rabat, Stanley had inherited, and with Stanley about to meet his maker and if he could succeed with the illusion that Stanley's brother might be back from the dead, and drive Stanley a little crazy, there was a fortune to be had. Illusion was everything. He was about to take his share; it was waiting for him right now in a Moroccan bank. As soon as the last act was complete and Stanley was dead, he'd get the code to complete the transfer. It was as brilliant as it was frag-

Chapter Fifteen

Shortly after Jade's conversation with him, Stanley went to lie down, claiming a headache.

Three quick knocks on the door. It was her and Zafir's agreed-upon alert.

She opened the door, and snow sifted into the small room, along with a blast of cold air that swirled around her ankles. She backed up. "It's gotten worse again out there."

"I can't believe this weather," Zafir said as he came in. He stomped snow off his feet. "Not that I'm surprised. In fact, I'd planned to do some snowboarding before all this came down." He smiled. "Faisal got me into it on the last trip." He took his boots off and then gave her his full attention. "What's up?"

"Sit," she said in a quiet tone. Knowing that his banter was only a screen in case their client was listening. "He's sleeping."

He came into the living area and sat down on the couch.

"Did you find anything at the van?"

His gaze roved over her like he knew her secrets. The thought of that sent a tingle through her that made her look away.

"There was evidence that someone else had been there. Not that that alone indicates anything, but the rancher gave me these." He held up the pack of matches from the Rabat hotel. "I went back to speak to the rancher and he confirmed that there was a man there who took off as soon as he saw him. In fact, it was earlier this morning. Ironically, I missed him by a matter of hours. He said that he was foreign and he was pretty sure that was who dropped the matches. He found them in the ditch. Anyway, Moroccan, I'd say from the look of these matches." He tossed the matches, and she caught them with one hand. "He also mentioned that the man was like me."

She looked at him with laughter in her eyes. "I'm betting, being the open-minded type he seemed to be, that didn't make him too happy."

"Not at all. Anyway, looks to me like we've only got one man after Stan."

"A Moroccan. Matches the airport security info," she said thoughtfully. "So he landed here and then made his way to Jackson following Stanley."

"He's our shooter?" she asked.

"Good possibility."

"The question is, where is he now?"

"And why does he want Stanley dead? Mohammed doesn't inherit. He has to have something to gain, but what?"

There was silence in the wake of the questions. They had no motivation, only too many coincidences.

"How'd Stan react to the news about his uncle?" He glanced over her shoulder to the bedroom where Stanley was snoring softly. "Did he finally come clean while I was gone? And told you not to tell me, too, I'm betting." He smiled, slow and lazy.

"He knew a lot more than we thought." She leaned back against the hard little sofa. There was a distance of only a few feet between them, and yet it seemed like there was no space at all. "In fact, it's a lot more complicated than we thought. He has the family from hell."

Zafir ran the back of his hand along his chin, where he had a good start on a beard.

She stood up and went to the window. Sleet drove in a white curtain, angling across the street and adding a white backdrop to everything. She turned from the window.

"Stanley revealed a lot while you were gone. He didn't want me to tell you," she paused. "I think you intimidate him."

"Enough to keep him in line," he gritted.

"We can only hope," she said with a smile. "Anyway, it appears he has a trust fund that he failed to tell us about."

"A trust fund?" Zafir looked at her with a frown.

"He claims it's recent and he didn't want it but his elderly uncle, who he apparently takes care of, insisted on it. One hundred and fifty thousand US dollars a year for life. All he has to do is continue to take care of the uncle."

"Explains the trust."

"Not totally," she said with a smile. "Seems Stanley is a dog lover. Promotes and donates any spare money he has to a dog rescue he supports. He's giving the majority of the trust to the rescue. And oddly, I don't think he knows anything of the inheritance."

"Doesn't know or won't admit?"

She shook her head. "I think he's telling the truth about that."

"So his cousin follows him here to kill him," Zafir said with a note of speculation in his voice.

"Possibly," she said. "Money aside, the interesting thing is the message on that phone, 'by the ears.' Turns out his brother was a sadistic..." She shrugged. "There's expletives that would fit but I'll leave it to your imagination until you hear the rest. Anyway, he'd torture animals often just to upset Stanley, who was an animal lover from way back. 'By the ears' was what he'd say to taunt Stanley before he either hurt him or a pet or another animal."

"So the message displayed on the phone is rather like a voice from the grave?" he said with a hint of irony in his voice.

"Possibly someone wants to have us believe that."

He nodded. "So we need to do some research on his brother's death. Maybe there's a connection we're missing. Another witness—something. What did Stanley say about it?"

"Not much. He was pretty young when it happened and, as we know, his brother had been confined to a psychiatric hospital where he eventually died. While Stanley originally told me it was an accident, he finally admitted that the family was told it was a suicide. There was no funeral and he has no official record. And we already know that there's nothing online. But the Marrakesh office has confirmed that there's a chart notation but no official record of his death in the institution where he died and that it was suicide"

"He died twenty-five years ago. That's a long time."

"It is and sadly I don't think there were many tears

shed when he died. Before he was institutionalized, his brother's abuse was pretty horrific. Stanley claims that he still has scars. Sounds to me like his brother, Chasi, was unbalanced. I can't repeat all the stories, maybe Stanley can tell you, I... It's horrible."

"It's all right, Jade. If Stanley is up to it, I'll let him tell me. First hand is better anyway."

She looked at him with relief. "There's more. I mentioned the will, he claims to know nothing about it."

Zafir let out a soft whistle. "I think we need to have a long talk with Stanley.

After that, for a time, neither of them slept. There was too much to consider, too much to reconfigure and consider again. But in the end, they realized it was Stanley who might have the answers, the final pieces of the puzzle, and his snores were still filling the small space.

Finally, as the night waned, they catnapped, in shifts, one taking over from the other.

It was an hour from daybreak when Zafir's phone rang.

Minutes passed before the call ended.

"They have a house that has everything we'll need. Thirty miles from here. The team is securing it now. It will be ready—" he looked at his watch "—later today."

"I hope we can keep him safe. That whoever—"

"Jade, it will be fine," he said, cutting her off. "Your success rate is one hundred percent. Any of our agents would kill to have you on their team, you know that," he said.

It was odd hearing the praise, for she knew that sort of thing was rare for him. There wasn't much she didn't know about him. And as she thought that, she missed the fact that he had closed the space between them. But those thoughts were pushed aside as he moved close, too close. His hands were on her shoulders, and she couldn't think or say anything. She could only instinctively respond to the hot need that erupted as his lips crushed hers. She knew that it wasn't in her power to stop him. She wanted this as much as he did, and all she could do was kiss him back. The kiss deepened, and he was demanding as much as she was wanting. It was a dance that was causing her body to tingle, her core to crave and her being to want more of him. Her breasts were crushed against the hard, toned wall of his chest. Her arms were around his neck. Her fingers tangled in the soft curls that wove seductively between her fingers. His tongue stroked the seam of her lips like an artist.

She melted deeper against him. She forgot all the reasons why she shouldn't do this, where they were, who they were…

It was the last thought that stopped her.

She pushed him away. Holy Hannah, this should never have happened, and it definitely couldn't happen again.

"Stanley," she reminded him.

"Is a name I'm beginning to dislike," he replied. The wry humor in his voice seemed to drift between them. But the space between them didn't cool. The hot, smoldering look he gave her said everything. It was as if he were willing to take her here and now as if… Her palms felt damp, and her heart tripped slightly at the thought of what she felt and what she suspected he wanted to do.

SHE TURNED AROUND and walked past him. Zafir watched her and really wished he hadn't for his gaze couldn't help going down to a perky butt that… That was twice he'd been caught by that part of her anatomy. He needed to pull his gaze away, to take his thoughts from the soft, rounded… It took everything he had.

Curves.

He wrapped his palm around the back of his neck as if a stranglehold massage would stop his thoughts. But his hand was only hurting his neck and doing nothing to stop the overwhelming awareness of her as a very attractive female. He wasn't sure what would help, but physical pain wasn't doing it. He dropped his hand.

He was unable to drag his eyes from her. Her figure curved in all the right places. He wanted to run his hands over her. He wanted to do so much more.

He couldn't.

He pushed the thoughts from his mind. They had a case to solve and a client to protect. He turned around, heading for the bedroom. He knew she'd gotten information from Stan, but after what he'd learned, he thought it was time they both sat down and had a long talk with him.

"Damn!"

Jade turned from the kitchen window and as she did, he met the question in her eyes. He stood in the doorway of their client's room, his fists clenched, all thoughts of passion or attraction forgotten.

"He's gone."

Chapter Sixteen

Jade pushed past Zafir. The window was open; the blinds were rolled crookedly. A gust of wind knocked them back and forth. They hit the wall with a dull *clunk*, waited a second then two and then clunked again. It was like each *clunk* was reminding them of the danger. Her heart pounded so hard it hurt. Her mind screamed that this could not be happening again. She took three calming breaths. It didn't change the fact that he was gone.

Oddly, she didn't blame Stanley. They'd been here for too long; he'd been cooped up too long. He was tired of it. He'd told her about his disappointment and, at one point, even his heartache at not being able to take the photographs he planned. He'd also demanded to go home. But he'd given his promise, and that meant something to him, she knew that. He'd made that quite clear in the beginning.

"He's left a note," Zafir said. He held up a scrap of paper that looked like it had been torn from the cover of the magazine he'd been reading. "It says he won't be gone long. Don't bother looking for him."

"Don't bother looking for him?" she repeated, not sure that she'd heard right. "What is he thinking?" She couldn't believe that it had happened again. What had she needed to do, chain him to the bed? "We screwed up. Stanley's no ordinary inexperienced guy."

"Excuse me?"

"Inexperienced, yes. But we didn't factor in that he's royal," she said. "He has royal attitude. He thinks he can do things for himself, that he has that right."

"According to this note, he's left to do what he came to do," Zafir said. "He cites some advice you gave—as in manning up." There was a grim twist to his lips. "You said that to him? Don't you think that the lingo for one is rather, well, sexist?"

"Unfortunate wording. But it was just in the context of a long conversation, not as something he should do now," Jade said, striding toward the door. "I didn't expect..." She shook her head. "I told him that he needs to learn to be independent, it was part of manning up..." Sometimes she just talked, the words alone calming, and with Stanley that's what she'd done. And the truth was that they'd spent a lot of hours together, alone. She admitted now that there may have been things she'd said that would have been better left unsaid. But there was no going back.

"We don't have time to waste," she said. "We need to hit the street and get him back."

She strode back into the bedroom. She sensed or maybe just hoped that there was something else, something they'd missed, some clue. She stuck her head out the window.

She looked up and down the street, but there was no sign of Stanley. The only thing that was clear was the silence and the fact that the sun was just beginning to rise.

She looked at her watch. It was 5:45 a.m. Stanley had been gone less than an hour, because he'd come out to get a glass of water an hour ago.

"I should have seen this coming. I spent the most time alone with him." She gritted her teeth, pushing back from the ledge, but she was still reluctant to leave the window as if there was a clue there they'd missed.

"He had his camera with him," Zafir said.

She turned around. "How do you know that?"

"The dresser is empty except for his photography magazine, and that's where he kept it."

"I'm betting he wants a good picture of the aftermath of the storm at daybreak. I'm betting this is also his way of showing us that he can be independent. Take care of himself." She backed out of the room. "Could it be as simple as that?"

"So he jumped out the window to do so?" Zafir looked at her disbelievingly as he followed her out of the room. "Really? I think it's more likely he's going to leave town."

"Let's skip the airport run for now. He's had no time to book a flight, and I have his passport."

"You do?" he said with a smile. "Brilliant."

"Besides, my gut says that his intention is innocent. He likes to take photos in the early morning. Considering my earlier conversation with him, I don't think he's left never to return. He's not stupid. He's already felt what it was like to be shot at and to be on the run. I think he plans to come back. In fact, I'm positive. He knows he needs us."

"Convince me of that," he growled.

"There isn't any time. There's a good possibility that whoever tried to kill him in Jackson is here in

Casper. This isn't a big place." She grabbed her jacket and headed for the door. "For now we go with the simplest option. That he's only taken his camera to take pictures. The best place for that, if you don't have a vehicle, might be the park that's not that far away."

"I hope you're right," Zafir said. "When I find him I'm going to…"

"Do nothing," she warned. "Unless you want him to bolt for good."

"Wait," Zafir said. "Before we go anywhere, I just want to say that this would have happened no matter what either of us would have said or done. Stan is stubborn. He's also a grown man."

"You're trying to tell me that it's not my fault?" she asked. She shook her head. "Thanks for that, but I wasn't blaming myself. I know he makes his own choices. We can only guide him. We can't make him follow instructions. Besides, this happened on both our watches."

A hand on her shoulder spun her around. Before she knew what had happened he was kissing her, hot and so sensual that she could only sink deeper into the kiss. It ended as quickly as it began. "Let's go," he said.

Zafir pushed the outside door open, and a rush of cold air met them.

Daylight was still just a promise. The snow reflected the glare of the streetlights and prevented the street from being completely dark. It was snowing again, and the flakes were sharper, colder as they bit and stung, and were quickly dashing away any evidence Stanley might have left behind.

Zafir looked up and down the street, but there was no sign of Stanley.

"He can't have gotten far. He has no transportation, and it's not as if there's a cab waiting outside," he said. In fact, the street was silent, the nearby houses still in darkness.

"He's gone to the park," Jade said. "I'm sure of it. He was determined to take pictures. He loves this time of day, or at least daybreak." They were walking toward the Pathfinder. Zafir opened the driver's door.

"There's nowhere else," she said. "Let's just hope he's alone."

There was no one on the street, and yet as the night thinned, it seemed that the danger only settled even deeper around them.

She clutched her gun as if it not only offered comfort and protection but answers. They didn't know who threatened Stanley's life. They only had theories but no facts. She was very afraid that Stanley had just walked into the trap of whoever wanted him dead.

"Stan might be naive and problematic, but one thing he's not going to be is injured or worse. Not on our watch," he growled. "If I have to tie him to my side."

"That might be our only option," Jade said, but already there was a sinking feeling in the pit of her stomach. "Let's move."

She took three steps and had her hand on the door handle. "If I'm wrong, the other option is exactly what you said, that he's halfway to the airport," she said. "He is resourceful."

"I trust your instincts. But I draw the line at resourceful," he said. There was an edge of humor in his voice. "He leaned pretty heavily on you at the airport," he said as he pulled out. "And he can't fly without his passport."

"Need I remind you that he's slipped our radar for the second time."

The look he gave her might have leveled a lesser person, but Jade had faced that and more in her lifetime.

He turned a corner and the Pathfinder slid as he pushed it just a little faster than conditions allowed. He steered it easily out of the slide without losing any speed.

They passed through a newer residential area where the snow-covered front lawns and houses with attached garages, front porches and bay windows all looked alike. There was no movement on the street; everything was quiet. Like the earlier block, the occasional house light was on; otherwise there was nothing. She had her eyes trained on the road, looking for Stanley or a sign that he had been here. But there was nothing to suggest that Stanley had come this way at all.

"You've got to agree," she said, "socially inept or not he's proven himself to not be a stupid man."

"I never thought he was. But I know what you mean. With the information we have at hand, we could never have expected what's transpired so far. It all seemed laid-back and easy, and to be fair, it was presented as such by Prince Rashad who contracted us in the first place."

"A false presentation. Neither Stanley nor this situation is any of that," she said, thinking of all she'd learned about Stanley in the time she'd known him.

Ahead of them was the park. It was five blocks from the safe house. It was the only place within walking distance that was good for nature shots, the kind of photography that Stanley loved.

Zafir had turned off the lights before he pulled the Pathfinder over and parked. They were a half block away, a safe distance not to call attention to themselves.

Jade had been holding her gun with one hand. She put both hands on the Colt as if that were somehow reassuring. But in a way it was—she had a love affair with her gun that no one understood, at least no female in her life. She'd always had different interests. Her mother had once said that she'd make a better son than daughter. It was true, except physically, and that was the part that made this job a challenge. She didn't have the physical size of a man, and thus she had to rely on her wits, her self-defense knowledge and her skill with her gun.

"Ready," Zafir growled, breaking into her thoughts. "Hopefully this is where…"

"I see movement," she cut him off. "To the right. It's hard to tell. We're going to have to get closer. It could be anything, a stray dog…" But that seemed unlikely considering the neighborhood they had just driven through. It was a neighborhood where the dogs were designer and contained, not stray and unpredictable.

A flash of light streamed in a thin line across the snow and then was gone.

"A camera flash," she guessed, and gripped the door handle with her free hand. "A good chance that it's Stanley. We need to go in."

"Not yet," he said. "I have a hunch."

Orders again. She gritted her teeth. She wasn't tolerant this morning. Maybe it was the fact that Stanley had managed to slip their protection for the second time. Maybe it was just because her head hurt from lack of sleep. But something felt like it was going to snap. She bit back what she wanted to say. This was no time for nitpicking. This was time to keep it together, to work together.

She ran her thumb along the barrel of her gun while her eyes swept the park. She glanced over to see that he had his gun in his left hand. But the casual way he was posed indicated that he wasn't so sure that the flash they'd seen was Stanley or that there was danger.

She wasn't so sure.

"Look," she said with a motion to their left. "We need to go, he's not alone."

The sun was rising and they could see Stanley just inside the park entrance. But it was the movement to his left, too distant to be clear, that had Jade concerned.

The unidentified man moved to Stanley's right. The sun was higher. There was enough light now for him to cast a shadow.

"Whoever is behind him means business. He's got a gun." She rolled down the window, prepared to lean out and shoot if necessary.

Both hands were on her gun, the weight of it almost a caress against her palm. Oddly a fleeting thought ran through her mind that the gun was a promise, a promise that it would not let either her or Stanley down. She leaned out through the open window, ready to go, to take it to the wall, shoot, kill, if necessary.

"We've got to go in," she said, knowing that the chances were slim that they could reach him unnoticed.

There was a glint of metal where the other man had slipped to the edge of a grove of shrubs. All they needed was for Stanley to turn. That could be deadly for him. But whether he turned or not, it didn't matter. The other man could only be after Stanley. She could see no one else in the park. It was a matter of time before he took him out.

Stay focused, she thought, as if somehow her thoughts could reach him. *Don't turn, whatever you do, don't turn.* She was afraid that if he turned it would trigger an attack. Right now the man shadowing Stanley seemed content to do just that.

"Hang on," Zafir said.

"What are you doing?"

"Providing a distraction."

He started the engine, the sound getting the attention of the men in the park, but before either could move, he'd gunned the engine and the Pathfinder spit snow as the tires spun. He let up on the accelerator enough to get traction. The vehicle bounced over the curb and into the park, moving fast enough that the two men had no chance to react immediately. Once they did, Stanley froze. The man shot at them, cracking the windshield.

"Down!" she screamed at Stanley. She was hanging as far out the window as she dared. She shot at the thin, dark-haired man holding the gun. The man who appeared to be stalking Stanley.

Missed.

"Get down," she screamed at Stanley again.

Stanley dropped into a crouch, his hands over his head as she fired again.

The other man shot once, twice.

Zafir slammed on the brakes. As the vehicle jerked

to a stop they were both out, using the doors for protection.

Meanwhile, Stanley was on his knees and then crouched down and moving. He dived behind a hedge and was out of sight and immediate danger.

The other man had moved far enough away, using a grove of bushes on the opposite side, that it was hard to get a clear shot. As they moved from the vehicle to the cover of nearby trees, he bolted into the open, stopped, and then turned to shoot wildly at them.

Gunfire echoed through the park.

Something threw her off balance and she almost fell.

"Are you okay?" Zafir was there, covering her as he stood over her, gun in hand.

"I…" She looked down, expecting to see a gunshot wound, blood—there was nothing. Only her jacket sleeve was ripped open. Otherwise, she'd been lucky. "I'm okay."

"You're sure?"

"Yes."

Zafir nodded. "I'm going after him. Get Stan out of here."

He grabbed her other hand and pulled her to her feet.

As Zafir took off at a lope after Stanley's attacker, she went over to where Stanley stood hidden in the midst of a thicket of shrubs.

"I can't take any more," he blurted out. "Why didn't you tell me that my own relative wants to kill me? My very own cousin. I can't believe this."

"Truthfully, we weren't one hundred percent sure

until now and if we'd told you, I thought you'd demand to go home."

"You were right, and you wouldn't talk me out of it," he said quietly. "Uncle needs my help. I don't know what is going on but I don't like it not one bit. If I'd known, but I didn't recognize him until I was flat on my belly in the bush, watching."

"You were safe…"

"Was I?" He cut her off. "My cousin Mohammed comes out of nowhere trying to kill me. Why is he here?"

She had him by the arm. "I don't know," she said.

"Something's very wrong. What's going on?"

"Let's get you out of here."

"I'm going home. I don't care what I promised." His lips were taut, and his eyes looked haunted. "I can't take any more," he whispered again.

She dropped his wrist and instead put an arm around his waist, as if somehow that would both comfort and contain him. "It'll be all right, Stanley."

He pulled away from her. "All right," he spat. "You call this all right. I've been shot at, hunted down like…" he stammered. "My cousin came out of nowhere and wants me dead." He laughed. The sound was dry and humorless. "Not that that is a surprise. He's hated me all my life. But why is he here?" His voice shook. "This is insanity. Craziness."

"The park's secure," Zafir interrupted as he joined them almost ten minutes later. He'd been running and he was breathing hard.

"I hit him once. Possibly twice. After that, he managed to elude me despite his injuries. Although I'd say that he's hurting badly. He dropped his gun. I've got it, so there's that."

"He's not armed," Jade said.

"Not that it matters much. I doubt if he'll make it. He's losing blood fast. It looks like an easy arrest or a morgue run," he said with a shrug.

Despite Zafir's harsh words, Jade felt no sympathy for Stanley's cousin. He was an assassin, more than likely a paid assassin. She just hoped that Zafir was right, that he was captured. She looked at Stanley. His expression hadn't changed. He didn't look shocked or saddened, just very annoyed. His cheeks were wind-reddened, his eyes bloodshot. The knees of his jeans were both ripped and his hair was mussed.

"I've notified the local authorities," Zafir said. "If he makes it, he'll need medical assistance. He shouldn't be too difficult to capture."

"Great," she said, and turned to Stanley. "Let's get you back to the apartment. It's freezing out here." She had him by the elbow as if preventing him from bolting again.

Stanley stopped at the edge of the park, pulled his arm free and looked at them with anger thinning his lips. "Look. I appreciate you saving my life, again," he said, contradicting everything he'd said before. "But I don't want a repeat of this. If I were you two, I'd drop this assignment while I was still in one piece."

He glared at Zafir. "Like I told Jade, I'm going home. This needs to end now. It's obvious that I'm the key to it all. I need to face whoever is orchestrating this. That's the only way it will stop."

Zafir said nothing, but he looked as if he wanted to wring Stanley's neck.

"Stanley," Jade said as she stepped between them. "For now, let's get back to the duplex." She took his elbow. "The rest can wait."

Chapter Seventeen

They were a quarter of a block away from the park when they saw a man calling to a dog that was off its lead.

"Stop!" Stanley commanded in a voice that expected compliance.

"What's wrong?" Zafir asked even as he stopped.

"The dog's going to get hit," Jade said with horror as she saw what Stanley had seen first. She was out of the vehicle, just behind Stanley. Ahead of them, a border collie was in the middle of the intersection and a truck was wheeling around the corner. It was doubtful that the driver had seen the dog or that he would be able to stop in time. Stanley dived and in an unexpected move grabbed the dog, rolling out of the way of the truck, which honked as it swerved around them.

"Gotcha, boy," he said as he picked up the squirming black-and-white border collie.

"You might want to keep him on a leash until you teach him to come when you call," he said to the grateful owner, who'd run up to claim his dog all the while thanking Stanley profusely.

"It only takes once and your dog is dead or seriously hurt," he said with an authoritative edge to his voice.

Jade and Zafir looked at each other. This was a completely different side of Stanley. He'd gone from near hysteria to determined rescuer in a matter of seconds.

"That's the other reason I need to go home," Stanley said five minutes later as he sat in the backseat for the short ride to the apartment. It was as if he'd read her thoughts. "The dogs need me. And I miss them more than I thought."

"Dogs? The rescues?" Jade guessed.

"Yes, I told you. Local shelter, I volunteer there. I use my nickname and what it's associated with. Like I told you, Stanley was a cartoon character. The program is well known in Morocco. It's nostalgia for the older generation, but they're bringing back a new version that's catching on with the younger set." He looked at both of them and seemed to sense that they weren't connecting with what he was saying. "Stanley—you know. Cartoon, funny. The name is well known, and I dress in character for various events. It raises money for the local shelter. Turned no-kill last year as a result."

Jade glanced at Zafir. Stanley was evolving from socially inept royal to a man who was becoming more likable as time went on. It was hard not to like someone who had just escaped a harrowing experience and then had the compassion and foresight to save a dog's life.

Minutes later they were back at the safe house.

Stanley grabbed a can of Coke and sank down on the couch, slouching back as if his legs would no longer hold him. Zafir lounged by the doorway, his eyes on the window.

"I know I agreed to stay at least a few more days. I gave you my word, Jade. We shook hands, and that means a lot to me," Stanley said. And when no one spoke, his lips thinned and his eyes took on a determined sheen. "I know we talked about staying here just a while longer, and it made good sense then. But everything has changed."

He looked at both of them with an edge to his hazel eyes and a tight look to his usually full lips. "It's my money that's hired you," Stanley said, and neither one of them bothered to correct him, to tell him it was Prince Rashad. It was a moot point. "If I want to go to see my uncle, then I have that right."

"We'll discuss that later," Jade said firmly. "First we need all the cards on the table." She looked at Stanley. "Tell Zafir what you told me earlier."

Silence filled the room.

"Tell me what's going on," Zafir gritted out. "There's been enough foul-ups on this case."

"He already knows, Stanley," Jade said softly. "Fill in the blanks in your own words starting with the trust fund."

Stanley stood up. The expression on his face was pained. He folded his arms and then dropped them. He sat down, plopping heavily down onto the sofa.

"Uncle set it up for me. One hundred and fifty thousand American dollars a year for life," Stanley repeated what Jade had already told Zafir. "Some of that was for the rescue that I work with. He knew how important that was to me, and he used it as kind of a bribe." He shook his head. "I didn't want his money, but the truth is, the rescue desperately needed it." He worried his lower lip for a minute before continuing.

"So I agreed. Although, except for the rescue, I would have gladly helped him for free. But the truth is that I need to work and couldn't devote myself to Uncle like he wanted. It was kind of a catch-22. So Uncle fixed it so I could." He laced his fingers together, his brow furrowed. "In the end, we reached an agreement that we could both live with."

"The trust," Jade added.

"Exactly," Stanley said.

"When did this happen?" Zafir asked.

"We discussed it a few weeks ago. He told me what he wanted and what he planned to do. I agreed and the final papers were signed just before I booked the flight here," Stanley said. "It was completely unexpected. I mean, when he presented the idea to me. But he's getting on in years and he needs help." He looked at them, with troubled eyes. "I've always been there for him, but now he wants me to live on the estate and take care of him full-time."

"That's a lot of money, Stan," Zafir growled.

"It is, but Uncle insisted. He wanted to help support my cause, and he didn't want to go to a senior facility or have strangers taking care of him. I don't mind doing it." He looked frightened and determined at the same time. "The trust is for the duration of his life, and it ends with either of our deaths."

There was silence. Zafir strode to the window as if there were answers outside the walls of the apartment.

Jade was beginning to feel a connection to Stanley that she hadn't felt for any other client. But then, he was different from any other. Young for his years and naive, but now showing another side, a more mature side and one she could admire. It was her job to ensure that he lived to act on the courage and caring he was showing now.

"That cottage, that's my bachelor pad," Stanley said. "I was supposed to be there for the last week. Then I decided to take this trip sooner rather than later. Especially with our agreement. Uncle wanted me to move in with him as quickly as possible. I wanted one more taste of being free and single."

Jade turned, knowing the shock was registering on her face. "You never told me that."

He shrugged. "I didn't think it had any importance."

"So, Stan," Zafir said. "It's safe to say that your cousin Mohammed followed you here intending to kill you."

Stanley frowned, and his eyes looked almost haunted. "I don't know why. What did he stand to gain?"

Zafir looked at Jade. She mouthed one word and he nodded.

"Did you know, Stan, that recently your uncle redid his will, and you're his beneficiary?"

"Me?" Stanley sounded shocked.

Jade looked at Zafir. It was clear that Stanley hadn't known.

"Your uncle didn't tell you?" she asked with quiet assurance.

"No. I…" His face reddened. "It's too much. I don't want…"

"You can deal with that later, Stan," Zafir said. "For now we need to figure out what is going on here. We know Mohammed has tried to kill you. The question is why?"

Stanley shook his head. "I don't know. Moham-

med wasn't close to Uncle or me. In fact, he's not related to Uncle Khaled. He's from my mother's side.
When he was a child he visited a lot, but always with
his parents." He shook his head. "I don't want to talk
about this."

"Keep going, Stan," Zafir snarled. "Some of this
might very well save your life."

"Neither of us would choose the other as friends.
As children we didn't like each other. As adults we
haven't had much to do with each other. I don't know
why he'd try to kill me now, after all these years."
He stopped and worried his lower lip with his thumb.

Zafir's phone beeped.

"One minute," Zafir said, holding up his index finger as he stood up and moved into the kitchen area.
"Yeah, Tara, what do you have, sweetheart?"

Jade watched as his expression changed from wel-
coming to grim in the space of two minutes.

Zafir put the phone in his pocket and came back to
the common area, where he perched on the armrest of
the couch as if poised to go into action.

"Tell us about your brother, Stanley," Jade said. She
tried to ignore the fact that Zafir had just received information from that phone call. She could sense it from
the look on his face and from the little she'd heard from
his end. That would have to wait. It was critical that
Zafir know everything that she'd so recently learned,
because she sensed that they were running out of time.

"Everything, including what you didn't tell me."

He looked at her with surprise.

"No more secrets, Stanley."

She touched the back of his hand as if that would

sway him, encourage him. "Start with the recent text message on your phone."

"By the ears," he said. "It was a horrid thing my brother would say to me when I was a kid. That phrase meant he was going to hurt me or hurt an animal I cared for. And I cared for them all, even the strays." He looked away.

She guessed that it might have been worse even than Stanley told her. She wanted to walk away, not hear it again. She had no choice but to stay.

Stanley dropped his head into his hands before looking at them again. "It was the one thing he shared with me and no one else. My brother, Chasi, was the only one who ever said that phrase, 'By your ears.' That message on the phone was like a message from the dead." His voice threatened to break. "Those words, they're like seeing him again. But he's dead, so who else knew?" He ran the back of his hand across his perspiring forehead.

"When you saw the message on your phone, you thought it was him right away?" Jade asked. "Even though he's dead?"

"He's been dead for twenty-five years. But I don't think anyone else knew he said that. It was our little secret." There was a quiver in his voice, and his hands were in fists. His face was white.

"He was close to your cousin Mohammed?" Jade asked.

"Sort of. As close as he could get to anyone." He nodded. "I can't believe it," he muttered. "You're insinuating that he's alive, that he hired Mohammed. Then where has he been all these years?"

"Did Mohammed spend time with Chasi?" Jade asked.

"Yes, he did. He visited and stayed over many times when I was young."

"And he would have heard Chasi taunting you, maybe heard that strange phrase of his?"

Stanley shook his head. "Maybe. I don't know. What does this mean?"

"I don't have any answers for you, Stan, but I bet there's still something you're keeping from us," Zafir said.

Stanley shook his head, his face flushed. Silence pulsed through the room before he began. The stories of torture and cruelty that followed were more than he'd revealed before, and Jade felt sick just hearing it.

"They said he was an uncontrolled psychopath. I was eleven when he was committed by my parents," Stanley said softly. "That's how they referred to it back then. Committed," he repeated. "I was relieved. My life got better after that."

Jade looked at Zafir. What Stanley was telling them was unimaginable, but it was the classic pattern of a dangerous psychopath.

"What happened when your brother died? Is there anything that stands out in your mind?" Zafir asked.

"There was never a funeral." He shrugged. "At the time I didn't care. I remember that my father said that he thought something wasn't right. But there was never any proof of anything. I know my parents had no idea what went on in the asylum prior to his death. We had no contact after he was committed. Chasi refused to see either of them."

"There's no death certificate, is there, Stanley?" Zafir asked.

"I don't know about that. I've never looked," Stan said.

"Did anyone view the body?" Jade asked.

Stanley shook his head. "We never viewed the body, not that I know of. I had nothing to do with the burial, and I don't remember my parents attending, either. The hospital handled all of it, at least that I know of. I think my mother might have said a prayer or two. My father, he never spoke of him again."

"We just ran an official search," Zafir said. "There's nothing, Stan. As far as the Moroccan government is concerned, your brother's not dead."

He bit his lip and sank deeper into the couch. "It was all odd, everything about his death. At the time I didn't consider it much. I was too young to feel anything but relief. As far as the specifics, I never asked. I was told that he committed suicide at the institution and that he's buried there. That's all I know."

The humming of the refrigerator was loud in the silence that followed.

"Who stands to gain from your uncle's estate if you're not alive?" Zafir asked. "Who is your next closest relative?"

Jade looked at Zafir, wondering where he was going with this. They'd received a copy of the will that named Stanley as beneficiary, but nothing that addressed who he would bequeath his estate to if Stanley predeceased his uncle. That was odd, and it changed everything.

"What are you suggesting?" Stanley's gaze swung

between both of them. "I get the impression that you think my brother's not dead." His voice shook.

"Who inherits your uncle's fortune if you're dead, Stanley?" Jade asked again, softly. "Your uncle didn't specify a successor, so it would be his next closest relative."

"Uncle's not dead." His voice was ragged. "You told me…"

"He's not, but officially it hasn't been released who died when that cottage was destroyed. All they said was that an unidentified male died in that explosion. That's why it's so important to know who inherits next. Your brother might be a long shot, but we can't rule anything out."

The words hung between them as the seconds ticked by.

"If he were alive, Chasi would inherit, if how you say that will's written is right, if I were dead." He shivered.

"In the meantime, there's the trust. Who else knows about the trust?" Zafir growled.

Jade looked at him with a question in her eyes.

"The trust is evidence of a favored position. From it, one could easily assume that Stanley will inherit," Zafir said. "Even without knowing about the will. I'm betting that's why all of this has happened so soon. Someone got wind of what was going down."

"I think you're out on a limb on that one," Jade replied.

"And—" Stanley looked at Zafir "—in answer to your question, no one knows. At least no one was supposed to but…both of you and no one else." His voice broke. "Most of my relatives wouldn't care...they have money in their own right."

Silence filled the room as Stanley seemed to struggle to collect himself. "Now you see why I have to go home."

"I know," Zafir said. "And we'll get you there. But you won't be flying commercial."

"You'll be safe," Jade assured him, putting a hand on the crook of his arm as if somehow that would give him confidence.

He looked at her and smiled. "I know. It's about time I faced my brother."

"Let's not make assumptions, Stan," Zafir said. "Officially, for all we know—he's dead."

Two hours later, the company Gulfstream was waiting for them on the runway. It was only a matter of them walking to the plane that sat two hundred yards away.

"I don't like this," Jade muttered as they stood on the edge of the Casper airport tarmac. "I think we need a decoy. I'll go..."

"No," Zafir cut her off. "I'll go."

"We'll all go together," Stanley broke in. "It makes the most sense."

Jade and Zafir looked at each other. Stanley was full of surprises these last hours, showing intelligence, a touch of courage and a modicum of common sense. He wasn't quite the man they had first assessed him to be.

"Let's move," Jade said as she began striding out onto the tarmac with Stanley behind her and Zafir bringing up the rear. But as she turned, scanning the area, making sure that everything was clear both in front and behind, she could feel something was off.

A movement near a luggage cart had her pulling Stanley close, her other hand on her gun. She wasn't ready to make an overt show of force, not here at the airport. That would be asking for trouble.

A movement to the right, and she could also see airport authorities moving around. No one was acting like there was any threat.

A luggage transporter moved slowly around a plane that idled on the tarmac. Seconds ticked by, and it was a full minute, then two, before either of them agreed to give Stanley the go-ahead. And as they did, a bag fell off a luggage cart, followed by three more. The noise made Stanley jump, and Zafir pushed past them so that he was in front, his hand ready to go for his gun. Jade grabbed Stanley, pulling him back between them. But it was nothing but what it seemed—falling luggage. There was no threat.

They were seeing danger everywhere.

Chapter Eighteen

"I never thought that I'd get a chance to work in Morocco," Jade murmured. "I'd hoped, but…I suppose I wanted to arrive under better circumstances. I mean, a case, yes, but… Oh, never mind. I'm rambling."

"You're excited. It's refreshing," Zafir said.

They were already three hours into the last leg of the flight, having landed briefly at JFK before continuing their journey overseas. It would be close to eleven in the morning before they landed in Marrakech.

Stanley had fallen asleep an hour ago.

"What if his brother is exactly that, dead?" she mused, talking quietly on the off chance that Stanley might awaken.

"I've got Tara checking out the next living relative. Stan wasn't too sure about the cousins on his father's side." He scrolled through his texts as his phone beeped. Five minutes later they had their answer.

"Barring the possibility of his brother's death being faked, the next in line is an unmarried cousin who hasn't set foot in Morocco in at least a decade."

"And…"

"From all appearances he has more money than he

needs. He's enjoying a lavish lifestyle, and his main residence is in Paris."

"Interesting," she said, and they were silent, each mulling over this new possibility as the plane took them through the night of one continent and into the daylight of another.

"I don't like the thought of you in the thick of this," Zafir said.

"It's what I do," she replied. "Just like any other agent."

But his eyes said something else. She couldn't look away. It seemed the most natural thing when he leaned over and put a strong, sun-bronzed hand on her knee. It was too soon and too intimate, but despite that, something shifted between them.

His brown eyes were hot with desire. He looked over at Stanley. "If it wasn't for—" one shoulder rose, indicating Stanley near the back of the plane stretched out on a small couch "—I'd make out…"

"Make out?" she whispered. No man she knew would have used such an outdated phrase in such a teasing, yet tantalizing way. "Are you…"

He leaned over and silenced her with a kiss as he pulled her tight against him. She could feel his arousal pushing against her, and all she wanted was to give in to every ounce of passion she had for him. But this wasn't the place, not here on a plane with their client only yards away from them. It couldn't happen, and she wanted so badly for it to happen.

Her heart pounded, and something deep inside wanted only to melt into him. Her mind screamed to pull away. It couldn't be—this was the wrong time, the wrong place, the wrong man.

She put her hands on his shoulder, creating a suggestion of distance between them.

"Jade."

"No." She shook her head. For as much as she wanted him against her, as much as she wanted his lips ravishing hers, as much as she wanted all of it and more, she couldn't. Again, she pushed him away.

This was crazy, unanticipated and completely out of control. She'd never felt like this about another man, and he was completely the wrong man to feel this about. She knew his reputation. His track record was a train wreck for any woman. She looked out the window where the only thing to see were clouds. They were no distraction at all. She had to get it together.

She didn't want any of this. At least, that's what she told herself. It was as if telling herself would control the feelings that were wild and difficult to contain. They were completely different from anything she'd felt with any other man.

He was like no man she'd ever known, even though he was an identical twin. She'd met Emir on one of his visits stateside. There was no comparison. For one, Zafir's handsome face bore a scar that ran the length of his left cheekbone to his jaw. It did nothing to distract from his good looks, but it made him even more rugged-looking than his twin. But it went deeper than that. Zafir had an aura about him. He angered her like no other, and yet she felt physically safe in his presence and emotionally wrecked, for he was too hot, too passionate and altogether too dangerous.

He was proving all that now. Making her pulse with need, making her want to bridge the distance between them and pick up where she'd forced him to leave

off—where she'd ended it. But it needed to be ended.
It could never be. Her thoughts needed to straighten
out. They were confusing and cloudy, almost dizzy-
ing. What was important was Stanley and his safety.
They needed to secure him and make sure he was
safe. What had just happened couldn't happen again.

"Let's go over our plan when we land," she said, but
her lips were sensitive from his brief kiss, even as her
belly fluttered. She was aroused in a way she hadn't
been in a very long time. Her body was acting out of
sync with her mind.

Zafir headed to the front of the plane, where he
grabbed a bottled water for each of them from a compact fridge. He came back a few minutes later. His
hand settled on her shoulder. "You're hot," he whispered in her ear.

His words, his nearness, had heat running through
her. She wanted him. She needed to pull back.

"Like no woman I've ever met before."

He slid into his seat and picked up the file as if he
had said nothing at all.

She was a puddle of molten attraction, trying to regain control. She needed to rein it in, and apparently,
she needed to rein him in, as well. And yet at the same
time, she only wanted to fall into his arms and let nature take its course.

So much for reining anyone in.

She wasn't sure how this would all turn out. When
the assignment was over, would his feelings be gone?
It was no secret that Zafir was a love 'em and leave
'em kind of guy. His broken trail of romances was evidence enough of that.

"What's with the look?" he asked.

His eyes were alive with desire. They seemed to take all of her in. If she said the word, if there were no Stanley—she knew exactly what they'd be doing on the butter-soft leather of a private airplane seat while they continued uninterrupted on their journey through the skies over the Atlantic.

Morocco.

Somehow that one word, a place where she'd never been and where she was about to land in just a few hours, brought reality slamming back into focus like nothing else could.

She met his gaze with steely determination. This was it. This was business, nothing more.

The tablet dinged a warning that a message had arrived. It was the second call to reality.

Now, the passion was gone, and instead that dark drive to close this case successfully was there—a seriousness that replaced the passion in a split second. She turned her attention to the tablet, skimmed her thumb along the screen, looking at the latest information that had come from the admins in the main office in Marrakech. It was rather an enlightening piece of information.

He looked backward as if to ensure that, despite the snoring, Stanley wasn't feigning sleep.

The plane hit a patch of turbulence and the interior cabin lights blinked.

"Fayad el Eloua, the only remaining nephew besides Stanley and one year younger, has just recently returned from Paris to Morocco."

He looked up. "That's interesting."

"Could the possibility of an inheritance have brought him back?"

"The research says that he inherited his family's wealth and lives a lavish lifestyle." He looked up. "Tara passed it on for an investigation into his bank accounts. She doesn't have the means to access something like that."

"You don't think…"

"Stanley's brother was always a long shot," he said. "But still can't be discounted."

The lights blinked, and the small silver communication box beside Zafir buzzed. He picked it up and nodded as he listened. A message from the pilot, Jade guessed, as she watched him receive whatever the message was through the earbud he was wearing.

"It'll be rough for the next few minutes," he reported to Jade while standing up to dim the lights over the still-sleeping Stanley. "He's buckled in," he said in a whisper. "Best get seat belts on ourselves."

She looked over at Stanley. "He's not used to what's happened in such a short period of time. But he's adapted amazingly well."

"He has," Zafir said, balancing easily as the plane jumped again before sliding into his seat and fastening his seat belt.

"We need the landing site secure," Jade said. She wasn't sure why she was stating the obvious.

Zafir ran a finger along her cheek, pushing a strand of hair back from her face, his touch velvety soft and hot. "It's secure," he said in a whisper that made his deep voice so gloriously seductive that it was impossible to focus on what he was actually saying.

She was doomed. Her growing feelings for him were impossible to put aside.

His dark eyes grazed lazily over her.

"What about my gun?" she asked, needing the distraction of something else.

"Royal sanction," Zafir said. "Our agency is authorized as part of our doing business."

He looked at her with surprise, as if accusing her of asking pointless questions for answers she already knew. He was right. She had been trying to divert the hot tingle of desire that was fudging her ability to think her way clearly through this case.

"We're two hours from landing. That's all the time we have to make sure the plan will be something we can get Stanley on board with," Zafir said.

"That's the key, isn't it?" Jade murmured as she took a sip of water and glanced at Stanley, who had only changed position but was still sleeping soundly. "A plan that will keep Stanley safe and one he's happy enough with to consider cooperating."

"In any other situation an easy task," Zafir said as he looked at her, this time with the passion of a challenge in his eyes. "But we've known that from the beginning."

"Let's do it, hit this thing with boots on the ground," she said with relief, her mind finally on their mission.

"And a cooperative client," Zafir said with a smile.

"And that," she replied.

They worked together like they'd done it for years, and in the end what they came up with, there was no question that Stanley would cooperate. They both agreed that there was no way he could not be happy.

He would soon be in Morocco, with his uncle and his beloved rescue dogs.

Now they only had to keep him alive.

Chapter Nineteen

Zafir's brother Talib was there to meet them at the Marrakech airport as they emerged into a private area.

"Good to see you, bro," Talib said as he clapped Zafir on the shoulder. "You lucked out. Emir and I have been running back-to-back cases that have been keeping us in Marrakech. Otherwise, you would have been on your own."

"Jade." Talib turned to her before anyone else could say a word. He offered her a smile that was solid and genuine. "Good to see you on this side of the ocean."

He held out his hand, which she shook warmly, and then he turned to Stanley, shaking his hand.

"I'm between cases," Talib said, leading the way out of the airport. They moved through a private corridor that was closed to most passengers and outside to a private parking lot. "Just got back from checking out a hotel."

"You're going into the hotel business?" Zafir asked with a laugh.

"As if," Talib said. "I'm trying to convince a friend of mine that it's a bad idea. But he's determined. If the deal goes through, he has me lined up to make sure the security is up to par."

Zafir's phone beeped.

"Your cousin Mohammed won't be a threat to you again, Stan," Zafir said a minute later.

"He's dead," Stanley said flatly.

Zafir nodded.

A look of relief washed over Stanley's face, but it was fleeting. He looked at Zafir. "It was your gunshot?"

"Unfortunately, I believe so," Zafir replied.

"Not unfortunate at all from all you've told me. He was no good." He took a deep breath. "I have to go to Rabat immediately."

"Your uncle's estate," Jade said. "That's…"

"We'll get you there." Zafir cut her off with an edge of impatience in his voice.

Jade gave Zafir a quelling look. One minute he was turning her on and the next he was pissing her off. Right now she was getting tired of his take-charge attitude. She didn't miss the amused look Talib gave them both.

"Now," Stanley said, redirecting her attention to him as he stopped and put his suitcase down, as if that made some kind of statement.

She went over to Stanley and took the handle of his suitcase, preventing him from picking it up without wrestling it from her hand. "You trusted us in Wyoming?"

"Yes. But…"

"We've got your back, and we know you need to get to Rabat." She looked at him and saw tears glistening in his eyes. "And we'll get you there. But we're going to make sure you're safe in the process."

"He's the closest thing I have to a parent. There is no one else. What if he's in danger?"

"He's fine, and we'll be there soon. This afternoon."

Stanley picked up his suitcase. "Okay." He nodded at Talib. "Let's do this."

A minute later they were getting into Talib's Jaguar. "British Racing Green, that's the color it's called," Zafir said with a laugh at her look of awe. He winked at her. "Talib loves luxury sport vehicles."

"Not more than he loves speed," Talib said, laughing. "Fasten your seat belt, folks."

The car was luxury on wheels, and Talib flirted with speed limits as they made their way into the heart of Marrakech and the asylum that had once held Stanley's brother.

Twenty minutes later, Talib rounded a corner and took them through a massive set of gates that looked like something out of the Middle Ages. The drive was wide and lined with palm trees, which made the whole approach rather strange, like they were entering a resort.

The asylum was old. It was built on the edge of the medina, where ancient walls separated the city's oldest neighborhood, once a vibrant trading center, with its narrow twisting streets, packed with vendors and shoppers, from the rest of the city. But despite the busyness of the area, the psychiatric hospital that had once been called an asylum stood alone on large grounds that gave it a feeling of isolation. It had been built at the turn of the twentieth century. Now the old facade remained, as well as the ten-foot wall of sun-bleached brick complete with a two-foot topping of barbed wire. It was a modern-day reminder of pain and suffering, but inside she knew that it had been completely changed. A fully modernized hospital now occupied the majority of the grounds.

The exterior, despite the fact that massive renovations had been done, was less inviting than a modern prison. The question that lay in all their minds was if Stanley's brother, Chasi el Eloua, had left those walls alive or if he had died as claimed twenty-five years ago.

Stanley had his hands laced together, and his jaw was tense.

"You don't have to go in," Jade reminded him. "Talib will stay here with you."

Stanley nodded, a grateful look on his face. "I'd prefer that," he whispered. "I've never been inside, and I'd like to keep it that way."

"I understand," Jade said, and she did, for she was also feeling reluctant to enter this grim-looking facility. She'd never been a fan of hospitals, having seen her father in one as a child. He'd died in palliative care of a neurological disease that had taken two long, drawn-out years. It had left a lasting impression.

"In fact," Zafir said, "why don't we meet you in the medina." He clapped his hand on Stanley's shoulder. "Maybe you can find a gift for your uncle in one of the souks," he said, referring to one of the numerous marketplaces within the walls of the medina. "I believe there's a souk just a few blocks away."

Stanley brightened. "It would take my mind off of this," he said.

They waited until Talib and Stanley pulled away before heading toward the building.

"The employee the administrator referred me to

is particularly knowledgeable about the earlier cases, those that aren't online," Zafir said.

She followed him as he turned to face the entrance. Like the rest of the outside, here the facade of age masked the modernized core of the psychiatric hospital.

"Are you okay?" he asked.

"Why shouldn't I be?"

"You don't like hospitals. I've read your file, Jade. I know it wasn't a good way to lose a parent."

"We've both had bad experiences. It was a long time ago. I'm fine, really," she said. She was shocked that he knew that much about her, that he cared enough to check it out and mention it, to make sure she was all right now.

"Then let's go," he said as he led the way through the doors where inside, they were overwhelmed by the liberal scent of disinfectant.

"The older section is no longer used, and there's a new area dedicated to psychiatric beds," Zafir said.

"Interesting," she replied.

"Is it?"

She stopped. "What do you mean?"

"That it has no relevance to the case. I was only making conversation."

His phone buzzed. "Wait," he said to Jade and took the call. A minute later he disconnected from their Marrakech office with a troubled expression. "Seems the bank records for Fayad el Eloua are looking grim."

"Broke?"

"Pretty much. Unless he's hiding it elsewhere there's not much left."

"That could change everything." She took in her surroundings. "Or so could this."

They approached the receptionist, who passed them on to another employee, who then passed them off to a young woman in a white lab coat.

Jade was intrigued as they walked briskly through a gleaming off-white corridor. It was as if they'd been dropped from archaic to modern in the space of seconds. The sleek lines of the updated area seemed to clash with the ancient brick and stone of the exterior they'd just seen.

"Even upgraded, it isn't very inviting," Jade whispered.

They stopped at an elevator. Jade crossed her arms and warded off a shiver.

"You'll find Omar on the basement floor in the southwest corner. He's our longest standing employee and considers himself our unofficial archivist," their guide said in Arabic. "Actually, we all do. He has more information stored in his head than we have in the records room," she said with a light laugh before turning to leave.

Zafir repeated the information in English to Jade.

"This is a problem, isn't it? Me not speaking the language."

"Let's hope we're not here long enough for it to be a problem," he said as the elevator doors shut. "Although there are many people who speak English or French, as well."

The elevator doors opened, and the musty smell of basement met them. Jade wrinkled her nose. For a second it felt like the past had wrapped a shroud around them. As they stepped out into the hallway, it was clear that the modernization had stopped in the basement. While the concrete walls had been painted white, the tile on the floor looked well worn. A battered gurney was against one wall as if it had been forgotten there and an exit sign glowed red at the end of an endless length of hall. They turned away from the sign and down the corridor in the opposite direction. Light filtered from a doorway and lifted some of the gloom. Just ahead of them a thin man stepped out of the shadows.

"Are you Omar?" Zafir asked and at the man's nod, he said, "Zafir Al-Nassar and this is Jade Van Everett."

Jade was surprised at how young he appeared. The only sign of the fifty years they'd been told that he'd worked here was his graying hair and a rather stooped posture, as if he'd sat at a desk too long. Although, she knew that wasn't the case as they'd been told that the majority of his work experience had been menial.

They both shook his hand, and he ushered them into a large room that was filled floor to ceiling with steel shelving holding boxes of files.

"Most of this has yet to be put online," he said with a wave of his arm. "You asked about Chasi el Eloua. He was committed a long time ago. But I'll never forget that case. It was the worst I'd seen at the time. Everyone talked about it."

"Worst?" Jade asked. "How?"

"He was violent, so violent. He had no empathy for anyone or anything. He didn't try to hide it, either. I'd never seen a patient like him. What the family told us was terrible. But here, it seemed to get worse. You couldn't turn your back on him. He broke an orderly's arm and hospitalized an aide the first week he was here. In fact, for his first months he was locked up in solitary confinement and, because of similar violence, off and on over the years that followed."

He shuffled through a box of papers and then turned around, scanning the room as if he'd lost his train of thought.

"You said you had proof of his death?" Jade interrupted.

He nodded. "He committed suicide, but not before threatening the lives of two staff members and fatally wounding two of the other patients. He partially beheaded one of them. I've never seen anything like it."

"How?" Jade asked, horrified at what she was hearing.

He shook his head. "Somehow he managed to escape his cell. Then he stole a carving knife from the kitchen. It took three of us to get control of the situation." He shook his head. "I was one of them. We weren't able to stop him from jumping from the fifth-floor window."

"You're sure he died?" Zafir asked. "That it was him?"

"No doubt," the man said. "I've had a lot of positions in my time. Then, I was in charge of removing the body and cleaning the cobblestones after." He shrugged. "It wasn't an uncommon chore."

He looked at each of them. "I'm sorry, that must seem harsh. Anyway, I was here when his father came to identify him." He looked at both of them. "There was no doubt that he was dead. As far as the legal registration, I don't know what happened there. It isn't a first, though, at least back then. So it doesn't surprise me. But one thing I can guarantee is that he was and is dead. A sad ending, but then maybe it was for the best." He handed them the chart. "See, it's notated here as I'm sure administration told you."

Zafir looked at the notation, and then glanced at the notes that proceeded it. There wasn't much there. In fact, what Omar had told them said so much more. "Date and time of death is here in the chart. That's about it," he said to Jade.

"Did he ever get visitors? From family or anyone else?" he asked Omar a few minutes later.

"Family, no, never. Except that one time for identification." He paused. "He refused to see his family. No one came that I know of in the entire time he was here."

"Thank you," Jade said as they shook hands and left.

THE VISIT TO the hospital had taken them less than an hour. Still, it was a relief to be away from the dank smell of the basement and the haunting remnants of lives destroyed by illness and outdated ideas about treatment.

Jade took deep breaths, as if that would remind her of life and hope. The hospital basement, the story of Chasi's sad ending, was haunting. It was impossible to forget that nightmare and it made her consider briefly what other horrific stories might be contained within that hospital.

"Stanley's cousin Fayad el Eloua is in financial straits and conveniently, he inherits if Stanley is out of the picture," she said as they walked. "I don't like the sounds of this." They crossed a narrow street and turned right, entering the medina, where it was mostly only pedestrian traffic; the streets were walled in and narrow. The buildings crowded close where the walls didn't. As they neared the souk, the street became more congested. Merchants and goods crowded on both sides. Tourist trinkets and local goods wove together as one shop seemed to merge into the next.

"Fayad might still believe that his uncle is dead. Information to the contrary hasn't gotten out yet, but I'm betting that if he doesn't know about Mohammed's death, he will soon," she said. "That means he will know that Stanley is alive. And he can track him here."

"I think from here on in we don't let Stan out of our sight."

"I agree," she said as she strode beside him.

"Talib just texted," Zafir told her. "They're waiting for us. We'll helicopter in to Rabat."

They walked the remaining block to the heart of the souk in easy silence. Although Jade found that her mind kept going back to the grim hospital basement and Chasi's last moments. They were a distraction. But the thoughts were soon driven away by the intoxicating scent of incense and spices. The warm scent of cinnamon laced through the sharp tang of cloves and the heavier scents of curry and turmeric. The noise of a multitude of voices and activity became an unidentifiable hum. As they got closer, the volume increased, and it was impossible to hear what each other was saying without shouting, so they walked in silence. The merchants had bordered the narrow street with their wares sprawled out in front of them, but now they entered an area crowded with both tourists and locals. Vendors and their goods lined one stall against another. There was motion and color and noise wherever they looked. Colorful robes hung from one stall, a brilliant display of scarves hung from a second and souvenir T-shirts at another. Barrels of spices were lined up in the next. A woman called to them, motioning them to come to her stall, to check out the red-hued pottery that was spread out in front of her. Across from her, another pottery seller also called to them. Her pottery hung from hooks, pitchers in vibrant colors and pots around her feet. A man in a beige-and-white-striped djellaba guided a donkey with woven baskets that bulged with red and yellow cloth. The merchants were crowded into the narrow space, many dressed traditionally, a few in modern attire. For a moment the smell of manure wove through the rich scent of spice, and oddly wasn't off-putting. She stepped sideways, dodging a donkey's fresh leavings.

"We're meeting Talib at the Spice Haven. It's owned by a friend of the family. The shop is another block from here," Zafir said.

A few minutes later, a woman pushed between them. Jade was jostled from the other side and turned to catch up with Zafir. In that moment they were separated by a man leading a pair of donkeys and a group of women who pushed ahead of the man and his animals.

A sinewy arm wrapped around her waist and yanked her backward. She was slammed back against someone. She couldn't see behind her. She could only hear rough breathing as she was dragged backward, to the edges of the crowd.

Just like that, she was pulled out of the main corridor of traffic and into the fringes. Here, transactions were made, of people, goods, animals, that went on unseen every day, in the shadows. Here, kidnapping and murder would slip by unnoticed. She had to get away. She needed a distraction. More than likely, she would have only one chance. She didn't fight. She wanted to let her captor think she was resigned, passive. She had a glimpse of Zafir twenty feet ahead of her. He was boxed in in the midst of the crowd.

A heavy hand clapped over her mouth, jarring her teeth against her lips. She took a breath, smelled stale sweat and without hesitation sank her teeth deep into the sweaty flesh. At the same time, she brought her heel down on his instep, her hiking boot slamming as hard as it could into the soft cloth of a sneaker. Luck was on her side. She broke free as her attacker cursed and eased his hold.

Through the crowd she looked sideways and could still see glimpses of Zafir. It was doubtful that he could see her, she was blocked by her captor. There was no time to contemplate that or anything else. To do so would be to lose the edge she now had. It was act now or never. She pulled her gun all the while knowing that she wouldn't use it in such a crowd except as a desperate measure, but her attacker didn't have to know that. She looked into his rheumy brown eyes and saw the disconnect she saw in many killers. This man saw her as nothing of value, as a thing, something to be removed in whatever fashion it took.

"You won't kill me," he snarled.

A shout just to her left. She was distracted for a split second, but that was all it took. He grabbed her left arm. She couldn't free it; instead she swung with her right, the one holding her Colt. She slammed the butt of the pistol against his temple. His grip loosened. Suddenly, she was completely free and her attacker was yanked off his feet. Zafir had one of the man's arms twisted behind his back. His other arm was crushing his windpipe. He looked over the man's shoulder, looking straight at her as if she was all that mattered, as if a filthy man with murderous intent did not stand between them.

"You're all right?"

She nodded. "Let's get him contained," she said as she pulled out a set of handcuffs.

Their captive cursed in Arabic.

Zafir answered him in Arabic.

"He wished me an unpleasant death, in not quite those terms," Zafir told her. He didn't say what he'd said in reply. She imagined it hadn't been friendly.

She snapped the cuff on the man's thick yet sinewy wrist. He spat, his dark hair glistening with grease, the scent of sweat clashing with the exotic smells that had been so enticing earlier, and the combination made her stomach curl.

"Over there." She pointed six feet to her left where there was a metal flagpole, held upright by a block of cement.

Zafir dragged the man with his arm tight around his neck. Her attacker didn't have a choice—either cooperate or choke. At the flagpole, he glared at her.

Jade gave the cuff on one wrist a hard yank. The man pulled back, refusing to get close enough to have the cuff close on the pole. Zafir was about to step in when she took their captive's legs out from under him with a hard kick to the back of his knee. He fell as she snapped the cuff onto the pole.

"Who hired you?" she demanded.

He spat. An expletive that was clear in any language followed. But he refused to look at her.

She lowered her gun, aiming for his crotch. "Five seconds." She warned. "One…"

"I wouldn't push her," Zafir said as he moved beside her.

She didn't take her eyes off the greasy character in front of her. He was a classic criminal for hire, not above doing anything sleazy, not smart enough to come up with the crime himself but more than willing to collect money for any number of acts. He glared at her, his thin lips tight with disdain.

"Three."

"Fayad el Eloua."

"Where is he?" she asked. "This time I'm not going to count." She brought the gun a few inches lower, a few inches closer.

He placed his hands over his crotch as if that would somehow make him bulletproof.

Behind her, Zafir chuckled. "I wouldn't want to be in your place," he said, but his voice was low enough that Jade doubted the man had heard.

"Where?" she repeated.

"I don't know," he gritted. "I was supposed to meet him in Rabat in two days."

"Where?"

He named a hotel in Rabat.

She turned around.

Zafir was on his phone, but he nodded at her. She stepped away from their captive as Zafir ended the call.

"The police will be around to release you," he said as he disconnected. "Although I doubt there will be much releasing happening. Maybe a ride to the cell block."

The man snarled and cursed.

Zafir looked at Jade. "We'll have this trash picked up in no time."

A man began to clap, and a woman whistled as if they thought this was a play put on specifically for them.

"Time's running out," Jade said to Zafir. "Let's get moving."

Chapter Twenty

"Security found a breach at the Marrakech Menara Airport," Zafir said. "A mechanic alerted Fayad el Eloua of Stanley's arrival. From there it was a series of informants marking our path all the way to the psychiatric hospital."

"He's resourceful," Jade said. "The question is, where is Fayad now?"

"That's what we don't know. What I do know is we need to get Stan's uncle out of there and keep both him and Stan close until we get this man contained."

They were standing on the edge of his family's compound in Marrakech. In another circumstance, Jade would have been in awe. The grounds were massive; behind them an infinity pool stretched, seeming to touch the distant edges of the mansion that was the family home. As it was she only noted the details and focused on the helicopter that would take them to Rabat, where they could make sure that Stanley's uncle would live out his remaining years.

They took off ten minutes later from the Al-Nassar compound. Zafir flew them in while Talib took the copilot seat. If anything went wrong, it was agreed that Talib would be getting Stanley and his uncle out.

Nothing would go wrong, Jade thought. She clenched her hands in her lap. And even as she thought that and glanced at Stanley to make sure he was okay, she knew that they couldn't assume anything. They didn't know where Fayad el Eloua was. He'd rented a rattrap apartment in one of the poorer areas of Rabat. Whether or not he was there now, they had no idea. The first priority was securing Stanley and his uncle.

No one was saying much. Everything that could be said, at least in front of Stanley, had been said. Instead, Jade watched Zafir's easy maneuvering of the aircraft. It didn't surprise her that he was an accomplished pilot. She wondered if there was anything that he wasn't accomplished at.

"Stint in the Moroccan air force," he said, glancing back at her, answering her unasked question.

"I didn't ask," she said with a laugh.

"But you thought it," he replied as he steered the helicopter into a turn, dipping it slightly to the right. "Even without that, I probably would have acquired my license. It's kind of the family path. Each of us learns to fly and joins the business."

"Tara?" she asked, referring to his sister.

"Maybe. Someday," he said with a smile.

"Never," Talib said.

She turned to look at Stanley. "Have you managed to contact your uncle yet?"

"He's not answering," he said. "But he said when I spoke to him earlier that he'd be here waiting for me. He was looking forward to a visit."

"I don't like it," Zafir said. "You said there was no answer from our agent on the estate."

Talib nodded. "I'll try again."

"Uncle could be in trouble, is that what you're saying?" Stanley asked.

"No," Zafir said.

"What don't you like?" he persisted. "What does it mean?"

"It means you should stay in the helicopter while I get your uncle and fly you both out," Talib said. "Jade and Zafir are well equipped to deal with any trouble."

"You mean my cousin? Is that the trouble?"

"No," Talib said patiently. "I mean exactly what I said. Any trouble."

"My cousin Fayad," Stanley muttered. "I haven't seen him since I was a boy. I remember he was distant even then. I thought he was living the good life in Paris. That he was like all my relatives, most of them, anyway—rich."

"He kept up a good illusion," Jade said.

They arrived in Rabat at three in the afternoon and landed in a small field a mile behind the stone mansion Stanley had told them about during the flight. It had all gone exactly as planned. Except that not only was their agent not responding, but a third call to the mansion went unanswered. The estate seemed deserted. The land seemed to breathe silence.

It was clear even from this distance that something was wrong.

"Get Stanley out of here," Zafir said to his brother. "I don't like any of this."

Talib nodded. It was the first rule of Nassar Security to protect those you could as quickly as possible. Otherwise the damage could amp up, fast.

"My uncle?"

"Will leave with Zafir and me, Stanley," Jade said. She only hoped that was the truth.

"Promise me," he said as Talib took his arm, keeping him at the helicopter. He protested again, weakly this time, for it was clear even to him that Talib was not beyond using more force than he already was.

"SOMETHING'S NOT RIGHT," Jade said. The helicopter had taken off with Stanley and Talib over fifteen minutes ago. Now she was crouched fifty feet from the main house near an outbuilding. Ahead of them was the remains of the stone cottage, and between that and the mansion stretched silence.

Seconds turned into minutes. The estate seemed to be empty, and that was warning enough that there was trouble. Unidentified trouble, the worst kind.

"Get down!" Jade barked at Zafir, getting lower and moving in his direction even as she scanned the area and motioned with a flick of her right wrist.

A shot rang out from somewhere near their right and closer to the mansion.

"Split up," Zafir said as he waved her farther away. Later, he'd regret that command. He'd regret it for the rest of his life. For now, he was concentrating on keeping them alive.

Another shot kicked dirt up a few feet from where he was sheltered behind the tires of a small tractor. He moved deeper into the yard and closer to the mansion where they suspected Stanley's uncle was. Jade had moved ahead of him and was using a small shed for cover.

But the closer they got to the mansion, the more broken and rusted farm implements they found. It was a strange state of affairs, but possibly spoke to Khaled el Eloua's state of mind.

Another shot rang out. This time it took out the side window in the small shed directly in front of Jade.

Minutes ticked by, and the next shot told them that their sniper had somehow moved. The bullet kicked up dirt ten feet to his right. Whoever had them pinned was using the graveyard of implements as cover more efficiently than he could ever have imagined.

"Zafir," she hissed. With the shots now coming from another angle, she'd had a chance to look into the shed, searching for a sign of their agent or Stanley's uncle. She moved away from the shed and back toward Zafir.

"I've found Anthony," she said, referring to their agent as she moved in beside him where he took cover behind the wheel of a tractor. "It's not good," she said. "He's not moving. I couldn't get inside, but I think he's dead."

Zafir spit out an expletive.

As he'd instructed earlier, Jade moved away, intent on covering the area from a different angle.

He had no time to consider the ramifications of what she'd found as he saw movement near the main house. He waited. A dark head. It was not Stanley's uncle. He fired once, twice, three times. Shots were answering his, and then it all stopped. A minute, two, he turned, checking for Jade. It was a mistake, something he wouldn't do with another agent. He couldn't help himself. He needed to know that she was okay.

A bullet whistled inches from him.

He nodded at Jade, now thirty feet away and just ahead of him, making her closer to the main house.

He motioned with his right hand for her to move back, to shadow him, hopefully boxing in the man they suspected was Stan's cousin.

She fired before moving back. The bullet was low and did nothing but bite dirt.

Now the shots all seemed to be coming from a small outbuilding that was close to the house. Another shot, but this time it went wild and was followed by seconds that turned into a minute of silence.

A shot from his left, Jade's position, and a thud ahead of him like their assailant had fallen. That was followed by silence.

Time seemed to spread out, seconds felt like minutes, and suddenly it appeared to be over. The gunman was down.

Jade stood up, took a step forward. There was movement ahead of him but it all happened so fast. And before he could warn her, even as he knew it was a mistake—it was too late.

"Get down!" he shouted. But everything was happening at lightning speed. The bullet spun her around and drove her to the ground. He crawled to her despite the danger.

"Blood," she whispered as her hand lifted from her chest.

His heart seemed to stop as he took her gun in his hand. Her weapon, his hand, everything was slick from her blood. With his gun in his right hand and her Colt in his left, he stood. It was a crazy thing to do but all he wanted was to begin shooting like a madman. To kill the son of a desert dog who had taken Jade down. Despite the insanity of what he did, he was lucky. For a split second he had a visual. That was all it took to take him out.

He heard his name or maybe he dreamed it, dreamed that she was calling for him. Maybe he wished so badly to hear her voice once again that he had made fantasy a reality. He turned, crawling to her, but even as he assessed the damage, he saw the never-ending blood. And he knew that even a miracle might not be able to save her.

Chapter Twenty-One

A Nassar employee had died in the line of duty, and another lay close to death. It was a sobering fact but the facts didn't get better.

Jade Van Everett was fighting for her life. Zafir didn't know what he would do if she died. He wasn't sure how it had happened, how he had failed to protect her or how he'd fallen in love with her.

With her down, he'd taken out Stanley's cousin, Fayad el Eloua, in a way he would never recommend to any of his agents. He had risen to his full height, thrown convention and reason away, and fired one shot after another until his magazine and Jade's was empty. In the end, the man had taken two fatal hits to the chest that had finally killed him.

It was over, but in a way it could never be over. The agent who had secured the estate had only recently been hired and trained. Anthony now lay in a morgue, and Jade's life hung in the balance. She was in intensive care with a bullet still lodged in her chest. It was touch and go whether she'd make it or not. The news ran through the agency with a sick kind of shock that only bad news can bring.

Zafir was tormented with remembering. In those

horrible seconds after she'd been hit, he'd leaped out of character and shot again and again, without thought, without reason. He'd been driven by anger, rage and disbelief. He'd reacted instinctively, as no Nassar agent ever should.

Later, he'd refused to leave Jade's side. He'd used his own shirt to make a field dressing. Stanley's uncle had watched from a corner room in the mansion, ironically the one place his geriatric hearing couldn't hear the phone ring. It was there that he saw the man who threatened his life lose his. He had called for the emergency response team and immediately run out to help Zafir—talking constantly, a trick he said he'd learned in the army. He'd said that it was critical she remain conscious. Zafir hadn't remembered any of that at the time. They were memories that came back now in fits and starts as the long wait threatened his very soul, if not his sanity.

All of that had been the beginning of the nightmare. It felt like he'd been here, in this hospital, waiting—forever. A woman in a lab coat that drifted open and revealed lush curves walked by. He noticed because it was his job to notice, but for the first time, he had no interest. Jade was all that mattered. She had to live. He would die without her.

He didn't remember much of what happened in those first hours that stretched to days. It seemed like he was living in a movie that had been fast-forwarded, the actors switching and changing as the hours went on. And through it all, he stood with Jade's blood staining his shirt and the life of the woman he loved in someone else's hands. He knew now that if she died, there was no reason for him to live. He loved her that much; he loved her that wholeheartedly, that unselfishly. How or when this had happened, he didn't know. But when she took the bullet to the chest, he'd felt like the life had been ripped from him. He'd acted like a madman and fought back with all the firepower he had and with a deadly accuracy that had killed all that threatened them. He had taken out the one man who had done it, and then he'd taken her in his arms, trying to phone for help with one hand while trying to stop the bleeding with the other. He couldn't do it. He remembered the phone being taken from his hands. It was all a blur. In the hospital, he refused to leave her, and Talib had stuck around to make sure that he didn't kill himself in the process by forgetting to eat or sleep.

Even now he couldn't believe it. Somehow it felt like he had made this tragedy happen and as much as he knew that wasn't true, the thought wouldn't go away. He'd prided himself on keeping his agents safe. The fact that it had been Jade who orchestrated the assignment, the fact that every safeguard had been in place, none of it eased the responsibility that weighed heavily on him.

"You did everything you could," Emir said as he arrived an hour after Jade emerged from surgery. He patted him on the back.

"An agent is dead," he said grimly. He didn't say anything about Jade; he couldn't. For to admit that she was fighting for her life felt like it would make the worst happen.

"It's not your fault. Anthony was ordered to pull out, to wait for backup," Emir said. He shoved his hands in his pockets and met Zafir's look head-on. "You were in transit. There was nothing you could have done. It was Anthony who made the call, who reported Fayad's appearance. I don't know why he defied orders. But it definitely wasn't your fault. You had no say in any of it."

Zafir could feel his twin's pain. He knew that his heart ached at the outcome of his order. He almost wanted to say no, don't finish. But he knew that wasn't what needed to be done. Emir needed to say this.

"He was supposed to take Khaled, Stanley's uncle, and get out before any of this came down. But somehow something screwed up and he didn't go when he should." Emir shook his head. "This is on my shoulders."

"It's on no one's shoulders," Zafir said. "You made the best decision you could. If you hadn't, more people might have died. There are so many other scenarios that could fall out, you know that. You can't predict the future. You can only do the best you can."

"I know," Emir agreed. "And I'll work through it."

After Emir left, Zafir was on his own again. He remembered what Emir had said. It didn't make what happened right, but as he told Emir, he could live with it, because the reality was there was no other choice, for either of them.

THE FIRST VOICE Jade heard, the first face she saw, the first hand she touched, was Zafir's. What she saw in his eyes, the connection that ran hot and electric between them, changed her in ways she'd never thought possible. Lust was one thing, but what she felt now was so much different. It was more powerful, more intangible than anything she'd felt for any other man. It went beyond lust or even love.

"Why are you here? Why aren't you on a case?" It was the first thing she could think to ask.

"Because I'd rather be with you," he replied.

She almost smiled. The spiritual connection that ran so deep only a few seconds ago was replaced with the familiar. His voice, molten tones of bass, his simple words of concern, seductive despite their surroundings. In fact, they brought a reality that took her away from her surroundings, from the doctors, the nurses, the needles and the pain.

They didn't talk much that day or the next. The pain and discomfort were too great. But a week after she was fully conscious and sitting up, they talked.

"How long have I been here?"

"Weeks," he said loosely.

"And you've been here all that time?"

"Where else would I be?"

She blinked and seemed not to focus on him. It was as if she were seeing something or someone else.

"It was you?" she said. "Every time I woke up. I could sense you."

"You knew I was here," he said softly.

"I needed you here," she replied.

She closed her eyes and slept.

Chapter Twenty-Two

The last weeks had been tough. But Jade was finally well on the road to recovery. In fact, only two days ago she'd been discharged and by the end of the week she'd be clear to fly. But they were taking it easy, and at the end of the week Zafir took her on a shorter flight. They made the trip out to the estate near Rabat where Stanley was now living. The case they had been assigned to protect Stanley had been closed with the shoot-out that had almost killed Jade. There was no one alive who was a threat to Stanley or his uncle any longer. Now it was time to say goodbye.

Stanley sat on the sprawling front veranda of the mansion of his uncle's estate.

"This is goodbye, Stan," he said as he approached. It had been three weeks since they'd first stepped foot in Morocco, intent on closing this case. "How's your Uncle Khaled?"

"Doing great. I'm glad I'm here for him. That he survived my cousin's greed." He smiled.

"And you survived to keep his legacy alive."

"I did. Thanks to you and Jade. Odd, my relatives, except for him—" he glanced over his shoulder where his uncle was walking toward one of the outbuildings, a dog following slowly behind him "—are so twisted. My brother, two cousins." He shook his head. "Makes you think it could be genetic."

"You turned out fine, Stan," Zafir assured him. "Anyway, it's over, and we just wanted to come and say goodbye and let you know that next time you visit Wyoming it won't be quite as hair-raising as your last visit."

"Is that an invitation?"

"It is," Zafir said with a smile.

"I may take you up on that. Maybe even next year, but if I do, I'll look you up." He shook his head. "In fact, I'll hire you."

Zafir laughed. "The danger's past, Stan."

"I don't know about that," he replied with a smile. "My crazed cousins might be gone, but there's still a rancher or two that I wouldn't turn my back on."

Zafir smiled. He held out his hand. "Deal. Till next summer."

He turned, looking to where Jade was chatting with Stanley's uncle. The old man laughed and clapped a hand on her shoulder.

"She's something, isn't she?" Stanley asked the question not like a man who had any romantic interest in a woman but more with a hint of admiration. "If I had a sister, I'd want her to be just like her."

"She definitely had your back this whole time," Zafir said. "Nassar is lucky to have her."

"You're lucky to have her," Stanley said. "Don't think I haven't seen what's going on between you two." He smiled.

"What's going on?" Jade asked as she came up to the two men.

"Nothing," Zafir said, feeling heat crawl up his neck

as if he'd been caught doing something he shouldn't have been. He hadn't had that feeling in a very long time. "Stan was just saying how great you are at your job."

"I'm going to miss you, Stanley," Jade said. "You definitely keep things exciting."

"What, by offering near-death experiences?"

Jade laughed. "I love the new Stanley."

"Stan," he said. "I prefer Stan." He stood up from where he was sitting on the steps. "Thanks, both of you."

He reached out and shook Zafir's hand. "Do you mind?" he asked.

"I don't care what he says, I'm not leaving without a hug, Stan," she said with a smile.

"I never thought it would end like this," Stan said a minute later. He wiped the back of his hand across his cheek as a large shaggy black dog shoved his head against his thigh, and a small brown mixed breed barked shrilly. "I'm back, boys. It's over."

THEY FLEW HOME later the next week. Jade was up and swearing she was fully recovered. But despite her protests, Zafir insisted on carrying her suitcase.

Now they were halfway home.

"I imagine this may be the easiest assignment we see in a long time," Jade said with a soft purr as she ran a finger down Zafir's chest. "At least it started out easy."

"I don't know about easiest. Maybe the most deceptive might be a better description," he said with a laugh. "Did I tell you I was elated when the case was upgraded and terrified for you at the same time?"

"Elated?"

"Chance to work with you, my love," he said with a contented growl as he pulled her into his arms.

The case had been one of the most challenging, but only because the growing attraction between them had been a distraction. His hands ran the length of her. His fingers were gentle as they moved down the silken skin over the sweet curves that had him hot and hard without the suggestion of anything but her nakedness beneath him. They had won this case together. And in the weeks that she had fought for her life, he had realized what she meant to him, and more importantly, what it would mean to lose her.

"You've got to quit doing that," she said.

"What?"

"Worrying, and worse, protecting me. We won't be able to work together otherwise."

"I'm not sure if I can do that, but maybe I can camouflage my feelings."

She laughed, the sound a light tinkle that stirred something deep in his heart.

"You're going to have to do better than that."

"I'll try," he said, and was surprised that he meant it. He knew how much Nassar meant to her, as it did to him. It was just that she meant so much more.

Now she leaned against the jet's butter-soft leather recliner seat and sighed at the feel of Zafir's fingers massaging her feet.

"Heaven," she murmured.

"Ah, my dear. Not quite, but one day I'll show you heaven, at least here on earth." He let go of her foot and stood up, leaning over to offer her a gentle kiss that only hinted at passion.

"Is it always going to be like this between us?" Her words were a throaty whisper, her breath hot and seductive against his neck.

MILLS & BOON®

INTRIGUE
Romantic Suspense

A SEDUCTIVE COMBINATION OF DANGER AND DESIRE

A sneak peek at next month's titles...

In stores from 18th May 2017:

- **Hot Zone** – Elle James *and*
  Son of the Sheikh – Ryshia Kennie
- **Cavanaugh Standoff** – Marie Ferrarella *and*
  Murder in Black Canyon – Cindi Myers
- **The Warrior's Way** – Jenna Kernan *and*
  Bodyguard with a Badge – Elizabeth Heiter

Romantic Suspense

- **Cold Case Colton** – Addison Fox
- **Killer Cowboy** – Carla Cassidy

Just can't wait?
Buy our books online before they hit the shops!
www.millsandboon.co.uk

Also available as eBooks.

His lips again met hers, this time claiming them as his own with a passion that he'd held back in that first kiss.

"I can't see it any other way," he said thickly as he lifted up on one knee and his caresses drifted to other places.

Her phone whistled, the sound signaling a new case. And despite his protests only a day ago, she'd taken her physician's last advice before she left Morocco and declared herself ready to work.

His phone whistled in unison.

"Timing," he muttered as his hand lingered on her breast, feeling the hardening of her nipple that offered so much more.

"Is always off," she finished.

Below them, as the company jet streaked across the remaining miles, the crystal blue of a Wyoming spring sky was alight with a promise that paled against the feel of her skin beneath his fingers.

And as she rose up to meet him, they both knew that no matter where this new case might take them, home was here, in each other's arms.

* * * * *

Ryshia Kennie's series
DESERT JUSTICE
continues next month with
SON OF THE SHEIKH.

You'll find it wherever
Mills & Boon Intrigue books are sold!

Join Britain's BIGGEST Romance Book Club

50% OFF your first parcel

- **EXCLUSIVE offers** every month

- **FREE delivery direct** to your door

- **NEVER MISS a title**

- **EARN Bonus Book** points

Call Customer Services
0844 844 1358*

or visit
illsandboon.co.uk/subscriptions

MILLS & BOON®
are delighted to support
World Book Night

World Book Night is run by The Reading Agency and is a national celebration of reading and book which takes place on 23 April every year. To find out more visit worldbooknight.org.